# Welcome to the novels of Jodi Thomas

"Compelling and beautifully written."
—Debbie Macomber, #1 *New York Times* bestselling author

"Tender, realistic, and insightful."
—*Library Journal*

"[Thomas's] often beautiful turns of phrase and eloquent writing impart truths we spend lifetimes gleaning for ourselves."—*All About Romance*

"A masterful storyteller."
—Catherine Anderson, *New York Times* bestselling author

"Thomas is a master at creating...appealing characters, and their expressions of love—as siblings, as friends, as partners—are intense and beautiful."
—*Publishers Weekly* (starred review)

PRAISE FOR

## CAN'T STOP BELIEVING

"Filled with bittersweet endings and new beginnings, this is a heartwarming and heart-wrenching visit to Harmony. Prepare to laugh and shed some tears." —*RT Book Reviews*

"Harmony, Texas, may be the most unusual series in the ever-growing subgenre of small-town romance."

—*The Romance Dish*

"[Thomas's] often beautiful turn of phrase and eloquent writing impart truths we spend lifetimes gleaning for ourselves . . . The best of the series so far." —*All About Romance*

## CHANCE OF A LIFETIME

"Tender, realistic, and insightful . . . Will appeal to fans of Debbie Macomber and Sherryl Woods." —*Library Journal*

"I've never met a Jodi Thomas book that wasn't absolutely dog-eared from being read many times. They are all like warm, cozy friends that just beg to be taken back from the bookshelves and revisited . . . [A] wonderful contemporary tale infused with humor and mystery." —*Fresh Fiction*

"Beautiful prose and a thought-provoking plot . . . [A] heartwarming romance and intriguing mystery. Like old friends, readers will love the chance to catch up with characters from previous tales." —*RT Book Reviews*

*continued . . .*

## Just Down the Road

"A welcome return packed with cameos from familiar characters." —*Publishers Weekly*

"This book is like once again visiting old friends while making new ones and will leave readers eager for the next visit. A pure joy to read." —*RT Book Review*

## The Comforts of Home

"Even for readers new to the series, the intricate relationships between these affable men and eccentric women are easy to follow and even easier to love. Thomas skillfully juggles the many subplots, and the relationship between Ronelle and Marty, which inspires both to trust again, is especially touching." —*Publishers Weekly*

"There's always something brewing in Harmony and each story just adds to the richness of depth of the characters and town. If you haven't had a chance to meet the fine folks of Harmony, Texas, what are you waiting for?"

—*Fallen Angel Reviews*

"If you're a fan of small-town settings, heartwarming tales, and out-of-the-ordinary characters, you don't want to miss this book." —*Petit Fours and Hot Tamales*

## Somewhere Along the Way

"A delightful story with as much love and warmth as there is terror and fear . . . This is terrific reading from page one to the end. Jodi Thomas is a passionate writer who puts real feeling into her characters." —*Fresh Fiction*

"Thomas once again brings to life this fascinating little Texas town and its numerous characters. The reader is expertly drawn into their lives and left eager to know what happens next." —*RT Book Reviews*

## Welcome to Harmony

"The characters are delightful, and a subplot about mysterious fires balances the sweet stories about being and becoming family." —*Publishers Weekly*

"A fast-moving, engaging tale that keeps you turning pages . . . Thomas's characters become as familiar as family or friends." —*Fresh Fiction*

"A heartwarming tale, with plenty of excitement, *Welcome to Harmony* is Jodi Thomas all the way—super characters, lots of riveting subplots, and the background of a realistic Texas town. Don't miss this terrific novel."

—*Romance Reviews Today*

*Titles by Jodi Thomas*

A PLACE CALLED HARMONY
BETTING THE RAINBOW
CAN'T STOP BELIEVING
CHANCE OF A LIFETIME
JUST DOWN THE ROAD
THE COMFORTS OF HOME
SOMEWHERE ALONG THE WAY
WELCOME TO HARMONY
REWRITING MONDAY
TWISTED CREEK

***

PROMISE ME TEXAS
WILD TEXAS ROSE
TEXAS BLUE
THE LONE TEXAN
TALL, DARK, AND TEXAN
TEXAS PRINCESS
TEXAS RAIN
THE TEXAN'S REWARD
A TEXAN'S LUCK
WHEN A TEXAN GAMBLES
THE TEXAN'S WAGER
TO WED IN TEXAS
TO KISS A TEXAN
THE TENDER TEXAN
PRAIRIE SONG
THE TEXAN AND THE LADY
TO TAME A TEXAN'S HEART
FOREVER IN TEXAS
TEXAS LOVE SONG
TWO TEXAS HEARTS
THE TEXAN'S TOUCH
TWILIGHT IN TEXAS
THE TEXAN'S DREAM

*Specials*

EASY ON THE HEART
HEART ON HIS SLEEVE
IN A HEARTBEAT
A HUSBAND FOR HOLLY

# A Place Called Harmony

JODI THOMAS

BERKLEY BOOKS, NEW YORK

**THE BERKLEY PUBLISHING GROUP**
**Published by the Penguin Group**
**Penguin Group (USA) LLC**
**375 Hudson Street, New York, New York 10014**

USA • Canada • UK • Ireland • Australia • New Zealand • India • South Africa • China

penguin.com

A Penguin Random House Company

A PLACE CALLED HARMONY

A Berkley Book / published by arrangement with the author



For information, address: The Berkley Publishing Group,
a division of Penguin Group (USA) LLC,
375 Hudson Street, New York, New York 10014.

ISBN: 978-0-425-25078-5

PUBLISHING HISTORY
Berkley mass-market edition / October 2014

PRINTED IN THE UNITED STATES OF AMERICA

10 9 8 7 6 5 4 3 2 1

Cover art by Jim Griffin.
Cover design by George Long.
Interior text design by Kristin del Rosario.

*This book is dedicated to*

*Jay Wilson*
*For all his help researching everything from medicine to cars.*
*Thanks for putting up with a writer for a friend.*

*Dear Readers,*

*I've been wanting to write this book since the day a place called Harmony came into my mind. Many of you have traveled this journey with me and grown to know and love the people of Harmony.*

*Now we're going all the way back to the beginning, to the start of the town. For those of you who read the series, you'll love knowing how it all started. For those who haven't visited Harmony yet, you'll be stepping into a community at the birth of not only a town, but of friendships that will last for lifetimes. If you enjoy this tale, you might just stay awhile and read the rest of my stories.*

*I've always loved historicals. For me, early heroes in Texas always walk off the pages and into my heart.*

*I think you'll feel that way about Clint Truman, who believes he doesn't have enough heart left to break; and Gillian Matheson, who has loved one woman since he first saw her; and, of course, Patrick McAllen, who is young enough to believe that love comes easy.*

*Many books I write take on a life of their own. In this one I felt like I was meeting these men and their wives, not making them up. Truman stepped onto the pages with a stubbornness that his descendants had in later books: Matheson's strong need to protect and help others is deeply rooted, and Patrick's laughter shows through in every scene in which he appears.*

*So climb into the covered wagon and come along with me to Texas. I promise, this story will keep you reading long into the night.*

*With love,*
*Jodi Thomas*

# Prologue

DEAD OF WINTER

HARMON ELY LIMPED OUT OF THE TRADING POST HE'D BUILT where two streams crossed in the panhandle of Texas. He'd suffered through a fire that burned his first building to the ground, two robberies, and a dozen winter storms that almost froze him out.

"It's been a good ten years, Davy." He grinned at the hairy yellow dog a few feet away.

The hound looked up at Harmon with sad eyes that called the old man a liar.

Harmon laughed. "I know you're gonna be surprised, but I figure it's about time we had a little company, and I don't mean the beef herders and saddle tramps I usually see. I want families, kids playing around the place, and a town growing up on all this land I bought after the war."

The old mutt named after Davy Crockett still didn't look interested.

Harmon lifted a board as high as he could and hammered it up on the front of his store like it was a picture. "I've been thinking. We'll need a lawman, and someone who knows a thing or two about building a town, and a carpenter to carry it all out. I wouldn't mind having a few cooks and kids and throw in a schoolmarm to teach them what's right and a preacher to make them feel guilty if they don't follow along."

Davy spread out like a rug on the slice of sun-warmed porch.

Harmon lifted a can of paint. Slowly, he wrote *Population* across the top of the sign. "I don't care how long it takes, I'm gonna have me a town."

In the middle of the sign, he painted a big number 1. Then down at the bottom he added in smaller letters, *and one dog.*

"A town," he said to himself, since Davy was snoring, "that even my family would want to come to. A nice place where folks will pass by and say, 'There's old Harmon Ely's town.'"

# Chapter 1

FEBRUARY
HUNTSVILLE, TEXAS

CLINT TRUMAN HIT THE FLOOR SO HARD HIS TEETH RATTLED, but, as always, he didn't have the sense to stay down. He came up swinging, ready for another round.

The next hard blow from the miner he'd decided to fight sent him flying through the saloon's swinging doors and into the muddy street. He slid several feet, picking up horse shit along with the mud as he dug up the road. Then he just lay still, letting the rain beat on him for a while.

When he tried to straighten, a heavy boot landed on his chest, holding him down like a boulder. Clint stared up, but the rain and clouds offered him only a shadow of the man above him. A wide shadow.

"Evening, Truman." Sheriff Lightstone's voice matched his three hundred pound body: big and frightening. "You drunk enough to listen to me now?"

"Soon as I finish the fight, Sheriff," Clint promised.

"The fight's over." Lightstone lifted the gun belt that

circled his ample waist. "We need to talk, Truman, before you kill someone and I have to arrest you. Now, we can do it here with you in the mud, or we can do it with you behind bars, but we're going to have a talk."

"Hell," Clint said, hating both choices. "How about you buy me a cup of coffee before you get into telling me how to live my life?"

"Fair enough, but clean up first. Between the blood and the mud, there ain't an inch of you left unaffected. I'm tired of standing in this drizzle anyway. You've got ten minutes to meet me at Maggie's. If you don't pass her inspection to get in, I'm putting you in jail and letting you dry out until the mud flakes off and the bleeding scabs over."

Clint stood and watched the sheriff head toward the only café willing to serve drunks in Huntsville, Texas. He hated being bossed around, and he wasn't trying to kill himself by fighting. He just had a ton of anger built up in him and needed to get it out. In a town like Huntsville someone was always looking for a good fight.

Walking over to the horse trough, he dunked his head in and shook, guessing the horses wouldn't appreciate him bloodying the water. He pulled the plug at the bottom of the trough and let water run out into the river already flowing in the street.

Thunder rumbled and the sky dumped buckets down on him. Clint turned his head up and took the full blast. "Give it your best shot!" he yelled, waiting for the lightning. Life couldn't get any more painful. He probably wouldn't feel a direct hit.

A kid of about ten ran past him, bumping into his outstretched arm. "Sorry, mister," he shouted over the storm. "Didn't you notice it's raining?"

"Hell," Clint answered. "It's been raining all my life."

He replaced the plug in the trough, then walked to a bench outside the saloon and lifted his saddlebags from where he'd left them three hours and several drinks ago. He might not have the sense to come out of the rain, but at least he'd left his horse in the barn.

Reluctantly, Clint headed to the back door of Maggie's place. Once inside the mudroom, he stripped off his shirt and dried with a towel the owner tossed him.

Maggie watched from the doorway of the kitchen as he cleaned up. "You're one hunk of a man, Clint Truman. If you ever gave up fighting and turned to loving, you'd make some woman very happy." Her inspection wasn't shy. "That scar running across your hand, or the one on your jaw, don't take nothing away from that perfect body. Broad shoulders, slim waist and . . ." She grinned. "Wouldn't mind if you turned around so I could finish my description."

He growled at her.

Maggie held up her hands and tried her best to look innocent. "Just making notes to pass along to some woman looking for a new lover."

"There's no more loving left in me, Maggie." He said the words as if he were swearing. "You mind turning around while I change my pants?"

"Not a chance. An old widow like me don't get to see a full-grown man strip but a few times, and I'm not missing this opportunity. My first husband used to wash in the creek and come back to the house naked, but he was so hairy I thought he was a bear heading my way half the time."

"You got anything to drink, Maggie?"

"Sure." She stepped away and he exchanged soaked trousers for damp ones from his bag.

When she returned she handed him a cup of coffee, and he frowned.

"Trust me, honey, you need this. That bull of a sheriff is out front waiting and he don't look happy."

Clint downed half of the hot liquid that tasted more like the mud outside than coffee. He'd known this talk with the sheriff was coming, so he might as well get it over with.

Thanking Maggie for the towel and the coffee, Clint stepped through the kitchen door to the café. Sure enough, Lightstone sat by the window staring out at his town.

Clint took the seat across from him without saying a word.

"You eat today?" the sheriff asked.

"I'm not a kid. I don't need mothering," Clint snapped. At thirty he'd about decided he didn't need anything from anyone.

"You ever wear anything but black?"

"No. Why the hell do you care?" Clint needed a drink. He had a feeling this wasn't going to go well.

The sheriff ignored his comment. "I heard you fought with Terry's Texas Rangers during the war. Some say you were a crack shot. Maybe even the best in the South."

"Some talk too much. Most of what I shot was game for dinner. I don't want to talk about the war. Wasted years. We lost, you know. The whole damn country lost."

"I know how you feel. I thought I was fighting for Texas. For rights, then found out later it was all about slavery. By then, it was too late and I was mostly just fighting to stay alive." He stared down at his cup as if looking for the answer. "What'd you do when you got home?"

"I drifted for a while, trying to shake ghosts following me. My folks kept a little farm going during the war, so I finally settled there. I helped them out for a few years until they passed on. Then, I thought I'd marry and start a family." Clint didn't go on. He couldn't. The memory of his two little girls crying still haunted his dreams.

Lightstone waited for a while then added, "I know enough to fill in the details, Truman. I heard your wife and daughters died a few years ago of the fever. Folks say you burned the house and the barns the morning after you buried them."

Clint didn't comment. He felt like his whole life was simply acts in a play, and some days he didn't want to step on the stage. Sometimes he thought the ache to feel his wife, Mary, by his side would collapse his chest, or the need to run his hand over one of his daughters' curly hair would almost take him to his knees. They were gone so fast, like his parents and all the boys he'd joined up with to go to war. Some nights, in his nightmares, he felt like a time traveler going back to them all. They'd smile at him and wave, then curl up and die like dried leaves caught in a campfire.

Clint took a long drink of his coffee and waited for the sheriff's lecture. He'd heard it before: different people, different towns. If he had enough caring left in him to change, he would try one more time, but he no longer saw the point.

"Truman," the sheriff began. "I need your help with a matter."

Clint raised an eyebrow. He hadn't expected the sheriff would want a favor. Lightstone was only passable nice to him on a good day, and the huge man had very few of them in a town like Huntsville.

"Now, hear me out before you decide. Promise. This is me asking for something, not me telling you what to do. You make up your own mind."

"All right. I'll hear you out," Clint answered. He didn't plan to walk back over to the saloon until the rain let up anyway. He had no other clothes to change into.

Lightstone leaned back. "I got a friend I fought with during the war who wants to build a town. He's been running a trading post up in the wild part of Texas where the Indian Wars have been going on for ten years. He makes good money, thanks to the cattle drives coming through and crazy settlers who wanted to move that far north, but he wants more. He wants to have a community. He says his wife refused to go with him because that part of the state is too wild. Thanks to Colonel McKenzie and a new fort moving in, it may be settling down."

"How does this affect me?"

"My friend is a good businessman, but the war left him crippled up. He's been robbed several times, and once they shot him and left him for dead. If he's going to do this, he'll need someone good with a gun working for him. I've heard, even if you don't usually wear a gun belt, that there is no better shot in the state."

"I'm not a hired gun, Sheriff. Not interested."

"Oh, you wouldn't be that. He's offering every man who comes to work for him forty acres and a house to live in. If you stay two years, he'll deed the place over to you. He'll pay a fair wage and you help him build the town. A real town where folks can walk the streets without worrying about being robbed or shot."

Clint was low on money and knew he'd have to look for a job soon, but he never planned to settle anywhere again. He might get attached to folks if he did that, and he never, ever planned to let that happen again. Signing on to be his friend or loved one was a death warrant.

"You'd be hauling supplies and running cattle and who knows what else, but you'd also carry a gun. You'd be protecting hardworking folks and running off those who are looking for trouble. This time you'd be fighting to keep people alive. That part of Texas has very little law of any kind. Trouble will ride in at full gallop more than once over two years, I'm guessing. You'll earn that house and land."

Lightstone leaned halfway across the table and yelled for Maggie to bring them a couple of meals. He didn't have to say more; she only served one choice a day.

She yelled that he needed to stop yelling at her.

The sheriff smiled. "I'd marry that woman if she'd have me, but she says four husbands were enough."

Clint didn't want to picture the two in bed, but the image came all the same. Both were built wide and thick. Maggie told him once that she was simply big-boned. Proof of dinosaurs, he remembered thinking at the time. If she and the sheriff ever did get together and make love, they'd shake the house.

Lightstone drew him back to the conversation. "What have you got to lose? The trip north, even if you decided not to stay, would do you good."

"All right. I'll go." Clint had nothing else to do anyway. He could be packed in an hour. "But I make no promises that I'll stay two years."

The sheriff nodded as if they'd made a bargain. "Oh, I forgot, you have to take one thing with you."

"What's that?" He was thinking maybe his own horse, or rifle.

The sheriff smiled and added, "A wife."

# Chapter 2

HUNTSVILLE, TEXAS

CLINT TRUMAN FINALLY SOBERED UP ENOUGH TO REALIZE just how crazy the sheriff's plan was. He didn't mind traveling across the state to look for work, but picking a wife from the women being released from prison tonight was loco.

Yet somehow, here he was standing next to a mountain of a lawman waiting for the prison gates to open.

Sheriff Lightstone stood close, probably making sure he didn't run. The night seemed smoky with low clouds, and so much moisture lingered in the air Clint could feel it on his face.

"Now it's not that hard, Clint. I've seen fellows do this before. Last month a man I've known for years met a little pickpocket outside these gates. He never had much luck with women, but they talked all night, then at dawn woke up a preacher. She had to pay, of course. Somehow my old friend couldn't find his money."

Clint didn't laugh. He had no idea if the sheriff was telling the truth or making a joke.

"Way I see it," Lightstone continued, "marrying you will look better to a woman on her own than her taking the only other choice." He pointed with his head at a wagon pulling up twenty yards away. "If no one picks them up, that guy, who goes by Harden, offers them employment at a whorehouse down near Houston. He makes regular runs picking up women leaving prison. Once they step in that wagon there's no going back to a regular kind of life."

Clint looked at the two women waiting in the back of the wagon as the sheriff continued, "He bailed them two soiled doves out an hour ago from county jail. One knifed a guy. They kept her in jail until they were sure her customer wasn't going to die. The other lady of the evening stole money from a patron at Harden's place. She looked fine when Harden picked her up, but judging from the bruises on her face he made her sorry she caused him trouble. Women leaving prison and climbing in that wagon know exactly where they're going."

As Clint stared, the one with a black eye lowered her head. Neither woman looked to be eighteen, but both were worn down by life. He doubted either would make it to thirty.

Several other people waited around the gate, looking more like mourners than greeters. One man sat on a bench playing with his knife, striking it again and again into the corner of the bench. Clint noticed an old couple and a kid of about sixteen close to the locked door.

The gate rattled and a guard stepped out.

"Might not be many tonight," Lightstone whispered. "Sometimes there is trouble in the prison and they don't let out many. Used to let them out in the morning, but too many people complained about them walking the streets. County gives each enough money to take the stage out of town, but some spend it on drinks the first few hours they're out." He frowned. "I was kind of expecting one woman to be released tonight. She'd be worth considering even if we have to come back next week."

Clint had already decided that he wouldn't be coming again. This idea was far too crazy to repeat. Once the sheriff saw there was no wife material here, he'd drop the plan.

"This is a bad idea. Getting married because the job description says to bring a wife just doesn't seem right," Clint mumbled to himself, guessing the sheriff wouldn't be listening. "How do I know one of these women hasn't killed someone, like maybe her first husband?"

"I doubt any have done more than they had to, or more than any one of us did during the war. Toward the end we all stole to eat and killed to stay alive. I'm guessing they did the same."

Clint didn't argue, but picking a wife this way seemed like scraping the bottom of the barrel. He looked down at his worn boots and decided he was already at the bottom. Half the townspeople thought of him as a drunk, and the other half felt sorry for him and offered to buy him a drink. If he married an ex-con, some would say he was marrying up.

The first woman out of the gate ran toward an old couple standing as close as the guard would allow. All three hugged and cried. No matter what she'd done, she obviously was still their baby.

The next two walked out together, yelling for Harden to pull the wagon closer and take them home. One of the women winked at Clint as she walked by. "Come on by tonight, honey. I'm offering rides for half price to celebrate."

Clint stared at their flimsy clothes. They were dressed for work already in ragged lace and see-through silk.

Lightstone filled him in on facts. "The women can wear what they were arrested in home, or the prison gives them one of the dresses they wore in prison. Most have worn that outfit for far too long already, so if they have anything else they change out of prison clothes."

A middle-aged woman came out in what had to be the uniform she'd worn in prison: a tattered apron over a gray dress with a plain collar. A shawl made with little skill was tied around her shoulders but looked like it would offer no shelter from the rain.

The man with the knife stood and waited as she walked to him. "'Bout time," was all he said as they turned and walked into the night.

Clint thought if he ever wanted a lower level of melancholy than he had every day, he'd come back and watch this scene again.

The last woman out was tall and dressed in a gray traveling suit that appeared finely tailored, but it was wrinkled. She looked almost a proper lady, but her clothes seemed a few sizes too big and her shoes were dilapidated and scuffed beyond repair. She held a bundle in her arms and another slung over her shoulder.

Clint glanced at a kid by the gate, thinking maybe he was meeting her, but he just shrugged and walked away. She obviously wasn't someone he was looking for.

The woman raised her head to glance around, but her eyes were dull as if she had little hope. Her hair was too short to pull back and hung down, dark and lifeless, across part of her face. Anyone seeing her would guess she'd been ill. Prison thin. Moonlight pale.

Harden whistled and signaled that she could join him in the wagon, but the thin woman shook her head.

The guard shooed her along. "There's a hotel down the road that'll let you sleep there if you give them a day's work come morning. They don't take in most of the women who get out of here, but I'm guessing they'll take you, Miss Karrisa. You tell them Sam said you paid your dues."

"Thank you," the woman in gray said, pulling the bundle she carried in her arms closer as if sheltering it from the rain.

Clint found himself staring and wondering what she'd done to end up in prison. She couldn't be more than twenty-two or twenty-three. Her movements were slow, as if she were testing every step like an old woman on uneven ground. Maybe she'd been hurt or sick, or beaten.

Surely no one beat her on her last day of prison.

The thought turned his stomach.

Lightstone took one step in her direction and she moved away. "Miss," he said too loud, then lowered his voice. "I'm the sheriff over in Huntsville and will be happy to give you a ride to the little hotel the guard mentioned. You'll be safe with me, and I promise you'll be safe there for the night."

She looked up and Clint saw that she didn't believe Lightstone. How many people must have lied to her, Clint wondered. Frightened round eyes set into dark circles looked his direction for only a moment.

"I might have a job for you if you're interested," the sheriff rushed on. "I could tell you about it and then you could pick which one you wanted: hotel work or my choice."

Clint saw it then, pure fear so deep she couldn't speak. He thought he was beyond feeling sorry for anyone but himself, only right now in the moon's watery glow, he felt sorry for her. She had no one and nowhere to go. If one person had cared whether she lived or died, he would have met her here tonight.

Harden's wagon rolled past. "You can have her, Sheriff; she's too thin to satisfy a man. I'd lose money on her keep and that baby will be yelling, waking folks up."

Clint saw the bundle move and realized what she carried out of the prison: a baby so small it had to be a newborn.

The guard closed the gate but turned to stare through the bars. "If the sheriff says he has a job, he probably does. I've never known the man to lie."

The woman he'd called Karrisa took a step toward Lightstone. "I'd appreciate the ride, Sheriff, but I don't know about the job."

"Fair enough."

Lightstone walked around the wagon while Clint followed the woman. When they reached the side of the wagon he offered to help her up, but she stepped back, out of reach.

As she climbed onto the bench, he again noticed her slow measured movements as if she were in pain.

Without asking, he tugged the bag from her back and tossed it in the wagon.

She raised her thin fingers from the bundle she carried in a slight wave of thanks to the guard. If she'd been mistreated in prison, it hadn't been by him. The guard looked hard as stone, but he'd shown her a bit of respect.

Clint also nodded at the guard and climbed in the back of the wagon. She stared at him as if she feared he might be a wild animal, then slowly settled on the bench. Without a word, he draped his duster over her shoulders, shielding both her and the baby from the rain.

The ride into town was silent. The hotel would have been a long walk on this dark, rainy night. Clint tried not to stare at her sitting as still as stone next to the sheriff. For the first time since his family died, he thought of someone else. Karrisa.

Maybe she was a murderer, or a bank robber. Women were usually given far more leniency than men, so whatever she did, she must not have served long. Their prison was small and crowded. Some said it was more like a workhouse with guards. Like the men in prisons, the women grew their own food, made their clothes, and took care of stock. If the crop was poor, they ate little. If the crops were good, some was sold off to offset expenses. Life was hard everywhere in Texas, but it must have been near hell in prison.

The hotel, at the edge of town, wasn't much. It looked like it had been an old stagecoach station and catered to mostly prison visitors or lawmen delivering new inmates or maybe travelers looking for a cheap place to stay. Clint would have passed it by and slept out under a tree, even on a night like this. Putting up with damp ground would be better than fighting bedbugs.

Sheriff Lightstone yelled, "Hello the inn," as they neared.

An old man stepped to the doorway but didn't call back a greeting. He had an apron tied around his waist and a shotgun lowered to the side of his leg.

"You got a meal for travelers, innkeeper?"

"We got stew, Sheriff. What you doing this far from your office?"

"Just came to eat your cooking. Hope that wife of yours made pie. Her buttermilk pie is worth the stop even on a night like this. I'll buy three bowls of soup if you still got it warming."

The old man moved inside with a nod. Like most folks since the war, they'd learned not to be too friendly.

Clint jumped out of the wagon and offered Miss Karrisa help down, but she didn't take it.

When she turned to reach for her bundle, he grabbed it first. "I'll carry it in for you, miss."

She turned away without arguing, as if the bag were of little value to her.

They moved into a dark cavern of a dining area. Long, poorly made tables ran the center of the room. Clint removed his wet coat from her shoulders, and without a word she sat down close to the fire.

Again Clint couldn't help but feel sorry for her. How long had it been since she'd stood close to a warm fire or had enough energy to care about anything?

The baby made a little sound and Clint remembered when he'd held his own daughters just after they'd been born. Probably as close to heaven as he'd ever get, he thought. That one moment, that first moment.

No one spoke until the innkeeper rattled into the room with a tray. "This is the last of the stew, Sheriff, so I won't charge you for it, but the pie will be two bits a slice."

Clint noticed neither the sheriff nor the lady asked if she could work for her board. Maybe the sheriff wanted to toss out his great idea first or maybe she didn't want the job. She probably wanted to wait until she heard the sheriff's offer before deciding.

When the food was spread out, they sat at a little table by the fireplace. Clint wasn't hungry, but he ate, taking a bite every time she did. Her manners were polished.

"Where you from, miss?" He finally broke the silence.

"Nowhere, really." She put her spoon down and stopped eating as she rocked the baby.

He didn't want to ask her any more questions, but he hated that she seemed so tense. Maybe if he talked she'd relax. "I grew up on a farm about thirty miles from here. My folks came in the fifties to homestead. My dad wasn't much of a farmer, but they survived even after my brother and I went to war. My brother didn't come back. He died at Shiloh."

She picked up her spoon as he continued, "I still own the land, but I thought I'd sell it. The soil's good but the house burned. Farmer next door said he'd buy my place anytime I was willing to sell."

Lightstone looked at him with a raised eyebrow as if he wanted to add that houses usually do burn when a fire is set in the middle of the parlor.

Clint continued when she took another bite. If she'd eat, he'd talk. "I'm thinking of taking a job up north near the panhandle where the Indian Wars are probably still going on." He'd tell her of their plan. The sheriff would only frighten her. "They say the weather gets cold enough to snow up there, and the sunsets spread out across flat land for a hundred miles."

The sheriff kept frowning. He probably wasn't sure if Clint was trying to talk her into going or out of going. Clint just felt like he had to be honest. If either of them was going to think of stepping off this cliff, they had a right to know what the ground looked like below.

"The sheriff's got a friend up there who wants to build a town, and he's making an offer that is hard for a man to turn down. Especially one who has nothing to keep him here. I got no family, miss, they're all dead. Maybe living on the edge of civilization is where I belong."

The sheriff finally interrupted Clint's rant. "You got any family to go to, miss? 'Cause if you do, I'll put you on the train come morning."

She set down her spoon again and lowered her head. "None that I'd want to see again or who would welcome me."

"You got any prospects for work or any money that will tide you over?"

She shook her head, making her straight black hair almost brush her shoulders.

"Well then, I might as well tell you what I've been thinking. Clint here ain't a bad man when he's sober. He's thinking of taking that job he told you about; problem is, the man building the town wants married men."

She looked from the sheriff to Clint, not saying a word. He held her gaze for only a moment, but it was long enough. He couldn't miss the fear in her eyes. Hell, he was surprised she didn't run.

He saw that as a good sign. She wasn't the type of woman he'd ever love, but there was something about her that made him want to take care of her. She had nowhere to go, no money, no one who'd look after her. As thin as she was, she'd probably be dead in a week if she didn't eat. If she wanted to go with him, he'd see she had food and wasn't cold. She probably wouldn't be much company and, if she ran off, he wouldn't miss a mouse of a woman like her. Maybe the idea of taking her along wasn't as bad as he feared.

"I'll let you two talk," the sheriff said as he stood. "I'll go find some of that buttermilk pie."

When the big man was gone, Clint just sat staring at her as she held the newborn close. He had no idea if he was making the right decision. He'd made so many wrong ones lately; maybe it was time to try something different.

"It's a crazy thing to spring on you, you just getting out of prison and all. If you need time, I'd understand. Until you walked out I was against the idea myself, but knowing you might need this new start as badly as I do got me to thinking that maybe it might be worth a try. I wouldn't be much help with the babe, but I'd do what I could."

She didn't move. She held herself so tight, as if she feared she might fall apart if she relaxed even one inch.

Clint tried again. "I'm a hard worker when I work and, until my family died, I'd never had more than a few drinks."

He hoped she didn't glance up and give him that look that said she didn't believe him.

She remained frozen.

"I'll be honest. I'll never love you. I haven't got any left to give. But, if you'll go along with me I can promise I'll always try to be kind. My wife, Mary, used to swear there was a kind side of me, though most folks probably wouldn't agree."

Slowly her chin rose. "You'll never ask me about my past or the baby? I'll tell you when I'm ready or not at all. That has to be up to me." Her voice was soft.

"Never, if that's what you want. Seems fair enough. From this night on, if you come along with me, the baby is ours as far as folks know. No questions."

"You'll never hit me?"

"If I do, you have my permission to shoot me." It crossed his mind that maybe she'd already done that to another. If not being hit was so important to her, maybe she'd killed the last man who tried. Only he wasn't going to ask. They'd already agreed on that point. Talking about his past was too painful, and learning about hers might keep him up at night.

"You'd never force yourself on me?" Her voice sounded a bit stronger.

"I'm not the kind of man who would do that." In truth, he hadn't even thought about the bedding part of the marriage. "We can sleep in separate beds. I'm looking for a wife in name, not in bed."

She didn't look convinced, or even interested, but he was coming around to the idea. "If you'll go with me, miss, I'll keep you and the babe safe. We may be poor and the work will probably be hard, but I promise you'll have no call to be afraid. While I breathe, no one will hurt you or the baby."

She looked up at him then, tears bubbling over. "Then I'll go with you if you'll offer one more thing."

He frowned. He didn't have much to offer.

She straightened. "Sewn into the folds of my traveling clothes are seeds. You'll give me enough land to plant a few apple trees if I come. You'll swear that you'll never cut a single one of my trees down."

He smiled. "I'll do that. You'll have land enough for an orchard if you want." Of all the things he thought she might ask for, a spot of land never occurred to him, but if that was her price, he'd pay it gladly.

# Chapter 3

HUNTSVILLE, TEXAS

WHEN THE SHERIFF CAME BACK INTO THE HOTEL'S DINING area, he was muttering something about having eaten the last of the pie as he wiped his mouth with his wrinkled bandanna.

Clint Truman slowly stood.

"We're ready to go, Sheriff. I know a place in town where Karrisa can stay that won't mind the baby. If you'll take us there, I'll get her settled in and ride out to wake up my neighbor. He'll be happy to know my land will be his as soon as we can do the paperwork."

Sheriff Lightstone looked surprised. "You two already agreed on everything? That didn't take long." He looked at the woman cradling the baby and rocking slightly. "Truman here didn't talk you into some pie-in-the-sky dream, did he?"

She shook her head. "He said we'd be poor and the work would be hard, but he promised I'd be safe with him."

The sheriff turned to Clint, but his words were for her. "Some say he's the best shot they've ever seen with a rifle or a handgun. I reckon if he says he'll keep you safe, he will. If that's all you want?"

She raised her head, and dull blue eyes as pale as summer clouds showed little sign of caring one way or the other what might happen to her. "That's all I'll ever need, Sheriff. I'll ask for nothing more than he's offering."

"Well." Lightstone shrugged. "I guess being safe is important."

A thousand words floated unsaid in the air between them. Clint decided if Karrisa wanted to keep her secrets and fears, he'd let her. Digging up memories wouldn't do either of them any good.

He offered his hand and to his surprise, she took it. He helped her stand, tucking her thin fingers against his elbow as they walked out. When he lifted her into the wagon he couldn't believe how slender she was. Skin over bones, nothing more.

No one said a word until they got to Quaker House. Martha and James Adams had lived in Huntsville for as long as Clint could remember. They were good people who ran a small boardinghouse for women.

While the sheriff waited with Karrisa, Clint knocked on the door and then explained to Martha that his future wife needed a room.

Martha hadn't been born with an ounce of curiosity, but the good Lord had doubled her up on kindness. She welcomed the thin woman in and hurried her off to a room.

Clint waited in the parlor until Martha returned. "I'll pay you for her room when I get back tomorrow, if that's all right? We're marrying as soon as possible, then heading north."

"That's fine, Mr. Truman. Only don't come to get her for a few days. That poor dear needs rest."

He knew all about women birthing babies; he'd helped deliver both his daughters. "How old is the baby?"

"Two days, maybe less. He seems healthy, though small." She hesitated, then added, "Your woman is still bleeding, Mr. Truman." Martha whispered her last few words knowing women didn't talk to men about such things. "If she travels north tomorrow, she won't make the journey. You'll pay me for three days and she'll stay longer if need be. I'll see she gets the care she should have had the minute the baby was born."

He nodded. Arguing with Martha would be like disagreeing with a saint. "Tell my future wife that I'll be by for a visit tomorrow, but it may take a few days to sell the land so she'll have to stay here. I don't want her thinking she's slowing us down."

Martha seemed to understand. "Come by for supper if you like. You'll be welcome."

Clint smiled. "I'll do that." It had been a long time since he'd been around kind folks and it felt good. "And I'll be sober."

Martha smiled and winked. "I wouldn't let you in if you weren't."

CLINT AND KARRISA WERE MARRIED BY A JUDGE AT THE courthouse four mornings later. The sheriff and Martha Adams were the only witnesses. Karrisa wore her same gray traveling dress.

She stood beside her new husband, feeling almost alive for the first time in eight months. She'd taken a long hot bath every morning, as though it took several baths to wash away eight months of being unclean. She'd eaten all meals plus the morning breads and the afternoon tea cakes Martha insisted she have every day.

When Karrisa washed the dried blood and afterbirth off the baby that first night at Quaker House, she'd studied him by candlelight, amazed at how perfect he was. One of the women in the prison helped her deliver, but there had been no clean water for either of them to wash afterward, and Karrisa had been afraid to say anything or the warden might not have let her leave.

What brought the baby to her had all been ugly, but he was wonderful. She thought back about the rape, the murder, her arrest, her time in prison. Someone she'd trusted had attacked her, then lied, and somehow she'd lost everything: her friends, her job, the life she'd had. The baby growing inside her had kept her sane through the dark days in prison. Despite all that had happened, she wanted him, needed him, needed to know that he might be the last piece of her family to live on.

This morning, her wedding day, she'd wrapped his bottom in clean strips of cloth, then put him in one of the little gowns Martha gave her. The man who was now her husband brought a blanket and a basket for the baby that she could carry on her arm. He said he would rig up ropes to hang the basket inside the covered wagon they'd buy so the baby would be rocked to sleep during the last part of their journey.

She looked up at Clint Truman as he signed the marriage license. He was trying to act as if they were just a regular couple getting married. After sitting across the table from him for three nights, she didn't know if he was a good man or not. She'd lost her compass for such things.

Every night since she'd left prison, she'd curled up in a big rocker and held her baby as he slept. She'd spent hours trying to make sense of what she'd agreed to do. Truman's offer was her only choice. None of her mother's family had answered her letters, and she doubted her father would open a letter from her. No friend responded. She'd been totally alone when she'd walked out of prison with fears that she'd be dead of starvation or cold within days, but strangely, Truman treated her as if she'd done him a favor by agreeing to marry him.

Silently she promised she'd be as little trouble to him as possible. Maybe she'd even find a way to help him if he was half the man he seemed to be.

"Are you ready to go, dear?" he asked as he lifted his hat from the rack. The endearment hadn't flowed easy from his tongue, but she understood he was trying.

"Yes," she said, bundling up her baby as she watched him shake hands with the sheriff. Truman had a strong jaw and broad shoulders beneath his black coat. There was a hardness about him. The scar crossing from his ear to almost his chin and the deep slash of twisted tissue across his right hand spoke of a violent past.

She had a feeling he didn't care about anyone in the world. Which might make them a good match because no one in the world cared about her.

When he'd slipped the plain gold band on her finger, she thought of her mother and father. They'd seemed happy when she was growing up, though her mother had always cherished her only child to the point that Karrisa often felt her father was jealous. When her mother died six years ago, something died inside her father as well. It was as if all his love washed away in tears of grief. She'd been sixteen, almost an adult, but he'd sent her to live with his half brother, where she'd learned to make a living in the mills. She'd always thought that she looked too much like her mother for her father to bear.

When she'd hugged her father good-bye, she'd known that she'd never see him alive again. He hadn't even noticed that she'd bought a fine gray traveling suit, or that she'd sewn seeds into the padding so that she could take her mother's apple trees with her wherever she went. Her only contact with him over the years had been a hurried note at Christmas to tell her how busy he was.

No one could have guessed how far Karrisa would fall, not even her in her worst nightmare. She'd long ago given up thinking about how her life would have been so different if her mother had lived. Her mother would have never stopped loving her, and her father wouldn't have known grief so deep that he gave up his daughter.

*You're a grandmother.* In her mind, Karrisa whispered to her mother as if she were in the room. *You always said that would be a dancing day when it happened.* A tear drifted down Karrisa's face and landed on the baby's blanket. *I'm married*, she added, *to a good man, I hope.*

*Don't think of the past*, she reminded herself. Whatever this new road held, it had to be better than prison. Better than New Orleans and living with her half cousins. Better than living in fear.

This strong man before her was promising he would keep her safe, and that meant more to her than anything in the world. She could live without love, but she never wanted to live in total fear again.

Clint cupped her elbow with his long fingers. "It's time we moved to the train."

Karrisa blinked away tears, unsure that this marriage wouldn't be another kind of prison.

"I forgot to say, 'You may kiss the bride,'" the judge shouted as they walked out of his office.

She froze as her new husband leaned down and kissed her lightly on the cheek.

It wasn't so bad, she reasoned. The slight kiss was almost polite. If he was polite, then she could handle being married.

"We need to get moving," the sheriff said. "Train leaves in an hour."

Clint lifted his suitcase, then glanced at her as if just noticing she had nothing but her bag of ragged clothes. "We've time to stop at the general store and pick my wife up a few things she'll need for the trip. When we get to Dallas I'll buy a wagon and you can collect what we'll need to set up housekeeping. The last ten or so days we'll have to travel by wagon."

Karrisa nodded. She'd had nothing for so long; anything more than the small broken comb she carried would be a luxury.

When they got to the general store, she was glad the sheriff remained in the wagon, saying he needed a smoke. Truman took the baby in one arm before helping her down. When he handed back her precious bundle, a smile blinked across his stern face for a moment before he turned away.

"Does the boy have a name?" Clint asked as he held the door to the store open for her.

"No," she answered. "There's time."

He nodded, and she realized this hard man, with his claim that he'd never love her, wouldn't resent her baby. He seemed to accept her child as a part of the bargain, nothing more.

Walking among all the stacks of clothes, she felt overwhelmed. She'd had nothing for so long that all this seemed far too much.

To her surprise, her new husband seemed to understand. "How about we start with a bag?" He pulled a carpetbag from the shelf. "Do you think this one would be big enough?"

She nodded but didn't reach for it.

He opened the bag and moved to the counter with the clerk following on his heels. "We'll need a comb, a brush." Glancing back at her, he added, "And a few combs for her hair."

The clerk pulled out a card of hair combs and Karrisa pointed at the two cheapest.

Clint frowned but didn't comment. For a moment they just stood, neither seeming to know what to do or say.

She knew she couldn't go forever without talking to this man, so she managed, "I'd like to pick out a few underthings and a gown alone."

"Of course," he said, and moved to a row of nails holding gun belts and spurs. "If you find a dress you like, you might want to pick it up here. I doubt there will be much selection in the small towns up north, and the train often stops in a town so late the shops are closed."

When she returned with simple underthings and a gown, he asked about the dress.

"It will be less expensive to buy material and a small sewing box. Then I'll have something that will fit me." She'd figured out after looking over the dresses that all would be too wide and too short. She could make two dresses and a few aprons for what one of the store dresses cost.

While the clerk cut material, her husband went back to looking at guns.

Once she returned with material, thread, and a bit of lace, she noticed that he'd picked up lotion and soap.

The clerk put together what he called a train lunch made up of canned peaches, a small loaf of bread, hard-boiled eggs, and cheese. When he started to add it all up, Clint put cookies and a small sack of hard candy atop the pile.

"Is there anything else you need?" he asked without looking at her.

She shook her head as the clerk fitted all they'd bought in

the bag. She had no idea how much money Clint carried, but he'd been generous, even adding an extra blanket for the baby.

"There's room for a few more things," the clerk said, obviously trying to run up the bill.

Karrisa looked up at the man she'd married, and he nodded once. She turned to the basket at the edge of the counter and picked up two skeins of yarn and a pair of knitting needles.

"That's good wool, miss," the clerk said. "Spun by a lady right here in town."

"It's Missus. Mrs. Truman," Clint corrected as he shoved the gun belt and Colt that he'd been looking at across the counter. His words had seemed so cold they froze the room.

The clerk suddenly seemed nervous. "I'm sorry, sir and missus." He wrapped the gun and belt in brown paper. "Will you be wanting bullets for this?"

"Yes, two boxes," Clint said as he paid for everything.

He picked up her carpetbag, now completely full, and the brown paper package. He walked out. She had no choice but to follow. The man had asked her to marry him, yet mentioning her being his wife seemed to have made him angry. Maybe he was having as much trouble as she was realizing what they'd done with less thought than they'd put into their purchases.

When he got to the wagon, he put her bag next to his in the back of the wagon and unwrapped the gun belt. While she watched, he strapped the belt on and loaded the Colt.

"How long has it been since you wore a gun, Truman?" the sheriff asked as he watched from the wagon bench.

"Since the war," Clint answered, but the skill he showed told her that he hadn't forgotten the feel of a weapon in his hand.

She couldn't help but wonder if this cold man would hold to his word to be kind.

# Chapter 4

FEBRUARY
GALVESTON, TEXAS

A RUSTLER'S MOON SEEMED TO FOLLOW PATRICK MCALLEN and his brother as he moved silently down the shoreline road toward the Spencers' place.

"Seems as good a night as any to kidnap a bride." Patrick's voice carried in the midnight breeze off the gulf.

Shelly, who hadn't spoken a word since birth, bumped his brother's knee.

Patrick laughed. "I know it's not exactly kidnapping when she walks half a mile to meet me, but you can bet Solomon and Brother Spencer will think so. I wouldn't be surprised if our old man doesn't come after me and bring half the congregation along to watch. He'll have murder in his eyes again and a death grip on that bullwhip of his."

Just enough light shone on Shelly's face for Patrick to see worry lines forming as his brother's hands tightened on the reins.

"I'll make it this time." Patrick tried to sound as if he

believed his words, but the sound of his father's whip ripping into his back and the smell of his own blood made his voice shake. "I'll make it or die trying. I swear."

His brother nodded. Shelly might never speak, but Patrick knew he could read his thoughts. They had until dawn for Patrick to escape and Shelly to make it back to the farm. Solomon McAllen would never know where his youngest son had disappeared to, but by Sunday Patrick had no doubt that Solomon would be telling everyone that his son had gone to the devil.

As they moved slowly, Patrick's thoughts were racing with plans and full of fears. When he'd applied for a job as carpenter to help build a town way up in West Texas, he knew his father wouldn't allow him to go. He knew what would happen if he tried to leave home. But this was his one chance to be his own man. To live free from Solomon McAllen's constant threats and demands to control.

He glanced at his silent brother and wondered if the last time he'd tried to leave was on Shelly's mind as well.

Patrick had been fifteen when he'd signed on for a cattle drive leaving Galveston. He'd thought it would be a grand adventure and hadn't listened to his father's rant. Only, the day the drive pulled out his father found him and dragged him back home. Solomon had strung Patrick up in the barn and almost beat him to death while preaching all the while about how a son should obey his father.

Shelly had been almost seventeen then and tried to stop the beating. Their father had blacked his eye and broken two of his ribs before he yelled for the women to hold the dummy down or he'd kill him.

Shelly had struggled against his four older sisters, but they'd held him until Patrick's back and legs were raw and Solomon's youngest son was more dead than alive. After weeks of nursing him back, Patrick's stepmother had simply said he should have listened. As Solomon's favorite target, she probably thought she knew best, but from that day to this Patrick had planned his next escape. Now, at twenty, he was making it happen.

Since he'd talked to Spencer's oldest daughter and she'd agreed to marry him, everything had gone as planned.

Shelly and he had loaded the extra wagon with the bare necessities he'd need on the trip and left it in the north pasture until tonight.

Patrick took his bath and laid out his Sunday clothes as he'd done every Saturday night since he could remember. But tonight he'd also packed a grain sack with his other clothes and waited by the window until everyone in the house was asleep.

All had gone smoothly during the week. Their father accepted Shelly taking over the weekly mail pickup but didn't speak to him when Shelly brought it in. To Solomon, Shelly was less than a son because he couldn't talk. Their father didn't seem to think that he could hear either. He'd blamed their mother for the birth defect and chose to ignore his own son.

Patrick had tried to tell their father that it was Shelly, not him, who was the gifted carpenter, but Solomon didn't listen. They'd gone as boys to help their big brothers build houses and churches in the area. When their two oldest brothers died in the war, and the middle two, only five years older than Shelly, ran away, Solomon told everyone in his small congregation that they'd gone to the devil, and he'd kill his own flesh and blood before he'd lose another son to Satan.

Patrick smiled, remembering his father's words. Come morning Solomon would lose another son, and there was nothing he could do about it. He took a deep breath of the humid Galveston air, thinking that tonight he could smell freedom, and at twenty it was about time.

The old buckboard was too light to leave noticeable tracks. Once they made Houston tonight, their trail would mix with a hundred others and no one would be able to track them.

"You don't have to go with me to the ferry," Patrick said to his brother. "I know what you're thinking. I need a best man. But we'll be lucky to find a preacher still awake in Galveston."

Shelly simply nodded. He'd obviously made up his mind. He would guard his brother until Patrick was off the island.

"It'll take you half the night to walk back home." Patrick did what he always did when nervous: He talked. "Did I tell you about how Annie Spencer came out to the barn after I delivered the firewood to her place? She's got it worse than we do stuck in the house with her stepmother. The old lady treats her bad. They don't even give her time off to go to church with the rest of the family. I told her once when I was delivering eggs that I wished I could leave Galveston 'cause Solomon gets crazier every year. She told me if I did, she wanted to run away with me."

Patrick was silent a moment as if listening to Shelly's answer, then added, "I know what you're thinking. I don't love her and I doubt she loves me and she ain't very pretty, not like those two stepsisters of hers. Those girls downright sparkle. Too bad they don't have a full brain between them."

Patrick drove the team, plotting out his life aloud. "I'm going to marry Annie. It's only right if she's agreed to go with me. Harmon Ely said I'd need a wife if I take the job, and she'll be a good one." He noticed Shelly's grin and added, "I know what you're thinking: Annie's older than me by a year so she's probably smarter."

Shelly nodded.

Patrick pulled the wagon up to the crossroads. No light shone from the direction of the Spencer house. If Annie was coming she'd be walking the path in almost total darkness.

"I hope she comes," he said to his silent brother. "She's got the prettiest eyes, and did I tell you she can cook?" He tried to relax, but the fear that she'd changed her mind weighed on his thoughts. "I'm going to be good to her. Better than Solomon was to either of his wives. And I'll listen to what she has to say, 'cause I have a feeling she's got a good head on her shoulders."

"I'm glad to hear that." A whisper came out of the darkness.

He looked down and saw Annie standing only a few feet away. "You came," was all he could think of to say.

She held up a pillowcase full of her things and then another long, feather-light pillow. "I came."

He swung off the wagon bench and put his hands gently around her waist. She was a tiny thing, barely five feet and less than a hundred pounds. Her long honey-colored braid hung down so long she could easily sit on it.

Awkwardly, he bent to kiss her cheek but missed and touched her ear.

She laughed and he lifted her up, saying, "Shelly wanted to come along as best man. Hope you don't mind."

To his surprise, she hugged Shelly. "I don't mind at all."

Then, as if she'd done so a hundred times, she scooted next to Patrick and circled her arm around his. "No one will miss me or my sister's new pillow until they wake without the smell of breakfast cooking in the morning."

She looked toward Shelly. "Don't look at me like that. I collected the feathers and made the pillow. Even if she claimed it, I figure I'd consider it a wedding gift she forgot to offer."

Both men laughed and Annie settled her small rounded frame between the two tall, thin McAllen brothers.

An hour later they drove the wagon onto the ferry and locked the wheels. Patrick hugged his brother but didn't say a word. He didn't need to. Shelly knew his thoughts. As they moved away Shelly stood on the dock, the only one watching them go. He raised his hand and held it high. Patrick did the same until the night separated them completely.

A young priest who worked at the hospital in town married them between helping with injured drunks. No flowers or well-wishers. No rings. Just simple words and a hurried blessing. The marriage didn't seem real, but now, as they left the last of their family behind, the truth of what they'd done seemed to weigh on them both.

"Do you think your brother will join us one day?" Annie asked, still waving at a man she could no longer see.

Patrick shook his head. "He doesn't like strangers, and after tonight he'd have to cross hundreds of miles of strangers to get to us."

As they moved over the water between Galveston and the rest of the state, Patrick told Annie all he knew of where they were going. "Not even a train passing near the place," he said. "Right now it's only a trading post, but the man who owns it wants to start a town. I'll work for two years at a fair wage to help build it, and then he says he'll give me land."

Patrick brushed the money packed away at the bottom of his sack of clothes. "I have money saved for more land. I'll build us a nice house and a proper barn. I'd like to run cattle on our land. A few at first, but eventually a huge herd."

He put his arm lightly across her shoulders. "What do you want, Annie?"

"I already have it," she answered. "I'm away." She moved her fingers over his hand resting on her shoulder and pressed hard, as if wanting to know that this was real and not a dream.

"Are we crazy?" he whispered.

"Probably," she answered. "But I'm not going back."

"Me either. Not ever." The sound of the whip still snapped in the back of his mind. Solomon had sworn that day that he'd never beat Patrick again. As he'd dropped the whip across his bloody back, he'd said simply, *Next time I'll kill you.*

That promise had haunted Patrick for five years, but it all ended tonight. Now he was free.

He didn't have to ask what problems Annie was leaving. He'd seen just a blink and that was enough. When he'd held her hand during the ceremony, he'd felt calluses. When he'd kissed her lightly in front of the priest, tears flowed down her face. She wanted this dream as much as he did. He'd seen it in her eyes for a year. Every time their paths crossed in town, he knew they were both thinking of the time he'd told her he wanted to run and she'd asked him to take her with him.

He'd never even walked out with a girl and now he had a wife. The only blessing seemed to be that she probably didn't know any more than he did about what marriage was all about.

He leaned down and kissed her gently, thinking he liked doing so far better than he'd thought he might. When she didn't pull away, he pressed his lips against hers and felt her sigh pass between them, and the kiss turned into something different. Something warm and welcoming.

When he finally moved away, he whispered, "I could get used to this, Annie."

"I think I feel the same. Do you think you might kiss me every night?"

He pulled her gently against him. "I'd like nothing better." They probably had a million things that were more important to talk about in this marriage, but kissing every night seemed a good place to start.

He'd heard Spencer say once that his oldest daughter never shone like his other two did, but there was a beauty about Annie that Patrick knew most folks didn't see. "In fact, if you've no objection I think we should set some rules down to this marriage, and the first one should be that I kiss you good morning every morning and good night every night."

"That's a lot of kissing." She giggled.

Patrick straightened. "I'm up for the task. Now you get to set the next rule."

"Fair enough. You have to promise never to lie to me. Not ever. Not about anything, big or small."

He agreed, thinking that an easy promise to keep.

About three in the morning, they docked. They followed the wide moonlit road, passing dark farmhouses and closed stores. Finally, after dawn, he let her off at the first mercantile they passed and went down to the livery to trade horses. By the time he got back she'd placed all they needed for the trip north on the bench by the store's door: pots, blankets, canned goods, dried beans, and coffee.

When he climbed down to load it all, she whispered, "Do we have enough money for this much?"

He nodded, thinking she'd be surprised at just how much money he carried. When he'd been alone in the barn, he'd taken the time to pull a few bills from his money pouch. No one seeing him pay at the store would guess he had more than just enough to buy what his wife needed, thanks to small carpentry jobs he'd done over the years.

For the rest of the day, one took a turn driving north while the other napped. Finally, when the road grew narrow and hard to see, they found a place to make camp.

Annie unfolded the bread and cheese she'd bought and they ate without talking, both too tired to make coffee. The night was cold, but they built no fire. They'd already decided to sleep in thc wagon bed.

He watered the horses while she combed out her hair,

then gave her more time so she could undress. When he returned, she was sitting on the back of the wagon holding her pillowcase.

"Everything all right?"

Annie shook her head. "I forgot to pack a nightgown."

"Oh." He almost laughed, thinking he'd tell her she could sleep without it. But he didn't figure that would work. "I got an extra shirt. You could have that."

"Thank you." She grinned. "I think I've found a kind husband."

What she didn't add hung between them. A bride should have a wedding dress and a proper gown for her wedding night. Even his older sisters, who'd never been able to step out with any man, all had lacy gowns they were saving.

He sat down beside Annie. "We'll pass a few towns before we get to where we're going. How about you buy one that you like, or maybe two. A proper married lady should have at least a few and a warm robe to wear on cold mornings."

She agreed. "Do we have the money?"

"We do," he answered, but she still didn't move.

Finally, he added, "Until we buy your nightgowns, we'll save the wedding night." He wasn't sure he could say more. He just hoped she'd understand what he meant.

"I'd like that," she said as she took his shirt, and added, "I wouldn't feel a proper married lady without a nightgown." Her long, straight hair waved gently below her round hips as she disappeared into the shadows.

He moved in the bed of the wagon where she'd spread the blankets flat and placed her one pillow in the middle. There was room for both of them on her makeshift bed. Without a word, he lay down on his back and stared up at the stars. A few minutes later he forgot all about the heavens when the silhouette of his wife moving beside him wearing only his shirt and her stockings appeared.

After a minute, she curled next to him, her head on the other half of the pillow and her shoulder pressed against his.

"It'll get cold before morning," he said as he spread the blanket over them both. "You might want to cuddle close."

"I'll do that." She laughed softly like women do when they're happy. "Good night, husband."

"Good night, wife," he answered with a smile.

They'd been married a day and nothing terrible had happened. This marriage thing wasn't near as hard as he thought it might be.

The sound of a bullwhip whispered in his mind as he drifted off to sleep, but Patrick paid it no mind. The fear that his father might be following faded a little. If Solomon planned to track him down and kill him, this wouldn't be a bad way to spend his last night on earth.

# Chapter 5

## Patrick and Annie McAllen

AFTER A WEEK ON THE ROAD, ANNIE DECIDED SHE AND her new husband worked like a well-oiled machine. They'd moved into marriage both accepting the other unconditionally, and their marriage rules grew, along with the laughter.

No going to bed without her socks on. He claimed he couldn't take the shock of her cold toes touching his leg in the middle of the night.

The one who drank the last of the coffee had to wash the pot.

He should always drive in the morning when the horses were fresh.

Each had their private time to wash and dress each day while the other stood guard.

As the list grew longer, so did the kisses. They'd both lived with so much criticism and so little affection that an overdose of kisses seemed the only cure.

Patrick, maybe because he had four sisters, seemed to understand women, or at least her. He never told her to do anything, only politely asked. He did most of the talking as they traveled slowly toward their new home, but she decided that was probably because he'd done all the talking for Shelly when they were growing up.

The only shadow she saw in his eyes was when he mentioned his brother.

One morning when she saw him staring down the road they'd traveled the day before, she whispered, "Shelly will come."

Patrick shook his head.

"He will."

"How do you know, Annie? He said he wouldn't."

"He misses you as much as you miss him. He'll come."

Patrick didn't look like he believed her, but he tried to smile. "I hope so." Then as if in a hurry, he said, "We'd better get going."

They traveled faster that day. Memories of home flew around them like the winter air. Both talked of their childhood and their fears. He told her of his four older brothers. Two had been old enough to fight in the war. The other two couldn't stand it at home so they left. Solomon said they went to the devil, but he and Shelly were working in Fredericksburg last year when a German asked them if they were kin to the McAllens farming over near Victoria.

"I like to think they're happy, not running around wild like Solomon says," he added. "Now I guess I'll be the old man's third son to go to the devil."

"No, you won't, because if you do I'll have to go along with you."

He moved the reins to his left hand and put his right arm around her. Pulling her close, he kissed her forehead. "If he ever does find me, I wouldn't put it past him to kill me. I've seen him turn away from people before. Cut them off like they were dead. He did that to a new widow who swore against God when her husband died. She and her children almost starved before anyone dared go against Solomon."

"He sees his family as part of him. And right now I'm thinking he sees me as a part that's now rotten to the core."

She kissed his hand. "When we were in school I used to watch the way you always stood up for Shelly. You might have been younger and smaller than the boys who picked on him, but you never backed down. You were a good boy, Patrick, and you're a good man."

"Just promise me if Solomon does ever come, you'll hide or run away, Annie. I don't want him hurting you. I don't think I could stand that."

"Don't worry about it. He'll never find us." Annie didn't turn loose of his hand, because she knew he was probably also praying her words were true. Solomon would never find them. Never hurt Patrick again.

They moved on, with the weather turning worse by the mile. By midafternoon it began to sleet and they knew they'd have to pull off the road and find shelter for both them and the horses.

A run-down farmhouse set back from the road was all they saw. Patrick turned the wagon onto a path marked with a downed fence. As they neared, even the snow couldn't hide the barn in need of a roof and a house with the porch sagging low at one side as if frowning.

Patrick knocked twice before a woman opened the door a few inches.

"Sorry to bother you, ma'am, but we'd be much obliged if you'd allow us to shelter in your barn for the night."

The woman looked from one of them to the other and must have decided they posed no threat. "You're welcome to come in and share my fire. You can put the horses in my barn, but I have no feed for them."

Annie had seen people on hard times all her life. When she'd been small, her mother would take loaves of bread to the widows barely surviving in Galveston. Only this woman was in rags and her place was almost empty of furniture.

"I have some potato soup, if you'd like some." The woman limped to the fire and pulled a pot away from the coals.

Annie looked at Patrick and saw that he felt the same as she did. Taking the woman's food seemed cruel, but hospitality demanded she offer and they accept.

As they sat and ate, the woman added a log to the fire. "I'm sorry I don't have more to offer. My husband died in the war and my son hasn't made it home yet. I've been just barely getting by since."

Eleven years, Annie thought. This woman had waited eleven years believing that her son might have survived and would someday make it back. Thousands had died and no one recorded their deaths except in numbers. How could she have kept hoping after a year, or even two?

As she talked about her boy and how good a son he was, Annie figured it out. Hope was all she lived on.

When Patrick offered to pay for the night, the woman, who introduced herself as Mrs. Dixon, shook her head. "You kids need your money to make a start. I'll get by."

Annie saw the pride in her as she straightened.

Patrick must have seen it also because he said, "The weather may be too bad to travel for a few days. Looks like a bad norther is coming in. I'd be pleased if you'd let me work off our keep. I'd hate to be caught out in the storm without shelter."

This Mrs. Dixon understood. "All right. My back door needs fixing. I'm not strong enough to do it myself. The roof leaks and with this bad leg I can't climb the ladder. You fix that, Mr. McAllen, and we'll call it even."

They'd settled on a plan. After supper, she showed them to her son's room. The bed was small, but everything was clean and in place as if she expected him any day. She might have sold everything of value in the rest of the house, but this was her only child's room and it would be ready for him when he returned.

Patrick went to put the horses and wagon in the barn while Annie changed into the shirt she'd claimed as her nightgown. When he returned, he stripped down to his long johns and climbed in beside her.

Annie cuddled beside Patrick and they whispered their plans for the next day. They'd do far more than fix the door. Mrs. Dixon needed wood chopped and fences mended.

While they talked, he gently stroked her hair. Annie wasn't sure why he did it, but the gentle touch seemed to relax them both.

She was almost asleep when Patrick asked, "Annie, would you mind if I touched you?"

Since she was pressed up against his side on a bed not big enough for them both to lie on their backs, she guessed he was already touching her, but she tried to wake up enough to understand his question. "Where?"

He was silent for so long, she thought he must have given up on the idea and fallen asleep. Then he said, "On your breast."

Now she was wide awake. "Why?" For almost two weeks they'd cuddled and kissed a few times each day; now out of the blue he wanted to touch her.

"Forget it," he said, and would have probably rolled over if he wouldn't have fallen out of bed.

She sat up, making room enough to turn and look at him. "I guess it would be all right, if you want to." Touching a breast wasn't making love, so they wouldn't be making a baby. And, since she was his wife, she knew at some point he'd be touching her.

She could feel him staring at her in the darkness, but he didn't say a word.

The light from a small window spread a dim yellow glow over her as she unbuttoned the front of the shirt he'd given her to wear. She opened it, exposing both of her breasts.

For a while he didn't move, and then very slowly he raised his hand and pressed his palm over one of her breasts. His touch was warm and tender. After a while, his fingers began to move, outlining the curve of each.

Her breathing grew rapid, but she didn't move away. When his full hand pressed over her, she drew in a breath of surprise.

"Does this hurt you?" he asked, his fingers still.

"No," she answered. "It's just that no one has ever touched me like you are now."

"It's something husbands do, I think?"

She nodded, unable to trust her voice.

"If you don't like me to touch you there, just let me know, Annie, but I have to tell you it's like you're giving me a great gift letting me do this."

He rose to his elbow and leaned close, gently kissing the fullness of each breast. When he lifted his head, he smiled. "Thank you. You're so beautiful, so soft there."

Annie didn't know how to take the compliment. No one in her life had ever said she was beautiful. When he leaned back, she buttoned the shirt and slipped in beside him once more. His arm circled, pulling her close against him.

He kissed her forehead and whispered, "Are you sure it didn't hurt?"

"No, it didn't. In fact, I think I liked it."

She was surprised when he laughed.

"I've been avoiding accidentally touching you in the wrong place since the night we married. Just wanting to has driven me crazy." He kissed her cheek. "Now I know how wonderful they feel, would you mind if I touched you there, not by accident, but on purpose now and then?"

"I wouldn't mind at all."

His mouth covered hers with a kiss that warmed her all the way to her toes. When he finally pulled away, she sighed and said, "We'd better get some sleep."

He agreed, but she had a feeling his heart wasn't in the idea.

When she awoke at dawn, his hand rested on her breast and she guessed it had been there all night. To her surprise, she didn't mind. In fact, she felt cherished. She didn't know much about men, but she figured Patrick McAllen, all six feet of lean muscle, was a good man and worth the loving. Right there, in the tiny bed, in the run-down house, Annie decided she'd love him the rest of her life.

By the time she helped Mrs. Dixon make breakfast, Patrick had fixed the back door and repaired the steps outside. Though the day was cloudy and promised rain, he kept working. Annie saw his skill in everything he did, not just repairing the barn and the house, but making it better than it had ever been. He even repaired the chicken coop, though Mrs. Dixon had not a chicken in sight.

On the third day the sun returned, but Patrick insisted on hunting so they'd have meat for the road. The deer he killed would give both them and Mrs. Dixon food for weeks. That night they huddled around the fireplace and talked about their families. Patrick told the old lady all about his brother Shelly. When Annie talked about her sisters and their fights over nothing, Mrs. Dixon laughed so hard tears rolled down her wrinkled cheeks.

As they had every night, Patrick took Annie's hand and led her to the bedroom. She'd change into the shirt with her back to him, and then they'd get into bed. Without a word, he'd kiss her good night as he slowly unbuttoned the shirt. His hands were bold now, caressing, pressing, and running his thumb over the tips of her breasts.

"I've waited all day for this, Annie," he'd whisper in her ear. "Touching you like this feels so right. You belong to me."

She giggled. "No, Patrick, you belong to me. I've already decided."

She let him take his time, never dreaming such a small thing would mean so much to him. Again and again he'd kiss her softly as his fingers moved over her.

Deep into the night she woke enough to feel him moving her to her back as he lowered his head between her breasts.

When she cried out in surprise, he moved to her ear and whispered, "It's all right, Annie. I'm sorry I woke you. I just can't sleep without one more taste of your beautiful body. It's so nicely rounded in all the right places."

"Kiss me first," she whispered. "Before you gobble me up."

He laughed. "Even if I do, you still willing to come along with me on the journey?"

"Yes," she whispered.

The next morning, when they finally hitched the wagon to head north, Mrs. Dixon hugged them both and wished them well. They'd told her their story about running away. As they climbed in, the widow gave them a box, saying it was a small wedding gift, but they couldn't open it until they had a house.

Annie didn't care what was in the box. It was a gift. Her first and only real wedding gift.

Three hours later, when they passed a small cluster of buildings that seemed to be built with no order, Patrick stopped in at the general store and ordered a dozen chickens to be delivered out to Mrs. Dixon's place along with ten pounds each of potatoes, sugar, and flour. While the owner, a man named Brown who'd lost the use of his arm in the war, gathered up everything, Annie added seeds for Mrs. Dixon's garden next spring and two nightgowns for herself.

When Patrick said he'd done some carpentry work out at Mrs. Dixon's place, Mr. Brown said he didn't even know anyone lived out there, but now that he did he'd stop by when he made deliveries out that direction and check on her.

As they loaded up to leave, Mr. Brown followed Patrick out and asked, "I got a load of furniture that came in three weeks ago. Factory shipped it in parts. With this limp arm I can't manage to handle it and hammer at the same time. Can't sell it when all it looks like is a pile of firewood. Any chance you'd stay a few days and help me out?"

Patrick hesitated. He'd like to help, but two days' more delay could cost them if, on a long shot, Solomon was following them.

"I could pay," the owner added.

Patrick figured he had plenty of money and a job already waiting for him.

"How about I pay in chickens to the old lady? A crate every fall and spring for three years if you'll work a full day."

Patrick glanced at Annie.

She smiled, reading him easily. "All right. I know you want to. I'll even help."

An hour later their wagon was pulled behind the store and they were working. Annie might not be able to lift a man's load, but she was a great help, and talking as they worked made the time fly. Before dark they'd completed all the furniture. Patrick, with his carving skills, carved the store name on a long board over the door. The owner offered them supper and breakfast and, of course, six crates of chickens as payment.

They ate, collapsed in their wagon bed, and slept until dawn. Just in time to eat again before they headed out.

As they moved on down the road, Annie said, "You know, Patrick McAllen, I think I'm falling in love with you."

He winked. "It was bound to happen, wife. I always figured I'd be irresistible if I ever stayed around a girl long enough for her to discover it."

That night, when she opened her nightgown just as she'd done the shirt for several nights, he smiled. "I'm afraid I may have started something. If we're not careful this nightly thing we do could become a habit."

"You're no longer interested in touching me?"

He pulled her down in the wagon and covered them both with a blanket. "Wife, I promised I'd never lie to you. I'd have to be dead not to be interested in you. All I think about is what might happen after dark."

She giggled, knowing that tonight they'd be giving up sleep while they got to know each other better.

"Can we take our time?" she whispered. "I want to remember everything about tonight."

His hand slid over her hip. "I've many parts of your lovely body to explore if you'll allow me, but you don't have to remember everything. I'll be happy to repeat each step."

She cupped his face in her hands. "You make me feel beautiful."

"You *are* beautiful, Annie. You always have been, just no one took the time to tell you." Patrick whispered his first promise again. "I'll never lie to you, remember."

# Chapter 6

## Captain Gillian Matheson

MARCH

CAPTAIN GILLIAN MATHESON DIDN'T BOTHER TO SLEEP. He'd been out hunting outlaws for three months only to find trouble waiting for him at the fort. His wife had sent a letter saying he had to join her at a trading post run by Harmon Ely by the second week in March. No details. Just the place and time.

Hell. It was already the seventh of March. He'd have to ride hard and fast to be on time. He dug his fingers through black curly hair that was so dirty it looked brown.

She hadn't said why, but Gillian knew it must be life or death. She'd never leave her family farm in Kansas otherwise. His wife, Daisy, was the most nesting woman he'd ever seen. He usually couldn't even talk her into going into town for supper when he was home on leave.

He swore as he stuffed a clean uniform into his saddlebags. He had to get to her. She might refuse to travel with him, but she was his wife. If she needed him, he'd be there.

His blond, beautiful, smiling Daisy. Her pure sunshine

had blinded him the day they'd met and he'd tumbled straight into love five years ago. They'd been married two weeks after they said hello, only to discover she wanted him to quit the army and stay on the family's farm. He thought she'd pack up and go with him.

He'd left her after a short honeymoon, planning to return on his next leave and change her mind. Only she'd been with child when he returned, and the option of her being with him was dropped.

Somehow, with time and another baby, they'd settled into a life apart. He'd always thought someday she'd change her mind, and he guessed she felt the same. Now, if she was in real trouble, it might be too late for them. They were both in their twenties. He'd figured they'd have years together eventually.

Gillian walked out of the bunkhouse at dawn and headed to the livery to saddle his horse. She wouldn't be dying, he decided. She couldn't be dying. The letter might be a month old, but he'd get to her in time. She'd already traveled half the distance between them; he'd make the rest. If she was dying, he'd not leave her side.

Sunrise sparkled along the horizon as he tried to think. The commander had told him to take all the time he needed. Gillian wished it were a battle he faced now. He could handle that, but he wasn't so sure he could deal with losing Daisy. He picked up his step, knowing the sooner he got to the trading post, the better.

The girl Gillian had found in an outlaw camp last week was waiting for him at the corral. She hadn't spoken to him all the way into the fort, but now she looked like she planned to talk to him.

Sergeant Watson's wife stood beside the girl. She must have outfitted her in a coat, boots, and wool trousers. All looked two sizes too big. The wild girl didn't look happy to be cleaned up. In fact, she'd shown little emotion at all since he'd loaded her up with the two Osborne brothers he'd arrested and brought here. The only time she looked interested in anything was when her eyes darted toward the gate, as if she planned to bolt as soon as possible. Who knew how many years she'd been with the outlaws or where she'd been before that? For all he knew she might be more wild animal than human. He'd seen it before.

The sergeant's wife didn't waste time with hellos. "She's older than she looks, Captain. I'm guessing fifteen, not twelve like you thought. Commander told me to have her ready at dawn and tell you to drop her off at the mission. He says it's on your way south."

Gillian shook his head as he saddled the first horse. "I haven't got time, Livia, I have to meet my wife."

"Well, with my five kids, I ain't got time to keep up with her. We can't just toss her out. You found her. She's your responsibility." Livia was a woman few men argued with. At five feet ten she stood eye to eye with Gillian. "She ain't said a word to me, but if I were you, Captain, I'd sleep with my weapons handy."

He gave up and started saddling another horse. "If she don't talk, that's fine with me as long as she can ride well enough to keep up." He'd seen kids like this before. Maybe they were captured during the war and didn't remember where they were from or who they were, or sometimes their parents died and they were taken in by first one family, then another. For all he knew she could have been born in the outlaw camp, though it would have been hard for a baby to survive.

Since the war, the orphanages were crowded and no one kept a record of every child born.

Gillian looked down at her. "Want to tell me your name, girl?"

She shook her head.

"All right. I guess it don't matter much anyway." She hadn't cared when he'd shot one of the outlaws she'd been with, or waved when he'd hauled the two Osbornes away. They were nothing to her and, as far as he knew, so was he.

"Climb up if you're going with me," he said, and watched her jump up onto the mare. At least she understood what he said. That was enough. He didn't need to talk to her. The only word he'd probably need to say to her was good-bye when they reached the mission.

They rode until full light, and then he passed her a biscuit he'd lifted from the mess hall.

She ate it, but didn't even nod a thank-you. Her mud-colored hair hung at different lengths, and with the big hat he'd probably never see her face again.

By dark, he was feeling more like he was riding alone across the open country. She kept up, never got in the way, and never complained. Without her saying a word he'd learned a great deal about her. One, the sergeant's wife was right; she must be small for her age because she handled a horse with far more skill then a twelve-year-old would have, and two, she knew how to live off the land. She never over-watered her horse or went too fast down a ravine. She moved over the prairie leaving no sign she'd passed.

When they made camp, he asked her to water the horses while he built a fire. By the time she came back he'd made coffee and warmed beans, *and* had time to worry that she might not return. He'd watched her all day and guessed she was waiting for the right moment to run. Watering the horses had been her chance, but she'd stayed. Gillian guessed she'd been studying him too and figured out that when she did run, he wouldn't chase her.

As usual, she didn't say a word as she sat down on her blanket and stared at the fire.

Gillian was tired of the silence. "This place I'm taking you to isn't so bad. The priests from the mission run it. When my family was all dead, I went to a place just like it."

He didn't add that he ran away after two weeks and caught a freighter wagon back to the fort where his dad had last been assigned. The soldiers decided to let him stay and he worked with the blacksmith until he turned seventeen and joined up. Back then he'd been too young for the soldiers in the barracks to pay much attention to, so he used to curl up with books while they talked or played cards until lights out. The post had a set of law books, and by the time he was grown he'd read them all several times.

Gillian glanced at the girl. He decided she might not have the options he had. This country was hard on women.

"They feed you regular meals at the mission and make you go to school every morning, and then everyone has a work duty in the afternoon." He thought of adding that it was the most boring two weeks of his life, but he guessed that wouldn't be too helpful. "You could learn to read and maybe cook or sew." Any skill might give her a chance. "You could become one of the sisters. They have a quiet life, I think."

She didn't answer. He gave up trying.

She rolled up in her blanket while Gillian tossed a few logs on the fire and decided to worry about Daisy's letter. If she was dying, a part of him would crumble. He might not see her often, but she was the keeper of all the goodness in him. The kindness. The laughter. The love. And he had never told her that. If she died, he'd have two boys to raise. It wasn't fair to drag them from fort to fort but, like his father, he didn't know any other life.

Prairie winds kicked up, making the fire dance in the starless night. Gillian stood and tossed his blanket over the girl before walking away from the fire. He needed the night's blackness to count all the things he'd done wrong. Daisy's face kept drifting through his mind. Her big sparkling green eyes. He could have stayed a week longer last time. He could have made time this summer to ride back to her. He could have explained how hard it was to be in the middle of her huge family when he'd never known any family except his dad.

They all loved her back at her family farm. Gillian wasn't sure his own father loved him. Every time he'd ridden off, he'd yelled back for Gillian to stay out of trouble and make himself useful and be a good soldier. Then, one day when his father hadn't come back, Gillian had done exactly what he'd been told. He'd become a good soldier.

Only he'd been a lousy husband. He hadn't been a father at all. And now it might be too late. Maybe one or both of his sons were hurt or ill. Daisy had written once that they both had his black hair, his good looks, his ornery nature. He barely knew them.

He pushed hard the next day. The girl never complained. When they reached the mission, he had to pull her off her horse. Much as she seemed to dislike him, it appeared she hated the idea of staying at the mission more. She fought, but in the end, she stayed.

Gillian rode away feeling as if he'd added another layer of guilt on like paint. If there had been time he would have tried to settle her with a family. Maybe they'd treat her as one of their own kids. She still had a year or two of growing up to do. Or maybe they'd treat her like a slave. He'd seen it before.

He'd left her the little mare at the mission, asking the brothers to let her have it to ride when she'd settled in. The mare wasn't much, but at least the girl would have something to call her own.

By dark, he'd crossed farther into Texas and was riding hard. He didn't bother to build a fire when he finally stopped. He just staked the horse and curled against a rock. Out of the wind, he slept solid, dreaming as he often did of green eyes and silky blond hair filling his hands.

The next day dawned sunny for a change. The traveling was easy now over flat land. About noon he shot two jackrabbits and decided to stop before dark so he could build a fire. Another few days and he'd cross the road heading south that would lead him to the trading post. It might be little more than wagon ruts, so he'd need to be alert. In this part of the country there was a good chance that anyone he encountered would be more outlaw than law abiding. Even teamsters traveled fully armed. The uniform he wore would keep outlaws at a distance, he hoped.

When Gillian returned from watering his horse, one of the rabbits he'd staked for roasting was gone. For a moment, he frowned, wondering how someone could get so close without him hearing. It didn't take much to figure it out.

"Come on out, girl. I know you're there. You might as well be warm by the fire."

The girl he'd delivered to the mission moved out from the brush, a half-eaten jackrabbit-on-a-stick in her hand. "If you take me back I'll just run again as soon as I get the chance. I don't want to go anywhere with you, but I wouldn't mind riding along until you hit civilization. After that, I can take care of myself."

Fat chance, Gillian thought as he sat down, leaned against his saddle, and started eating. "I agree that taking you back would probably be a waste of my time, so I vote we ride together for a while." Someone would have to keep her out of trouble. In this country a girl could wander around forever without bumping into a town. "Glad to see you can talk. How long did it take you to break out after I left?"

"Two hours. You were easy to track, but hard to catch."

"Why follow me?" He wouldn't have admitted it to her, but he was glad to see her. Talking to himself had been downright depressing of late.

"I ain't got nowhere to go and you seem in an all-fired hurry to get somewhere. I'm not joining up with you and I won't cook or clean up after you. I'm just headed in your direction."

"You got family somewhere?"

She shook her head. "All dead."

"You got a name?"

"Jessie, just plain Jessie. I don't have a last name."

"All right, Jessie, you can ride with me, only you cook every other meal, understood? I don't have time to turn around and take you back. I need to get to my wife. She's meeting me at this little place where two streams cross. Once we come across the wagon tracks all we have to do is head south to find it. So you can come, but if you give me any trouble or slow me down, I'll leave you out here for the coyotes."

She nodded.

He watched her in the dying light as she struggled to take off her saddle and care for her horse. No matter how grown she thought she was, Jessie was small, about the same size he'd been when he'd found himself alone. He couldn't help but think that for a boy it was hard, but for a little girl alone in this country it would be impossible.

Whether Jessie liked it or not, he'd find a way to help her.

The next morning she shared the bread she'd stolen from the mission with him and they were in the saddle by full light. As the days passed he learned more about her. She didn't like to talk and hated answering questions. She didn't know how old she was. She never remembered having a real family, just a mom for a while.

Gillian liked having someone to talk to, even if he was carrying most of the conversation. He also knew how she felt, all alone and homeless, so he gave her the only gift he could. He taught her every survival skill he knew, including how to fire a gun. She'd need them all if she planned to make it to adulthood in this country.

The morning they finally crossed the wagon tracks that served as the only road for a hundred miles, Gillian began to have the feeling that someone was watching him. Jessie must have felt it too, because she pulled her mare closer to him.

He looked back once and thought he saw a thin line of dust that one horse traveling fast might have kicked up. But nothing else. Not a sound. They were moving into open land with few hills or valleys. By tomorrow he'd see trouble coming from miles away. By tomorrow they'd be safe. If they had to, they'd leave the road and circle down, then come into the trading post from the south. Gillian didn't like the idea that he might be leading trouble right to the place where his wife was meeting him.

The sky clouded over before dusk, and a slow rain began to fall. Jessie pointed out a place where rocks formed a rise in the earth big enough for them and their horses to take shelter. A cliff protected them from the rain, but not the wind. Without fire or anything to eat, Jessie settled in among the saddles and went to sleep.

Gillian stood guard even though he couldn't see more than a few feet beyond the rain. He couldn't shake the feeling that someone was tracking him, and he'd made enough enemies to know that if he wasn't careful he'd be dead by dawn.

Finally, when a watery light spread across the horizon, Gillian closed his eyes and leaned back against the wall of rocks. The rain had stopped and the earth seemed newborn and silent. He was thinking of Daisy and how she wrote all her thoughts in a book every night before they went to bed.

She'd had schooling, all the way to the tenth grade, and she'd said someday she wanted to teach.

The click of a gun being cocked brought him full awake. He reached for the Colt he'd left beside him.

The gun was gone.

Slowly he opened his eyes. Nate, the youngest of the Osbornes, who'd gotten away over a week ago, now stood five feet from him, a rifle pointed toward Gillian's heart.

"You're a hard one to track, Captain Matheson." The outlaw grinned with teeth yellowed and broken. Nate Osborne couldn't be out of his twenties, but he'd grown up in a rough family.

"You could have gotten away, Nate." Gillian kept his voice low and level. "I had my hands full with the others. You could be holed up somewhere safe. Why track me?"

"Yeah, I thought I might keep going. You never would have tracked me down. But you had something of mine." He tilted his head toward where Jessie was still sleeping between the saddles. "She ain't much, but she was promised to me when she finished growing. I wouldn't let any of the others touch her. Never had me a virgin before. I'd been chasing her around the past few months so she could get used to the idea of me bedding her regular when she fills out. I'm thinking once I have her, I'll use her every night till she wears out, then I'll trade her off. She's small, but I guess she's pretty enough and she's quiet. Never could stand it when a woman screams while she's being used. The last woman I climbed on was a screamer. I made her sorry she made so much noise. I want to see if the next one I try will be, but women in these parts are hard to find unattended."

Gillian sat up. "And you're telling me this because?"

"Because I want Jessie to tell me if you bothered her. 'Cause if you did, I'll gut-shoot you and let you die slow." Nate turned his head slightly, but his rifle remained pointed directly at Gillian. "Girl! Get up and come over here. I got a question for you."

When Jessie didn't move, he yelled, "Girl! Unless you want a few blows in your middle, get over here."

Nate smiled at Gillian. "I don't never hit her in the face." He said it like he was bragging about how considerate he was of the kid.

Jessie stood, showing no sign that she'd been asleep. She took a few steps toward Nate without looking at Gillian.

Nate laughed. "I come to save you, girl."

She faced him. "I'm not going with you. I know what you got planned for me and I ain't going."

Nate frowned as if surprised she'd dared to talk to him. "You belong to me. You can't just decide to go off with this captain. I traded a horse for you, so you're going with me. It's about time you learned a few more ways to be useful."

"I ain't with him." She pointed to Gillian. "We're just riding together. He's nothing to me. He didn't touch me. There is no need to shoot him."

Nate raised the rifle. "Oh, but it's his time to die and I ain't bargaining with you. He was a dead man the moment he rode into our camp. He just didn't know it yet."

The next few seconds of Gillian's life passed in slow motion.

He saw the barrel leveled toward his head.

Jessie moved sideways, swinging her arm in front of her. The morning sun flashed on his Colt in her hand. In the space between heartbeats, she fired at the same time Nate pulled the trigger on the rifle.

Gillian felt like a horse kicked him in the head. He tumbled backward from the force. The last thing he saw before all went black was Nate crumbling as if boneless.

For a moment, as the shots echoed off heaven, Gillian searched the darkness for Daisy. If he died here, now, she'd never know how much he'd loved her. She hadn't been just a part-time wife; she'd been his only wife. He might not have known how to be a husband, but he'd been true to her and kept her in his heart.

He'd always planned to someday go back to her.

He fought through the pain and concentrated on her green eyes. If he died here today, he wanted Daisy to be the last thing he saw in this world.

# Chapter 7

## Trading Post

Daisy Matheson tried to talk her family into letting her go alone to join her husband, but they wouldn't hear of it. Finally, she simply started packing, leaving them no say in the matter.

All her brothers, and every one of her nephews over fifteen, volunteered to go with her to Texas. If she was moving to Texas, they planned to make sure she got there safely.

She loved the company, but they were bound to find out that she'd lied if they met up with her husband, so she had them deliver her earlier than she'd told Gillian to meet her.

The family didn't need to know that Captain Gillian Matheson hadn't quit the army and wasn't planning on joining her. In fact, he didn't even know his wife had forged his signature on an agreement to work for Harmon Ely. She'd been writing the trading post owner for four months, and all her letters were signed with her husband's name.

She'd been the one who'd applied for and accepted the job

to help build a town. The dream of joining her husband in a newborn town had been just too good not to gamble on.

So, she loaded her four little boys, with black hair and blue eyes like Gillian, and all her household goods in two wagons. The trip took a month, but with her two older brothers driving the wagons and four of her teenage nephews riding along to scout and hunt, the journey was an easy one. Her parents insisted she take two milk cows and a crate of chickens. The men also brought extra horses, planning to leave some with Gillian and ride the others back home. They'd get her to Texas and settled, then ride back to the farm in time to help with the spring planting.

Daisy, who'd never been more than a few miles from home, was both excited and terrified. The last time Gillian came home he hadn't begged her to go with him, but she hadn't been brave enough to leave. Her mother had told her if she held out, eventually Gillian would stay on her family's farm. Only he didn't, and each time he rode away, more of her wanted to go with him. When he hadn't made it home for Christmas, she knew she was losing the little piece of him she thought she had.

She had to change. She had to go to him. Standing up to her family had been far harder than the monthlong journey. They'd all taken their turn listing all the reasons she should stay, but Daisy kept packing.

In the end, they'd all stood and watched her go. She'd silently cried every night for the first week, and then slowly an excitement built inside her. She'd never been brave, but she was now doing one brave thing.

During the journey, the weather was cold and the days boring, but she'd made it to Harmon Ely's trading post by the first of March. Like her family, Harmon believed her husband would join her within two weeks. He put her and the boys up in his own room beside the kitchen and left her wagons packed in the barn. The owner of the trading post took one of the small rooms upstairs that he'd added on for his children. He said his family would come as soon as the town was built.

Daisy settled in and waited. Her handsome captain would

come. He would stay with her and they would start a new life together, she kept telling herself, but deep down she feared he might not join her. If he didn't, she'd go back home and call herself a widow for the rest of her life.

Harmon Ely was a grumpy old man in a fifty-year-old body. His hair seemed to have slipped off the back of his head. The few remaining strands hung tightly to the last of his scalp in long, fussy, gray ringlets. After eating his cooking for two days, Daisy offered to take over the kitchen as part of her board. Though Mr. Ely lived alone, he had a habit of inviting anyone riding by to stay for supper, and with Daisy cooking, he did so proudly.

As soon as the settlers passing by tasted Daisy's food, they began to shop later and stay for another meal. In exchange they brought apples, peaches, and butter. So apple pie quickly became a standard at the trading post table.

Daisy didn't mind the extra people at the table. She was used to cooking for a dozen or more. Only a few of the men smelled so bad she made them take their supper on the porch.

On warm days she roped off the back porch and let the boys play while she baked bread and did laundry. Mr. Ely claimed just the smell of her bread doubled his sales. More often than not, when he wasn't busy with a customer, the old man was playing out back on the porch with her sons. He was a man who loved children and talked about how his were growing up without him.

"As soon as I get this town built, my family is coming," he'd say over and over.

In the evening, after the dishes were done and the boys were asleep in their bed, Daisy always went to the rocker on the front porch. Mr. Ely had tried his best to make the rebuilt trading post look like a respectable mercantile. He told her he'd always seen the store as the first of a dozen along a street welcoming everyone to the little town.

This place might be in the middle of nowhere with mostly hunters, teamsters, and dirt-poor farmers as customers, but she loved the sunsets. It was like God was making up for all the plainness of the land by putting on a grand show every night.

On the third night she was there, Harmon Ely stepped onto the porch with a can of paint. Without a word he painted over the "1" on the population sign and replaced it with the number "6."

Daisy giggled. She and her boys had just been added as residents.

She waited for Captain Gillian Matheson. Staring to the north every evening until it was full dark. Hoping. Willing him to come. Longing to change the sign to read "7."

# Chapter 8

MARCH

CLINT TRUMAN, DRESSED IN THE SAME BLACK SUIT HE'D BEEN married in, sat beside his wife on a train heading north. She'd held the baby the first few hours, and then she'd lowered him into the basket lined with a blanket. He slept as the train rocked him.

Clint watched her, not missing how she cared so gently for a child she hadn't named. When he moved closer to the window, she set the basket between them. He wished he'd been close enough to offer his shoulder for her to sleep on, but he doubted she'd use it. Karrisa, so prison pale, held herself so stiff he almost expected her to snap.

He decided she'd once been pretty before prison thinned her so and life hardened her to stone. She rarely made any effort to speak. They could have been total strangers riding the train and not man and wife.

At noon the train stopped long enough for folks to go into the train station to eat lunch away from all the smoke. Once they settled on a back bench, he opened the meal and offered her half.

She hesitated. "It's too much. I only need a little."

"You'll eat, Karrisa, for the baby's sake. If you don't take in enough food you won't make enough milk to feed the baby." He wished he could think of something to say besides an order, but nothing about her manner seemed to welcome conversation.

She must have understood his reasoning, for she took what he offered. When she finished, she surprised him by leaving the sleeping child with him while she made a trip to the washroom.

He caught himself smiling at the baby when no one was looking. The little fellow had a spot of dark hair on top of his head and blue eyes that hadn't learned to focus.

"Your first?" asked the woman sitting down on a bench facing him.

Clint could do no more than nod. If he lied and said yes, it would be as if he were forgetting his daughters, and if he said no, he'd be saying the baby wasn't his and he'd promised to all they met that he'd claim the boy as his.

The memory of his girls flashed in his mind, blinding him to all around him. They'd been four and five with hair so light it was almost white. It didn't matter if he'd been gone a day or an hour, they'd always run to him and he'd swing them up into a hug.

The last memory stomped through his brain. They'd both been crying, begging him not to leave when he'd hurried out to get the doctor. Only a few miles from town. Only a short wait for the doctor. Only a few miles back to his farm. But it had been too late.

He hadn't hugged them that last time. He'd been too worried. He'd been in too much of a hurry.

Clint moved his scarred hand across the blanket, gently patting the baby with no name as he tried to push his regret into the shadows. Would a minute of hesitation have mattered? The hugs he never got to give would haunt him until the day he died. But he'd not let them break him. He'd not drink them away this time. He might never know love again, but he had a mission. A simple reason to live. He'd keep this baby and his mother safe.

He was thankful Karrisa returned before the woman could ask more. When the old woman tried to start a conversation with her, his wife shook her head and whispered something in German.

Clint did his best not to smile. Clever way to avoid conversation.

When they walked back to the train, he whispered, "German?" Hoping she'd tell him a little about herself.

"I also speak Italian and, of course, a little French and Russian."

"So, you can *not* speak to me in three languages," he stated simply.

For the first time he saw the hint of a smile on her pale lips.

When he offered his hand to help her onto the train, she took it even though she didn't say a word.

At dusk he'd climbed off the train at a water stop and refilled his canteen. With each stop the car had emptied more until now they were the only two in the last car. He stood in the dark and watched her breast-feed. She was careful, very discreet, but still he watched the touching sight and remembered the wife he'd loved. She'd been his world, his happiness, and every thought of missing her was like a gaping wound he'd never be able to heal.

But he wouldn't compare her with Karrisa. He couldn't. It would hurt too much. This was his life now. His only life. He might have no love or joy, but at least he had a reason. Sheriff Lightstone must have known that was what he needed. Clint would help build this town in the middle of nowhere, and he'd take care of this woman who wouldn't talk to him.

When he finally joined her as the train started up, his mood was so dark he didn't look at her. He simply pulled his hat low and pretended to sleep until they reached the next stop along the line heading toward Dallas.

There, they had to find a hotel. In the summers people would camp out on the platform for the night, but it was too cold for that now. He carried their bags and she carried the baby as they walked across the street to the only place still open.

Clint booked them a room using only his name.

The clerk glanced down and said, "Welcome, Mr. and Mrs. Truman."

Neither of them answered. Clint simply took the key and headed up the stairs. The place was so poorly built the whole staircase seemed to sway with his weight.

Their room was small, but warm and clean. He insisted she take the bed, and he pulled a chair up to the foot of her covers. Propping his feet on the bed, he leaned back in the chair so that he could see both the door and the window. He'd heard stories of thieves robbing travelers as they slept. Anyone coming in would have to step over him.

When he lowered the lamp, she whispered, "I learned to speak German and French in a factory I worked at in New Orleans. Women, mostly immigrants, were hired to run the machines and do the handwork on all kinds of clothes."

He couldn't see her in the dark. "Did you like working there?"

"No, but learning the languages helped pass the time. It turns out I have an ear for it. I hear a word a few times and I remember it." Her voice came gently across the darkened room, refined and educated without the hint of an accent. A lady, he thought, only ladies don't walk out of prisons.

He knew she was making an effort to talk to him, but he was so out of practice he didn't know how to keep a conversation going. "That's good," he finally said. "We'd better get some sleep."

Neither bothered to say good night. Near dawn, when she woke to feed the baby, he grabbed his hat and told her he'd go downstairs and order breakfast.

Half an hour later when she joined him, she had used one of her tiny combs to pull her hair back on one side, but it did little to improve her looks. If the woman were any paler, she'd glow in the dark.

He offered to hold the baby while she ate.

They didn't talk. She ate and he patted gently on the

baby's blanket. A tiny hand swung out of the covers and clamped onto his finger.

Clint couldn't hide the smile. "Hello, little fellow," he said. "Nice to shake your hand. I'm your papa, so it's about time you said hello."

He waited to see if Karrisa would object. He'd said he'd claim the boy, and he just had. When she didn't comment, he continued talking to the child. "We're heading north to a town that doesn't even have a name. The sheriff said it's a place where two rivers cross. Soon as you're big enough I'll take you fishing, if your mother doesn't mind."

For some reason talking to the baby was easier than talking to her. As she ate her breakfast he kept telling the newborn things about all that was going on in the north. "I'm thinking this may be my chance to start all over, and I'm going to do my best to do it right. I'm going to take care of your mother. Of course, she can speak three languages, so if I do something wrong she can cuss me out three different ways."

When he heard the whistle blow, he looked at his wife. "Finish your meal, dear. We need to be on our way."

For a moment he thought she might argue, but then she ate the last few bites and tucked the extra biscuit in her napkin.

"You called me *dear*," she said as they walked toward the train.

"It seemed the proper thing to do. *Mrs. Truman* might be a little formal and the use of your first name doesn't feel just right on my tongue yet."

"*Dear* is fine, Truman."

Clint smiled. Apparently his first name didn't sit just right on her tongue either.

When they boarded, they found themselves alone in the car except for two young salesmen playing cards on their boxes of goods to sell. He rode, watching the scenery, and she laid the scraps of cotton she'd washed in the sink at the hotel out to dry on the empty backs of seats. By the time they made the first stop, all the cotton squares were dry and folded back into her bag. The baby would need them soon enough.

Several cowhands climbed on at the stop, and she used

his coat to cover her when she fed the baby. Clint moved to the seat nearest the aisle and placed his legs on the seat opposite them. His body formed a barrier, protecting her.

When she put the baby back in the basket, she made a tent with the extra blanket and set the basket next to the window where the sun warmed the seat. Then she leaned her head on Clint's shoulder and fell asleep.

For a while Clint didn't move, and then he tucked his coat over her. She was a brave little thing, he'd give her that. The baby was barely more than a week old and she hadn't complained once. He'd heard her moan in her sleep last night. Tiny cries as if something haunted her dreams. She'd said she worked in a factory, yet the traveling suit she wore was far too finely made to belong to a working-class girl. She'd been educated before she worked in a factory. He'd bet on it. Maybe even pampered. But now she had nothing but a few worthless squares of cotton for the baby to call her own.

They reached Dallas before dark and he thought of getting a carriage and going to a good hotel a few blocks from the station, but she looked so tired, he settled for the best room at a small place a hundred yards from the tracks.

While she rested, he checked out liveries that sold buggies or wagons. The buggy would be more comfortable for her, but the wagon would be far more useful once they got where they were going.

He settled on a wagon with a cover so she could sleep if she needed to. He bought two horses to pull the wagon and another for himself. He had no idea if Karrisa rode but guessed she wouldn't be doing any for a while.

When he returned to the hotel, he was told that his wife was taking a bath and had asked not to be disturbed. He waited a half hour, then tapped on the door.

One of the girls he'd seen in the hotel's café opened the door. "You're just in time, mister. I just brought up your supper."

He walked in and saw two plates set out by a small fireplace. Karrisa was sitting in one of the two chairs with the baby asleep in her arms. She had on her nightgown. Though the gown buttoned to her throat, he didn't think it was quite right that he have dinner across from a woman who wasn't dressed. Then he reminded himself she was his wife. The fact was in his brain, but the feeling hadn't registered yet.

For once, she looked up at him and repeated his thoughts. "I know it's not proper to have dinner in my nightgown, but I washed my traveling clothes and haven't had time to make another dress."

"You don't have to explain." His words seemed to relax her a bit, and she nodded slightly. "You're the lady of the house, even if this is just a hotel room. You can set any rules you like."

"I'm not sure what you like to eat, so I ordered two different plates."

"I don't much care as long as it's food. During the war I ate peanut soup and bark stew. You cook and I'll eat once we get settled. As long as it's not peanut soup I'll probably like it just fine."

He washed his hands at the stand while she put the baby down to sleep in his basket.

When they sat in front of the fire, the room seemed overloaded in silence. As always, she picked at her food, testing the first few bites as if she feared it might be bad.

"Roast is good," he offered. "You need to—"

She raised her fork and pointed it at him as if it were a weapon.

He waited, thinking this might be how she had killed someone. So far she'd left no hint of how she'd landed in prison. He'd never heard of a fork murder, but it was possible.

"Please, Truman." She lowered her fork. "Don't keep telling me to eat. I'll try, I promise, but don't keep ordering me."

Her words were a request, as if what she asked was not her right to demand.

"All right," he said, thinking that this was the first time she'd looked like she might live more than a few days. "I'm not in the habit of ordering anyone. I'm also not in the habit of talking to a lady. You may hear an order, but I'm thinking I'm making a suggestion. No matter what I say, you have no call to ever be afraid of me. Ever."

"I'll try to believe you, Truman, but it may take some

time." Her shoulders straightened a bit as if he'd just handed her an ounce of power.

He saw how hard she was trying to be brave. "Tomorrow, I'd like to leave as soon as we stock the wagon. We'll have about ten days, maybe less on the road, so we'll need blankets, food stores, and tools. Anything you want for the trip, I'd appreciate it if you'd let me know."

She nodded and they ate the rest of the meal in silence. He'd expected her to go to bed, but she gathered up her sewing and began measuring out a dress. He watched her working, careful not to waste an inch of material.

As the fire grew low, she wrapped one of the baby blankets over her shoulders and kept working.

"You need your sleep, dear," he finally said in a voice he hoped didn't sound like an order.

She didn't look up from her work. "If I can get this one dress cut out, I can sew it on the road tomorrow. May I work a little longer?"

"You don't have to ask," he said. "I was just making a suggestion. You're free to do as you will." It crossed his mind that she might still decide to leave. They were barely more than strangers.

Clint fell asleep watching her work. A few hours later, the wind woke him as the windows rattled. She'd gone to bed and the extra blanket was resting over his body. He pulled the other chair closer to prop up his feet and went back to sleep.

The next morning while she fed the baby, he collected the wagon. The cover over the wagon bed was tall enough to stand in, and someone had built a fold-down cot on one side. With the flap pulled down in the back the covered wagon reminded him of a flimsy cave, barely strong enough to hold out the wind and rain, but cozy inside.

He bought plenty of supplies, not knowing how many trading posts would be along the trail of a road heading north. Huge wagons left out ahead of him carrying lumber toward Fort Elliot. The man at the livery said the tent fort on the edge of the Indian Territory would be a real fort by summer. Once that happened, the traffic on the north road would double.

For all Truman knew, double could be from ten to twenty. After all, the man called the trail of wagon tracks a road.

At the last moment, he purchased a small rocker and put it in the back. It would rock along when the wagon was moving and give her privacy when she fed the baby.

Clint told Karrisa the news of the new fort when he picked her up. He hoped she'd feel safer, but what his wife feared seemed to lie behind her, not in front of them. Now and then he noticed her glancing back as if to see if her past followed her.

He didn't comment about her fears, for he often felt the same way. A few of the things he'd done during the war to save lives had been considered spy activity. When all the Southern men who fought were given amnesty, those who committed acts of spying were left out of the pardon.

It had been eleven years since the war. Surely no one was looking for him now, and no more than a handful of men knew he'd crossed into northern territory a few times to spy. Most of those were Southerners who'd never testify against him, and the few who weren't would be living up north, not down here in wild Texas.

Still, he froze now and then when a shadow crossed his path. That was why he didn't settle down when he first came home. Why he'd moved his wife twice in the five years they'd been married. But no one had ever called him out or knocked on his door. Eleven years. He was safe.

As they traveled farther north, he guessed he did ninety percent of the talking. She worked on her dress, then knitted a blanket for the baby. He drove the wagon, took care of the horses, and built the fire every night. Then, to his surprise, every evening she handed him the baby to hold while she cooked. The meals were simple. He never complained or complimented. They were simply each doing their job.

She slept with the baby in the wagon and he slept on the ground by the fire. Every night he'd hear her cry out softly in her sleep as her nightmares came to claim her rest. Once, after she'd woken him, he heard her crying. Clint listened to her, knowing he wouldn't be welcome if he tried to comfort her.

Hell, he thought, he wouldn't know how to comfort a

woman anyway. He'd learned that there are some things in this life that can't be smoothed over with kind words, and whatever she was crying about sounded like one of them.

During the day he'd learned that if he ended his orders with *dear*, she was much more likely to do whatever he needed her to do. "It's time for you to rest for a while in the back, dear." "Finish your meal, dear." "Let me help you with that, dear."

She was not dear to him, but the one word made orders into requests.

The journey from Dallas was uneventful until the last day.

# Chapter 9

MARCH

PATRICK MCALLEN TOOK HIS TIME MOVING DOWN THE road on the cool winter afternoon. He knew they were close to the trading post, far closer than he wanted to be. The days on the journey had been a dream. It had taken them almost a month by wagon from Galveston, but he felt like he'd passed from one life to another. He'd become a man. A husband. Nobody's boy.

Sleeping out under the stars with Annie by his side on clear nights and cuddling close to keep warm on cold nights was a kind of heaven, he'd decided. They'd bought what they had to along the way, and he'd hunted a few times while she'd made camp. Both loved talking, sharing, and best of all, they'd made love so many times they'd both lost count.

They laughed often, saying they hoped they were doing this marriage thing right. They'd sing songs until she complained about him being tone deaf. So he'd sing louder until she started beating on him. He'd finally give in, ending his performance until she was almost asleep, and then he'd whisper his song in her ear. She'd giggle and fight him for the one pillow to put over her head.

Now and then a wagon would pass. Every time Patrick would ask how far it was to Harmon Ely's trading post. Finally, this afternoon, a man had said simply, "A few hours."

The stranger's guess took Patrick by surprise. He'd thought they had another day or two. He thanked the man and moved on, slowing his pace rather than hurrying.

"You afraid to get to Harmon Ely's place?" Annie asked at the same time she bumped his shoulder with hers.

He wasn't surprised she'd read his mind; she'd been doing it often lately. "All I ever thought about before this trip was getting away and starting a new life. I thought I'd push the horses as hard as possible the whole way, but that was before you. Part of me wants to stay on the road forever, just me and you. We could become Gypsies and never talk to others or settle on a town or have to work. We could pass the years growing old as we always turn down the less-traveled road when we come to every fork in life."

"I'd love that, but eventually we'd run out of money."

"But I don't know what's ahead of us, Annie. What if building this new town is terrible? What if we hate it? There are outlaws and Apache in this part of Texas. I'm good with a hammer or a plow, but I've never been much of a shot and I've never worn a holster."

She cut him off. "If it's terrible, we'll hitch the wagon and find another town. And as far as handling a gun, I'm fair. I'll ride shotgun for you."

"It could take a long time to find where we belong. Most of the towns in this part of the country are populated by prairie dogs."

"But this place doesn't sound so bad. I want a house to really cook in and a real bed to sleep in and children to raise and . . ."

He smiled. "Just think, when you married me a month ago all you said you wanted was to be 'away.' I was the one who wanted everything. Now, all I want is you. I'd be happy with campfire food and the sky as my roof if you were next to me, Annie."

"Not me. While you were sleeping on me last night, I was sleeping on the ground."

"I don't remember you complaining last night. I barely had the energy to keep going, wife. I think people who do what we did last night must age twice as fast."

"If so, we'll be dead by summer."

He grinned. "I wouldn't complain."

He watched her stretch as she whispered, "I think we may have had a little too much fun last night. My whole body is sore. I don't think people are supposed to make love on the ground."

"I'll build you a bed, Annie. As big as you like, just as long as I can find you in it." He studied her. "It's not just what we share in bed, you know. I love being with you. I think I was a very lucky man that night you asked me to marry you."

She smiled. "You asked me, Patrick McAllen, and don't you forget it. I won't have our children thinking—"

Annie froze, her brown eyes growing huge in fright as she stared straight ahead.

"What—" He looked in the same direction. For a moment he thought what headed toward them was a horse pulling a pile of rags between two poles tied on either side of an empty saddle. Then he saw the girl walking beside the horse, her head down, her coat spotted with dried blood.

Patrick shoved the reins toward Annie and reached for the rifle under the seat. "Stay here, Annie, and keep the rifle ready."

He jumped down and ran toward the girl. "Are you all right? What happened? Can I help?"

Forcing himself to breathe, Patrick calmed. He was a grown man. He could handle this. If he got too excited he'd probably frighten the girl covered in blood.

She stared up at him with eyes that looked hollow from lack of sleep. "I've been walking for three days but I'm not hurt, just tired." She rubbed the front of her coat. "This blood belongs to the captain. He was shot in the head and I can't stop the bleeding."

Patrick knelt down beside a man bundled in dirty blankets. He rested on branches tied to the poles that pulled him along. Blood was everywhere, but the man she'd called the captain was still breathing. He wore the uniform of a soldier.

"Annie, fire off a shot. If the trading post is close they might send someone to help." Patrick placed his hand on the man's chest and felt a strong heart pounding.

The sound of one round of gunfire seemed to echo off heaven. Then silence.

Annie climbed down from the wagon and lowered the rifle. She moved slowly toward the man wrapped in blankets.

The girl started to cry. "Please help the captain. Please help him. He was just trying to protect me. He didn't do nothing wrong to get shot."

"We will," Patrick promised, having no idea how to keep his word.

Annie knelt down and pulled the blankets from his chest. "No blood here," she said. "I think he's just shot once in the head, like the girl says." She pulled the scarf from her neck and wrapped it tightly around the soldier's head.

Patrick watched, unsure of what to do.

Annie's voice came through to him, giving Patrick direction. "If we can get him in our wagon we can travel faster. We can't be far from help." She put her arm around the girl and guided her toward the wagon. "This one may not be bleeding, but she's about to drop. I'll get her up in the wagon first."

Tears bubbled in the girl's eyes, streaking her face. "I'm so tired, I must have missed the trail north of here. When I realized it I decided to circle around, hoping to come across the wagon ruts going to the trading post. I hoped any trail I took would lead me to folks who might help. The captain said he was meeting his wife at Harmon Ely's place. I got to get him there. It's all my fault he's hurt."

"We're heading that way." Patrick finally got a handle on his fear. "Annie, clear a place and I'll carry him to the wagon."

Before they could lift the captain, they heard horses

heading toward them fast. Patrick reached for the gun and stood beside Annie. The half-grown girl disappeared amid the supplies.

Briefly, he thought of jumping in the wagon and making a run for it, but whoever was coming might be the answer to their call for help. Or—a thought crossed his mind—anyone coming might think that he'd shot the captain.

There was no time to run, and the captain's life might be at stake. There was no time to waste. Patrick widened his stance and prepared to face whatever was traveling at full speed toward him.

A quarter mile away he saw a wagon about the size of his, only with a bonnet covering the bed. A man and woman were on the bench. The man driving handled the wagon like an expert.

"Help," Patrick whispered. "Help is coming."

The tall, wide-shouldered stranger dressed in black and wearing one gun while carrying another jumped from his wagon and hurried forward. Before he could ask questions, Patrick told him what he knew.

The stranger nodded once and handed his rifle up to his wife.

It only took a minute for them to lift the injured captain into Patrick's wagon.

"I'll follow you," the stranger said to Patrick. "We need to move fast. I don't know how much time this man has, but we've no time to waste."

As Patrick moved onto the bench and took the reins, the stranger added, "My name's Truman. Don't worry; I'll keep you covered until we're all safe. Whoever did this may still be out there."

Annie and the girl sat beside the man as if buffering him on either side.

As Patrick pushed the team into action, the stranger who'd said his name was Truman stripped the makeshift travois off the tired horse and tossed it aside. The flimsy stretcher on poles fell to pieces as it tumbled down toward a stream.

Glancing back, Patrick saw that Truman had staked the animal a few yards off the road. The horse could graze and reach a stream. He'd be fine until they had time to get back to him.

Within a few minutes, Truman was close behind Patrick as they raced across the dried grass. When they saw the roof of what had to be the trading post, Truman pulled even with Patrick. "That's it, kid. I'll pull up first. You hang back a little to make sure whoever shot the captain isn't at the trading post."

Patrick yelled back as he fought to control the horses. "Truman, we're the McAllens. Patrick and Annie."

The man named Truman touched his hat in greeting to Annie and then pulled ahead to lead the way.

Patrick drove as fast as he could, thinking that whatever lay ahead of him might be trouble, but at least it would be interesting. This was the most excitement he'd had in his life, and suddenly all the world looked like an adventure.

Glancing at his new wife, he knew she felt the same way. It was as if they'd been asleep since birth, just waiting to start living. He saw fear in her eyes, and excitement and love. Wherever he was going, she planned to be right by his side.

Annie sat in the back of the wagon cleaning away blood from the man's face using the last of the canteen water.

When the man called the captain asked for a drink, she took a deep breath for the first time. "Hang in there, sir, you might just make it."

"Daisy," the handsome officer muttered. "I have to get to my wife, Daisy. She may be dying."

Annie gave him another drink. "Don't worry, Captain, we'll get you to your Daisy."

Patrick looked back at her. For a moment their gazes met and he knew they were both thinking the same thing. He hoped her promise was true.

# Chapter 10

HARMON ELY'S TRADING POST

JUST BEFORE DUSK, ON AN EVENING ALMOST TOO COLD TO sit out on the porch, Daisy Matheson moved to the rocker. Her sons were asleep. Time to sit and wait, and hope that her Gillian was heading toward her. Tomorrow would be the ides of March, the day she'd said she would be waiting for him. Her note hadn't said what she would do after March 15 if he didn't show up, because Daisy had no idea. Going home seemed her only option, but going back to her family didn't seem right when her heart only wanted Gillian.

She could close her eyes and remember every detail of how he'd looked when he'd ridden up to her family's farm that winter five years ago. She'd been barely into her twenties and thought he was so handsome in his cavalry uniform. He'd been a few years older and a lieutenant then, riding with four of his men from farm to farm. They were looking for a band of outlaws who'd been causing trouble.

Her father had winked at her when he'd invited the soldiers to supper as if he were giving her a gift. By the time she handed Lieutenant Gillian Matheson his dessert, she was in love. It had been mid-December and when her father heard Gillian had no family to go home to for Christmas, he invited the young soldier to stay with them. By New Year's they were married.

Daisy thought of how simple it all seemed at first. Since he had no family, she'd shared hers. They all welcomed Gillian in. On a large farm another set of hands was always needed.

When he left for an assignment she thought he'd come back to stay soon, even though he talked about her joining him at one of the frontier forts. But one year turned into two and then three, and his visits grew farther apart each year. The last time he came home they'd argued, crushing each other's hopes. He wouldn't stay and she wouldn't leave. She'd known it would be a while before he came back, but after another year passed, Daisy knew she had to act. By accepting this job for him and moving here, she'd find out if Captain Matheson was staying away from her family or her. She'd crossed more than the distance he'd have to ride from Fort Elliot, but he'd have to come the last hundred miles to her.

She was no longer a girl. Daisy was twenty-six and the mother of four sons. If Gillian didn't come, she knew she'd be his wife until the day she died, but she'd stop waiting for him. If he didn't come, she'd go back home and raise her sons.

She'd never sit on the porch again, watching the night, hoping he'd come back to her.

Pulling her shawl around her, Daisy leaned forward as the sound of horses came through the evening shadows like a rattle on the wind.

Standing, she saw two wagons moving toward her. The first one was covered, driven expertly by a big man in black. The second looked to be a work wagon like her family used on the farm. A younger man drove the second wagon and two women, one more girl than woman, sat sideways in the back.

The second wagon pulled ahead of the first. In the two

weeks she'd been at the trading post she'd seen no women, only soldiers or men hauling supplies to the forts, or cowboys moving cattle to the markets north. The sight of females rushing toward her surprised and delighted her.

Daisy stood, an uneasy feeling turning over in her mind. Mr. Ely had told her two more couples would be coming, but these wagons were pushing hard as if trailed by trouble.

Picking up the lantern, Daisy moved down the steps. Without turning back, she heard Harmon Ely move through the door of the store and stand on the first step. His bulk always made the first step groan.

She guessed he'd have a rifle at his side; he usually did when visitors arrived late. Both times he'd been robbed, trouble had come at dusk.

The half-grown girl in the back of the first wagon looked up. She must have seen Daisy standing on the steps. In the jingle of harnesses and stomping of horses, she called, "You Daisy, miss?"

Daisy saw that the girl and a woman had something between them. Something wrapped in blankets, about the size of a body.

"You Captain Matheson's wife?" the girl called again as the wagons pulled to the front of the store.

Daisy couldn't move. She knew that the body in the wagon bed was her husband. Her mind knew, but her heart wouldn't accept it. Gillian was a strong man who looked quite handsome in his uniform, the perfect image of an officer.

The body wrapped in dirty, bloody blankets could not be her man.

"Miss?" the girl said in a voice that sounded like it hadn't been used in days. "Mrs. Matheson? I brought the captain to you."

Daisy lifted her skirts and ran toward them. Deep down in her very center she knew it was Gillian. She knew even before she saw his face.

The lantern in her hand swung wildly, giving flashes of the man in only blinks of light. Blood on the blankets. Blood shining in his black hair. His hand lay across his chest, holding on to a Colt as tightly as he seemed to be holding on to life.

"It's Captain Matheson, lady. I sure hope you know him 'cause neither one of us is going to make it much farther."

The two men who'd been driving the wagons circled around her and began moving the body out of the wagon bed with great care.

"We found them on the road a few miles back," the younger of the two men said.

Daisy turned the lantern up. "I'm his wife," she announced, as if they wouldn't let her touch him if she wasn't kin. She wanted to scream or run from the horror of it all, but she had been raised on a farm. When trouble came, be it illness or accidents, everyone went to work on the problem. On a farm, no matter how many were in the family, there was never time to panic or hesitate.

Questions could wait; she had to get Gillian inside.

Harmon Ely's rough voice snapped orders as if he knew the man carrying her husband up the steps. "Get him to the back room. Spread him out on the kitchen table. We'll clean him up and have a look at where he's hurt."

As they passed Ely, the old man looked at the youngest stranger. "McAllen, right?"

The tall, thin young man nodded, his face reflecting a menagerie of emotions from excitement to worry.

Ely turned to the other man, in his early thirties. He was almost as tall as McAllen and looked wide with muscles, but his face gave no emotion away. "Then you're Truman," Ely said.

"I am," was all the big man had time to say before they passed him.

Daisy cradled her husband's head as she guided the men through the store to the back room. She wanted to pull back the corner of the blanket covering half of his face, but she feared what she might see.

It took all three of them, but they maneuvered Gillian into the kitchen without bumping into anything. Blood and mud seemed everywhere. The girl started crying and muttering her disjointed story. "I didn't know what to do. He got to shaking like he was real cold. I figured he'd die if we stopped to build a fire, so I just kept moving. When it got cold I piled mud and leaves on him, hoping it would keep him warm."

A woman a few years younger than Daisy and almost the same height stood beside her and whispered, "I'm Annie McAllen. We're going to need a doctor for both your husband and the girl."

"Ain't got no doctor out here, miss," Harmon Ely snapped. "Up until a few weeks ago the population of my town was one."

While Ely got the doctoring box, Daisy glanced toward the child who'd brought Gillian to her. The girl looked frightened and about to drop.

Daisy offered her hand to the girl and led her to a chair by the potbellied stove. She covered the girl with her shawl and drew her a dipper of water from the bucket. Daisy needed a moment to comprehend all that was happening around the table.

"Will you be all right here for a while?" Daisy whispered.

The girl nodded. "He talked for days about how we was heading south to you. Then, when he got shot three days ago, he kept saying your name like I might forget to take him home to you." The girl looked up. "I didn't forget."

Daisy touched her shoulder. "You did good getting him here. Now rest. I'll take care of him for a while."

As she stepped to the table, the men backed away. They'd stripped Gillian to his waist and pulled away all the blankets. His chest had a few bruises, nothing more. As Daisy's gaze rose, she braced herself but still took a step backward when she saw the wound along the side of his head. It looked as if someone had taken a blade and scraped an inch-wide trail from the edge of his forehead into his thick black hair, leaving nothing behind but bloody open flesh.

He'd always been so alive, so perfect, her young lieutenant, her strong captain. Her husband. Her only lover.

Now he was broken. His face ghostly pale and his eyes closed. No longer perfect. No longer strong.

Ely began laying out supplies while Daisy washed away the last of the blood.

"It looks like a bullet wound grazed the left side of his head just above his ear." Ely announced the obvious. "Some of the wound has scabbed over, but it'll need cleaning. That place on his forehead is still dripping blood."

Daisy went to work. Around the wound the skin was red and puffy as if infection had already set in.

She never considered herself much of a nurse, but she'd seen enough wounds to know that if she didn't get it cleaned fast, blood poison would kill him. His skin was already hot to the touch. Another few hours and he would be on fire.

She cleaned the area as best she could using chloride around the wound and lye soap where it wasn't bleeding. "Hold him down," she whispered to the two men who'd brought him in. Then, with a new scrap of cotton, she dabbed iodide on the wound.

The captain gritted his teeth, refusing to scream. After one final jerk to break free, he passed out.

The woman who'd hugged Daisy when they first brought Gillian into the kitchen now stood beside her, silently helping whenever needed. Annie McAllen was younger than Daisy, but she didn't seem a stranger to working through emergencies.

The two men and a tall, thin woman had backed away into the shadows of the kitchen. All were silent. All watched. The thin woman had been so quiet she almost seemed like a shadow in the background.

Daisy had little idea who any of them were, but she felt like they were all somehow connected. Like strangers in a lifeboat or lost miners in a dark tunnel. Their lives depended on one another, and right now it was Gillian's life that was in danger.

After they'd cleaned the wound and wrapped a bandage around his head, she finally took time to look at her husband's face. Always before, when they'd been together, there had been a slight smile on his mouth, in his eyes. Now, his eyes were closed and pain twisted his handsome features into someone she barely recognized.

She cupped his whiskered face in her hands. "You're

going to be all right, Gillian. You got to me in time. I've got you now. Just sleep until you're ready to wake up and tell me of this latest adventure. You know how I love hearing all about them." She knew others were listening, but she had to add, "I love you, darling. I always have and I always will."

He didn't answer, but her words seemed to calm his breathing.

"You've been working three hours, ma'am," the younger one of the tall men said softly. "If you'll sit a spell, Truman and I'll put a nightshirt on your husband and move him to a bed."

Daisy looked up at the two men who'd brought in her husband. "I'm sorry I didn't have time to introduce myself. I'm Daisy Matheson and this is my husband you may have saved from death's grip. His name is Gillian, but most folks just call him Captain."

Both men nodded a greeting.

"Like I said in the middle of all the panic earlier, I'm Patrick McAllen and this is my wife, Annie." He pulled the chubby little woman who'd stood by Daisy's side for hours closer to him. "We're from Galveston, but we've come here to build a town."

"Hello." Daisy smiled, noticing the way they clung to each other. There was a time she and Gillian had been that way. Those first few weeks they were married they couldn't stand to be apart.

The other man straightened. His features were harder, his eyes weary of life, and he wore a Colt strapped to his leg. "I'm Clint Truman, but most people just call me Truman. My wife is feeding our baby in a corner of the store." He seemed to hesitate as if forgetting something before he finally said, "Her name is Karrisa. Karrisa Truman."

"Thank you all. Mr. Ely told me you were coming." She turned back to her husband. "Tomorrow, when the captain wakes up, I'll tell him all about how you saved his life. Right now, if you'll move him very quietly into my bedroom, I'll sit up with him. It must be close to midnight and I'm sure you'd all like to get some sleep."

Clint Truman and Patrick McAllen did as she'd asked while Patrick's wife took the girl into the store to find a nightgown. Daisy could do nothing but watch. Gillian looked like a huge rag doll as the men moved his arms into a nightshirt and then pulled off his muddy boots and trousers.

Daisy smiled. Her husband had never worn a nightshirt. He'd be surprised to wake up with one on in the morning. She followed as the men carried him to the room beside the kitchen that had been Mr. Ely's bedroom.

Now the old storage room was crowded with beds: two small cribs she'd brought with her, one regular bed, and a set of bunk beds for her oldest two sons.

Patrick smiled and whispered, "Reminds me of home. I'm the youngest of six brothers and we all slept in the same room. My mom used to say we slept in the same room so long we snored in harmony."

As they carefully lowered Gillian into the bed, Patrick asked Truman, "How about you? Did you come from a big family?"

The man in black didn't smile. Truman simply said, "No."

Patrick nodded as if he'd figured out something. "I guess you and the missus are planning to have a big family. Give that baby of yours lots of brothers and sisters."

"No," Truman said. "I think we'll only have one. Might get one that talks too much if we keep going."

He glared at McAllen so hard Daisy almost laughed before she shooed them both out of the room. The last thing she needed was for the babies to wake up. Abe at four and Ben at three would probably go back to sleep, but the twins would be up the rest of the night.

"I'll sit with your man awhile, Mrs. Matheson," Ely said from the doorway. "You might want to check on the girl. She's welcome to sleep in the kitchen close to the stove. To tell the truth I don't think she wants to be any farther away from the captain."

Daisy thanked him. Old Ely wasn't a naturally friendly man. Most days he didn't say one nice thing to anyone, but he cared about children. She'd seen it in his worry over her boys and now about the girl.

When Daisy found the girl, who said her name was Jessie, she was cleaning away the mess they'd made doctoring Gillian.

Without a word, Daisy hugged her and they both cried. Finally when Daisy pulled away, she said, "Thank you for bringing him to me."

Jessie nodded. "I knew he'd die if we didn't keep moving. Except to let the horses rest now and then we haven't stopped moving for three days. Yesterday, sometime, I think I must have fallen asleep on my feet. The mare the Captain bought me must have wandered off, but I didn't have the time to go look for her."

Dark circles shadowed the girl's eyes and her hands were raw from gripping the rough rope.

Daisy sat her down and cleaned her hands, covering the tiny cuts with lanolin and wrapping the palms with soft cotton. Then she warmed soup and sliced bread for Jessie.

While she watched her eat, Daisy slowly pieced together what had happened. The girl looked too tired to chew, so Daisy helped her to the cot and said good night.

"Will I have to leave come morning?" Jessie asked.

"No. You're part of our family for as long as you want to be. We'll not hold you if you want to leave or ever turn you out."

Jessie smiled and closed her eyes as Daisy layered blankets over the girl, then walked out to the store where she heard the others talking.

The sense of family covered her once again. Three couples who would build a town had finally come together.

Daisy thanked them all once more and showed them upstairs to their rooms. Ely had moved his few belongings into the first room off the landing. The other two rooms were farther down a hallway with a bathing room at the back.

As she walked, she talked. "Mr. Ely told me he has three kids and these will be their rooms when his family comes.

His wife said she's not making the trip until there is a town. He's spent years building his business at the trading post. I've been here for two weeks and am surprised at how many people pass through."

Truman pointed to the back bedroom. "We'll take this one, dear," he said to his silent wife.

She nodded and moved inside.

Truman turned to the others. "Any idea what the old guy has planncd for us?"

Daisy grinned. "I don't think he has much of a plan, just a dream, but I've been talking to him." She turned to Annie. "If you can help me with breakfast in the morning, we can all talk about a plan then."

"If the kitchen is stocked, I can manage breakfast for eight, ready to eat by dawn." Annie straightened with pride. "I'm used to cooking for a group. I'll cook and you watch over that injured man of yours."

Daisy agreed. "It's stocked, but if you need anything there is a store a door away."

Everyone except Truman laughed, relaxing for the first time.

The young couple, Patrick and Annie, took the middle bedroom and said good night as Daisy walked back down the stairs. In an odd way she no longer felt homesick. She was surrounded by her new family, and they'd help her watch over Gillian until he was whole again.

After stoking the fire in the kitchen stove, she slipped out of her dress and lay on the other side of the bed from Gillian.

He was so still she wasn't sure he was breathing. Putting her hand on his chest, she whispered, "Get better, my one love. Get better. We've much to do here."

# Chapter 11

TRADING POST

TRUMAN CLOSED THE DOOR TO WHAT WOULD BE HIS BEDROOM until the homes were built. It was small, with a bed, a desk, and a chair. He felt like a giant invading the room of one of the seven dwarves. Ely had built the upstairs room for his three children, but they wouldn't come until the town was finished. There were no curtains on the windows or rugs on the floors, but the place was warm and dry. It would serve fine.

Folding his black coat over the chair, Truman tried to relax. He hadn't carried a bleeding soldier since the war. Tonight brought back the hell he'd lived in for four years. The smell of blood. The chaotic panic of trying to fight death for a man's life.

Karrisa set her bag on the bed and pulled out a nightgown. "If you'll watch the baby, I'll go down the hall to the washroom and change."

"You don't have to leave the room to change. I am your husband." He didn't know why he'd said such a thing. Maybe because the other two couples seemed to be really married, not simply pretending to be. Karrisa was playing her part, but they still were far more strangers than friends.

When he met her gaze, he saw fear in her eyes again. They'd been together long enough to have developed a bit of trust between them, but she still looked at him as if he'd try to kill her at any moment. She was the one who'd gone to prison, not him. If anyone should worry about waking up dead, it should be him.

"Forget I said that," he snapped. "I need to go down and take care of the horses. Take your time in here. I'll bring in enough blankets to make my bed over by the window and the basket for the baby to sleep in. Anything else you'll be needing tonight?"

"No," she answered, then stood frozen as he passed her and left the room.

Clint made it to the barn before he shook the anger with a list of swear words mostly aimed at himself. He might have been her last choice for a husband, or more likely her only choice, but he'd been kind. He'd never yelled and he'd tried not to make everything he said sound like an order. He even traveled slower than usual so she wouldn't tire out on the trip.

The least she could to do was not brace for a blow every time he was within striking distance of her.

Suddenly realizing someone must have hit her several times to cause such a reaction, Clint calmed.

Swearing again, Clint decided he'd put a bullet in the man if he ever came across him. That would probably have him thinking twice about hitting a woman, if his cracked skull could hold a thought. Clint considered that the guy could have been a prison guard, but she had no bruises when she walked out. Her body was frail from bad food and delivering a baby, not beatings.

Questions, he thought. Questions he'd never ask his wife about.

He fought the urge to go back for one of the bottles of whiskey he'd seen on the shelf at Ely's store. A few drinks would take the edge off his life. He had no idea how the job was going to work out now that one of the men was down. Or how long he could stay married to a woman who obviously hated him. She never said one thing to him that she didn't have to. If liking being around him could be measured on a scale of one to ten, Clint figured he'd be sitting on zero.

Every time he saw her rocking the baby he thought of another time, another wife, another baby. Part of him wanted to tell her that once he'd had a woman who thought he hung the moon and didn't freeze every time he got within three feet of her.

Only he couldn't talk about his Mary. He'd sworn he'd never bring up his past or Karrisa's. But somehow this not talking didn't seem the way to start. They couldn't very well spend the rest of their lives not speaking, not touching.

Or could they? He decided that being around someone who didn't want to be there was worse than being alone, and he'd become an expert at being alone.

After he brushed down the horses, Clint walked through the barn taking inventory. Whatever his job would be tomorrow morning, he needed to know where things were. The old guy was well stocked with what looked like enough hay to last the winter and enough lumber lining the back wall to frame out at least one house. Two years didn't seem long enough to build a town, but the old man seemed to think that if they put up the buildings folks would be like ants at a picnic. They'd just move in.

When he finally walked back to his bedroom upstairs, Clint heard the young couple in the middle room whispering and laughing softly. They were no more than kids, but Patrick and Annie seemed made for each other. They touched every time they got within three feet of each other. Patrick was tall and she was short and rounded, but somehow they fit together.

Turning the doorknob on the last door, he slipped into his room, surprised to find the lamp still burning low. Karrisa was in bed with the baby tucked in beside her. Her eyes were closed, but he doubted she was asleep.

He moved to her side of the bed. "I brought you up a cup

of well water. Thought you might get thirsty after the baby nurses."

"Thank you." She shifted and took the cup. "I know you don't think so, but you are good to me. I've no complaints, Truman."

He didn't know what to say. How bad must all the men in her life have been for her to think a hard man like him was good to her?

"You all right with this setup, dear? I don't think I heard you say a word to anyone tonight."

"I'm fine." She set the half-empty cup down beside her bed.

"That's all?" He wanted her to say more.

"After watching Daisy doctoring tonight, I think the first thing we will need in our new house is a medicine box."

"All right." He waited for her to say more.

She looked a little frightened, as if she'd been put on the spot. It took her a while, but she added, "Everyone seemed nice."

They were on safe ground now. They could talk about the others, and for a change he needed to talk. "The McAllens are young. Little more than kids. Old Ely said he's a good carpenter, but it bothers me that he doesn't carry a gun. With Captain Matheson down, if trouble comes, I may have to handle it alone."

"Can you do that?"

"I can," he answered without hesitation. "I was barely seventeen when I ran off to the war. I was trained very well over the years." He hesitated, not knowing how much to tell her. "I'd rather face a half dozen men alone than have to worry about McAllen getting hurt trying to help. So if a fight comes, I'll do my best to keep him out of it."

She asked no questions.

He walked over to the window and stared out at the moon, remembering the times he'd killed. In self-defense, to save others, because he was ordered to. The reasons didn't matter. The ghosts of those who died would always haunt his nights.

After a while, he spread his blanket out and lay down on the floor. Before he fell asleep, the baby began to fuss.

Karrisa sat up and opened her gown. As she began to breast-feed, Clint realized she hadn't turned around or covered herself with one of the baby blankets. She had no idea if he was awake or asleep in the shadows. The light from the moon came through the window, crossed above him, and shone on her.

Her breasts were full and nicely rounded, her skin as pale as her gown. When she finished she tucked the baby in the basket he'd left by her bed, and then she buttoned up her gown. As she slipped the last button in, she raised her head and stared directly at him. "You are my husband," she whispered. "I've no reason to turn away when dressing or undressing."

He'd lost the ability to speak. All he could do was stare and wonder if she could see him watching her. Had she been talking to him, or herself?

The next morning, while he held the baby, he pretended not to watch as she removed her nightgown and slipped into her clothes. After all, he wasn't interested in her as a woman. She was a wife in name only. Plus, she wasn't beautiful. Way too thin with hair that had no shape at all.

When he handed her back the baby, he said simply, "Now you are ready, it's time we go down to breakfast, dear."

She followed him out of the room and down to the little kitchen behind the store. Leaves had been added to the table to accommodate ten chairs, but there was barely room to walk.

As promised Annie, Patrick's wife, had made what she called a farm breakfast, complete with pancakes, eggs, and ham. She told anyone who listened about how her father had her cooking for his new wife and her daughters by the time she was eight.

Daisy was already at the table and smiling. Her husband hadn't opened his eyes yet, but his fever was down and he seemed to be resting easy. "The captain won't stay down long," she repeated to everyone, as if saying the words made them true.

Ely joined them, saying that the girl, Jessie, had asked if she could sit with Captain Matheson for a while. The old man couldn't stop smiling. His dream was about to come true. He filled his coffee and picked up his plate. "I eat in my store at sunrise. Open seven to seven every day but Sunday. Expect all of you to work the same hours except a week off if you need to plant a garden in the spring. Anything you grow or make can be sold in the store. You keep the profits as long as I keep one out of every ten things, be it pies, eggs, or carrots, to stock my kitchen. Any questions?"

Patrick, who'd been helping his wife put the food on the table, asked, "What am I going to do with all my free time?"

Everyone laughed, but Clint had the feeling Patrick had asked an honest question. In truth, he wondered the same thing. Seven at night to bedtime seemed a long while to spend in a little room with a woman who never talked to him.

He pulled her chair out and waited for her to sit down. As usual, she didn't say a word. He really didn't care. Being sober made him aware of how much time people waste talking.

Clint didn't miss the four chairs at the far end of the table filled with tiny little boys who looked just like their father, Captain Matheson. Daisy introduced them with a wave of her spoon. Abe, who could talk, said he was four. Ben, who spoke in some indecipherable language, sat beside his older brother. The other two didn't look old enough to walk and were both tied in their chairs with apron strings.

"Twins?" Clint asked the stupid question.

"No." Patrick pulled up the chair next to him. "Why would you say that, Truman? What was your first clue?"

All the women, even his wife, laughed at Clint.

"Look, kid, I was just trying to make conversation." Clint decided he could dislike Patrick McAllen if he half tried.

"Don't call me *kid*," Patrick said politely. "Name's Patrick."

Clint saw a touch of steel in the kid's green eyes. "You got it, Patrick." Maybe the kid was worth liking after all. Clint respected men who stood up.

They ate breakfast like they were all half starved. Patrick's wife, Annie, said shyly that she'd cook more tomorrow. "Since I'm the only one without children to worry about, it makes sense that I'll cook the meals. Breakfast at dawn. A simple lunch at noon and supper when you get in at seven. Fair enough? I'll try to make desserts as I cook and they'll be left on the table if anyone gets hungry between meals."

No one argued. It had been so long since Clint had a dessert, he wasn't sure what they were. Maybe he'd try to come in every afternoon that they were working close by and have coffee and dessert with his wife. She could stand to gain a few pounds.

In the silence, Clint was surprised Karrisa spoke up. "I'll do the dishes after every meal and make the bread as needed. I'll also keep the water buckets filled in both the kitchen and the dressing room upstairs."

Daisy jumped in to offer help. "When the boys take their naps, I'll help out in the store as soon as the captain's better. Ely has a good business, but he'll be the first to admit that his books are a mess." Daisy glanced from Annie to Karrisa. "We'll work everything out here. It'll be easier than building a town."

Patrick moved his plate aside and spread out a piece of brown paper. "I talked with Ely early this morning. He has no idea how to start, so I came up with some ideas for building that need working on before spring. For the time being I suggest we use the kitchen as our meeting place and headquarters. I thought I'd start on the buildings that would benefit us all the first week and move to the houses next. We'll need a better smokehouse, a forge, and there's work that needs to be put in on the barn to hold not only our stock but our supplies."

Clint listened to Patrick. The kid knew what he was doing. They had less than two months to build before spring planting. Soon, a town would need streets marked off. A hotel for folks to stay over. A café. A church. A school. Once the buildings started to go up, there would be people who'd either buy them or rent them from Ely. Either way, the money would pay for more buildings. In two years either Ely's grand plan would be a bust, or Ely would be a rich man. Either way, Clint figured he'd have a house and forty acres to call his own.

He slid his hand along the money belt he still wore. At the

end of two years maybe he'd buy more land or maybe he'd move on, but either way, he'd have enough to start over again if need be.

Ely passed through the kitchen for another cup of coffee. He stopped at the door and said simply, "Build your places as soon as you can. I don't know if I can stand all you hanging around once the weather warms."

Patrick pulled out another piece of paper he'd had rolled in his his pants pocket. "I drew up some simple houses we can put up within a few weeks each. They'll be small and plain. All will be made so we can build on. I figure we might as well start with two stories for the Matheson clan, but Truman, yours and mine can start off as little more than cabins. As we move along with the town and begin to hire men on to work, we'll move a team over to add the extra rooms on."

Ely nodded. "Then pick your land, men. The houses will sit on my land for two years, and then, if you stay, I'll deed the forty acres you pick out over to you. Any of you think you'll want a house in the new town? I could make a bargain . . ."

All said no at once.

Ely passed through the door without another word.

Patrick stood. "I'm thinking we start with what needs doing here first. We've got lumber, but no stoves or sinks or a dozen little things that will make the house more than a shack. They'll have to be ordered and driven up from the nearest train station, so we're stuck here together until they come in. A forge between the store and the barn would probably be useful to us and travelers. With all of us eating, I could put up a smokehouse in four days. We'd have time to mark off streets later. With the creeks crossing through this place it won't be easy, but we can start with a town square once we're settled. Ely may be dreaming, but he claims if we build a courthouse, he might get the county seat. That and a post office and we'd be on the map."

Suddenly everyone was talking at once. Everyone except Karrisa. She sat silent beside Clint.

He reached his hand beneath the table and closed his

fingers around hers. "You all right with this?" he said in his best effort to whisper.

She nodded as she held his hand tightly for only a moment before she let go. Instead of pulling away, she leaned forward and whispered, "When you pick your forty acres, make sure it has water for my trees."

Clint nodded. "I haven't forgotten, dear. Apple trees. As many as you want to plant."

He and Patrick stood and went to take inventory of all supplies. Clint didn't want to leave her alone with strangers, but he had to. With luck, these women would become her friends.

When he was alone with Patrick, they walked off where to build the forge and the smokehouse and then inventoried supplies. Plenty of wood, not near enough nails. Ely seemed to think all they'd need to build was wood. He didn't stock stoves, doorknobs, hinges, or glass for windows.

"We can use river rocks to build the chimneys, but some supplies will have to be ordered in." Patrick sat down in the shadowy barn and started a list of all they'd need. "I wish my brother were here," he said for the third time. "He's the one with all the brains."

Patrick had been talking for an hour, so Clint asked, "Let me guess, he's the quiet one?"

The kid's head shot up. "He doesn't speak. He can hear, but something happened with his voice. He's not dumb, though; he's smarter than me."

"I've no doubt." Clint didn't even know the brother, but he didn't want to argue. "So you've done the talking for both of you all your life?"

Patrick shrugged and went back to work. "Yeah, I pretty much talked all day and he listened. Annie's noticed that too. If I didn't have her, I'd miss Shelly something terrible. You'd like him, Truman. He's one person who talks less than you."

"I'm sure I would." Truman answered. "I feel like I know him already. Let me guess, he's older, right? But, of course he looks a lot like you. Maybe an inch or two shorter than you. Maybe not quite as thin. Only his eyes are gray, not green, and his hair a few shades darker brown."

"Unbelievable, Truman, you described him exactly. What are you, one of those mind readers?"

"No," Truman answered. "But I've always had good eyesight."

Clint couldn't stop smiling as Patrick turned around and looked at his brother standing behind him. The McAllens hugged, taking turns lifting each other off the ground, and then Patrick started asking questions.

Shelly pulled a note from his pocket and handed it to his brother as if already guessing what he'd ask.

Patrick took a minute to read the note and glance up at Truman. "He says it wasn't any fun without me in Galveston, so after a week he saddled up and rode out. He made faster time because he didn't bother to stop and visit. He writes that he passed a few places where he saw my work along the way."

Truman wasn't surprised. "I like your brother already. How about we go to work? Old Ely might not make him the same deal he did the three of us, but I'll bet he'll hire Shelly on until the captain gets on his feet."

Patrick explained the layout of the forge to Shelly, and Clint wasn't surprised when the silent McAllen took out his pencil and began making improvements. It seemed Patrick did all the talking even when the brothers argued over changes. Only, strange as it might sound, it was usually Shelly's suggestions that were used.

By noon, Clint decided to skip lunch and seek the silence of the upstairs bedroom. On a good day, he'd never been all that interested in construction, and with Patrick talking nonstop to his brother, Clint didn't consider this a good day.

He wasn't surprised to find that his wife was also in their room. Every day since they'd married, he'd insisted she rest at midday. It was helping. She had more energy and wasn't quite as pale as she'd been those first few days out of prison.

He tossed his hat on the chair and stretched out beside her

on the bed. When she opened one eye, he said, "Do me a favor and don't say a word."

Karrisa didn't even move. The baby was asleep in the basket, making little sounds babies make in their sleep. For the first time all morning there was peace and Clint simply wanted to drink it in like fine whiskey.

He took stock of his surroundings. The baby had woken him twice last night. Harmon Ely, down the hall, snored until almost dawn, and the young couple next to him must be part squirrel from all the moving-around noises coming from their room. Downstairs four little boys were yelling or crying or banging by first light.

On the bright side, he had a job and a hint of a future to plan for. His wife was letting him lie in bed without screaming, which was nearer to normal than they'd been since the wedding. Despite Patrick's talking and Shelly's silence, he liked both the McAllen brothers. He was stone-cold sober and for the first time in years he'd laughed.

Clint was afraid to ask if his wife was happy, so finally he simply said, "Do you feel safe here, dear?"

"Yes, Truman," she answered as she patted his shoulder.

# Chapter 12

## Trading Post

With Annie cooking breakfast and Karrisa cleaning up, Daisy had time to take care of her husband. The morning after he arrived, while the boys played on the roped-in porch, she washed Gillian and bandaged his head wound with clean strips of cotton. It looked much better and not near as red, but she knew there would always be a scar along his forehead. There were other scars he'd collected in the months they'd been apart. The year had not been easy on him either.

She couldn't stop staring at Gillian, touching him. How could she have allowed over a year to pass without being with him? Her family had told her that if she'd hold strong about not leaving the farm, eventually he'd wise up and come home. In his letters he'd talked about places they could live, but he'd never mentioned Kansas or the little home in sight of her parents' house as being one of them.

Gillian Matheson was a man she didn't understand, but she couldn't love him less for it. If he didn't like this plan she'd come up with of meeting halfway to build a town, they'd think of another way. She wanted his sons to know their father. She wanted to sleep beside him every night until they grew old. She wanted *him*.

Tears rolled down her cheeks unchecked. She'd wasted five years waiting. That was over. No matter what they did from now on, she would be by his side. He was a man of honor and duty. He'd never promised he'd stay with her in Kansas; in fact, she could still remember the hurt and surprise in his eyes when she'd told him she wouldn't follow him from fort to fort. The first time, she'd used the excuse that she was going to have a baby. A year later, she'd used the same excuse. When he'd left over a year ago, he hadn't known about the third pregnancy, and she hadn't told him. Gillian had no idea he was the father of four sons, not just two. She'd thought to surprise him, but in his weakened state the shock of twins might kill him. Only there would be no hiding the children once he woke.

When she looked up at his bandage, steel blue eyes peeked from beneath the white cotton.

"Daisy? Are you here or am I just dreaming about you again?"

"I'm here, Gillian."

"Good." He closed his eyes and took a deep breath. "Mind telling me where *here* is? Last thing I remember was hitting the ground so hard lightning split through my mind."

"Did you get my letter?"

He slowly nodded, then groaned. "You were in danger. I was riding hard to get to you. Thought you, or one of the boys, might be dying."

"No, Gillian, I'm fine and so are the boys. The lightning you felt was a bullet flying along your skull. After you were shot, you made it to us thanks to Jessie. We're all here at Harmon Ely's trading post."

"I've been to that place a few times. It's in the middle of nowhere." He lifted two fingers and caught the tail of her long blond braid.

"You're here now. You're with us." She cupped his chin with her palm. "You came to me, and I came to Texas to be with you."

His eyes were closed for so long she thought he might have gone back to sleep, yet his fingers still held tight to her hair. Finally, he whispered, "I want to be a real husband, Daisy. I got two boys who need a father. I want to be more than a man who rides in for a few weeks once a year."

She couldn't stop crying. He was saying the very words she'd wanted to hear for years. "You've been a good soldier on the frontier for years, Gillian. You've made your father proud. Now it's time for you to try something new. Something that will let you come home every night to your sons and to me."

He took a deep breath as if relaxing for the first time in years and drifted back to sleep.

Resting her cheek on his chest, she listened to his heartbeat, remembering when they first fell in love. He'd told her that the beat of his heart and hers were in time with each other and neither one would ever be happy unless they were close enough to hear the other's heart.

Daisy slowly straightened and smiled. He'd been right. It took both of them five long years, but they'd come to the same conclusion. They belonged together.

A light tapping sounded against the door. Daisy looked up, feeling ready to face anything since she'd finally talked to Gillian.

Jessie, the girl who'd brought her husband to her, stood at the door holding a ball of yarn and a crochet hook. She seemed afraid to come into the bedroom.

"It's all right, Jessie, he's asleep." Daisy waved her in.

The girl moved closer as if needing to see for herself that the captain was alive. When she reached Daisy's side, she whispered, "Mrs. Truman taught me how to crochet. She said I needed to practice with this yarn. If you want, I could sit with the captain and practice. If he wakes, I'll run and get you."

"That sounds fine. I need to check on the boys. Maybe I'll

take them out back and let them chase chickens for a while. If they catch one, we'll have chicken pot pie for supper."

Jessie smiled at her. "The captain's better, ain't he?"

"Yes, he is. He even talked to me a little. He's going to be all right, you know."

"Yes, ma'am. I sure do hope so."

As Jessie began to play with the yarn, Daisy moved to the midday warmth of the kitchen. She couldn't stop smiling. This place, this time might be their only chance left.

There seemed far too many questions and far too few answers, but one thing she knew. Gillian still loved her; she saw it in his eyes. And, for Daisy, that was all that mattered.

# Chapter 13

TRADING POST

WHEN CLINT TRUMAN AND THE MCALLEN BROTHERS CAME in for supper, they were exhausted but feeling good about what they'd done. Patrick was right about his brother. Shelly was gifted. Clint had always considered himself a fair builder. He'd been part of barn raisings a few times growing up and even built a room onto his parents' house before he'd gone to war. But the McAllens were way ahead of him in skill. After ten minutes of trying to add his two cents into the mix, Clint wised up and simply followed directions.

They washed up and walked in the back door. Patrick was first, grabbing his wife and swinging her around as he said, "I've got a surprise."

His words were drowned out by Annie's scream of joy when she saw Shelly follow his brother in.

Clint watched the reunion. He could think of no one he knew that he'd be particularly happy to see come or sad to see go. These three were dancing around like long-lost family, not three people who'd seen one another less than a month ago.

Clint glanced at his wife. She wasn't even looking at him. She obviously hadn't missed him. He pulled off his gun belt and hung it on a high nail by the door. While they were eating he wanted the Colt far out of the little Matheson boys' reach.

Everyone except Karrisa crowded around the table and talked as they passed bowls of food. His wife took her time putting the baby down in his basket on the counter, then joined them without a word.

Daisy reported that the captain was doing better. He'd even talked to her a few times between sleeping.

When Ely joined them, Patrick filled everyone in on the details of what they'd been working on. When he predicted the smokehouse would be ready in two days now that Shelly was here, Clint offered to go hunting as soon as the roof was on. The group around the table would need meat soon or they'd completely deplete Ely's supply for the winter. A few days of hunting should keep them supplied for a month if game was good, and give Clint treasured silence.

"When you get back, Truman," Ely said, finally getting a word in, "I want you riding shotgun on the supplies coming in. I sent the order today with a teamster heading south. Within four or five days, I want you riding toward Dallas. It may take you a few days, but I want you to check the supplies, hire drivers, and make sure it gets back here."

Truman didn't have to ask. He knew Ely's shipments were sometimes robbed. One of the men he'd talked to when he'd bought his wagon had told him that there were outlaws who stopped the smaller loads crossing open land and tried to charge a toll.

Harmon Ely continued to talk. He seemed happy to have Shelly but had no idea where to put him up. When Shelly wrote that he'd be happy to sleep in the barn loft, Ely nodded.

As the meal moved to dessert, Karrisa picked up her knitting. She was sitting beside him, but Clint never made eye contact with her. She seemed to be the invisible person in the room. Even Shelly participated by nodding, or shaking his head if he disagreed, or even jotting notes down and passing them to his brother.

Clint's thin wife only watched.

Daisy took her boys, one by one, to bed while the others fleshed out a dream they all shared of a town on this land where two waters crossed. Only Karrisa remained quiet as she worked on her knitting and checked on her sleeping baby beside her.

Clint knew his job would be protecting this group. He didn't know how to tell them that he had no goals beyond keeping Karrisa and her baby safe. He'd done the homestead dream once before and all his plans hadn't turned out.

He was thankful when Ely stood and announced it was time for bed. They all climbed the stairs, saying good night to Daisy. She'd stay beside her husband downstairs. Jessie would stay close, sleeping in the kitchen in case Daisy needed help with the captain during the night.

Once they were alone, Karrisa handed him a new set of clothes. "When I washed your other clothes, they needed mending. I'll do it tomorrow, but you'll need clean ones to wear." She didn't look up at him as she talked. "I put these on account with Ely. I hope you don't mind."

"The account's open for anything you, or apparently, I need. I'll settle up with him at the end of the month. You buy whatever you want, dear. We are not rich, but we can afford the necessities."

She fidgeted a bit as if she'd been unsure she'd done the right thing. Or maybe she'd lived in a world once where the rules constantly changed.

"Thank you," Clint said, surprised that she'd worry about him. He laid his hand over hers that rested on the garments. All evening she hadn't said a word. And yet she was taking care of him, almost like a real wife. He didn't know whether to be thankful that she cared or irritated that she thought he couldn't see after his own needs.

Before he could comment, she added, "I took up the waist a few inches, but I think the length will be fine."

He smiled, realizing it had been a long time since a woman worried about his clothes. "I'm not even good at sewing buttons on."

He caught a brush of a smile crossing her lips before she added, "I noticed. One you'd sewn on your shirt was an inch off the mark."

"Did you get your dress finished?" he asked, liking that they were talking, even if it was about nothing important.

"Almost. I still have to hem it. Daisy said she'd pin it up for me in the morning after all the men leave."

"You like Daisy?"

She nodded. "Annie, too. They made me sit down and rest several times today. Daisy said she didn't get out of bed for a month when she had her first, but I feel fine, Truman, honest I do."

"Good." On impulse, he leaned over and kissed her forehead.

He wasn't surprised when she moved away quickly. Without a word she left the room and when she returned, she'd changed into her nightgown.

Clint picked up his new clothes and headed for the washroom. Since he'd never worn a nightshirt, he slept in his long johns and trousers. That way, if he was needed quickly all he had to do was strap on his gun belt.

As he lay down on his pallet by the window, he thought of what kind of trouble might find him on the road. The ride out would be easy. He'd be on horseback and have both a Colt and a rifle. No one was likely to catch him, must less bother him.

But on the way back, he'd have wagons to watch over. Clint decided he'd take his time hiring good men. Every wagon would have a shotgun beneath the seat. If any gang tried to stop them, they'd be risking their lives.

Tomorrow, while he hunted, he'd go south so he could check out places where he might be ambushed. Then, when he rode out, he'd ride the same trail the wagons would be traveling. He could gauge the miles. On the return, he'd be on horseback, constantly scouting ahead, making plans where they'd be safest at night, looking for any sign of trouble riding their direction.

Clint realized his mind had fallen easily into the pattern

he'd used during the war. It had been eleven years since he'd worn gray, but he still remembered every detail. He'd been little more than a boy then, but one mistake, one slip, and the mission would not be accomplished. Men might have died if he missed a detail. He might have died.

Only this time the mission wasn't war. It meant the survival of a town. No, more than that, it meant the survival of three families.

And one of them was his.

# Chapter 14

## Trading Post

When Jessie finished her hour of sitting with the captain, she walked outside and headed toward the creek. All the people at the trading post were fun to talk to and watch, but she needed to be alone. In the camp where she'd cooked she'd often spent days alone. The Osborne brothers never cared if they left her food, so she'd learned to survive. Once, soon after they traded for her, when she'd been about twelve, they'd left her for a month. She would have died of hunger if she hadn't found a stream. After that she saved the eyes of potatoes and made a crude garden at every camp.

She felt like she'd been just surviving all her life.

Without much thought that she might be seen, Jessie lay down on the winter grass and let the sun warm her. For the first time in longer than she could remember, she wasn't hungry. She'd eaten more for breakfast than she usually had to eat in a week. All three of the women were kind and willing to teach her things no one else ever had. If she stayed awhile she might learn enough to make it on her own.

"I love this place," she whispered.

Far down the stream she watched a tall, lean man moving in the shallow water. He had to be one of the McAllen men. The big man in black was Truman. His wide shoulders almost made two of the McAllens. Old Ely never ventured away from the shadow of the trading post, and the captain wouldn't be out of bed.

Jessie moved closer, curious why a man would stand in cold water.

Thirty feet away she saw his face. Shelly McAllen. The man who never talked. She'd watched him at breakfast. His brother talked and laughed, but Shelly seemed almost invisible.

Jessie liked him, though. He'd picked up his plate and brought it to the washstand when he finished eating. None of the other men had bothered.

As she walked closer, he looked up, nodded once at her, then went back to his work. Slowly, examining rock after rock before deciding, he lifted stones out of the creek and tossed them on the bank.

"What are you doing?" she asked.

He looked up at her, but didn't answer.

Jessie sat down and hugged her knees. "That was dumb of me. I know you can't talk."

Shelly McAllen looked up again. When his gaze met hers Jessie saw intelligent eyes.

"You mind if I watch?"

He shook his head.

"If I could read you could write down your answer like I've seen you do with your brother, but I can't read. Never got to go to school." She straightened, not wanting him to feel sorry for her. "I'm not ignorant, though."

He didn't look up, and she guessed he didn't want to see her lying. She watched him tossing rocks on the bank for a while. When he climbed back on the bank and started stacking them in a wagon, Jessie decided to help him.

"I'm not a kid, you know," she finally said. "I'm a hard worker."

Shelly didn't stop working.

"I figure you and me are more alike than you think. Everybody else has someone, but me and you are alone. Old Ely even has his dog." She hated herself for sounding like she needed to talk. "You think we could be friends?"

Shelly stopped, set down the rock he'd been carrying, and offered his hand. His strong fingers circled around her small hand as he nodded.

"Good," she managed, not quite sure why it was so important to her. "I'll come out and help you when I can, and if you don't mind, I might talk to you now and then."

He smiled at her and she saw the kindness in his eyes.

Backing away, she smiled back, thinking they were more alike than he knew.

# Chapter 15

GILLIAN FELT LIKE HIS LIFE WAS PASSING BY IN RANDOM lightning flashes. Sometimes he'd wake and it would be morning. He'd talk to Daisy a little before his thoughts began to jumble in his mind. The next time he'd wake it might be still morning, or it might be night. He was never sure if he'd been out for a minute, an hour, or a day.

Now and then he'd try to wake and only make it halfway. He'd be aware of people moving around him. Of little boys peeking over the covers at him. Of his head hurting.

Other times he'd just remain still and listen. Daisy wasn't the only woman around him. He seemed to be recovering in the middle of a train station, with people coming and going at all hours. Some old white-haired man kept sitting down by his bed and rambling on about roads being wide enough or asking if Gillian thought ten rooms were enough for a proper hotel. All the time he patted a hairy old yellow dog.

Once he woke and found Daisy sleeping on top of the covers beside him. He turned slowly and studied her every feature in the soft glow of a bedside candle.

She'd been the prettiest girl he'd ever seen. When she'd first smiled at him he thought his heart might explode. From that moment, he'd loved her. Once he'd seen Daisy, he'd never looked at another and he had a feeling he never would. The problem was, loving Daisy seemed easier than living with her.

Her family was huge and well off. Every one of her brothers and sisters had houses of their own, all within sight of the main house. From the moment they told the family they'd like to marry, Daisy's big brothers started planning his life for him. They'd marry and move into the little house where all the newlyweds lived during their first year. Like everyone else, Gillian and Daisy would have breakfast on their own, but lunch was always served in the field, or orchard, or barns where the men were working. Dinner was at the big house—*every* night with all the family.

Gillian had gone along with everyone at first. When they'd married, food was delivered to their door the first four days so they could have a honeymoon. Then Gillian was expected to quit the army and join the workforce.

He used up his month of leave trying to fit in but finally told everyone he had to go back to the fort. The thought that she wouldn't come with him had never crossed his mind, and he wasn't sure he believed it even when he rode away with her crying.

At first the fort was close and he could come home often, but as he was reassigned farther and farther away, he saw her less and less. Another fort always needed building. Finally the fights and arguments over where to live came down to two words every time he had to leave.

"Come," he'd say.

"Stay," she'd answer.

"Someday," remained their compromise.

Both their hearts would break as he rode away. He'd spend his nights at the barracks studying law and missing her. He had a feeling she did fine in the middle of her family, but he hoped at least when Daisy was alone in her bed, she missed him too.

Tonight she was beside him. Gillian grinned. He knew he wasn't dreaming because if he were she'd be under the covers and nude. He had no idea what day it was, or even where he was, but she was with him and that was enough.

"Daisy," he whispered. "You awake, honey?"

She opened sleepy eyes. "No," she muttered.

He smiled. "I love you, you know. You were pretty when I first saw you. Just a girl not old enough to know better than to fall in love with me. But now, Daisy, you're not just pretty anymore. You're beautiful."

"I know," she said, sounding more asleep than awake. "My husband tells me that every time he comes home."

"We're not home now, Daisy, but I'm still telling you." He brushed his fingers along her soft cheek. "You know, honey, anywhere you are is home to me."

"I came to be with you, Gillian. I packed up everything and came to Texas. I don't want to be without you."

"I know, you told me. We got boys to raise together."

She leaned forward so that her head rested close to his. "Gillian, is your mind with you?"

"I believe it is, Daisy, but then if it's not, I'd probably be the last one to ask."

She smiled at him, and as always he wanted to make her happy. "I can tell by that look in your eyes that we need to talk. So whatever you need to tell me, go ahead and get it out in the open."

"Promise you won't get upset?"

He laughed. "That sounds like something your mother would say to your dad. I don't think I have enough brains left to blow my top; besides, who could ever get mad with a woman like you so close?"

She nodded, almost bumping her forehead against his bandage. "Well, I remember you said your tour was up in January and you would have to reenlist."

"Right, but I haven't been there long enough to sign the papers. It'll mean more pay and there would be a nice house for the captain and his family, once they get Fort Elliot built."

She interrupted. "I was thinking you might want another job. One where you'd come home at night. One where I wouldn't have to worry about you being shot."

"I'm not moving back to the farm. I could handle my own place with you, honey, but for a guy with no living relatives, your clan frightens me. Plus, there's no challenge in waking up every morning and having one of your big brothers tell me what to do every day, all day."

A slow smile moved across her face. "I'm not going back to Kansas, Gillian. We came here to be with you. We can start that farm of our own right here and a lot more."

He wished it were true, but he didn't have near enough money saved to buy land. Plus, he wasn't sure he knew enough to make a go of farming. He understood army life in wild country and he knew a little about blacksmithing. He even knew law. But farming seemed like a hundred simple jobs that, if they weren't done just right, would cause total failure.

Lying back, he rested, wishing he didn't have to tell her that the dream they'd once talked about during their honeymoon days wasn't going to happen. Not yet. Maybe not ever.

In a calm voice she began to talk, telling him about seeing a small ad in a farmer's journal, describing how she wrote and asked for an application. Month by month she'd exchanged letters with someone named Harmon Ely. He wanted families and was willing to give up land to get them to stay.

Finally, she ended her story by saying she'd sent word to the fort for Gillian to come here to meet her the day she'd left Kansas with their boys. She knew she'd arrive early, but she wanted to be waiting for him.

He listened but he wasn't sure he believed.

"I've two wagonloads of furniture and equipment that we'll need to start. By the end of spring we'll have a house and land to live on. In two years there will be a town and we'll own the land."

Gillian didn't know whether to believe her. The offer Harmon Ely made sounded too good to be true.

"He hired Patrick McAllen, a carpenter, to lead the building, and a man fast with a gun to stand if trouble comes. Mr. Ely said you were the perfect man in the middle. You understand blacksmithing, which will come in handy early on. You're a soldier, so you'll know how to handle a gun, and, when the town forms, there will need to be a man to organize the town, maybe even run it so no corruption takes over."

She cuddled closer. "You could be the first mayor, or lawyer or county judge. I told Ely that you studied law. At first I didn't see how you'd be needed to start a town, but Mr. Ely said a captain in the army is exactly the kind of man he's looking for."

Gillian didn't answer. She was right, he did know the law, but this job would mean leaving the army, the only life he'd ever known.

"Just think, Gillian, we'll build a town. One of the first this far north. We'd be together."

He closed his eyes, picturing the life he'd always lived. It had an order to it, a routine. He'd be giving that up. He saw the outline of the first fort his dad took him to. No grass grew in the square of buildings and barns. Wooden walls framed everyone in and blocked the sunsets and sunrises.

He wanted more than what he'd grown up with for his boys. He wanted them to be able to ride free without worrying about making it through the gate before sunset. He wanted them to walk to the fishing hole and go to school with the same kids for years. Maybe he wanted too much.

He thought of all the men he'd known. Some strong leaders. Some dependent on the order of army life to keep them in line. Friends he'd known who rode out one day only to return draped over a horse. He remembered their widows' wails long into the night, and he remembered the men who died without anyone to stand at their grave to mourn their passing. Gillian thought of the thousands of dull days with little to do and the long nights on the road when fear kept him awake.

He'd known great men and he'd known men who stayed too long in the army. Old men broken down who were given odd jobs around the fort because they had no family to go to when they retired. Men who'd hardened from one too many battles until nothing was left inside.

Gillian thought of all he'd be giving up if he didn't reenlist, but most of all he thought of the one thing that he'd never had and would never have if he didn't step away.

He'd never have his family. Daisy would grow old waiting for him to come home, either at her family farm or at some remote post with the other wives.

All his life he'd known that being a soldier was making the world a safer place, but maybe there were other ways to make the world better. There were just so many times he could dodge a bullet or recover from a wound. One time he might not. He'd be one of the crosses beside the fort that no one visits. He'd be the crippled-up old soldier who never leaves because he has nowhere else to go.

"We could stay here, Gillian," Daisy whispered. "We could help McAllen and Truman build Mr. Ely's town. Our children and grandchildren will watch over this place and take care of it for hundreds of years."

He took her hand as he drifted back to sleep. Half dreaming, he whispered, "All right, Daisy, we'll give it a try."

She squeezed his fingers and he smiled, wishing her dreaming could be real.

The sun was up when he woke, but Daisy was gone. He tried to figure out if he'd really talked to her in the night, or if he'd just thought he had. She'd had a crazy idea of how they could live together.

The bed moved. A little head, chin level to the mattress, smiled at him.

"Morning, Abe." Gillian greeted his oldest son.

"I'm over here, Papa," a voice from near the window answered.

Gillian forced himself more awake. The little boy he'd left over a year ago had shot up. He sat in the windowsill. How could it be possible that Abe had grown to be four? "Sorry, son, I guess I was remembering you when you were younger. My brain is a little foggy."

Trying to focus on the head bobbing up and down at the end of the bed, he said, "You must be Ben. You were just walking good when I left." Over a year, Gillian thought. He'd been gone so long and they'd changed so much.

"Papa. You awake. Mom says we have to be quiet 'cause you sleep. I see your eyes. You are not asleep."

Gillian glanced at another boy sitting in the chair next to his bed. He was swinging his feet so the buckle of his shoe clicked like a clock on the leg of the chair.

"Ben talks too much, Papa," Abe announced as he slid off the windowsill. "Mom swears he was born talking."

"Do not," Ben shouted as he banged his feet into the wood of the chair.

"Do too." Abe joined in the shouting match.

Gillian's head was starting to pound in time with Ben's feet. "If you're Abe and you're Ben, who is that?" He pointed to the head that kept popping up and down at the end of the bed like a turtle in shallow water.

Both his sons moved closer and watched as if studying something foreign to their world.

"Hell if I know," Ben, the three-year-old, said.

Abe turned on his brother. "Mom told you not to say *hell*."

"Uncle Fred says *hell*," Ben defended.

"Momma says Uncle Fred was kicked in the head by a mule and isn't right. She says cuss words dribble out of him like snot. You don't want folks to say that about you, do you?"

Ben didn't back down. "If Uncle Fred can cuss, it must not be a bad word. Grandma wouldn't let him do it if it was."

"Just because Uncle Fred says them that doesn't mean you can say any of them. Momma says so." Abe straightened, as if his extra three inches made him more the adult.

Ben looked at his father and pointed at the bandage. "Papa was shot in the head. Will he say *hell*?" He leaned closer. "Papa, are you gonna be right in the head or go around dribbling bad words like snot?"

"Probably not, son, but who is that smaller version of the two of you at the foot of my bed?"

Abe answered, "I don't know, Papa. I never can tell them apart. It's either Charlie or Dylan."

As Gillian watched, two heads popped up at the same time. One was crying and one was laughing.

Ben wiggled his chubby little body off the chair and leaned close to Gillian. "The one crying is probably Dylan. Momma says he's always crying. She says she probably should have named him Dam because water's always flowing."

Before Gillian could comment, he was saved by Daisy. She ignored her older two boys arguing over whether *dam* was a bad word and the baby's crying. "Morning, darling," she said sweetly as she met his stare. "I see you've met the Matheson gang."

Gillian frowned and pointed at the end of the bed. "Where'd these two come from?" Since they looked just like Abe and Ben, he didn't plan on denying them, but still she could have told him.

"They came about six months after you left. I was pretty sick after I delivered them earlier than the doctor said they were due to come out. For a while, they were so small I feared they wouldn't make it, but once they started growing they've caught up. Since then I just didn't have time to write." She tugged Dylan's arm. "Come meet your papa. And be good. Your papa has had quite a shock already."

Gillian tried to think of which shock she might be referring to. He swore his life was tied to a lightning rod.

The boys only wanted on the bed. They showed no interest in Gillian as their mother pulled them up.

"I have four sons," Gillian whispered. He'd only been married five years. At this rate, if he stayed home and worked on it, they could have a dozen before Daisy saw her first gray hair. He'd be outnumbered. Maybe going back to the army and fighting outlaws wasn't such a bad idea. "Four sons," he repeated, lost in the reality of it.

Daisy laughed. "You're used to handling an army of men. How much trouble can four boys be?"

Gillian frowned. "Why do I feel unprepared for the assignment?" He raised an eyebrow. "There aren't any more surprises hiding under the bed, are there?"

"No." She picked up the twins. "I'll go feed these two while you visit with Abe and Ben. They've been asking me questions about you since we left Kansas."

Gillian didn't have time to argue. She left him alone with Abe and the cusser.

They just stared at him.

Finally, Abe said, "I remember you, Papa. You're a soldier."

Gillian smiled. "I remember you both. I'm thinking of giving up being a soldier and coming home to live. Would that be all right with you two?"

Ben nodded, but Abe just leaned his head sideways. "If you did, Momma wouldn't cry at night when she thinks we're all asleep. So I guess it would be all right."

Just like that the decision was made. Gillian would write his letter and resign. He had a town to build and boys to raise. He'd better get well quick. There was no time to lie in bed.

"Men," he said in a formal tone. "I'll need your assistance in getting dressed."

They rushed to follow orders.

Fifteen minutes later the captain sat down at the breakfast table with his wife at his side. The other two men already at the table stood and introduced themselves. Gillian caught himself almost saying *At ease, men* to them. Truman looked a few years older than him and far more serious in his black clothes, but McAllen, though tall, couldn't have been more than twenty. Patrick had an easy smile and a way about him that made folks like him right away.

"We've a town to build," Gillian said to everyone at the table, "and I plan to be strong enough to help within a few days."

The younger man, named Patrick McAllen, started going over ideas, but the one called Truman sat back and watched. Gillian had a feeling that Truman would get to know him first before calling him friend.

By the time breakfast was over, Gillian wasn't sure he could make it back to the bedroom alone.

Daisy must have sensed something was wrong. She held to him as they walked together to the bedroom. "I'll put the boys on the porch to play. Jessie likes to sit at the door and watch them. Don't worry, they won't bother you the rest of the morning. You can rest."

"I'll just lie down until the world settles a bit. Who is

Jessie?" He thought hard, trying to put pieces of a puzzle together in his mind. "Jessie, the girl who was with me?"

Daisy lowered him into bed. "Yes, that Jessie. She brought you to me. She ate early with Mr. Ely this morning. She likes to help him open the store. He pays her a dime every morning for the hour's work, so don't worry that he's taking advantage of her time. Mr. Ely says a girl her age needs a bit of her own money."

"I had orders to take her to the mission."

"If she wants to go, that's one thing." Daisy pulled a blanket over him. "If she doesn't, you're not taking her anywhere. She's part of our family if she wants to be and that's final. Now, you rest, Captain."

Gillian leaned back on the pillow. "Whatever happened to the sweet little Daisy I married?"

Daisy kissed him on the cheek. "You left her alone with four kids, Gillian. She had to become a sergeant to survive."

# Chapter 16

FOR TWO DAYS PATRICK WORKED WITH HIS BROTHER ON the smokehouse. The primitive one built against a rise in the ground was little more than a cave. He and Shelly laid out the plans for one that would hold a winter's supply of meat, and then they went to work. The first two buildings would be the smokehouse and the forge. The brothers knew each other so well, folks often said that the two of them could build a house faster than most teams of six men.

Truman drove a wagon back and forth with supplies from the barn, but he wasn't a carpenter, or a talker, it seemed. Working with him was like having two Shellys around, Patrick decided, only one couldn't build much of anything.

Patrick tried to guide Truman and not tease him, but once he learned Truman took the teasing in fun, he let him have both barrels. Truman would cuss and swear and then laugh at himself. Patrick often told him that while he might be teaching Truman a few tricks, Truman was teaching him a whole new vocabulary.

Once, when Patrick was alone with his brother, he whispered, "What do you think of Truman?"

Shelly made a sign as if riding a horse.

Patrick agreed. "I know, he's good with horses. Talks more to them than he does to his wife. It bothers me that he always wears a gun, even when we're eating breakfast. I've heard it's wild out here, but does he really need a weapon to tackle pancakes and eggs? I wouldn't be surprised if he takes a bath with that gun strapped on. Now that would be a sight I wouldn't want to see, and if I accidentally did, it would probably be the last sight I saw. He'd use that Colt and I'd be on my way to the hereafter with an image of Truman naked tattooed on my brain."

As always, Shelly listened, and Patrick continued, "I'm going to keep my eye on him. He's not much of a carpenter and, strange as it sounds, I don't think he cares. It's like he knows he was hired for some other reason."

They heard the rattle of rigging and knew Truman's wagon was delivering more supplies.

As they unloaded, Truman told them that he'd already picked out his forty acres and knew exactly where he wanted to build his house. "I'm going to take my wife out to see the land before dark."

When he told them the location, Patrick shook his head. "I don't want to discourage you none, Truman, but that land has more than its share of trees. Land ripe for farming or ranching is a few miles farther out."

"No, that land's not for me," Truman said. "I don't plan on farming more than a garden, and what cows I have will be milk cows. The water's good on the forty acres I picked and the ride into town won't take long. I'll plant my feet on the ground I picked. Who knows, I might plant a few more trees."

Since Truman was ten years older than him and always wore a gun, Patrick decided not to argue with the man. The money would be in crops and cattle, not a garden and a few milk cows. The only good thing he could say about the land Truman had chosen was that it was only a short ride from what would be town.

When they finished at seven, Patrick guessed he hadn't said ten sentences to Truman. The man in black didn't seem to need anyone. He never talked of his family, or his home, or what he'd been doing for thirty years. If Truman had been a book, all the pages would have been blank.

Patrick, on the other hand, couldn't wait to get home to his wife. Annie, he swore, grew prettier every day, and their favorite thing to do after they retired for the night was to cuddle up and talk about their day. She'd tell him all about what happened at the store and in the kitchen, and he'd tell her all about what he'd built. She'd laugh about things the Matheson boys did and they'd whisper about the somedays in their lives when they'd have children. All the time they talked, he'd be touching her rounded little body and thinking he was the luckiest man alive.

The days passed quickly. The smokehouse was completed. Truman left to hunt and the McAllen brothers started on the forge.

Two days after they started work, Patrick stopped to take a break and grab a dipper of water. When he raised his head, he saw Truman riding in. The pack mule behind him was loaded down with meat, and a spotted mare followed on a lead rope.

When Jessie saw the little mare the captain had given her, she broke into a dead run from the house. Patrick had never seen anyone get so excited about a horse. The girl laughed and cried and hugged everyone, including Truman.

Patrick slapped Truman on the back. "That was a nice thing you did, finding the kid's pony."

"Lucky I didn't shoot it and bring it in for food," Truman said without smiling. "Only, paints are never fit to eat."

Patrick glared at him.

Shelly laughed, and Patrick realized Truman was teasing. If he could have remembered a few of those swear words, he'd have been tempted to use them. "That wasn't funny, Truman. I ought to give you a piece of my mind."

"Keep it," Truman almost smiled. "You might need it."

When Shelly laughed louder, Patrick gave up and smiled. To his surprise Truman smiled back.

The day was warm and everyone joined in to help get the meat ready for the smokehouse, except Daisy, who stayed inside with her husband and the little boys. There were two wild hogs, a deer, and several wild turkeys. Everyone agreed that one of the turkeys should be cooked for supper.

By the time they'd all cleaned up, the sun was setting and what looked like a feast graced the table. Everyone laughed and talked. Captain Matheson joined them, but he grew tired and excused himself before the meal was over.

Ely offered up a bottle of whiskey, but no one drank. While Annie and Karrisa cleared the dishes, Shelly got out his harmonica and began to play.

Everyone listened for a while, and then Patrick asked Annie to dance. Ely politely offered his hand to little Jessie, and she giggled as the old man danced around her. Daisy picked up one of her boys and circled around the little kitchen.

Patrick watched as Truman finally offered his hand to his wife. She shook her head, but when he kept just standing there, she finally stood. Most of the time the Trumans didn't even look like they liked each other. Tonight dancing wasn't much different. He barely touched her and she was so stiff and thin she looked more like the Maypole than one of the dancers.

They both appeared relieved when the music ended. Mrs. Truman picked up her baby and Truman simply sat down beside her.

Shelly played on, beautiful music proving that he could hear. Sometimes when Patrick listened to his brother play, he thought Shelly must be a very old soul to make music that haunted through your mind for hours after he stopped playing. Since they'd been little, he'd played when he was alone, but never in front of the family. Patrick was the only one who knew of his talent.

Ely moved over across from Truman, and Patrick caught some of the conversation about Truman's upcoming trip to Dallas. It would be dangerous this time of year and Ely wanted him to make the trip as fast as possible.

While they talked, Jessie laughed and danced with the little boys.

Patrick watched them all, thinking about how in the few days they'd been together they'd formed a community. He'd never seen a group of people who all treated each other as equals. Each had their strengths. All helped the whole.

He leaned over to Annie and whispered, "You think this is what heaven must be like?"

She giggled. "A small trading post with a mismatched group of people who have no idea what they are doing? Yes. I think this must be heaven."

As Daisy took each boy to bed and Ely started snoring at the table, the others decided it was time to call it a night.

As he often did, Patrick took Annie's hand and they walked outside while the house settled down. In the moonlight they could be together without anyone noticing how he couldn't keep his hands off her or that she giggled every time he kissed her neck.

"Will you always love me, Annie?" he whispered as they stepped into the blackness behind the barn.

"Forever and ever and ever," she said. "And will you always love me when I grow old and fat and lose all my teeth?"

"Of course, because I'll be blind by then and won't notice."

They kissed as they always did before the night turned to passion. He liked to pretend that this was their first kiss, soft and innocent before they moved on.

As they walked back to the porch, he whispered, "Annie, if anything ever happens to me, will you go to Shelly? I don't want him or you to be alone."

Annie didn't answer, and Patrick didn't know if he shouldn't have asked such a thing or if she simply didn't want to answer. No woman had ever looked at Shelly. Maybe no woman, including Annie, ever would.

Neither of them mentioned his request again as they cuddled in bed and talked, but Patrick couldn't help but feel that his question lingered in both their thoughts.

After Annie went to sleep, he realized for the first time that he'd found something he couldn't talk about with his wife.

And he didn't know why.

# Chapter 17

"YOU'VE PLENTY OF MEAT TO LAST UNTIL I GET BACK," TRUMAN said as he watched Karrisa change into her nightgown. She'd avoided him all evening after they'd danced the one dance. Even now he wasn't sure she was listening to him. She was a woman who made no show of changing her clothes, but ever since he'd mentioned that wives did such things in the presence of their husbands, she'd stayed in their one room instead of going down the hallway to change.

All he could figure out that might have upset her was the fact he was leaving at dawn to meet the train and bring the supplies Patrick had ordered for the building of their three homes and the start of the town. She knew it was part of his job, so she probably wouldn't say anything even if she didn't like the idea of being alone.

If all worked exactly as planned, he'd be back in two weeks. But what if rain slowed his ride to the station? Or the supplies weren't waiting when he got there? Or he had trouble finding good men? Or they ran into outlaws on the way back?

Clint clenched his jaw. He could think of a dozen other things that might slow him down. Not just the rain or outlaws, or time schedules, but a broken wheel might cost them a day, or swollen streams might make them have to go miles around where they'd planned to cross.

Hell, he swore to himself. Even thinking about all that could happen didn't bother him as much as leaving her. There, for one moment, when she'd been in his arms at the dance she'd almost felt right. Like she belonged there. Like he wanted her so close.

Even thinking of her as his for one moment wasn't right. All he needed to worry about was her safety, nothing more. That was all he'd agreed to do and all she agreed to accept.

"You'll be safe enough here with the McAllens and the Mathesons. Nothing will happen to you or the baby. The captain's well enough to walk around now. If anything even hints of being wrong, Ely will put him on the porch with a rifle. No one's likely to get past him. If he fires one shot, Patrick and Shelly will come running."

She didn't look at him. Clint had no idea what to say or what she wanted to hear from him. Part of his job was guarding shipments, and it was what he did best. "When I get back we can all start on the homes. With four of us working, it won't be long until you have your own house. I've been talking to Shelly about adding on a sewing area from the start." He glanced around at her box of knitting and the desk covered with a dress she was cutting out for the girl Jessie. "I'm thinking you'll be needing it sooner rather than later."

He wished she'd complain a little so he would know what she was so worried about. Or maybe she wasn't worried. Maybe she just didn't want to talk to him tonight. Maybe she had nothing to say.

He liked watching her undress even if she didn't talk to him. There was a grace about her thin body. She'd gained a few pounds over the three weeks he'd known her. Her cheeks were not so hollow and her ribs no longer stuck out.

Her hair looked better too. It always hung over her face

when he left for work, but when he got home one of the other women had usually braided the sides and pulled it back. The dull charcoal-dust black was gone and, thanks to good food, her midnight hair was beginning to shine.

When she didn't say anything as she climbed into bed, he made himself turn and walk out of the room. He would have stayed if she'd said one word, but sometimes the loneliness of being with her was too much. He would have made up some excuse about where he was going, but he didn't think she cared.

When Clint reached the bottom of the stairs, he could hear Patrick and Gillian still talking in the kitchen. The captain had managed to make it to the table for supper. Another week and he'd be able to do light work, maybe help out in the store so Ely could go work on his dream in the afternoon. Ely might be twenty years older than any of them, but he seemed strong as a bull despite his limp. He'd built this business after the war, and not even being shot during a robbery had slowed him down. For Ely every building that went up was like Christmas morning. He laughed with joy when they finished the smokehouse out back and was so excited about the forge that he ran out to check the progress every hour.

Clint bypassed the kitchen and walked out the front door.

"Evening, Shelly," Clint said as he passed Patrick's brother sitting in one of the rocking chairs on the wide front porch.

Shelly nodded once and went back to his whittling.

Clint leaned against the new railing that made the trading post look more like a mercantile in town. "I'm heading out at dawn tomorrow."

Shelly nodded again.

"Thought I'd ask you to keep an eye on things. If you hear or see anything that doesn't seem right, let the captain know right away. He may be weak, but he can handle a gun. I was thinking of asking him to wear one while I'm gone. You and your brother will be busy building the forge."

Like Karrisa, Shelly didn't seem interested in what Clint had to say, so Clint said good night and walked back inside.

When he made it up to their little room, the baby and his wife were asleep. Clint stood, his hands on either side of the window, and stared out into the dark night. Clouds hid the moon and stars, and not even shadows moved in the wind tonight. The entire world seemed asleep but him.

The loneliness Clint wore like his great black coat over his shoulders seemed heavy tonight. Sometimes he feared he'd be the last man left alive on earth. It would somehow be his punishment to forever live and walk alone. His memory of his Mary was fading, moving into the shadows of his mind, leaving him somehow more alone every night.

Sheriff Lightstone would probably be surprised that he hadn't had a drink since they'd talked in Maggie's café less than a month ago.

Clint didn't hear Karrisa until she was standing beside him. When he turned he could barely make out her slender outline.

The room, the world, was so still tonight, he decided not to make a sound. The slow, steady breathing of his wife whispered like an echo in the air.

She moved between him and the window, her white gown brushing against his black shirt.

He tried not to breathe. She'd never been so close.

Slowly she raised her arms and circled his neck, and then she leaned in, pressing her body against his. Her cheek rested against his shoulder. He felt the tears he couldn't see.

She was crying.

Carefully, as if she were glass, he wrapped his arms around her, pulling her against him, needing the feel of her as much as she must need him.

They stood, her nestled against him for a long time. He felt her breathing slow as she relaxed. Part of him wanted to see her face, to be able to see what she was feeling. Part of him was glad he couldn't. If he'd seen fear again, this time it would have shaken him.

Her silent tears stopped, but she didn't pull away. She hadn't said a word, but he no longer felt the loneliness. This one contact was enough, maybe all that either of them could handle.

When noise came from the hallway as Patrick climbed the stairs and retired, the spell was broken. Before she could pull away from him, Clint moved his arm below her hips and picked her up. As before, he was shocked at how little she must weigh.

He carried her to the bed and gently laid her down. After he covered her, he kissed her on the forehead, then walked to his bed on the floor. For a long time he knew she was awake, just as he was, thinking about what had happened. He didn't know why and he guessed she probably didn't either, but something had shifted in their relationship.

Trust was born tonight, he decided just before he fell asleep.

When he awoke at dawn, she was gone.

For a moment, he panicked. Then he realized there was nowhere for her to go except the washroom or the kitchen downstairs. Her clothes were still in the room. Her knitting. The basket for the baby.

Still, he hurried, wanting to know she was all right.

When he walked into the kitchen and saw her helping feed the two toddlers, he felt his heart slow a few beats. People in his life tended to disappear, and he didn't want to turn around and lose another one.

Daisy saw him before Karrisa did. "Morning, Truman. You have time to eat before you leave. I made cinnamon pancakes this morning."

He'd planned to leave at first light, but he sat down next to his wife and said, "If you got it ready."

Daisy passed him a plate. "I was just packing your supplies. You'll have bread, cheese, and the last of the apples for the first few days. After that you'll have to survive on jerky and hardtack till you get to the railroad, unless you want to take time to stop and build a fire every night. If you plan to do that, I'll put in beans and coffee."

"I'll be riding as fast as I can. Ely says I may have to go

in search of the supplies once I get to town." When he reached for his coffee cup, he brushed Karrisa's arm.

She didn't move away, so he relaxed back in his chair with his shoulder pressed lightly against hers. He almost felt like they were together, maybe not like the other couples, but still together. The memory of the way he'd held her for a few minutes last night drifted through his mind.

The pancakes could have been sawdust. He wouldn't have noticed. The feeling of being near another human was so foreign to him he decided not to even try to carry on conversation.

Thanks to Patrick and the captain joining them, no one noticed Clint's silence. Patrick was busy asking questions about Gillian's days on the frontier, and the captain was enough of a storyteller to enjoy making the life sound interesting.

The conversation shifted to the work that Patrick and his brother planned to do while waiting for Clint to get back. "We'll level off the land for the house and decide where you want your front door, and then we'll use the wagons to haul rocks from the streams for the fireplace. You got any preference as to where you want the fireplace, or the house for that matter? Forty acres doesn't narrow it down much."

"Wherever my wife says will be fine with me," Truman said between bites.

She didn't say anything or have time to think before Patrick added, "I wish I could be that way, but Annie and me have been arguing about which direction the front door will face. I want to sit out front and watch the sun rise, and she wants to sit in the same place and watch it set. That's going to be mighty hard to build."

Annie turned from the stove. "I'll get my way on this, Patrick, or we'll be building two bedrooms."

Patrick's grin was so wide it almost reached both ears. "That settles it. We'll watch the sunset from our front porch."

Everyone laughed.

The captain slapped the back of Patrick's head. "Way to stand up to the little woman, McAllen."

Patrick kept grinning. "It's the lying down with myself that didn't look so appealing, Captain."

"Good point." Captain Matheson winked at his wife while everyone else acted like they didn't notice.

Clint finished his meal and said good-bye to all but Karrisa. When he turned to grab his hat, he looked at her. "See me off?" he said in what he hoped didn't sound like an order.

She nodded once without looking up as she lifted the bag of food Daisy had packed for him. After checking on her sleeping baby, she stood, ready to go.

He waited for her to walk out first, but when she didn't, he went through the door and hoped she would follow. Every time, she waited for him to make the first move, almost as if she feared making a mistake.

Ely stopped Clint as they passed through the store. The old guy had a few more bits of advice to give him, but nothing Clint hadn't heard every day since they'd planned the trip.

When they were finally in the barn, Karrisa stood silently as he saddled his horse.

After he finished, he turned to her, having no idea what to say to the woman. Until last night when she'd hugged him, living with her hadn't been much different than living with a ghost, and Clint was an expert at living with ghosts.

Frustrated, he grumbled, "I'll come back. I promise. I don't want you worrying that I'll get killed out on the road somewhere or just ride off and leave you here."

Swearing under his breath, he decided his good-bye talk probably wasn't doing much to cheer her up.

She stared at his boots, but she didn't move, so he figured their conversation wasn't over even if she wasn't exactly holding up her half.

"You still afraid of me?"

To his surprise, she shook her head.

"Well, then come over here and hug me good-bye." He guessed if he'd stepped one step in her direction, she'd probably bolt.

He hadn't planned on touching her again. He wasn't sure

how he felt about the way she'd come to him last night. Two lonely strangers hugging because they didn't want to be so alone hadn't helped either of them.

She took two steps toward him and handed him the bag.

He looped it over his saddle horn but didn't reach for her. "I'm guessing a man should kiss his wife good-bye," he said, trying to lower his voice. "You have any objections?"

Raising her head, she met his eyes.

He saw uncertainty, shyness, but no fear. *Not hating him* didn't exactly mean love, he told himself, but if she wanted to act the part of a wife, he could do the same and act the part of a husband. Hell, for all he knew she thought the others might be watching.

Deciding to play the act out, he whispered, "One more step, dear."

She moved closer, still looking at him with eyes that might burst into tears at any moment.

He slowly lifted his hand to her shoulder.

She didn't move. He wasn't holding her, just touching. She could run if she wanted to.

Leaning down, he kissed her forehead, thinking that her hair smelled like honeysuckle. Then, with little determination and no need, he lowered his mouth to her lips.

When she didn't pull away, he tasted her lips. They were far softer than he'd thought lips were supposed to be. Not that he was an expert. He was thirty and could count on one hand the women he'd kissed.

As his mouth pressed her soft, welcoming lips, he felt like it had been a lifetime since he'd kissed a woman, and Clint had forgotten it ever feeling so good.

His arm slid behind her shoulders and he drew her close as his tongue slipped along the seam of her lips. She was stiff in his arms, but her mouth tasted so good he couldn't make himself stop with an innocent kiss. He tugged at her bottom lip until it puffed, and he pulled it slightly into his mouth for a better taste.

Then, as if realizing what he was doing with a woman who'd never even called him by his first name, he pulled a few inches away. "I—I didn't mean to do that." Her eyes were closed, her head still lifted as if waiting for him to continue. "Did you mind that?"

When she didn't answer, he ran his thumb over her bottom lip. "Did you mind the way I kissed you just now?"

"No," she answered. "I've never been kissed like that before. I found it quite pleasant."

Several questions popped into his mind. *How could a woman with a baby not know a man's kiss?* for one. But he'd sworn not to ask about her past, so he had little hope of being answered.

"Open your eyes," he said. "I want you to know that it's me kissing you again."

She followed his order. "All right."

When he saw no fear in her blue depths, he lowered his mouth over hers once more. The taste was still there, warm and sweet. Her lips were plump, welcoming and wet from the last kiss. He took his time learning the feel of her, enjoying something so newborn and familiar at the same time. When she sighed, he parted her lips and the kiss deepened.

She didn't protest but seemed to be offering him a gift freely given. He raised his free hand and cupped the side of her face as he pulled away just far enough to look at her.

Her eyes were closed again, but she didn't move. Her mouth remained slightly open and her lips were swollen and wet.

He ran his thumb over her mouth, enjoying the feel of what he'd just tasted. "One more," he whispered against her as he kissed her again. This time harder, faster. A kiss good-bye.

When he finished, he left one arm around her as he grabbed the reins of his horse and began walking out into the morning sun.

"Now you remember to eat," he said, thinking that he should have said something else. Something kind. Something endearing. But he wasn't that kind of man. "And take care of that baby. When I get back I want you to have thought of a name. If you can't, we'll start through all my relatives and maybe one will suit your fancy."

"I will." She matched her steps with his.

"And when I get back, dear, I expect, if you've no objection, to try another kiss." He figured he'd be thinking about the few they'd just shared for most of the trip.

"Of course, Truman."

The other families were moving onto the porch to wave good-bye. Even the dog's fat tail was thumping on the boards. There was no privacy now. Clint simply gripped her shoulder for a moment before turning loose and swinging up into his saddle.

He looked down. "I'll be back in a few weeks."

A slight smile brushed those lips that tasted so good he might get addicted. As if she could read his mind, she blushed and lifted her fingers to her mouth.

Truman tipped his hat to the group and kicked his horse into a run. If he didn't leave fast, he was afraid he'd think of another reason to stay a little longer because, if he stayed longer, he'd have to have another kiss.

As he rode, he calculated in his mind. Four days of hard riding and he'd be in Dallas. One, maybe two days to get the crew and then, if he pushed a little, they could make the trip back in ten or eleven days. The first thing he planned to do when he got back was get his silent wife alone and see if the kiss that still lingered in his thoughts was as good as the memory of it.

# Chapter 18

THE ROAD TO DALLAS, WHICH HAD SEEMED CALM AND relaxing when Truman drove his new family north to the job, now took on a completely different light. The little wagon with their few belongings had easily taken the streams and uphill climbs, but wide, loaded wagons would be harder to move across uneven ground. The mules would be slower than his pair of horses, but they'd be able to pull five times the load. He carefully mapped out every mile as he moved toward Dallas.

Skills he'd learned while still a boy in the war served him well now. The first night he didn't bother with a fire, but the second day turned cloudy and he stopped in time to have a fire going before dark.

He thought sleep would claim him, but it didn't. After he ate the last of the food Daisy had insisted he bring, Clint rolled up in his bedroll and stared at the fire. His mind turned back to the kiss he'd shared with Karrisa. He still didn't think of her most of the time as his wife. A wife seemed like so much more than someone who mended his clothes.

She probably didn't think of him as much of a husband either. But now that he'd had time to think for a few days, Clint guessed she was trying her best. He didn't know her past, but he'd bet she'd never been married. That meant the baby was a bastard.

Clint swore. *Was* didn't matter. The boy was his kid now and he'd stand against any man who said he wasn't.

Slowly the truth, standing on no facts, came to him. She'd never kissed a man who cared for her, but she had a baby. That meant she'd been forced. Raped.

The things she'd asked for before she agreed to marry him came through loud and clear. That he wouldn't hit her. That he'd never force her.

She'd been forced. Raped more than once, he guessed from the amount of fear he'd first seen in her eyes. Whatever she'd done after that, be it a crime or not, must have been justified. Maybe she'd killed the attacker, or maybe she'd stolen to get away.

Another realization tumbled in his mind. When she walked out of the prison that night, not one person, family or friend, waited for her. They'd all turned their backs.

Rage like he hadn't known since the war boiled in Clint. Rage so great it wiped away all his own sorrow and self-pity. He wanted to ride back to her and demand she tell him all about what had happened to her, and then he'd make a list of all the people he planned to get to the hereafter faster. One man might have raped her, but others stood by and did nothing.

She must not have had a father, or a brother, or any man who'd stand up for her. If she had, they would have done the killing of the man who got her with child.

That was why she couldn't think of the baby's name. She didn't know one good man to name him after. Clint stared at the fire, guessing that she was no one's daughter, no one's sister, no one's love.

But despite all that had happened to her, she was trying to be his wife. She'd mended his clothes. She'd cooked his food even though he'd never said a word of thanks. She'd even dressed in front of him when he told her that's what wives did.

And she'd let him kiss her. Without fear, she'd let him kiss her. Not because she loved him, or probably even liked him, but because she wanted to be his wife.

The *Why?* ached inside him until it finally gave birth to one fact he knew for certain.

She'd married him; she stayed with him because she had nowhere else to go. He had a wife because she had no other home; no one else cared if she lived or died. He didn't love her, or even notice her all that much. He wasn't kind, but he'd promised to keep her safe. And that was enough for a woman who had nothing.

Maybe letting him kiss her was Karrisa's way of showing him that she was no longer afraid of him. In her book, that probably made him one man in a million. A man she could trust.

Trust wasn't much to build a lifetime on, but for her what he offered was priceless.

With that, Clint finally relaxed and let reason rule. He couldn't go back. He was halfway to Dallas. People were depending on him and needing this load. He had a job to do. He had to get the wagons safely back to the trading post.

Once he did, he'd build his wife a house. He'd give her that little square of land she wanted for an orchard so she could plant the apple seeds she carried hidden in the cuffs of her traveling clothes.

The next day Clint rode through a drizzle of rain. By nightfall he was passing the settlements north of Dallas. As the rain began to pour, he stopped at a livery in some town he didn't even know the name of and paid for a night. The livery boy said he'd rub the horse down and feed him hay and oats.

Clint thought of sleeping in the barn but decided to run across the street. Sleeping in a real bed sounded good.

The room wasn't particularly clean, but the hotel was quiet. He ordered a meal delivered along with a hot bath and hung his clothes up to dry before falling into bed. As he drifted to sleep he dreamed of his Mary and their daughters playing beneath an old cottonwood. The branches were so low that his daughters vanished in and out of his sight as they danced around the tree. Mary smiled at him, but she too faded in and out, almost as if the late sun were blinking on and off in the meadow.

At dawn he woke sore from not moving, but smiling. Clint couldn't remember how long it had been since he'd slept the night away. He dressed as he had since the day his family died, in all black, and went downstairs. After eating two breakfasts, he walked over and picked up his horse. Travel this day would be muddy, but he didn't care; he'd be in Dallas before afternoon.

Something had settled in his mind during his days alone.

# Chapter 19

TRADING POST

GILLIAN ROLLED OVER SLOWLY AND FACED DAISY. HE guessed it was long after midnight. "Honey," he whispered. "You awake?"

"No, Captain, I'm asleep," she answered.

He smiled. When she was next to him he usually slept soundly, but Daisy woke even when he rolled over. Maybe that was part of being a mom. "I think I'm about recovered, honey; you don't have to worry about me."

He'd stayed up all day today, even helped Ely in the store. For some reason Gillian was the one the old man told his dream to. McAllen would build it and Truman would protect it, but Ely thought it would be Gillian who would make the town work.

Daisy touched his arm. "Worrying about you has become a habit. I sometimes think I do it in my sleep."

"I know. I think about you in my sleep too, but it's not usually worrying that keeps me awake. Daisy, why don't you sleep under the covers?"

She shook her head. "When we have a house and the boys are in their own rooms, then I'll sleep under the covers."

Gillian frowned. "That could be weeks. I'm not waiting weeks to sleep with my wife."

He'd said the words a bit too loud. One of the twins woke up and started crying, which woke up the other twin.

Without a word, Daisy moved off the bed and picked up both boys. "I'll be in the store until they fall asleep again."

As she left, Gillian frowned. Apparently he wasn't going to sleep with his wife. First, he tried to think of an argument that would change her mind; then he decided it might be easier to build the house she wanted.

The next morning, after breakfast, Gillian insisted he was strong enough to work. All the others argued, but it was Ely who came up with the answer. "The captain can help the McAllens for a few hours; then he can relieve me in the store." Ely wanted to help, but he didn't want to be gone all day.

All agreed.

Daisy had told Gillian that the trading post books were solid but wouldn't stand the building of a town. Sometime soon they'd need to sell lots in town to keep building. They'd need more supplies as well as more workers. If this plan was to work, Gillian knew he had to think big, not small. He had to see Ely's dream coming true, not just a few houses standing next to the trading post, but a town with streets and businesses.

For a few days, the plan of him and Ely splitting the outside duties worked. Gillian ran the store and usually watched over Abe and Ben while Daisy fed the two little ones and got them down for a nap.

Gillian didn't risk talking in the middle of the night again. He hated that he never had a moment alone with his own wife. Seeing her and not being able to touch her was worse than missing her. When they were in their room, four little ones were also there. By the time they got the boys to sleep, people were in every other room of the trading post.

Each morning Gillian got up more determined to work. After a few days he and the McAllens finished the fireplace at the Trumans' place and moved to the next square of land.

Gillian chose the next farm. With luck it would grow out in two directions and become a real ranch. But right now the forty acres was flat, rich land with lots of open space for the boys to roam. He talked Ely into holding the land that ran toward a canyon wall. "I can't pay you now, but someday I will buy that land all the way to the canyon even if I have to do it ten acres at a time."

Ely grinned. "You men are doing just what I hoped you would do; you're wanting more land. The more you buy, the more likely you'll stay, so I'll sell it to you low. Truman gave me a dollar an acre for another hundred acres. I'll hold a hundred running next to your land for ten dollars."

"Fair enough."

"You all three get your land where we're cutting the road, but you can go as far out from there as you like."

Shelly walked into the store just as Gillian and Ely shook hands on the deal. Shelly had been clearing the road that would lead to all three farms. Without a word, he laid a piece of paper and ten silver dollars on the counter.

Ely picked it up and smiled. "You got yourself a deal, Mr. McAllen. Now get back to work on that road past the lone oak."

Shelly nodded once and walked out.

"What was that all about?" Gillian wondered aloud.

"Shelly McAllen just put down ten dollars on a hundred acres on the other side of Lone Oak Road, straight across from his brother. He writes he'll give me half his salary until the land is paid off and he'll build his own house when he has time. He named the road and I guess he had a right, he's building it." Ely put the ten dollars in a box on the top shelf. "Captain, looks like we just increased the population of my town to thirteen."

Gillian watched Ely pick up his paint bucket and go outside to repaint the sign as he sat down behind the counter to work. He wanted everything legal from the first. There were papers to draw up and have signed. He'd have his work cut out for him to keep everything in order.

A week passed, Gillian discovered that some days no one stopped in, and other days wagons stopped and men hung around the stove drinking free coffee and talking for hours.

Wagons coming from the north were few, but they arrived with long lists. They were the settlers who liked the solitude of the open country. Most had ranches. A few raised sheep. Ely's trading post was the closest most came to civilization.

During quiet times, Gillian worked on his map. If the town was planned well it would be easy to get around in. A hundred things had to be taken into consideration. He wanted a town square where businesses would be close to one another and quiet streets where families lived and children could walk to the schoolhouse without having to cross major roads.

Gillian almost laughed aloud. Planning a town was far more fun than planning a fort.

# Chapter 20

## Patrick McAllen

AS THE DAYS PASSED, PATRICK WAS SURPRISED BY HOW MUCH he missed grumpy Truman. Patrick never knew when he was going to hit a nerve and Truman would let out a string of cuss words. He'd heard people talk about men who weren't comfortable in their own skin, but Patrick wasn't sure Truman was comfortable on the planet. It wasn't like he was afraid of something. It was more like Truman feared nothing. Not even his own death.

But Patrick missed Truman all the same. He'd noticed the way Truman watched the sky for a change in weather and how he seemed aware of every stranger who rode near. Patrick couldn't tell if he was looking for someone or looking to avoid someone, but Truman was definitely a man who missed little in his surroundings.

Patrick watched Shelly sawing away. "You ever wonder why Truman doesn't talk to his wife?"

Shelly shook his head and continued to work.

"I know what you're thinking." Patrick pointed at his brother with his hammer. "You're figuring that maybe Truman reads her mind the way I read yours, but I doubt it."

Shelly kept working and Patrick kept thinking aloud. "I thought maybe he beat her, but we're right next door and I've never heard a sound coming from their room. Not even cussing, and I find that hard to believe that Truman doesn't cuss around her. But then, he never cussed around the other women either. Maybe it's just me and you that draw the words out."

Shelly looked up and raised an eyebrow.

"All right, maybe it's me." Patrick smiled. "He sure did think up a few new words for me when I asked him how many times he and his wife did it before she got a baby growing inside her. I was just curious, but he was touchy about something as simple as a number. Besides, how else am I going to know if he doesn't tell me? It wasn't something I could ask Pa about. If I wasn't proof to the contrary, I'd swear Pa never did it with either of his wives."

Patrick tossed his hammer from one hand to another. "I love getting Truman's goat. I know you're wondering when he's going to draw that Colt he has strapped to his leg and shoot me, but I'm betting it'll never happen. I think he likes having us around."

Shelly finally laid the saw down and picked up a branch so he could write in the dirt.

Patrick leaned over to read, "Get back to work." He looked up in surprise. "I thought we *were* working, Shelly. Sometimes I swear your mind wanders."

Shelly laughed and rolled his eyes.

As the week passed, Shelly and Patrick finished the last details on the forge and worked on the fireplaces for the houses. Just for fun, they often worked on the front of the trading post in the evenings. The ladies had put curtains on all the windows and painted everything out front, including one of the Matheson twins from the looks of him.

Harmon Ely complained about all the fuss, but they saw the pride in him when folks stopped by and said the place looked grand.

The days were getting longer and warmer. When they moved to Truman's land to work on his fireplace, Karrisa always came out to bring them lunch and stayed to tell them details she wanted in the house. She was shy and somehow seemed deep-down sad. Patrick had no idea if Truman was the source of her sorrow or the cure.

Jessie liked to ride out and watch them work. She loved her mare. Patrick didn't know her story either. He'd noticed she liked to talk to Shelly. Maybe because he was the only one around who didn't talk back?

Patrick's favorite time was after supper when everyone gathered around to talk either on the porch or in the kitchen. Karrisa mostly sewed and listened, but Patrick had a feeling she enjoyed the company. Old Ely would tell one story after another, and then when he got tired, he'd announce it was bedtime as if no one else would ever figure it out unless he mentioned it.

Some nights Ely would order them all to bed, saying he needed his sleep even if they didn't. The old yellow dog would guard the store while everyone else found their beds.

One afternoon Patrick brought up missing Truman again. "He's been gone nine days."

Shelly shook his head and held up ten fingers.

"Ten days," Patrick corrected. "I'll be glad when he gets back. You figure he's all right? I think his missus is worried about him. I see her sometimes standing in the window upstairs just staring out as if she might see him coming."

As Shelly often did when he was working, he seemed to turn off his ears. Patrick gave up trying to carry on a conversation.

That afternoon, when they returned from Truman's place, they were surprised to see that the captain and Ely had started a real corral. Matheson was growing stronger every day. Somehow he'd organized the women and Jessie. They carried the boards while he and Ely hammered.

As they walked up, Patrick started bragging on their progress, but Shelly stopped and helped Annie with the board she was dragging.

She smiled her thanks at Shelly.

The thought that Annie should go to Shelly if something ever happened to him crossed Patrick's mind again. The two of them were friends, he was sure of it. They'd help each other if he died. The pops of a bullwhip had faded in his mind, but he couldn't quite shake the feeling that his father would someday find him. The old man's anger must be festering like an open wound. If he came, Solomon would kill him. If that happened, he wanted his last thought to be that his Annie was safe.

Pushing the dark thought aside, Patrick forced himself to silently say three times that nothing was going to happen to him. Nothing. Nothing. Nothing. But still, didn't people start thinking about their own death right before it happened? He seemed to remember folks at funerals saying things like, *He told me he didn't think he'd make the winter*, or *He was worried about dying for weeks.*

Maybe the dark thoughts were haunting him because he was so happy. All his life bad times always rained down when he thought the world was bright. Right now, he had so much to lose. So much to live for.

"You feeling all right?" Annie asked as she passed by with another board for the corral.

"Why? Do I look sick?" *Oh great*, Patrick thought, *others are starting to see death's shadow over me.*

"No, you look fine. You're just so quiet."

Patrick forced a smile. He was being an idiot. He should just count his blessings and not worry about trouble coming. Truman was the one on the road and maybe in danger. Matheson had suffered a close call getting here. Ely was near about fifty; he could kick the bucket anytime.

Maybe he could buy one of those rabbit's feet that Ely kept in a box. They were supposed to be good luck. But they hadn't been much luck to the rabbit.

Patrick told himself he had nothing to worry about. "Nothing. Nothing. Nothing," he said aloud for luck. His thoughts had simply wandered off in the wrong direction.

That night when he made love to his Annie it was so sweet. So perfect. While she slept on his shoulder, he worried that maybe life gets perfect before you die young. That would make sense.

No, that didn't make sense. Most of the people who died young didn't seem to have figured out anything. If they had, maybe they would have figured out how not to die?

Finally relaxing, Patrick decided that when Truman got back he'd ask him about why people think they're going to die young. Who knew, after the big guy finished cussing him out for asking, he might offer a bit of insight. Truman had been in the war. He had scars on his hand and chin. He must have been near death. Hell, dressed in black, he looked like the devil's brother. Surely he'd know something.

Then as midnight passed, Patrick started thinking that if Truman died on the road he'd never get his question answered.

Patrick finally decided maybe he should just go back to worrying about Truman getting killed and forget about his own looming death.

# Chapter 21

DALLAS TRAIN STATION

THE STREETS OF DALLAS WERE FAR DIRTIER THAN CLINT remembered when he'd passed through with Karrisa. Maybe he'd been more worried about getting her and the baby safely out of town and on the road. Those first few days with her had been hard for them both. She hadn't trusted him, and he kept wondering what kind of a fool picks his wife among women getting out of prison. Even now sometimes he'd look at her and wonder if they weren't still both thinking the same thing.

Only difference was now he couldn't wait to get back to her. One kiss shouldn't have mattered, but it did. The sooner he could get his business over and be on his way north, the better.

Rain hung in the air, making everything damp and adding a layer of cold his jacket couldn't seem to keep out. He moved among the shipments and men unloading freight at the train station. Buyers with carts picking up lobster and fresh produce for restaurants, cowhands unloading cattle, families collecting their goods and packing everything they owned into wagons, all mingled amid passengers changing trains.

It took Clint an hour to find the several boxes that Ely had ordered shipped in and another hour to locate the lumberyard where he'd ordered most of the building material. Apparently, Ely figured that if Clint was picking up building supplies, he might as well pick up everything needed for the trading post.

By dark, Clint had three wagons loaded and stashed in the nearest livery. He'd hired two drivers who came with the wagons the livery owner rented him. The third wagon also belonged to the man who owned the livery but had no driver. The barrel-chested owner called himself One-Eyed Buford. He was a round little man with a black patch over one eye and no teeth, and, like most men over thirty, he'd fought in the war.

Buford apologized for not having the third driver. He said the driver who usually manned the third wagon had worked for him for almost a year, but the guy was a drunk and kept falling off the bench. Buford seemed far more worried about his wagon than his former employee.

"Find me a sober driver," the livery owner said, "and I'll pay his salary for the trip back with my empty wagon. That way if he don't bring my wagon back, he won't be paid."

"What if my shipment takes a fourth wagon?"

Buford smiled. "I got the extra wagon, but you'll have to find yet another driver." The livery owner knew he was asking Clint to do his job for him. He also knew Clint was in a hurry and that left Buford with the advantage.

Clint agreed, guessing that finding a new driver wouldn't be easy. The cattle drives were organizing and heading out. An able-bodied man could make twice as much money herding cattle as driving a supply wagon.

Buford pointed Clint to a saloon about a hundred yards down the road. "You might start there. Folks post work for hire on the board by the bar. Tell them where to find you or write that they can report to One-Eyed Buford. Everybody in town knows me. If there's a man available, he'll report in within a day or two."

Clint thanked the man and headed out. He had three more stops to make in the morning, so he needed to put an ad out for drivers tonight if possible.

Ely bought clothes to sell from a little factory on the south side of Dallas, leather goods from a saddle maker near the courthouse, and staples, like flour and sugar, from a wholesaler near the station. Since Clint had no idea how big each of the orders was, he'd pick them up early tomorrow, then decide if he needed another wagon.

The saloon looked dirty and smelled as bad as an outhouse. He thought of all the bars he'd been in since his wife died three years ago. He'd even passed out and slept on the floors in a few. Now, when he looked down, it turned his stomach to think of his wasted days before Sheriff Lightstone straightened him out. Truman was no fool; he knew Lightstone had probably saved his life. Every fight he got into as a drunk took more out of him. There hadn't been much left of the man he'd once been that day the sheriff gave him a choice of heading north or going to jail.

Clint was beyond caring, and he had no one and nothing to keep him from failing. Now, after over a month of being sober and eating regular meals, he felt like a different man. He told himself he hadn't spent three years on the bar floor. He'd drifted, worked cattle for a while, even signed on with a stage line for a year. Only, every night and every day off, he'd drunk until his memory blurred. Eventually, he'd lose whatever job he'd gotten and then he'd just drink until his money was gone and he had to sober up and get another job so he could drink again.

During that time he never sold his farm. He kept the land and he kept circling by it. A spot of land with a burned-out barn, a house in ruin, and a hundred-year-old cottonwood were all he'd had left. He never stayed on the land he owned. He rarely visited the three graves on the hill beneath the tree. He'd been their hero and he couldn't bear to think of them seeing him drunk.

The smell of whiskey pulled Clint farther into the saloon, and he tried to push out the memories of his wife and girls dying so easily of a fever. They were all there with him one day, and the next he was digging graves.

He tried to think of his new wife now. Karrisa must be stronger than she looked. She'd survived prison and the birth of a child in conditions that must have been horrible. She'd put up with the trip and the crowded conditions at the trading post without one complaint.

She was his wife. She and the baby were his responsibility. He'd told her he had no love left in this lifetime to give, but he'd keep her safe. She had food and a place to sleep and him to watch over her. That night at the prison gate he'd known that he had only two paths left. He could help her, or he could find the energy to dig his own grave beneath the old cottonwood.

"You want a drink, mister?" a tired bartender snapped.

"No," Clint answered. "I want to post a job opening."

The bartender pointed with his head toward a board and moved away. He wasn't interested in talking to someone who wasn't buying.

As Clint walked the few feet to the board at the corner of the bar, he watched the crowd. Saloon girls trying to make money. Drunks sitting alone. Several men talking, a few arguing. Poker games going on at every other table. The one nearest him had a big hairy guy, with his back to Clint. The guy was dealing from the bottom of the deck. The other players were too drunk to notice but sober enough to complain when the dealer raked in the pot.

Clint moved on, putting up a note saying that he was looking for a long-haul driver. He left his name and his hotel's name at the bottom of the note along with One-Eyed Buford's name.

Before he could walk away, a woman in a faded red dress looped her arm around his. He looked down, fighting the urge to fling her away. She was short with breasts so big and pushed up they looked like a shelf beneath her chin.

"You want to buy me a drink, mister?" Her words were slurred, indicating she'd already had her share of drinks for the night.

"No," he said. "I was just leaving." He tried to untangle her arm without being rude.

She cuddled close. "I could go with you. You look like you could use a little company, and I'm real good company."

"No," he snapped. The woman smelled of cheap perfume and whiskey. "I'm a married man."

She laughed a rehearsed laugh. "I can do things your wife never thought about doing."

Before he could disentangle himself, she reached up and cupped her hand on the back of his neck. "How about a little kiss before you make up your mind?"

Her laugh clanged in his ears.

She'd jerked his head down a few inches before he realized what she was doing. Her thin lips were painted the same red as her dress and her mouth opened as it drew closer.

Clint reacted, pushing her away, and then, too late, realized he'd used more force than was needed. She tumbled backward into the group of drunks playing cards a few feet away.

Cussing and threats blended with annoyance as drinks spilled across the chips in the center of the table.

The big man who'd been cheating stood. He didn't offer to help the woman. He turned on Clint and in a low guttural voice demanded, "Who do you think you are, stranger, shoving a lady into our game?"

Clint met the stranger's stare and saw something he recognized from his past. The man had aged, hardened with life, but Clint knew him, or had known him once in another time, another place.

"I'm no one," Clint began, knowing he had to get away fast. "I'm sorry to have bothered you gentlemen." He tossed a double eagle coin to the bartender and said, "Buy them and the lady another round."

The bartender smiled. Clint had just paid double for a round and they both knew he wouldn't be staying around to pick up his change.

He turned and headed out. The big guy at the table either didn't recognize him or was too drunk to move fast enough to follow. Clint didn't look back to make sure, but he heard no footsteps behind him as he exited.

As soon as Clint reached the fresh air, he lengthened his stride and headed for the hotel as memories caught up with him.

The big man had been a sergeant with a fighting group from Arkansas. He'd been maybe twenty-eight or thirty when Clint met him the first year of the war. Some men fought for honor or the pay or out of fear, but Dollar Holt fought for the joy of killing, and so did the men who followed him. They didn't answer to anyone and were often used for jobs no soldier wanted to do.

Clint was newly trained and hadn't seen his eighteenth birthday. His commanding officer ordered him to go with Dollar one night on a secret mission.

They crossed the lines and headed into northern territory. Clint had been told Union troops were holding stolen supplies meant for the South. He had followed orders and taken out the guards with his rifle only to discover when Dollar and his men moved in that the guards weren't in uniform. They'd been older men guarding a shipment of whiskey.

He'd killed two innocent men for a load of whiskey.

Dollar had laughed at him for getting sick. The raid hadn't been for the Southern cause. It had simply been theft, and he'd been a part of it.

After that, he asked to be transferred, and for the rest of the war he made sure he was fighting soldiers, not civilians. At first he told himself he was killing men who'd killed his brother, Daniel, but he knew he lied. After a while he used his skills to hunt food for the troops. He was so good at it, he managed to finish the last two years of the war firing at nothing but wild game. But he never forgot the night he'd been tricked into killing or the man who'd laughed at what a naïve fool Clint had been.

Dollar Holt. Time had twisted his smile into a smirk and extra weight had pooled around his middle, but evil never changes. Clint had no doubt Holt was still robbing and killing.

That night, atop a real bed, Clint didn't sleep well. The nightmares wouldn't leave him alone. He'd been running from what he'd done for eleven years, and one man in a saloon in Dallas had brought it all back as if it were yesterday.

He was dressed and down at the café on the ground floor of the hotel by dawn. He wanted a chair where he'd have his back to the wall and could still see out the window. If Dollar figured out who he was, the man might be gunning for him.

As Clint drank his third cup of coffee, he thought of the woman in red who'd tried to kiss him. The moment he realized what she planned to do, he knew that the only woman he wanted to kiss was Karrisa. His shy wife, who only talked to him if she had to, who mended his clothes and had danced with him once. Karrisa, whose lips welcomed him when her words never had.

When he got back to her, he planned to kiss her again if she was still agreeable. It had been so long for him, he knew he was out of practice. He was afraid he'd forgotten how to be gentle. But he'd like to try to be when he kissed her again. Maybe she'd even be agreeable to letting him hold her close, or lcan hcr against thc door of thcir littlc room and prcss gently into her, covering her body with his while his lips touched hers. The thought of her letting him kiss her just like that lingered on the edges of every thought he had.

He remembered her shy little smile just before he rode away and the way she'd touched her lips. She'd liked the kiss also. She'd be waiting for him to get home. He'd never push her into anything. If they could just share this one thing now and then, it would be enough.

A shadow moved across the window, and Clint knew Dollar was coming for him. Pulling the Colt from its holster, he rested it on his leg as he lifted his coffee cup with his left hand and acted like he was simply drinking.

He didn't have to wait long. Dollar walked into the empty café and headed straight for Clint's table.

He leaned back, the Colt in his right hand, his finger on the trigger.

"It took me a while, Truman, but I finally remembered you." Dollar stood in front of the table. He was a man used to intimidating people with his size, Clint guessed. "You've grown some since I last saw you, but I'll never forget those cold eyes that stared at me once like I was lower than dirt."

"You're still lower than dirt, Dollar." Clint knew it would do him no good to act like he didn't know the man.

To his surprise, Dollar laughed and took a seat across the table as if he'd been invited.

"I ain't here to pick at old scabs, Truman. I'm here on business. I've done some checking. You've got three, maybe four wagons heading out of here as soon as you get the drivers."

Clint waited. If Dollar asked for a job, he'd simply say it

had been filled, but somehow he didn't think the big guy was here for work.

Dollar ordered a coffee and as soon as the waitress disappeared he said, "The livery owner says you work for a rich old man up north who thinks he wants to build a town. Now, I'm not greedy, but, since we were old army buddies, I thought you wouldn't mind it if a few barrels of goods got accidentally left in the livery. It'd be like insurance to make sure you get safely along that road north without anyone bothering you. There's danger at every bend in that road and no help for a hundred miles."

"That your line of work now? Robbing wagon trains?"

Dollar smirked. "Look at it this way, Truman, a few barrels will be a lot cheaper than losing a whole wagon and maybe a man or two along the road. Accidents happen. Stray shots come out of nowhere. Wagon wheels break in the middle of the night. Stock gets spooked."

Clint nodded. "Seems possible."

Dollar smiled. "Then we agree?"

Clint leaned forward. "I have another deal. I leave no barrels behind and if you fire one shot at my wagons I'll hunt you and your gang down. Don't bother telling me you travel alone. Cowards always travel in packs. Before I'll be in range of any of your best guns, I'll pick every one of you off. I'll leave you gut-shot to die in the middle of nowhere just for the trouble it caused me to track you down."

Clint saw fear flicker in Dollar's eyes, and then he laughed. "You've hardened since the war, boy. There was a time you couldn't stomach killing." He raised an eyebrow. "You were the best shot I ever saw, though. I'll give you that."

"I still can't stomach killing and my shooting has improved over the years. I also learned that you don't give a snake another chance to bite. If you so much as raise a weapon in my direction, you're a dead man. I've got orders to deliver the wagons north and I plan to do just that."

Dollar stood. "I guess our business is over, Truman. Don't look like your load is worth the risk. Maybe I'll catch you next time when your pockets are fuller and you're not so worried about another man's load of goods."

The big man walked away, never letting his hand get close to his gun.

Clint left money for his coffee and Dollar's untouched cup, then headed for the livery.

One-Eyed Buford looked frightened when Truman walked out of the sunshine into the shadows of the barn. He jumped up from his stool and hurried over. "I just told him the facts," Buford said before Clint had time to ask a question. "He comes in here early asking all kinds of questions, but I just told him the facts."

"It's all right." Clint didn't blame the livery owner. "He would have found me anyway. I just dropped in to rent a buckboard so I could pick up a few more things."

Buford nodded and hurried off to harness a rig.

By ten o'clock Clint had collected everything except the store-bought clothing Ely wanted. He stopped at a small factory to pick up two dozen shirts and pants, six dresses, and six coats in different sizes. As he stood waiting for the clerk to fill his order, Clint looked out over the rows of sewing machines with women leaning over them. Their fingers moved the material along as their feet pumped away at the pedals. He couldn't help but wonder if Karrisa had worked in just such a place. The windows were dirty, letting little sunlight in. The place was noisy.

"Where do the women come from who work here?" Clint asked the clerk.

The young man shrugged. "Mostly immigrants who don't speak English. Dumb as rocks, if you ask me."

"You ever try talking to them, learning their language?"

"Why? They just work here until their men get jobs, then they quit and have babies. Lucky for us, jobs for those who can't understand English aren't easy to find, so the women stay on for a while. We've even had them work while heavy with child and then drop their babies right on the floor." He smiled. "Boss gives them a week off with pay if they don't take time off before the baby comes."

Clint didn't ask any more questions. He just stared at the women, young and old, who were working away. His Karrisa had taken the time to learn how to talk to them. Maybe she'd taught them enough English to get by. When he got back home, he'd tell her about this factory and that would be something they could talk about.

As he drove back toward the livery, he passed a cobbler and remembered how worn Karrisa's shoes were. They'd tried on all the pairs Ely had at the trading post, but her foot was long and slim. None fit her. On impulse, he stopped and bought a fine pair of lace-up boots for her. The leather was soft and would do a much better job of keeping her feet and calves warm than the cracked shoes she had.

By noon he had all the local supplies and was back at the livery. Buford still looked nervous.

"I'm going to need that fourth wagon," Clint started, then paused, seeing the livery owner glancing back at the door. "Any problem?"

"No, sir," Buford answered. "As long as you have the drivers."

"I will," Clint said. "Have the wagons loaded by dawn tomorrow—and, Buford, I want everything on the wagons. You understand?"

"I understand." He moved closer. "Mr. Truman, I should tell you, there ain't many men who argue with Dollar Holt and live to tell about it. Law can't prove anything against him because there ain't never a witness. I'm thinking there won't be many men who'll want your hauling job knowing that a man like Dollar is not happy with you. The road north is long and lonely."

"Don't worry about it. If Dollar comes after me he'd better take his best shot because he won't have time to fire twice. Now, all I have to find is two men to drive and I'll be on my way home in the morning. You do your job and I'll do mine. We'll be moving out long before Dollar Holt even notices us gone."

Clint stopped by the hotel, but no one had asked for him. He walked over to the saloon only to find that his sign had been taken down. When he asked the bartender, the man told him not to bother putting up another one. It would be a waste of time.

For a while Clint walked the streets hoping to find another place to leave a *Help Wanted* note. All he could think about was Karrisa waiting for him to come back. If he didn't find men by morning, a day would be wasted. He could put an ad in the newspaper, but it wouldn't be out for three days. He tried asking at other liveries, but most told him to check with One-Eyed Buford down by the tracks.

It was almost dusk when he walked past the factory where he'd bought the readymade clothes. The women were getting off work and all looked exhausted, their shoulders rounded from leaning over sewing, their eyes red from the odor of the dyes.

He walked along with them for a block, thinking of his wife and how she saw them as people, not just immigrants. There was good in his shy bride, more than he'd seen at first.

Playing his last chance, Clint shouted, "Does anyone here speak a little English? I got a job for two men."

Most of the women kept walking, passing him as if they thought he was a fool preaching on the streets to people who didn't understand.

Clint waited as the sea of skirts passed, and then he yelled again.

Nothing. A few glanced his direction with fear in their eyes. If they had husbands at home needing jobs, all he had to do was get through to them, but how did he do that?

"I have a job for two men," he said again. "It's—"

A tiny woman stepped in front of him. She was in her forties but looked strong and healthy. Her layers of shawls and scarves made her seem fat, but her thin hands and face gave away the truth. "I speak'a da English but my husband, no. He die on the way to America. He no speak'a nothing."

Clint lowered his voice. "I need two men to drive wagons north. To make the trip will take a few weeks round trip, but the pay is good when you get back. Can you help me find men wanting work?"

"How will'a these two men eat on the road?"

Clint hadn't expected the questions. "They'll cook, I guess. They can bring their food along or I'll hunt and we'll cook what I shoot." He made a mental note to buy canned peaches, beans, and jerky. That should be enough. Add coffee for him and four men. Maybe they could trade off on the cooking.

The little woman shook her head. "They no speak'a the English. How you tell'a them what to do?"

He was starting to feel like he was the one being interviewed. "I just need two men who can drive wagons north. It won't be easy, but it's simple. All they will have to do is follow the two wagons in front of them. Tell them I'll provide the food, but they don't get paid until they drive the empty wagons back to Dallas. If we make the trip there in less than seven days, I'll pay every man a ten-dollar bonus, but I'm leaving the rest of their salary with the livery owner."

Clint had no idea why he kept walking with the woman. She didn't look like she would help him. Maybe she just wanted someone to practice her English on.

They turned the corner and Clint saw two young men jump off the steps of an old boardinghouse and run toward him. They both looked ready to fight, or rob him, or maybe defend their mother.

He waited while the woman spoke what sounded like Italian in rapid fire. Both boys listened, nodding in agreement.

Finally, the woman turned to Clint. "My boys will drive'a your wagons if the pay is fair. I will go along and cook'a for the same amount of pay."

Clint almost laughed. "I don't need a cook." He could almost hear Patrick laughing when the wagons pulled up with a cook on board.

"You must need'a drivers bad if you stand on the street and yell. We make'a the deal. Two drivers and a cook."

She was right, Clint realized. One extra salary was a small price to pay. "All right. I'll meet you at the Buford Livery in the morning at seven after I buy food."

She shook her head. "I cook. I buy food. I need'a thirty dollar. I get all'a we need. If you hunt, you skin. I cook."

Clint wrote down the name of the livery while she talked to her boys. They looked to be in their late teens and were obviously excited. He shook hands with them and walked back to his hotel thinking he wished he'd been able to hire seasoned drivers who could handle a gun, but this was better than nothing.

When he passed the livery, on impulse, Clint went inside. His gear was still stowed away with his saddle. He lifted the blanket from atop his pile and climbed on one of the loaded wagons. He'd sleep there tonight. If anyone wanted to bother him, they'd have trouble finding him. If anyone wanted to bother the wagons, they'd have *no* trouble finding his Colt.

At seven the next morning Clint stood talking with the livery owner and the two seasoned drivers, Jack West and Harry Woolsey. One-Eyed Buford had recommended them both, and Jack said he'd traveled the north road several times.

All of them, including Clint, were agreeing with Buford that Clint had probably been cheated out of thirty bucks by a little woman when two young men walked into the stable. One carried a bag and the other had boxes piled so high he could barely see.

Their mother came next with an old carpetbag in each hand. Tucked in her arm, she had a bag with long thin loaves of bread sticking out. Behind her was a little boy of about eight and an old woman who could have been a hundred. Both carried bags. A mangy dog with one worthless leg limped behind the boy.

"We ready," the mother said. "I bring'a my own pots and I buy food for all'a you with your money. My name is Filicita Roma, but you can call me Momma Roma."

Clint frowned. "The deal was for two men and a cook. Don't we have a few extras here?"

She smiled. "Don't'a worry, I not charge you for my momma or the boy. They work free. They are my assistants." She said the last word slowly as if just learning it.

Clint shook his head. "I don't think so."

"They no go, we no go. They have no place'a to stay here." Filicita waved her hand over the old woman and the boy, then pointed at her older sons. "We family. Stay together."

He knew he was beat. If he didn't take them, he'd spend at least one more day looking for help with two drivers standing around getting paid. With Dollar Holt bullying everyone in town who'd think about driving for Clint, there was a good chance it would take him a week to find drivers brave enough, or dumb enough, to go along.

Looking at the old lady, he wondered if she'd even make the trip. "What's that thing at her side?"

"That is my momma's musket. It'a old flintlock."

"I know what it is, Momma Roma." Clint hadn't seen a weapon that old in years. "It only shoots one shot at a time."

"That's all'a she ever need. We call'a her Granny Gigi but you no call'a her. She not answer to you."

Clint nodded.

The little woman frowned at him and he knew she wasn't finished with her bargaining.

Her words came slow as if she needed to make sure he understood every word. "I cook, do notta suggest I do anything else for you or Granny Gigi will use her bullet on you."

"Fair enough. I'm Truman and you should know that I'm a married man."

"That no stop'a the foreman at the factory. He know the women can't afford to say no. Women need to feed their families. They can no get fired. The young ones he forces, and if they fight he makes them fall down. Sometimes many times. He know they go'a home hurt but only tell'a their family that they fell. If they too hurt to work, he fires them."

Anger climbed in Clint. He made a promise that if he ever came back to Dallas he'd visit that factory again and this time it wouldn't be a woman who fell down. But right now he had his pockets already full of trouble and the safest thing to do was get out of town fast.

Clint told her to translate to her sons all the orders needed as they loaded up. She rode with one son; her mother and the little boy rode with the other. The dog rode on top of one of the wagons that was covered with canvas to protect their stores from the rain.

As they pulled out, Clint was all business; but when they left town behind, he couldn't get what Filicita had said out of his mind. *If the women didn't agree to the abuse, they fell down many times.* They were beaten.

The list of questions he couldn't ask his wife was growing.

# Chapter 22

BETWEEN DALLAS AND THE TRADING POST

BY THE THIRD DAY ON THE ROAD NORTH, CLINT TRUMAN decided the smartest thing he ever did was hire a cook. He couldn't pronounce half the food, but it tasted great. The two regular drivers from Buford's livery, Jack West and Harry Woolsey, said they'd make a haul anytime Truman needed drivers. One even claimed that the reason the man Buford fired last week drank was that he couldn't stomach the bad food on the trail.

Momma Roma was a worker, Truman would give her that. She was up making coffee before the others crawled out of their bedrolls. After breakfast she'd pack up a snack for each man while her mother scrubbed the pots. When they stopped at dusk her little boy would make the fire while she cooked up food that seemed far too fancy to serve on a campfire menu. When she wasn't busy trying to teach her sons to speak English, she sang.

Truman could hear her voice from a mile away. Though he couldn't understand the words, he smiled, thinking how nice it sounded.

Her sons made up in effort what they lacked in skill, and the old dog they brought along barked at everything that moved near the wagons.

On the fifth day, they stopped by a stream a few hours before dark. The day was sunny, the air still. Everyone needed a break.

Clint took a bath and switched into his other set of clothes, the ones Karrisa had mended. He ran his hand along her fine stitching and thought that she'd cared enough about him to sew up all the tiny rips he'd simply gotten used to. She'd altered the new clothes she'd bought too. He was a big man, slim in the waist and wide in the shoulders. The new clothes fit him better than any he'd ever had.

With the good weather and steady progress, they'd be home in three days, ahead of schedule. He wasn't sure he'd thanked her for the clothes, but he'd remember to do that when he got back to her.

Neither of the regular drivers had brought along extra clothes, so they simply pulled off their boots and waded into the water with a bar of soap. Without taking off a stitch, they washed body and clothes at the same time, then lay in the grass to dry.

Momma Roma and her mother rigged up a tent between two of the wagons. She boiled water in her pots, and then the women washed in privacy.

The Roma boys didn't move toward the water. Apparently they'd just gotten their winter coat of dirt and didn't plan to wash until spring. Truman did his best to communicate with the young men using hand signals and the few words they knew. *North, south, right, left. Hello. Thank you.* They were good boys who earned their pay and respected their mother. That went a long way in Truman's book.

The next afternoon he rode away from the camp, planning to shoot a few rabbits and take a good look back. If anyone followed them, he wanted to know before they got close enough to fire off a shot.

The rabbits were easy to find but he saw nothing, not even a dust devil along the road behind them. Still, he couldn't shake the feeling that something, or someone, was out there watching.

After a supper of the best hare stew he'd ever eaten, Clint climbed up a rise about a quarter of a mile from camp and studied the horizon. This time of day, just before dark, the wind settled and all the land stilled. If anything, or anyone, was out there, his best chance of catching sight of them was now.

Something had kicked up dirt toward the north, but trouble wouldn't be coming from that direction. Clint decided wild ponies must have been running, or deer.

A thin line of smoke rose toward the western sky, almost too thin to be a campfire. Clint watched it disappear and thought of a dozen things that could have caused the wisp of smoke: a low-hanging cloud, an animal darting across fine dust. Or maybe his nerves were simply causing him to see things.

In the shadows he watched one of the drivers, either Jack or Harry, who must have walked away from the camp earlier and was now strolling back. Clint had seen the same shadow moving other nights and guessed whoever it was liked to make sure he was alone when he visited nature's outhouse, or maybe one of the drivers drank a little and wanted no one to see him. After all, the last driver had been fired for drinking.

Clint made a note to watch them both carefully. He didn't care about the drinking at night, but he wanted both men alert in the morning.

He flattened against the earth and listened as he watched his small band make camp within the square of four wagons. He knew how men hunted, even those who hunted other men. If anyone tried to move in on the camp, he'd see them long before they saw him. Also, there was a good chance the dog would bark or one of the men in camp would spot something moving. Since the first night he'd had the men guard in two-hour shifts.

The boy's dog barked suddenly and ran out of the square of wagons. Someone let out a whistle and the mangy animal returned to the camp. They were settling in for the night.

Clint watched and waited. Two days, three at the most and he'd be home. Strange how he could think of one room above a trading post as home. The supplies he carried would build his house, but home was where Karrisa stayed. The little farm they were starting would be awfully quiet with just the two of them in a house. He'd kind of gotten used to all the talking and laughing at the trading post. He wouldn't miss Ely's snoring, though.

A little after midnight, he moved down into camp. With a low whistle he let the man on guard know that he was returning.

One of Momma Roma's boys whistled back.

Clint took care of his horse but didn't move close enough to the fire to feel the warmth. He'd put up with the cold in trade for the ability to be unseen.

As he had every night, he climbed up on one of the wagons and stretched out.

Watching the silent shadows of the night, he thought of his wife. Funny, in all the days they'd been together she hadn't been on his mind as much as she was tonight. Maybe folks don't see the good or bad in people until they step away.

He tried to stay alert. If trouble was going to come, it would probably come by tonight. After that they'd be too close to the trading post. Clint didn't close his eyes all night. Everyone else must have felt the promise of trouble following them, for they were up and ready to move soon after dawn.

The progress went well all morning and into the afternoon, but as evening approached so did the clouds. By the time they stopped for the night, Clint couldn't see twenty feet beyond the circle of the wagons.

Everyone was tired. Momma Roma didn't sing and none of the men talked as they ate their supper and turned in. By dark the low fog seemed to blanket them in and the cold frosted their breaths.

If outlaws were near, this was the break they'd been waiting for. It didn't matter how good a shot Clint was, if he couldn't see the target, he couldn't fire.

Lack of sleep from the night before wore on them all. Clint took the first watch, knowing that he wouldn't be able to stay awake long. With his rifle on the crook of his arm, he walked around the wagons. They'd pulled the mules inside a wider circle tonight and hadn't even tried to keep the fire going. Though embers still offered some light, Clint knew that by midnight they'd be in total darkness.

Most of the crew elected to sleep on top of the wagon loads. It might not be as comfortable and could be deadly if someone rolled off in his sleep, but the height seemed to offer a bit of safety. Anyone storming the camp would be looking down for bedrolls, not up.

Clint guessed if it started raining, they'd all move under the wagons. He swore. How had he become a mother hen to this group? A month ago he could barely take care of himself and now he had seven people and a dog to worry about. He'd even made Granny Gigi a place between the boxes where she and her old musket would be out of the wind.

While they all slept, the mutt followed Clint on his rounds. Every time Clint stopped to stare into the fog, the dog stopped too as if somehow helping.

A little after midnight, when Clint was waiting for Jack to replace him, the dog growled low.

Clint lifted his rifle even though he guessed it was probably Jack circling around the outside of the wagons looking for him. Only, the dog usually didn't growl at anyone in the group.

"Jack?" Clint whispered. "That you? You're late taking watch."

No answer.

Maybe it was a rabbit or groundhog or snake getting too close to the camp?

Clint moved between two of the wagons and continued to watch the night as the dog stared into the fog at something he saw. The hair on the back of the dog rose. Clint sensed trouble he couldn't see.

Curling his finger around the trigger, Clint waited. Anyone coming up in this fog wouldn't be a friend.

A sound came from the tall grass on the other side of the wagons. The old dog turned his head and barked but didn't leave his watch.

Trouble was approaching from two sides and Clint couldn't see five feet in front of him. He did hear movement above him and guessed the dog's bark had alerted the others. Clint wanted to yell for them to stay put. To stay safe. But if outlaws were moving in, he didn't want to give away his location.

He circled, the rifle ready. If rushed from all sides, he'd have time to get off one shot, maybe two, before they reached him or a bullet found him. No one else on the caravan claimed to be much of a shot except for Granny and her one bullet, so he had to make his few shots count.

A swishing sound reached him a second before a board creaked above him. Something hard and flat slammed into his head. He tumbled forward, losing his hold on the rifle a moment before he saw stars in the cloudy night.

Clint hung on to consciousness by a thread and remained still on the ground. Several men were moving around him. Shuffling in the dirt, whispering orders about where to look.

A guttural voice came through loud and clear in the still air. "Where in the hell are the others, Jack?"

The realization that Jack West had betrayed him hurt far more than the knot on Clint's head. He'd trusted Jack. Even looked the other way when he thought the man was drinking.

"I don't know." Jack's voice was low and close, a whine in the night. "I thought they were all on top of the wagons or bedded down by the fire. The old woman sometimes sleeps underneath, but even she's disappeared." He swore and added, "She's a hundred years old, she couldn't have gotten far."

"They couldn't have all disappeared." Dollar Holt's voice came through, angry and impatient. "Find them."

"In this fog? I was lucky to even see the top of Truman's head." Jack's words held a hint of panic. "He's the one you want. Who cares about the others? Let's hitch the wagons and move out."

"Not before I end Truman's miserable life." Dollar laughed. "A couple of you men grab him and shake him awake. I want him to know I'm the one killing him. I plan to shoot him in both legs so he'll beg before he gets the final bullet. He caused me a hell of a lot of trouble and I plan to repay the favor."

As two of Holt's men lifted him up, Clint heard Jack whisper to Dollar, "We got to kill Harry too. He knows me. The others will probably die out here, and even if they manage to find a post, no one will listen to them. But Harry, he'd be a witness. He might be standing ten feet away watching right now. Before we move out, we got to kill Harry."

Dollar laughed. "That's your problem, Jack. When you decided to go in with us, you took your chances. He probably doesn't know you're involved. Ran off with all the others would be my guess. Maybe you should stay behind and pick them off one by one while you try to stay alive walking to the trading post."

"No." Jack puffed up, ready to argue. "I go with you. These four wagons will bring a good price and I want my cut. I'm not in this for the fun of it. After all, I'm the one who told you about this shipment in the first place."

Clint was pulled to his feet by two thugs. He raised his head just in time to see Dollar draw his gun from his holster and shoot Jack West in the heart. The driver crumbled as if boneless.

Dollar stood over him and fired another round, making the body seem to twitch in death. "There. That's your cut. Never ask for your money before the job is done."

Clint straightened. If this was his turn to be shot next, he'd face it head on. Blood dripped from where he'd been clubbed, blocking out most of his vision from the left side. If he could get one arm free, he'd have a chance, but the men holding him were powerful enough to make sure that didn't happen.

Dollar still stood over Jack's body, as if fascinated by the dark stain of blood pooling in the dirt. Finally, he raised his attention to Clint. "You going to die so easy, Truman?"

"No," Clint said, showing no sign of being afraid. "I plan to haunt you all the way into hell, Dollar, just as probably all the other men you killed will. You're not worth the air it takes to keep you alive. You never have been."

Dollar Holt raised his gun, and Clint braced for the

bullet. He figured if he made the outlaw mad enough Dollar would forget about shooting him in the legs first.

Only before Dollar could pull the trigger, what sounded like a cannon going off behind them rattled the air as a flash blinked bright in the night before the world fell back into total blackness.

One of the men holding Clint let out a cry of pain and dropped to his knees, then fell forward in the dirt.

Clint saw his chance. He swung the other man around as the bullet from Dollar's gun fired, hitting the man in the back.

Suddenly, all was chaos. The old dog barked. A woman screamed and what sounded like blow after blow hitting flesh came out of the darkness.

Clint pulled his Colt but couldn't make out the shadows clear enough to fire. One shadow, bigger than the others, moved through the low clouds just beyond the wagons. Clint fired at the big man, once, twice, but it was too dark to know whether he hit his mark.

He heard running and swearing and then the sound of horses galloping away.

In what seemed like a blink, silence settled over the circle of wagons. Then whispers in Italian as Momma Roma checked on each of her boys. Clint didn't breathe until the third boy answered.

Slowly his eyes adjusted to the darkness, but he didn't move. One of Dollar's men could be ten feet away. Clint hadn't been able to count the robbers. There could have been four, or five, or maybe even six if he counted Jack. He couldn't tell how many had ridden away. Two, maybe three.

In the stillness, he heard the strike of a flint and saw the flicker of flames. The little boy was lighting a fire. A minute later the campfire ignited and the inside circle of the wagons was visible. The mules were still stacked at one side. The wagons were all in place. And his people?

Clint began to count. The two Roma brothers were sitting on a man who looked like he'd been beaten. Both boys had patches of red on their faces but were smiling as they tied the outlaw up. The man must have weighed as much as both of them, but they'd fought him and won.

Harry Woolsey, the other regular driver, was rubbing the back of his head and holding a rifle. "I had one of them cornered, but something hit me from behind. I was only distracted for a minute, but the one I thought I had for sure got away." Woolsey moved closer to Truman. "You mind if I put another bullet in Jack? He wanted me dead. I was close enough to hear what he said to the leader."

"I know how you feel, but no, you can't. It might scare Granny." Clint looked around. "Where are the women?"

Everyone started searching, well aware that the fight might not be over yet. It took only a few minutes to find the women. Momma Roma was leaning over her mother, crying softly.

"Is she dead?" Woolsey asked.

Momma Roma shook her head. "I think'a the kick from the old musket knock'a her off the wagon."

Gigi moaned and everyone let out a breath. Momma Roma shouted in joy and hugged Woolsey, who didn't seem to mind a bit.

Clint lifted the old woman up from where she'd fallen between the wagons and cradled her as if she were a child. "Tell her thank you for saving all our lives."

"I no have to. She know." Momma Roma straightened proudly. "I tell'a you she only ever need'a one bullet."

"You tell her that from this night on"—Clint said the words slowly—"tell her she and her family are my family."

Momma Roma cried as she translated, which made Gigi cry and then the boys, still high on adrenaline, start shouting.

Clint turned to Woolsey. "It appears I've claimed a very noisy family."

The next morning, the Roma boys buried three outlaws. Jack West was the only name scratched on a cross. The one Granny shot and the outlaw who took the bullets meant for Clint were buried as unknowns.

Clint walked out in the direction he'd fired last night. In the spot where he'd seen the big shadow of a man, blood dotted the ground until horses' hoofprints scattered the dirt.

He'd hit Dollar, but the man had managed to climb on his horse and ride away. From the looks of the trails, five men had ridden in and two rode out, with one dripping blood.

An hour later, with the one outlaw tied up and nestled in with the supplies, and Granny Gigi surrounded by blankets as she rested, Clint discovered another fact. Momma Roma, who didn't weigh a hundred pounds with rocks in her pockets, could drive a wagon as well as any of the men. Clint wanted to relieve her, but he needed to stay in the saddle and circle, making sure Dollar Holt and his one remaining gang member weren't close. They'd be fools to try to strike again, but Dollar didn't seem a man long on brains.

Late that afternoon Granny Gigi began to cough up blood, and everyone worried. They stopped to rest the horses, but no one wanted to stop for the evening. Momma Roma made coffee, but no one ate. As darkness settled in, the nightmare of the fight stayed with them.

Harry came to Clint and said he knew the trail from here on in and could lead the way, so long before dawn they were moving again. All with one goal: to reach the trading post as fast as possible.

Clint kept circling by the wagon that held the old woman. She tried to sleep, but pain kept her awake. By dawn she looked pale and the coughing was worse. The blow to her chest and shoulder might have done more damage than she was willing to admit.

When he suggested stopping for a while so she could rest easier, Momma Roma shook her head. "She say'a she want to get to the town you call'a Harmony."

Clint shook his head. "Harmon Ely owns the place. It's not even a town yet."

"Granny say she will not'a stop until she is in'a this place called Harmony. We must keep'a going."

# Chapter 23

THE MCALLEN LAND

"FOURTEEN DAYS," PATRICK MCALLEN SAID TO HIS BROTHER. "Truman has been gone two whole weeks. I'm sure he's lying dead somewhere and we're talking about him like he's alive."

Shelly glanced up and frowned.

"All right, Shelly, I'm talking about him like he's dead. I'll stop. I got a feeling the man would not be happy if he heard I was saying he kicked the bucket. Course, if he's dead, he wouldn't care one way or the other."

Patrick hauled a few more river rocks from the wagon to where they were working on a fireplace, and then he stopped to rest. "I don't know why I can't shake this feeling that something is going to happen. Something bad. It's like I can almost hear the fuse burning down and the dynamite is going to blow any moment. Something bad is coming and it's heading straight toward me."

He'd made it halfway back with another load of rocks when Annie pulled up with a lunch basket.

Patrick smiled. "Now that will cheer me up. I think I'll give up worrying for lunch." He waved as he walked toward her. "About time you got here. Shelly's starving to death."

He helped her down, swung her around, and loved the way she laughed. For Patrick, the day had suddenly gotten a great deal brighter.

As she set everything out on a blanket in the buckboard, Patrick looked back at their project. They'd finished Truman's fireplace a week ago and the two in Matheson's bigger house three days ago. If the weather held, Shelly and he would finish his fireplace in a few hours. "This fire will warm us all winter for a hundred winters."

Annie smiled up at him as she always did. "It's going well?"

He nodded. "Shelly loaded the wagon with wood this morning. We've got enough nails to frame in Truman's place before dark. If we can get the roof on we'll be able to keep working even if it rains."

"The captain says he's riding over after lunch and bringing his oldest boy. They plan to help with the framing." Annie straightened and kissed Patrick's cheek.

As always, she blushed. He didn't say a word about it or she'd only blush more or, worse, stop kissing on him. And kissing on him in daylight drove him mad. He tried to remember what they'd been talking about. Oh, yeah, the kid. "Matheson's little fellow can't do much beyond carrying nails."

Annie agreed. "Didn't you start out carrying nails for your big brothers when they built Solomon's first church in Galveston?"

"I did. My oldest brothers were almost grown before I could walk. They always worked as a team just like Shelly and I do. Even went to war together and died together on the battlefield. My other two brothers were five and six years younger, so they missed the war, but after they heard about the oldest two dying, they went wild. My father tried to control them but he couldn't. When they went to the devil, he swore he'd kill me before he gave up another son to Satan."

Annie looked from Shelly to Patrick and whispered, "You both think Solomon is coming for Patrick, don't you?"

Neither answered, but Patrick saw the truth in Shelly's eyes. A worry became a fact in one blink. His silent brother had been having the same thoughts. "You followed me here because you know he's coming, don't you, Shelly?"

Shelly shrugged, and for the first time Patrick knew that a shrug could be a lie. He'd seen it in his brother's eyes. Shelly had stayed behind a week. He must have heard his father's ranting. He knew what Solomon wanted to do and he'd come here to make sure it didn't happen.

Patrick didn't have to know the details; he could imagine them. Solomon must have gone into a rage and brooded for days after he woke that Sunday morning to find his son gone. Then he'd probably stormed out of his study and declared that he would find Patrick. That would have been about the time Shelly slipped away. He'd seen the map on the post office wall. He knew where to come. Knowing Shelly, he'd made sure to leave no tracks heading in the right direction. He may have even planted false notes or maps before he disappeared.

Their father was coming, not after Shelly, but for him. He was the one who was supposed to follow in his father's footsteps. Solomon had six sons, and as far as he was concerned they'd all betrayed him. Patrick knew there would be no beating in a barn this time, there would be a murder. His murder. Solomon would rather see him dead than free.

There was no need to talk about it. No need for him to worry Annie. Solomon was his and Shelly's hell. One fact bothered him more than the fear of death. If his father got to him Shelly would already be dead because he wouldn't stand by and watch another beating.

Patrick forced a smile. "Don't worry about it, Annie. He'll never find us, and if he does, he'll find men, not boys. We're not going back, not ever. Right, Shelly?"

For the first time in their marriage Patrick was lying to Annie. He told himself he had to. She would only worry. Only, when Solomon did come, it might be too late for Patrick to say he was sorry he lied.

Shelly moved over to pick up his lunch without looking at them, and Patrick switched the talk to house plans. "We got to think ahead, Annie. There's going to be lots of kids one of these days and we'll outgrow this two-room house pretty fast."

"Give it time, Patrick; we don't have to do everything at once. We've got years. After living in one room, this place will be a palace." She looked at the hearth. "Can I have a window that faces the sunrise and a flower box just for herbs?"

"Of course." Patrick smiled down at her, but the lead in his heart was still there. Somehow he didn't feel like he had time. Weeks maybe, but not years. "As soon as we get the door framed in I plan to hammer up a horseshoe and we'll catch all the luck we need."

"And I'll hang scissors just inside to cut any trouble that blows inside in half." She laughed. "My own house; just think, Patrick, I'll have my own house."

"Wait, I'll be there."

She frowned. "Oh yeah, I forgot. We'll have my own house. You can have the land and the barn, but the house is mine, unless you want to help clean it."

"No," Patrick said. "You'll have your own house. I'll just live there with you. As long as I'm sleeping next to you, I'm happy."

She handed him lunch. "I like that idea."

He took a bite of the biscuit stuffed with ham and tried to smile, but he noticed that Shelly tossed his lunch into the grass and walked down toward the creek.

The girl, Jessie, was there with her pony. Patrick had seen her talking to Shelly before and wondered what she had to say to a man who never answered back.

The faraway sound of a bell ringing seemed to clang in the air. For a moment they all listened. Matheson had hung the bell the first day he was able to walk out of the house. He said if there was trouble at the trading post, everyone should come running.

Jessie swung onto her horse and held her hand down for Shelly to join her. She dropped him at the wagon without slowing down and he climbed up.

Shelly took the reins of the wagon Annie had ridden out

in and headed at full speed toward the post while Patrick swung first Annie and then himself up. They were farther out by a mile than they'd ever been.

While Patrick bounced around on the bench trying to hold on to his seat and his wife, he tried to think of what might have gone wrong. The list was far too long to bother repeating to the others.

When they passed the chimney at Truman's place and rounded the last bend on what they all called Lone Oak Road, Patrick made out several wagons pulled up to the trading post. Wagons often traveled in groups, but these wagons looked to be loaded with lumber.

"Look!" he shouted, hugging his wife. "The supplies are here."

Truman was back. The real building could begin. Patrick almost felt like he could jump off and outrun the team traveling at full speed. Now the building of the town would really be under way.

Only, when they pulled up no one was celebrating or hugging. Patrick helped Annie down as they watched Truman slowly lift an old lady from the first wagon.

Truman walked, flanked by two young dark-haired men, toward the trading post. A tiny woman of about forty was talking to Karrisa in a different language and, to Patrick's surprise, Truman's wife seemed to understand.

"Put her in our room," Karrisa said as Truman passed inside. "I'll move our things out."

"No," Harmon Ely yelled from the porch. "Put her in my room. I'll sleep in the store. Tired of climbing the stairs anyway and that top room right off the stairs is the warmest one."

Patrick turned to say something to Annie, but she was no longer at his side.

He found her and Daisy a few minutes later in the kitchen helping boil water and getting towels ready to go upstairs. "What's wrong?" he asked to Annie's back.

But it was Karrisa who answered in her shy voice, "The old woman saved Truman's life but was hurt. They were attacked on the road. Her daughter says she's been coughing up blood for a while."

Matheson stormed into the kitchen. "Got the warm towels ready and a bottle of whiskey?" The captain in Matheson was taking charge. "Jessie, can you watch the kids?"

The girl who'd just stepped through the back door nodded as he continued, "We'll need blankets. Ely is staying with the store and there is not room for all of us in the tiny room. Daisy and Annie, can you handle the doctoring? Karrisa, I want you to keep talking to her since you know Italian. It may help her calm. Try to get a little whiskey down her. It might help with the pain."

All three women nodded.

"I don't know if it will help," Matheson added, "but once when I saw a man kicked by a horse, the doc wrapped his chest with strips of cotton soaked in starch. The starch made the bandage harden as the cotton dried. If we can keep her breathing shallow it might stop any more damage inside her chest."

When they hurried to follow orders, Patrick asked, "What can I do to help?"

"Get the wagons in the barn and the mules in the corral. Karrisa said one of the drivers speaks English so he'll help. The others will probably pitch in." Matheson glanced at the pot of stew. "Truman said they haven't eaten since yesterday." He looked from Shelly to Patrick. "Looks like we'll have to man the kitchen until the women have her resting easy."

Patrick and Shelly must have looked horrified at the thought of cooking because Daisy interrupted her husband. "After you take care of the wagons, wash your hands and start slicing bread and ham. That and the soup should feed folks."

As the women hurried away, the captain looked at the McAllens. "Can either one of you cook?"

Both shook their heads.

"We've got four older sisters still at home. Why would we be needed in the kitchen?" Patrick didn't want to appear a fool, so he added, "But I'm sure I'm a better cook than Shelly."

Since Shelly didn't comment, the claim stood.

"How about you, Captain, can you cook?"

"I've eaten in the mess hall all my life. All I've ever done is warm a can of beans over a campfire."

Patrick smiled. "That makes you the head cook. If the women aren't down in an hour we have bread, ham, and warmed beans."

Matheson headed for the door. "Great. We have a plan. As soon as Truman comes down I'll find out if there is a chance the outlaws may be following them."

"And if they are?" Patrick asked.

"Then we prepare to fight."

# Chapter 24

## Clint Truman

TRUMAN STOOD IN THE CORNER OF THE ROOM AND WATCHED Granny Gigi's breathing grow slower and slower. Every now and then it would be so long between breaths or her breathing would be so shallow he was sure she was dead.

She'd used her one bullet to save him. He had a Colt full and couldn't save her. Momma Roma knelt by her bed, holding her mother's hand and crying softly as she prayed. He understood how she felt. He'd been that helpless once. His Mary had died of a fever and his daughters were growing weaker by the hour. He'd decided to ride for the doctor one more time, hoping something could be done. He'd left, with their cries for him filling his ears. Only, when he returned with the doctor it was too late to save them, too late to hold them.

Clint closed his eyes and leaned his head against the wall. He hadn't slept for two days and nights. Silently, he pushed his daughters' deaths to the back of his mind and forced himself to think of them dancing in their summer dresses underneath the old cottonwood on his farm near Huntsville.

People circled past him, but he was barely aware of them. Daisy and Annie had done all they knew to do. Everyone agreed that the kick from the musket she'd fired must have collapsed her lung. Maybe it broke something inside that started bleeding. Maybe her lungs were slowly filling with blood. Without a doctor no one could be sure.

Truman had heard Harmon Ely mutter something about how the next thing this town needed was a doctor. No one argued. They were all strong and young but unprepared for illness or accidents. From the looks of it, a cemetery might be needed soon.

The one thing that made the sickroom bearable for Clint was that Karrisa was in the room. She'd changed slightly in the two weeks he'd been gone. Her face was a bit fuller. She'd gained a few pounds, finally rounding out a bit, but it was more than that. She was one of them now. She talked easily with the women. His wife was growing stronger, getting over the birth. Her eyes were brighter and her hair no longer dull. He'd rushed home thinking only of being with her and there hadn't been a moment he'd been alone with her. The need to kiss her again was a dull ache that never left now that she was so near.

She'd never be someone he could love, but he was glad she looked better. If Sheriff Lightstone could see her thriving out here, he'd think Clint was doing a good job of taking care of her. Clint didn't want to think about what would have happened to her if he hadn't been out by the prison gate that night. Would she have survived? Would he have?

The baby cried and Karrisa excused herself. Everyone in the room knew nothing could be done for the old woman. From now on it was just a waiting game. She might recover. She *might*, Clint reminded himself, wishing for the impossible.

The captain came in and suggested Clint go down and eat something. "It's going to be a long night, Truman, and you're no good to anyone if you fall over."

Clint didn't care about food, but he needed to do something besides measure the time passing between Granny Gigi's breaths. He'd been around far too much death in his life. Sometimes he thought death planned to keep stomping him in the gut until finally he'd feel nothing, absolutely nothing.

He expected to find Karrisa in their room; but it was

empty so he followed the captain's orders and went down to the kitchen.

Patrick and his brother were there serving dinner to the two Roma boys and the one remaining driver from Buford's livery. Harry Woolsey never had been much of a talker on the road, but because he was the only one willing to take McAllen's questions, he was now reporting on every day of the journey.

Clint noticed Karrisa over in the shadows feeding the baby and listening. She had a blanket over her shoulder and the baby. The men probably didn't even know what she was doing. He decided his wife was the most invisible person in every crowd.

Clint went over to her and blocked the men's view of her with his broad shoulders. "May I see the baby, dear?"

He thought she would lift the tiny boy up to him, but when she simply raised the blanket the sight of the baby feeding almost buckled his knees. The baby's cheeks were red, his eyes bright as he pressed against her creamy white breast.

Karrisa ran her finger gently along her son's cheek. "I still haven't thought of a name," she whispered.

He trailed his finger where hers had caressed the warm tiny cheek. "My brother was a good man. He loved to watch things grow and sang louder than everyone in church. He was older than me, but he never said a mean word to me. The day he left home he had big tears in his eyes when he hugged me. Daniel died at nineteen fighting in a war he didn't understand."

"Daniel," she whispered. "I like that name. We could call him Danny until he grows up, and then when he goes off to be a doctor, he'll probably change it to Dan or maybe Daniel like his uncle, Daniel Truman."

"Thank you, dear," he said, knowing that she'd just given him a gift.

"You are welcome, Truman." Her voice was soft, just for him. "Now eat your supper. We've a long night to wait out death's calling."

"You know it's coming?"

She nodded. "I've seen it before. I was only sixteen but I

remember sitting by my mother's bed and watching her pass away a little at a time like the old woman is doing now."

Clint knew she was right. He'd seen it also. Sometimes folks don't die all at once, but a little bit at a time.

"Her name is Granny Gigi. That's all I know about her," he whispered. "Except she saved my life."

He lifted the baby blanket and put it back on her shoulder. His scarred hand brushed against the side of her hair in almost a caress before he turned to join the others.

Patrick was busy trying to learn Italian in one night and managing to make the Roma boys smile.

Truman collected a bowl of stew from the stove and a slice of bread before sitting as far down the table as he could get from the others. He wanted a clear view of his wife sitting in the corner. She'd told him a bit more about herself tonight, but it hadn't been a surprise. He would have guessed her mother, maybe both of her parents, were long dead. Also, it didn't speak well of her father that she hadn't wanted to use his name. If he was still alive, he didn't mean anything to her.

Patrick spotted him and headed straight toward him. "Truman," McAllen said, "I've been waiting to ask you one question."

"Can it wait till I'm finished eating, because your questions usually make me so mad I can't eat for cussing?"

"This one is simple." Patrick looked serious. "Shelly and I tied up that outlaw these Roma boys caught during the raid. Now what do you want us to do with him? There's not a lawman for over a hundred miles and we don't have a jail, much less a cell. Since he was caught during the raid on our supply wagons, I'm thinking there will be no doubt of his guilt, but the captain says there will have to be a trial and we haven't got enough men for that. You bringing him into our town kind of makes him all our problem now. So we've got to think of something to do."

"I guess you'll have to shoot him," Truman said between bites.

Patrick jerked as if slapped by Truman's answer. "We can't just shoot him."

"You're right. Too much noise. We'll have to knife him in his sleep."

"No." Patrick took another step backward. "We can't do that."

"Right again, McAllen. Way too much blood to have to clean up. I guess we could choke him. That wouldn't make any noise or leave any blood. Only, wait to do it until he's close to his grave. A dead body always seems heavier than a live one." Truman took another bite. "It's like the blood cools down and turns to lead once a man dies. So, my advice is to choke him within a few feet of the grave."

Patrick paled a few shades. "You're joking?"

"Of course I'm joking," Truman snapped, half mad that McAllen had even believed him for a minute. "I'll take him back to Dallas when I return the wagons."

Clint didn't like the idea but he'd figured out while he'd been upstairs waiting that four wagons had to go back. Even if Momma Roma could drive the fourth one, it wouldn't be safe to send the one driver, two half-grown boys, and a tiny woman out alone. Much as he hated the thought, he'd be returning to Dallas.

"How about you and Shelly go out and feed the outlaw? One of you can hold a gun on him while he eats and the other can try to talk him to death. Maybe we'll get lucky and he'll kill himself to get a little peace and quiet." When Shelly grinned, Clint added, "I'll let you two figure out which one does which job."

Patrick shook his head and walked away saying, "I'm sorry I even thought I missed you, Truman."

Clint laughed and realized how good it felt. Every nerve had been twisted into knots for two weeks. Now finally, even amid all the mess they were in, it felt so good to be home.

Momma Roma came in before he finished eating. Everyone hovered around her, wanting to ease her load. She talked in her broken English about how her mother had insisted on coming to America.

Clint leaned forward and touched her hand. "This is all my fault," he began. "If I could have hired more men to guard the wagons, or if I'd figured out Jack West wasn't to be trusted." He didn't add that he should have at least left Dollar Holt in too bad a shape to follow him, or maybe he could have warned the sheriff in Dallas about Dollar's threat. "I should have been more aware of someone behind me. One blow to the head and I was no help. Your mother got hurt saving my life. I should have . . ."

Momma Roma pulled her hand out from under his and slapped his fingers. "No. No," she shouted. "My mother, she not saving you, she was'a saving all. We could never have'a fought them off without you. Don't you see? You were our one'a chance. She use her one'a bullet so you could be free'a to fight."

Clint understood. She was right. The grandmother had saved them all that night. He nodded and suggested she try to eat something.

Karrisa handed him Danny and sat down on the other side of the tiny woman. They talked in Italian, his wife's voice comforting and Momma Roma's heartbreaking—even though he couldn't understand the words.

As he rocked the baby on one arm, Clint watched Karrisa comforting first the mother and then her sons. They all knew sorrow waited at the door, and soon it would be time to let it in.

Carrying the baby, Clint walked out on the porch and stepped over the old yellow dog. All the people arriving hadn't affected Davy's sleep at all. The sun had set without him noticing and the air was warm tonight, hinting of spring. Harmon Ely had painted the population sign again: POPULATION 14.

"Someone else come?" Clint asked.

Harmon Ely shook his head. "Damned if I didn't count myself twice. We got four men counting me, three wives, one stray half-grown girl, and, counting your son, five boys. Seems to me we're a little heavy on boys."

"Tell McAllen to only have daughters." Clint smiled. He'd like to be around when that conversation happened.

Ely went back to his painting.

Truman tucked the blanket around little Danny. "You're getting heavy, son," he said in a low voice, and swore the baby smiled at him. "Did you take good care of your mother while I was gone? You need to work on making her smile. I have a feeling she hasn't done near enough of that lately."

Harmon Ely muttered something about everyone in the place going crazy. He picked up his paint bucket and went back inside.

Clint didn't care. He'd just as soon talk to Danny alone. Somehow knowing the little boy had his brother's name eased a sorrow that had followed him for years.

After a while, Karrisa stepped out on the porch and took the rocker next to him. She didn't reach for the baby or say a word. They just sat side by side as he rocked Danny to sleep.

Finally, in the stillness, he said, "I'd planned on kissing you first thing when I got back. Would you have had any objection to that, dear?"

"No," she whispered back.

He waited awhile, trying to figure out how to put his words in order. "I worry," he began, thinking he'd already started wrong. "I fear that my interest in holding you again might frighten you. I need to assure you that I would never hurt you or do something that you wanted no part of." His words were too formal, but he wanted everything completely clear. She owed him the effort to be a partner in this adventure, but nothing more.

She rocked for a few minutes before she answered just as formally, "I am your wife. A man should have a right to kiss his wife, providing she's told him such an act is not unpleasant to her."

"And is it, dear?"

"No, Truman, it is not."

He thought about kissing her right then, but people were everywhere tonight and they were not two kids in love like Patrick and Annie. He'd wait until the time was right.

An hour later, Granny Gigi simply forgot to take another breath and passed as if in sleep. Daisy came down to tell Karrisa, who told the family. They cried and hugged and talked of better times, but in the back of everyone's mind whispered one question.

How long until they too breathed their last breath?

# Chapter 25

TRADING POST

AT DAWN EVERYONE—EXCEPT THE PRISONER TIED UP IN THE barn—dressed and followed the coffin Patrick and Shelly had made toward a rise in the earth a quarter mile away. Patrick had carved a dove on the top of the box and Gillian watched Momma Roma cry when she ran her fingers along the wood. Patrick's thoughtful gesture had been simple, but it seemed to mean a great deal to Granny Gigi's daughter.

Gillian wore his uniform and looked like the polished officer he was except for the bandage still circling his head. Black curly hair in need of a trim hung over the bandage. He had walked the land at dawn and marked off the beginning of a cemetery on a hill that would someday overlook the town. If generations of Mathesons, McAllens, and Trumans were to be buried here someday, he thought it only fitting that their spirits watch over the place.

Daisy walked beside him, her hand in his, and their boys followed along like ducks. Charlie was dirty by the time they were halfway to the open grave, but Gillian doubted anyone noticed. Charlie was always dirty.

Abe, the four-year-old, explained what was going on to his younger brother as they walked. "She's dead, Ben, just like a chicken is when Momma wrings his neck."

"Will she run around for a while?" Ben didn't seem all that interested in a woman he'd never seen dying. "Chickens run around for a while even without their heads."

"I don't think so. Maybe. Maybe not." Abe answered as if he were an authority on everything. "That may be why they put her in the box. Just to make sure."

Gillian turned around, frowning at his oldest sons. "Stop talking, boys. Just march. No talking or running around at funerals. It's a rule."

The frown that sent new recruits running for cover didn't seem to affect a three- and four-year-old.

They both nodded, then forgot the rule while watching Charlie push Dylan over in the muddy wagon rut. Now both twins were dirty.

As the small procession reached the grave, Patrick and Shelly lowered the casket while the others gathered around. Gillian guessed it was his job to do the service since no one else volunteered. When he'd suggested Patrick might want to say the words, McAllen said no so fast he must have already feared being assigned the duty.

As Gillian read from the Bible slowly, allowing Karrisa to repeat the words in Italian, all the women and Harry Woolsey cried. Gillian didn't dare close his eyes for the prayer. No telling how many of his sons would fall into the grave.

"She lived a long life and was blessed with those who mourn her," he said. "Now may she go from Harmony to Heaven in peaceful passing."

Everyone said amen. They all waited as the dirt was placed in the grave, and Annie set a handful of spring flowers on top. Momma Roma sang a soft song that few understood, but they all politely listened. Then they all walked back to the trading post.

Daisy put her arm around Momma Roma in comfort, leaving Gillian to grab hold of the twins, who'd decided to toss mud clods at each other. As he gripped two muddy little hands, Gillian announced in his most military voice, "You two will be in for a round of reprimand when we get back to headquarters."

Neither looked like they cared. Charlie was trying to swing with Gillian's steps, and Dylan fell down so many times Gillian felt like he was dragging him most of the way. He was thankful when Daisy took them from him, only she frowned at him like she thought it was his fault they looked like mini mud men.

"These two have no discipline," he said, thinking it was lucky that he came home from the army to help. Daisy was outnumbered.

She just smiled as if she knew a secret. "Wait until they turn two and move into open rebellion."

His wife walked away with the mud boys before he could ask any questions.

Gillian joined the main group gathering in the kitchen for coffee.

They all sat at the long table drinking from tin mugs and eating biscuits with jam. Since most had had little sleep, no one felt like talking. One by one they all drifted off to take care of neglected business or to rest.

Gillian could hear Ely snoring in his comfortable chair by the old stove in the store. The McAllens went out to the barn, saying they had a little project to finish. Momma Roma told all her boys to get some sleep as they climbed the stairs. Truman hitched up his wagon and took his wife out to see their place before the low clouds dumped another round of rain.

The trading post was quiet. For a few hours, Gillian worked on his plans. For a town to work, every detail had to be considered.

When Daisy went to their bedroom to get the boys down for a nap, Gillian poured himself another cup of coffee and sat across from Jessie, who looked to be knitting a ball of knots.

The girl still looked frail, but he knew exactly how strong she was. She'd gotten him here all by herself. They hadn't had time to talk without others around since they'd been at the post, but Daisy had kept him up on what Jessie was doing.

"You all right, kid?" he asked her, wondering again how old she might be.

She nodded. "I like it here. You going to let me stay or try to take me back to that mission you dumped me at before? Daisy says I can stay, but she's not the captain of this camp."

Gillian shrugged. "I'm not so sure she's not the boss, but either way, you can stay. You saved my life, kid. I'm grateful. If you want to stay here with Daisy and me till you're grown, that's fine with us. You'll be treated like one of the family. You'll be expected to work like we all do, but whatever we have will be yours, too."

"I get to keep the money I make at the store?" She faced him directly, but he saw the uncertainty in her eyes. "I dust and put things where they go for Mr. Ely. He pays me a dime an hour."

"You keep that money. Daisy and I will buy what you need like clothes and such. That money from Ely is for what you want." Gillian still wasn't sure the girl liked him. The only time she talked seemed to be to the boys. "Are we all right with what happened out there on the trail?" He knew he didn't have to mention the man she killed. "You did what you had to do, girl, and there is no wrong in that."

"I know what Nate had planned for me," she whispered. "They caught an Apache girl once. I seen what they did to her. We were moving camp the next day and Nate said to just leave her tied up, but I cut her ropes before we left. When Nate noticed she was gone, he slugged me hard and told me my time was coming. If Nate were to rise up from the dead, I'd shoot him again."

"How'd you end up with them?"

"My mom used to cook in an outlaw camp over near the Indian Territory. One night she and this man she'd been keeping company with ran off with the latest haul of stolen goods."

The girl played with her hands, twisting her fingers together, then pulling them apart. "I ran after her, but she told me to stay. She said she'd come back for me, but she never did. Since I could cook, I got traded to first one gang and then another. I figure I don't got no one, but I ain't a dumb animal to be swapped around."

"Can you read?"

She shook her head. "Never saw no need. I like learning, though. Mr. Ely is teaching me to count money and Karrisa is showing me how to sew." Jessie leaned forward. "Can I stay here with you and Daisy forever, Captain? I swear I'll never be a bother. I've never known good people like all you folks. If my mom drove up today I wouldn't want to go with her."

Gillian nodded. "You can stay and we'll teach you to read. We'll build a schoolhouse soon and you can go to school."

The girl hardened a little, silently telling Gillian that she'd been lied to all her life.

"I'll stay for a while, but don't promise too much."

"Fair enough. Do you have any idea how old you are, Jessie?"

"The sergeant's wife at the fort said I was about the same size as her twelve-year-old, but she said the way I'm filling out I might be older and just small for my age."

"How about we start with fifteen? You can tell people that, and next spring we'll have you a birthday party and you'll be sixteen."

She frowned for a moment, then shrugged. "All right. Nobody ever bothered to ask me before about my age, but lots of folks around here seem to want to know, so now I'll have something to tell them." She stood. "I'm going to the store. There's work to be done there. I can't just sit around here getting older." She took two steps and turned back. "I'd like to know how to read and write. It might come in useful sometime."

He grinned at Jessie but didn't try to delay her, guessing she'd talked to him about as much as she wanted to talk. Standing, Gillian set his cup on the washstand and opened the door to his bedroom.

To his surprise every member of his family was sound asleep. With all the people at the trading post the boys were up early every morning and hard to get to sleep at night. Daisy was no exception. With the extra people, she'd been helping out more in the kitchen. Her day started an hour before dawn and ended when the last boy went to sleep.

He removed his uniform jacket and boots, then carefully lay beside her, pulling the blanket over them both as he leaned back. She was still sleeping on top of the covers every night, using excuses for not sleeping with him. Most nights both were too exhausted to talk when they finally settled all the boys.

Placing his hand on the side of her head, he felt her soft sunshine hair and the warmth of her cheek. He wanted nothing more in the world than to make love to his wife, but he knew this was not the time. The boys might wake or someone might come into the kitchen or it was too light or too late, or she was too tired.

He'd heard all her excuses except the truth. His beautiful wife of five years didn't want to sleep with him. Gillian couldn't figure it out. She'd uprooted the family, she'd traveled hundreds of miles, she'd risked everything on the chance that he'd stay with her here, but she didn't want him to make love to her.

Part of him thought he might try courting her again, but how does a man court the mother of his children? They might not have spent a great deal of time together, but she was his wife and his only lover. He knew her body in great detail, not only from memories, but also from his dreams.

He couldn't bring himself to wake her. He didn't want a hurried mating; he wanted the passion of before. He wanted his loving Daisy back, and he'd have her if he had to build the two-story house all by himself.

Then there would be no blanket between them if he had anything to do with it.

# Chapter 26

## Trading Post

Clint felt like he was walking in an ocean of sorrow. No one ate any lunch. The weather had turned too bad to take Karrisa out to check on his land and new chimney. He'd hitched up a wagon but wasn't surprised when she shook her head and took the baby back inside. He took the wagon to the barn, checked on the prisoner, who'd refused to say a word, and walked back to the porch.

No one came to the trading post, so Harmon Ely complained that he might as well close the store. If there were wagons on the road they'd probably stopped wherever they could find cover to wait out the rain.

He walked around the store, the kitchen area, the back porch with a roof that leaked, then back to the front porch where rain barred him in like a prison. Restless in the confined space with so many people, he circled again and again.

Matheson and McAllen were poring over what they called a city map as if the town were already built. The captain wanted to go out as soon as the rain stopped and measure the streams. The last thing they needed to worry about was flooding across the place they'd sectioned off as the town square.

For a while Clint stood around watching the women quilt as the Matheson boys played under the frame. Jessie and Momma Roma's youngest son were playing checkers on the floor of the store. By early afternoon Harmon Ely had taken up drinking with Harry Woolsey. Neither was a very enthusiastic drinker, but it passed the afternoon.

About the time Clint thought he might go up and take a nap, his wife asked him to try on the shirt she'd made for him.

They left Danny sleeping in his basket beside the women and went up to their room. The rainy day made the small room almost dark enough to need a light, but Clint doubted they'd be there long enough to bother.

He pulled off his worn shirt. When he slipped on the new one, he felt the difference in the fine cut of the shoulders and the sleeves. The material was probably the best she could find at the trading post, but she'd finished it like one of the fine custom-made shirts he'd seen in a Houston tailor's window. The shoulders had plenty of give and the sleeves were long enough not to pull when he moved. He was a man bigger than most and never could remember a shirt fit so right.

"I added a double row of stitches where the sleeves join the yoke so you wouldn't pull them out so easily," Karrisa said as she brushed her fingers along her work.

"This is nice, dear. Really nice. But you didn't have to go to so much trouble. I'm not a man used to being pampered. Maybe make something for yourself."

She stood in front of him and smoothed the material out as she buttoned each button. "I liked making it for you. I thought of you while I worked. The width of your shoulders that I slept on during the train ride. The way you move, always aware, always ready for trouble. I thought this color might warm the cold blue of your eyes."

Clint didn't move. She'd never said so much to him at one time. It was like she'd saved up all she had to say and said it at once.

On impulse, he leaned down and kissed her cheek. When she didn't move, he tilted her head up with one finger and gently kissed her lips. The kiss he'd waited so long for didn't disappoint. Her lips were every bit as soft and full as he remembered.

"Come closer," he whispered against her wet lips just before he pulled an inch away. He wanted her coming to him. He needed to know there was no doubt that she wanted this between them.

Her hands moved up to his shoulders as she closed the distance between them.

"Are you sure you want to be so close to me?" Clint gave her one more chance to back away. He'd made up his mind he wouldn't push this shy creature. If she came to him, she came of her own free will.

"Yes," she answered. "I want this between us."

That was all he needed to hear. His hands slid around her waist as he pressed her to him. His mouth tugged at her bottom lip and she opened to a deep kiss. The memory of their first kiss that he'd carried with him for two weeks blended with another memory he knew he'd keep until the day he died.

He could feel her heart beating against his chest. Lifting her off the ground, he straightened as her body rested on his. The feel of her pressed against him was quickly moving from being a longing to a need. When her fingers dug into his hair, he opened her mouth wide and explored.

There was so much he didn't know about her. But right now, with her in his arms, he knew that he wanted her. This shy, fragile woman with her secret past and fears deeper than he'd ever seen was the one person who made him feel alive.

This silent broken woman who didn't even look at him most of the time was willingly giving him exactly what he needed. Contact. He'd been so alone for so long that her body resting on his was almost too much for his senses to bear.

He felt her shiver in his arms and he lowered her back to the floor. Out of breath, he forced himself to pull away from her lips but not from the nearness of her.

"Too much?" he whispered against her ear, knowing that the kiss had been far deeper than he'd planned. "Am I demanding more than you're ready to give, dear?" He could have asked himself the same question. He'd allowed no comfort from a woman since his wife died. "You taste so good. You feel so good. I may drown in this pleasure you allow me."

She buried her face against his throat, her breath coming fast. "No," she whispered. "It wasn't too much. I just—I just never thought it would be like this. You make me feel warm all over. I'm not afraid of you. I don't want to stop. Please hold me."

Dear God, she was begging him. For two weeks he'd wondered if she'd allow him one more kiss and here she was asking for more.

He laughed and kissed her hair. "We need to ration kisses or I fear we may become addicted."

"Of course." She backed away. "If that's what you wish."

He tugged her into the circle of his arms. "But not yet, dear. Don't move away so fast. Right now all I wish is to have you against me, so close I can feel your heart beat."

This time she came to him quickly, surprising him. She wanted more and he was perfectly willing to accommodate her wish. If his brain exploded with the overdose, he'd risk it. The thought crossed his mind that he would risk anything to know he mattered to someone again.

He cupped the back of her head and turned her just right so that his mouth fit over hers fully. His hands moved from her waist up, stroking the sides of her body as he took her breath away with his passion. Her mouth was soft, timidly waiting for his kiss. He found her shy hesitance blended with her willingness to try intoxicating. She made him want to be tender.

When he finally ended the kiss, he'd become addicted to the smell of her, the feel of her, the taste of her. He moved to her throat, enjoying the rapid pulse as his mouth nibbled along her soft skin. He couldn't let her go. It wasn't time to end this with a kiss. He wanted more of her. "Lean your head back for me, dear," he whispered as he gently tasted her neck.

She closed her eyes and smiled her little smile as if

waiting for a gift. He knew she'd run if he stepped too far, but he wanted to please her and, if she wanted a little more, he'd do just that.

He tilted her over one arm as his free hand tugged at the buttons of her dress. Kissing each one as it gave, he worked his way down to the V between her breasts.

She stiffened at his boldness.

"Easy now, dear, I'm not going to hurt you. Just relax and I promise you'll enjoy it as much as I do. If you want to stop at any time, just say so. I'll go no further."

She nodded once, silently telling him to continue.

Her trust of him made him want to go slow, make it perfect for her. He moved his hand along the open collar. When her dress opened, revealing her undergarment, he lowered and kissed the rise of her breasts over her cotton camisole.

"I've always wanted to tell you how beautiful you are right here." He kissed her as his finger trailed along the top of her breasts. "So beautiful," he repeated.

She cried out softly with pleasure.

He straightened her and once more captured her mouth, wanting another kiss more than he wanted to breathe. She was liquid in his arms, moving with him as if they were slowly dancing, letting him hold her any way he wanted. As he journeyed to the valley between her breasts once more, he realized he'd never kissed a woman with such hunger. He was starving and she was his only way to survive.

She smelled so good. Like a warm summer day, fresh and newborn. He opened his mouth, needing to taste her throat. As he moved down, pressing his face against her throat, he heard her make a little sound.

Glancing up, he watched her rock her head back and forth as if she were drifting with a tide. Moving his fingers across her camisole and along the exposed flesh of her throat, he finally reached her now slightly swollen lips. When he pressed his thumb against her mouth, she didn't open her eyes but opened her mouth, letting him brush along her wet lips. Velvet, he thought.

He drew her to him then. Holding her against him as he

took in the nearness of her. She let him take his time, never pushing away, never holding back. Finally when she moaned, he knew he'd found exactly how she liked to be kissed and several places she liked to be touched.

The realization that if he didn't stop soon he wasn't sure he'd be able to sobered him, and he broke the kiss. Lifting her up, he walked to the one chair and sat down, pulling her atop him.

For a while he just held her, thinking of how this shy woman had affected him more than anyone or anything had in years. He moved his hands over her dress, feeling a body that, though still slim, was nicely rounded in places.

"Karrisa." He whispered her name as if the one word were an answer to a prayer. "Karrisa, I can't get enough of you." He held her close.

She cried softly against his shoulder. He didn't turn loose and she made no move to slip away.

"Are you all right, dear?"

"Yes."

"Then button your dress." He wasn't sure he could touch her so intimately and then walk away. "We should probably go back downstairs."

She straightened and fastened the buttons he'd kissed. When she slipped off his lap he didn't try to stop her, but his hand lingered at her waist.

"There is no need to cry. I didn't hurt you, did I?" Her hair was in her face again and he couldn't see her eyes. She was still so frail he feared he might have held her too tightly.

"No." Her slender hands moved over the wrinkles in her dress. "You can stop asking me that, Truman. I don't think you'd ever hurt me."

He waited, wishing she'd give him some reason why she'd cried, but he'd promised not to ask. If she'd never been kissed like a man kisses a woman or if she'd been abused in the past, he'd probably moved way too fast. Yet she believed that he wouldn't hurt her, even now when what they'd done made her cry. She'd trusted him and he swore he'd never hurt her.

He stood. Suddenly their little room seemed even smaller. "Are you ready to go down?" He needed time to think.

"Yes, Truman." Pushing her hair back, she looked at him. "I'm ready."

The woman who'd been in his arms moments ago now looked very proper. A lady, he thought. A proper lady with her dress buttoned up to the throat, showing none of the satin flesh he'd touched, and kissed, and tasted.

Karrisa turned toward the door, but his hand on her arm stopped her. "Tell me. How do you feel about what we just did?" He couldn't ask about her past, but he could ask this. If she hated what they'd done or was just kissing him because she thought it was her wifely duty, he swore he'd never touch her again.

She stared at her arm resting in his light grip, then raised her head and shook her straight midnight hair away from her face. "It frightens me a little, the way you make me feel all warm inside. The hunger you have for me. Only when you hold me I feel wanted, cared about. Cherished." His shy wife straightened as if trying to be brave. "I liked what we just did, Truman. If you have no objections, I'd like it if we do it again?"

Clint froze, trying not to show how deeply her words set his mind to rest. "I think we might, dear. Maybe tonight if you're not too tired." He let his hand move up her arm and slide along her back. "And you're right, Karrisa, I do find I have a hunger for you."

She smiled and whispered, "And I you, it seems. Will you unbutton my dress again tonight? I liked watching you do that very much. Clint."

"I will." He fought the urge to do it right now. The sound of his first name on her lips somehow spoke more than any words of passion. In his mind he was already kissing his way back down to the top of her camisole.

"That would be acceptable." She turned the handle, opening their door slightly. "And I'm glad I married you. You're an honorable man. You've been good to me and to Danny, but that is not the reason I let you kiss me."

"Want to tell me what is?" He liked the way she talked,

when she talked. A soft voice, gentle words like an educated lady.

"No."

"Then how about telling me why you cried?" he whispered from just behind her. He found himself drawn to her, but more than that, he wanted to understand her.

"No," she answered, and slipped into the hallway.

The door closed a moment before he leaned his forehead against it. He now had no doubt that she liked him touching her because the lady had no problem telling him no to any other form of communication.

Hell, he was no good at conversation either. Maybe they should just stick to kissing. They had no trouble there.

He grinned. *His silent wife had a hunger for him.* He felt half drunk and he hadn't opened a bottle. Karrisa, his Karrisa, was no longer a stranger he could ever think of leaving.

# Chapter 27

MAYBE IT WAS OLD GRANNY GIGI'S FUNERAL OR MAYBE Patrick had just stayed up too late the night before building the coffin, but he couldn't shake the feeling that death was stalking him. At twenty his life was about to end.

The cloudy day did nothing to cheer him as he stepped out on the trading post porch. He tried working for a while, then visiting with the captain about street plans in a town everyone was now calling Harmony, but his mind kept going back to the discussion just before he and Shelly had heard the bell ringing. The fact that he now knew that Shelly was worried about their father coming was no comfort to Patrick.

The fear of death became lead in the pit of his stomach. He could almost feel the life being suffocated out of him or his blood dripping out slowly.

He could think of only one person who probably wanted him dead right now, but surely his father wouldn't really come. His old man hated traveling, camping out, having to cook his own food. He wouldn't come. Not after a month. Not now when all was good in Patrick's life. Only he knew

Solomon. Once he got a mission in his mind, there was no turning back.

Patrick heard the door open and footsteps on the porch, but he didn't turn around.

"You all right?" Annie asked him as she handed him a cup of coffee.

"I'm fine. I thought I'd go out and check on our prisoner." Patrick didn't want to talk to his Annie. He was afraid if he did, she'd guess how worried he was. Lifting the cup, he added, "This will help warm me up for the run."

She smiled. "I'll have a blanket for you to wrap up in when you get back. Don't be gone too long, supper will be ready soon."

Patrick didn't want to leave her, but he felt like he was moving into a dark place in his mind and he needed to be alone and think. He needed to walk, and if he waited much longer it would be dark. Rain or not, he'd go to the woods and think.

When he passed the barn, he heard Shelly working on a door that would eventually go on Truman's home. Everyone else seemed to think that because there had been a funeral, no one should work today, but Shelly worked. He always did. Maybe he figured he'd have no family to raise, so he'd leave his mark on the wood.

Jessie was helping him. Maybe the girl would have more talent for working with wood than she did yarn. It was downright hard to compliment her on her knitting when no one had any idea what she'd made.

Patrick walked past the barn and turned off toward the trees when he thought he was out of sight of Shelly and the trading post. The rain was warmer than it had been. Spring was on its way.

He crossed over to where the streams met. The captain kept talking about this place as the heart of the town, and maybe it would be. The water from two streams mixed together for a hundred yards in a raging fight, then broke peacefully in two once again. Ancient rocks held the banks so they couldn't expand at the middle. Hundreds of years of water had worn the banks smooth as glass, only they still held their post.

This place was starting to grow on him. This town that the old woman had called Harmony. Sitting on the damp grass at high ground, Patrick could see where the streams united. In nature's dripping watercolors of the rain he saw the reflection of a future town. He wanted to be a part of it. He wanted his children and grandchildren to be the teachers, and bankers, and farmers around this place.

He'd build each building carefully, using all the skill he had. There would be no shacks with painted storefronts like he'd seen in other towns. He'd make sure there was a harmony in the buildings.

Only all he planned might not come true if his father rode in with his disciples ready to strike down the son who'd gone to the devil. There would be no reasoning with the man. Patrick knew what he had to do. The one thing he could do to protect Annie and Shelly.

He had to face his father alone. Even if Solomon killed him, Annie and Shelly would be safe. They would want to be at his side when he stood before his father, but Patrick couldn't, wouldn't let them.

To carry out his plan, he'd have to lie to Annie. The one thing he'd sworn he'd never do. The one thing she said she'd never forgive. But even if it cost him her love, he had to face his father alone.

Slowly a plan took shape. His father wouldn't show up by himself. He'd always been able to draw followers to help him do what he called "the Lord's work." Solomon would want to confront Patrick without anyone around who might be on Patrick's side. After years of lectures, he knew how his father would rage. Solomon might never listen to reason, but he wasn't a fool. He'd wait and watch until he could catch Patrick by himself, and then he'd bring his wrath down on his youngest son with no mercy. Patrick would pay for the abandonment of the other sons. In Solomon's mind they'd betrayed him and there would be only one punishment. Death.

All Patrick had to do was make sure that he was alone at different times of the day or night. Which wouldn't be easy. Either Shelly or Annie always accompanied him along with Truman and Matheson on work days.

He didn't want to think about dying, but even more than dying, he didn't want to be responsible for Shelly or Annie getting hurt protecting him. The thought was unbearable.

He'd face Solomon on his own and, if it came down to it, he'd die fighting. Patrick had briefly thought of strapping on a gun like Truman did, but in truth, he knew he could never fire at his father.

If he died, the only saving grace would be that he'd die alone.

# Chapter 28

MUCH AS HE WOULD HAVE LIKED TO TAKE KARRISA UP TO their room after supper, Clint stayed to talk with Matheson. Gillian had recovered from his head wound and ideas seemed to be dribbling out faster than anyone could write them down.

Clint had to remind the captain several times that he wasn't under his command. Captain Gillian Matheson always apologized in his formal way. In truth, it was hard to get mad at the man when he was right most of the time. Patrick McAllen might fly off into some wild idea now and then, but Matheson seemed to have a master plan for the town in his head.

Several times during the rainy evening talk, Clint had wondered why he was even here. He wasn't a great carpenter like Patrick or Shelly or an organizer like Matheson. Hell, until the sheriff made him head north, Clint had no plan for his own life, much less anyone else's. He really wasn't skilled at anything. He was good with a gun, but he didn't see that as any great talent. Once a doctor told him that his vision was far better than most folks. That probably explained the accuracy with a weapon. That and his steady hand. He rarely got nervous or excited or even afraid. Angry and bored seemed the range of his emotions.

Friends in another lifetime used to tell Clint that his first wife would never have married him if she hadn't known him since birth. They were probably right. She'd lived down the road from his parents. When he came home, she'd been widowed in the war. Their friendship kind of flowed into an accepting kind of love. She used to mock his grumpiness like it was an act. When she died, he settled into it as his personality.

The more he thought about how useless he was around the future town, the more determined he was to stay and find his place. He was tired of drifting.

Karrisa passed by and refilled his coffee for the fourth time. She rarely met his stare and never showed any affection, but he found he liked just knowing she was near. As long as she was in his sight, he knew she was safe.

While Gillian talked, Clint tried for the hundredth time to think of what she had done to be put in prison. If it was murder, he hoped she'd killed the bastard who'd raped her. What kind of man would do that terrible thing? What kind of family would put shy Karrisa to work in a factory?

Maybe they were all dead. That was why she'd walked out of prison alone. But when the sheriff had asked her if she had family to go to, she'd replied, *None that I'd want to see again or who would welcome me.* So somewhere she must have kin still living.

When Clint finally decided to pay attention to the conversation, the men were talking over the likelihood that Clint had to go back with the wagons. Not just for their protection but to deliver the outlaw to jail. If Harry Woolsey and the Romas didn't return, they wouldn't get paid. With empty wagons, the trip would be faster, but not much safer. Thanks to the rain, accidents would be more likely on muddy roads.

He'd already figured out he'd be going, so he saw no need to jump in the conversation.

However, the last place he ever wanted to go again was

Dallas. If Dollar Holt hadn't died from being hit that night, he was probably back in Dallas waiting—no, hoping that Clint would show up.

Clint suggested they wait a few days to leave. Maybe the Roma boys would help out with the building, giving their mother time to grieve.

Captain Matheson agreed. If they waited for one of the wagon trains that hauled lumber up to the fort to come by heading back to Dallas for another load, maybe they could join in. Army wagons always traveled with guards.

Patrick and Annie had given up their room for Momma Roma and her little boy. Her older boys agreed to sleep in the room where their grandmother had died. They claimed that if her ghost was there, it would be only to bless them. A few days' rest would probably do them all good.

An hour after dark, Annie picked up a few extra blankets for the night. Patrick swept her up in his arms and Shelly held the lamp. They made a run for the barn, yelling back that they planned to bore the prisoner to death by talking all night.

Watching them, Clint realized he never remembered being that young. He'd been twenty-one when he started drifting after the war. He'd felt scared and old even then. If he hadn't met his Mary a year later when he visited his parents, he wasn't sure he would have ever settled down. She'd been in mourning for a husband she'd married three days before he left for war. Clint remembered telling her that he'd wear black the rest of his life if she died before him. They'd been good friends. They'd understood each other. He'd forever miss the peace she'd given him those few years they'd been married.

Clint remained on the porch for a while, wishing the rain would stop. He'd be glad when his house was finished. The trading post was a beehive, with people moving and talking everywhere. He could hear Daisy putting her boys to bed and Momma Roma yelling something in Italian upstairs. Harry and Ely had passed out from a day of drinking. No one had bothered to pull them from their chairs. Everyone simply stepped over their outstretched legs when they walked through the store.

Clint thought he heard Danny crying and guessed Karrisa would be feeding the baby about now.

Leaning back against the porch railing, Clint wondered how he could be in the middle of so much life and feel so dead inside.

He grinned. Well, not completely dead. There for a while earlier today, he'd felt very much alive when he was kissing Karrisa. Only, passion didn't mean love. If it did, half the cowboys who walked into saloons and saw a half-dressed barmaid would be falling in love daily.

With Karrisa it was simply a surprising passion. It had to be. The only problem was he wasn't sure how to handle it. From the beginning he'd wanted to protect her, take care of her, cause her no more sadness. Now he wanted to touch her, but somehow it didn't seem fair when he knew he'd never love her.

Only, she obviously didn't mind just sharing the passion. In fact, in her shy way she'd encouraged it.

She hadn't cared when he'd said he had no love to give her. It was like she wouldn't have wanted it anyway. Maybe all she wanted was to be safe, and the passion was just a bonus they'd both discovered by accident. He would never settle for gratitude, but a little more touching from her was something he could handle.

Only he swore she'd get as much pleasure out of this passion as he took. That seemed only fair.

If all she wanted was to feel passion, he could give her that. In fact, it would make their life quite satisfactory. They wouldn't have to talk or argue during the day, and at night he'd hold her without words. He wasn't sure how far she wanted this new thing between them to go, but even if it just stayed where it was, he wouldn't complain. He might have to start dunking himself in the cold stream every night, but he wouldn't complain.

And if she didn't mind if it went further, he definitely wouldn't argue.

Tossing the last of his cigar into the rain, he went inside, stepped over Harry and Ely snoring in unison, and went upstairs.

Karrisa stood by the window watching the night when he opened their bedroom door. The baby was asleep in his basket close to the bed. She looked so alone and he wondered what she was thinking. If a thought could be bought for a penny, he'd give all he owned to understand this silent woman.

Clint couldn't think of anything to say. He felt like he'd been either talking or listening all day, and tonight all he wanted to do was feel.

With only one candle burning, the room seemed to dance in shadows. He walked across the room and stood just behind her, lightly placing his hands on her waist and loving the idea that she'd have no objection to the touch. A pale, watery moon sparkled silver into her dark hair as she turned. Her blue eyes were still hauntingly sad, but he saw the slight smile on the lips he'd grown quite fond of lately.

Tightening his hands on her waist, he drew her to him, liking the way she came to him without hesitation. When they were almost touching he lifted her up until her head was above his, and then he pulled her closer and let her body slide down against his. The feel of her was intoxicating.

When she reached his mouth, he kissed her with all the gentleness he could muster as he lowered her until her feet touched the floor. His hands tugged into her hair and pulled her face close so that the kiss could continue. The hunger for her was there once more, and the simple fact that she welcomed his kiss made him feel light-headed.

When he finally stopped, he held her away from him and watched her lean back on his arm as if floating. Her head remained back and her eyes stayed closed while his hands at her waist turned her. He loved watching her move as he pulled her close, then let her drift away only to come close once more. They moved in a private dance that their bodies were learning.

Finally, he picked her up and carried her away from the window.

Setting her gently on the edge of the bed, he knelt down

in front of her. Without a word, he began untying her shoes. The leather was so thin that the shoes almost fell apart as he tugged them off.

She watched him silently, the gentle smile on her lips encouraging him to continue.

"I brought you something from Dallas." He pulled the box out from under the bed.

For a moment, he just held her slender foot in his hand. The stockings she wore had been mended in several places.

He pulled the finely made kid boots from the box and slipped the first one on her foot. The soft leather hugged her ankle and calf. They fit perfectly. Handing her the other boot to look at, he tugged off the one he'd put on. "They'll wear well in this country life."

"Thank you," she said, brushing her fingers along the soft leather. "It's been years since I've had new boots."

"No, Karrisa, don't thank me for what I should do for my wife. If you need anything, just put it on account here or tell me to get it for you. Only thank me if I ever give you something that wasn't needed."

He sat back and looked up at her as he handed her the box. "It looks like I'm going back to Dallas, so if you'll make a list of what we'll need for the house that you can't get here, I'll see that it either comes back with me or gets shipped on the first load headed this direction."

She slid off the bed and into his arms. "Don't go, Clint," she whispered as she kissed him.

When she straightened, Clint laughed. "That's the first time you've kissed me first, dear, and the second time you've called me anything but Truman. I find I like knowing that my first name is now resting easy on your tongue."

He cradled her against him. "I have to go, but I will return as soon as possible. I want you to remember to eat and take care of Danny." He liked holding her so close. "And I'll expect more kissing when I get back if you're still like-minded to the idea."

The little smile was back on her mouth. He knew his advance would be welcome.

"Now lean back while I unbutton your dress, dear." He guessed there were probably other words he should be saying, but he couldn't think of them now with her so close.

She leaned against his folded leg and remained perfectly still as he slowly unbuttoned the front of her dress. This time he didn't stop until he reached her waist.

She remained still as a statue while he slipped his hand around her back to undo the waistband of her skirt so the top would pull easily aside. Once he drew the fabric free, he pushed the straps of the camisole off her shoulders. When he touched the first tie of her underwear, he whispered, "I've seen you undressed before, but tonight I'd like to touch you."

He could feel the rise and fall of her quick breaths, but she didn't move.

Slowly, one tie at a time, he opened her undergarment and touched her soft flesh. She remained silent and after he'd warmed her with his light touch, he tugged her closer and kissed her tenderly.

She responded to the kiss, opening her mouth, but he kept the kiss light as his fingers brushed along her shoulder, then dipped to cup her breasts.

"You like this?"

She made a little sound of pleasure and he lifted her so her back rested against his chest. Moving his chin against her hair, he began to explore. His hand spread out, pushing material aside as he brushed over her waist and down to her tummy. There he stopped, letting his hand rest in the spot where her child had grown.

The thought of just how much he'd like to feel his child growing there surprised him. "Relax, dear, I only want to touch you tonight."

She nodded slightly as he opened his mouth over the side of her throat. When she stiffened in his arms, he spread his hands wide and moved them along her exposed flesh, warming her, exciting her, learning her every curve.

His chest was solid against her back as his hands pressed her to him until he felt her relax and move with the pleasure they were both enjoying. He moved his big hand along her leg.

She froze in his arms.

Realizing how bold he'd been, he pulled back and turned her so he could meet her gaze. She was looking at him now, not frightened, but nervous. "Close your eyes, dear. I'm not finished touching you."

She nodded slightly and his hand pressed against her skin just below her waist once more. Her body shook as he leaned forward and kissed the valley between her breasts as his hand pressed into her soft flesh. His fingers brushed her gently and he felt her breathing quicken.

He pulled her to him and kissed her cheek. "Did you like that?" he whispered in her ear.

He caught her answer in a kiss that lasted a long time. When he finished she was warm and relaxed in his arms, but he made no more advances.

"Thank you for letting me touch you, dear," he found himself saying as she rested against his chest. She was soft and relaxed in his arms, cuddled close, content not to make a sound. "If you've no objection I think we might do this again."

She answered by placing her hand over his, resting just below her breast. Her touch seemed far more intimate than anything they'd ever done.

He stood with her in his arms and carried her to the bed. When he laid her down, he kissed her again, harder, bolder, knowing that he might be bruising those perfect lips. As the kiss turned to fire, he pressed his chest down against her soft breasts, wanting her to know the weight of him above her. He feared she might be frightened, but she only sighed and wrapped her arms around his neck, pulling him closer over her.

God help him, he wanted his wife. This wife. He'd turned away from every woman who'd offered comfort or her bed, but he couldn't turn away now. She satisfied a hunger so deep in him he feared for his sanity.

Karrisa held tight as if her need for him were the same, but when he felt her tears, reason returned. He broke the kiss and held her gently as she cried.

When she stopped, he kissed her forehead. "Want to tell me why you cry?"

"No," she whispered.

He stood and pulled the covers over her. She hadn't invited him to her bed, and he wouldn't go without an invitation. "Good night, dear."

"Good night, Clint," she answered, already sounding more asleep than awake.

He walked to his bedroll by the window, realizing how much he cared for her. He'd sworn she would never matter to him. Only she was so wounded, maybe too wounded inside to ever recover. He didn't know if the passion they shared would help or hurt her, but he did know that he had to let her set the pace.

After he knew she was asleep, Clint silently slipped from their room and went downstairs. He stepped over Ely and Harry, still snoring, and walked outside, heading straight for the stream. The spring rain helped cool his desire for his wife, but he needed to dunk his body and stay under until he could calm all the fires burning inside him. He never would have guessed that a shy, thin woman who wouldn't even look at him most of the time would be the one to fill him with desire. He wanted her, needed her. When his hand spread over her tummy, he wanted his seed inside her growing. When he'd put her to bed, he'd wanted to stay forever with his body pressed over hers.

Without pulling off his clothes, he walked into the stream, guessing he was going mad. Completely drunk in need for a woman who barely talked to him. He'd never known such passion, such longing. Never.

Ten minutes later, when he walked into the shelter of the barn's overhanging roof, Patrick frightened a year off his life by stepping out of the shadows.

"Going swimming this time of night, Truman?"

"Not that it's any of your business, but yes." Clint tried to get his heart out of his throat. He'd been so deep in thought he hadn't even been aware of his surroundings. That was something that never happened, and it was dangerous.

"Only one reason I can think of that a man would go for a cold swim this time of night. You didn't even bother to take your clothes off."

"They were already wet from the rain."

Patrick laughed. "Like I said, strange behavior for a man who should be in bed with his wife about now. Something wrong? Maybe I could help."

Sorry he hadn't gone swimming with his Colt in tow, Clint answered, "I'm going back to sleep. McAllen, I suggest you do the same." When Patrick didn't move, Clint added, "It might be good for your health." He studied the man ten years his junior. "I'm up because I needed a bath. Why are you up?"

"I'm thinking about my own death," Patrick complained. "You ever can't sleep for thinking? I swear, worrying about when I'm going to die keeps me awake more and more."

Clint growled. "It's starting to keep me awake too. You're not going to die tonight, Patrick, so go back to bed."

"And you, Truman, are you going back to bed? Maybe try again to . . . sleep. At your age body parts are bound to have trouble working now and then."

Clint swore he could see the kid smiling even in the dark. "I take that back. There might be a chance, if you keep talking, that you could die tonight."

Patrick laughed, not the least frightened. "Don't worry, I've heard when you get older it's hard to keep up the pace. Once you're over thirty, it's all downhill."

When Clint reached for Patrick, he was gone, vanished back into the night, leaving only his laugh behind.

Clint headed for the trading post not knowing who was the bigger fool, McAllen for worrying about dying all the time or him for standing in the rain thinking of wringing his neck.

# Chapter 29

AS RAIN TAPPED AGAINST THEIR ONE WINDOW, KARRISA watched her husband come back into their tiny room upstairs. Soundlessly he removed his wet clothes. She'd studied him since the night they'd met and knew far more about Clint Truman than he probably knew about himself.

His body was strong, powerful, and well built, but that wasn't what she admired most about him. He'd never raised his voice to her or said one unkind word. He might storm at Patrick or cuss when he thought none of the women were listening, but there was a gentleness about him few saw.

He never looked in a mirror except the tiny one when he shaved. She guessed that if he had, all he would see was the scar running along the side of one jaw. A scar everyone else barely noticed.

He always asked about the baby and took Danny often to hold. This hard man loved children. When he'd touched her below her waist, she'd wondered if he was thinking that his child might grow there one day.

She liked the way he touched her, always hesitant as if he needed assurance that his caress was welcome, never demanding. He might not know much about women, but he knew how to make her feel cherished.

The watery moonlight danced across his wide shoulders. Her husband wasn't handsome like the captain, or fun-loving like Patrick, but he was exactly what she needed. The sight of his body made her long to touch him. Those strong shoulders seemed to hold the weight of the world on them. She needed not just to be protected from a world she'd found frightening, but she needed him to care for her. Somehow when her mother died and her father sent her away to live with cousins she didn't know, Karrisa had fallen into a pit. No one cared about her and she had few skills to survive.

A year ago when she'd screamed in pain, no one had helped her. Later when she'd cried and told how she'd been beaten and raped, they'd laughed and told her to toughen up; things like that happen when a girl has to work.

Now she knew if she ever screamed, Clint would give his life to protect her, and when she cried, he held her close. He was the one person who cared about her, but one was enough.

He cared. He might never say the words, but he cared. He had been gentle and kind from that first night. Once she lost her fear of him, she knew she had to open her heart to him. With each touch she knew he alone could wash away all the pain she'd been through.

He might never say he loved her. It didn't matter. He was showing her he cared and that was enough.

# Chapter 30

## Captain Gillian Matheson

THE MORNING AFTER GRANNY GIGI'S FUNERAL DAWNED sunny, and everyone seemed to want to be outside in the light. Gillian organized the men, trying to remember that they had not enlisted and he was no longer a captain, but his suggestions came out in typical military manner. He guessed they were all used to him by now or maybe respected him enough to follow orders. Or there was always the chance they thought him mad and simply didn't want to argue with the insane.

The Roma boys pitched in, heading out to Truman's place with the first load of lumber, but Harry Woolsey complained of a headache from too much whiskey the night before and stayed behind on the porch of the trading post. He promised to check on the prisoner, but driving a supply wagon seemed to be his only occupation and at forty he didn't want to start another.

With the McAllen brothers directing Truman, the Roma boys, and him, the frame of the first house was up by noon. When the women came out with all the boys loaded in the back of the wagon, lunch became a picnic.

Gillian, as he sat on a blanket with his wife, watched

Truman through the wooden frame. The big man was showing his quiet wife around their house. A kitchen big enough for a table by the window, a bedroom facing east, a small parlor, and a room just for her sewing ran the length of the house. She kept dancing around Truman as if she thought the place was grand and he'd been the only one hammering all morning.

Since Truman kept nodding and writing something on a piece of paper, Matheson guessed she was ordering furniture. They were the only couple who'd arrived with nothing but clothes.

When the Trumans finally joined the group, Matheson relaxed. Maybe Patrick would stop talking about death now that the women were present. The young man might be a gifted carpenter, but he'd been preoccupied far too long about this fear of dying. The others were worried. Gillian had seen it before in young recruits in the army. Usually, after a few battles they stopped worrying about dying and just started being happy to be alive.

Truman walked up behind the group as Patrick said, "I can't help it if I worry about things. Bad things happen and I figure it's about my turn to roll the dice and take my chances."

"About what?" Truman asked, as if he didn't already know the answer. Everyone knew the answer. Even the Roma boys who knew little English probably knew.

Patrick took the bait. "About my death. I can feel it coming and there's not a thing I can do about it."

Truman moved directly behind Patrick. "I say we test the theory right now."

Patrick straightened suddenly and lifted his hands. Worry blended with fear in his eyes as he looked at the others.

Everyone froze. Truman must have pulled his Colt on Patrick. Gillian opened his mouth to order the big man to stand down, but Truman spoke first.

"What's the matter, McAllen, you still worried?" Truman said in deadly calm as if he'd already killed this morning and one more wouldn't matter. "Death is knocking on your door right now, kid."

"I'm worried because you're sticking a gun in my back,"

Patrick whispered. "It's probably got a hair trigger and will fire if you breathe too deep."

"What makes you think I've got a gun pointed at you?"

Patrick's face paled, but his voice remained strong. "I know what the barrel of a Colt feels like."

"Good," Truman said. "If you believe life is predestined and you're going to die soon, then if I pull the trigger, your vision comes true, but if I pull the trigger and you don't die by some miracle, then you'll admit all this is in your mind."

"The feel of your Colt is not in my mind," Patrick whispered.

"Right. Now we're dealing with a fact, not a worry." Truman shifted slightly and everyone in the group saw the handle of a hammer he had shoved between Patrick's shoulder blades, but no one moved.

"So, settle your mind. Do you live or die?"

No one breathed as Patrick straightened, as if awaiting his fate.

Annie could not keep silent. "Patrick, he holds a hammer, not a gun."

Patrick looked back and relaxed, then grew angry. "That was a dirty trick to play, Truman. I could have had a heart attack or something."

Truman shook his head. "Even if it had been a gun, kid, you could have avoided death. Nothing's for certain. If you use your head and keep calm, you can walk away sometimes no matter what danger you face. Right, Captain Matheson?"

Gillian nodded. While the women finished lunch, he watched as the once-soldier showed McAllen how to swing his hand and twist if a real barrel ever rested at his back. Chances were good, if he moved fast out of the line of fire and hit the gun as he twisted, that the shot would go wild. From the way Truman demonstrated, Gillian would bet that he'd used the trick a few times. Truman probably had his own war stories to tell, but Gillian didn't know if they'd ever become good enough friends for Truman to open up.

"That's a skill they teach every soldier, Patrick." He stood and joined the others. "May you never have to use it."

As fast as he'd turned angry, McAllen went back to his usual happy self. "Thanks, Truman, for the lesson and the fright. You scared the worry right out of me." He shook Truman's hand. "You know, if I could just teach you to hammer a straight nail as quickly, we'd have this house done by dark."

Truman took a halfhearted swing at Patrick, and then they both laughed. As they helped the wives and kids into the wagon, everyone paused when Truman leaned down and kissed Karrisa on her cheek. She blushed and turned away, but Gillian caught her smile as Truman lifted her into the wagon.

Gillian watched, glad that the man had finally noticed he had a wife. The captain was learning his men. No, correction—he was learning his friends. Truman had been a fighter once; maybe he still was. McAllen was a thinker, a logical mind who'd age them all double time if he didn't stop worrying. Shelly McAllen had a real gift for building. They all respected each other, and together they'd build old Ely's town.

The wind was calm and spring warmed the air just enough to make the work seem easy. Late in the afternoon, Truman motioned Gillian over to the supply wagon.

When they were alone, he pointed with his head toward the south.

Gillian didn't pretend not to know what he was worried about. "I know, I noticed the smoke a half hour ago. Too close to be travelers. They would have come on into the post for the night."

"I agree. Someone is watching us." Truman kept his voice low. "Maybe Apache? Maybe Dollar Holt wasn't hurt as bad as I thought and he's waiting for his chance to get even with me? Hell, for all I know it's McAllen's father come to kill his fallen son."

"So what do we know?" Gillian had already been piecing the puzzle together, but he wanted to hear what Truman had to say.

"They are not strong enough to attack us out here, so I'm thinking it's four men or less."

"I agree it's a small party, but they might not have any

interest in attacking. They might just want to watch us." Gillian thought he was probably being too optimistic.

Truman kept going. "If they wanted money or valuables, they'd go after the trading post, and now, with most of the men here, might be a good time. Of course our women wouldn't stand by and let them take what they want. They'd get off at least a few shots. We'd know."

"Right, but Harry's probably still on the front porch and Ely meets guests with a rifle at his side. Daisy mentioned that a few army scouts riding north stopped by this morning and Ely invited them to lunch." Gillian dug his fingers through his hair. "Maybe I'm worrying about nothing. Just to be on the safe side, how about you and the Roma boys hang around for another day or two before you leave to take the prisoner and the wagons back."

"I was thinking the same thing." Truman grinned. "Course, if the strangers stay much longer Ely will change the sign and add him to the population."

Gillian laughed. Ely was so excited about having folks around he'd even count an outlaw.

A few hours later, when they loaded up and moved back to the trading post, everyone was tired but happy. Real progress was being made.

Gillian wasn't surprised the women had spent the day quilting, but he was surprised that Momma Roma had made supper. A feast was set for them, putting everyone in a party mood. When Patrick told Harry and Ely his story of Truman almost shooting him with a hammer, everyone joined in the laughter.

After the meal, Gillian helped Daisy get the boys to bed. He thought it would be easy, but Abe tried to reason that it wasn't time. Ben kept sneaking back into the kitchen, and the twins didn't understand a word he said.

The good news was that with so many hands in the kitchen, the dishes were done in minutes and everyone had wandered off to their beds by the time Gillian finished bullying the twins to bed. Jessie, as she always did, ran out the back door to go check on her horse. He decided if she loved that mare any more they'd have to move her cot from the kitchen to the stall next to the horse.

He poured the last of the coffee into two cups and sat down at the table as Daisy came out of the bedroom already in her gown.

"You want a cup?" he asked, guessing she did. "You look so pretty in the white gown, just like you did on our wedding day."

"I'm older now."

"And smarter. If you'd been much more out of your teens, Daisy, you probably would have been too smart to marry a soldier, even if he was crazy in love."

She shook her head. "I'd fall for you all over again today, Gillian."

He leaned over to kiss her cheek, but she pulled away and picked up her coffee.

He knew they had things to discuss and time alone was rare. Maybe he'd start with something easy and move into what was really bothering her. "We need to talk about our house. Patrick says he's going to stay behind tomorrow at Truman's place and do some of the inside work while we all move over to our land. I wouldn't be surprised if we don't have the first floor framed up by suppertime tomorrow."

Daisy downed a long drink and asked, "Did you tell them I want a big kitchen and a pantry?"

"I did. We'll have two stories, so it'll take longer than Truman's frame. Patrick thinks he'll have the outside up in a week, but the real work is inside. We may have to live with it roughed out for a while. He wants to get all three frames up before planting time."

"Makes sense." Daisy smiled. "I won't know what to do just cooking for you and the boys. Ely says he'll trade me all the apples and flour I want for a few pies a week."

"Do you want to do that? We'll move in as soon as the pump and stove are working. I told him to just floor the second story and we'll put in rooms later. I guess we should think about how many bedrooms upstairs."

"Four," she answered simply. "One for Jessie, one each for Abe and Ben, and then the twins can share."

"But what if we have more children, Daisy? Where do you plan on putting them? You seem to get with child every time you stand downwind from me."

She still didn't look at him when she added, "We'll only have four, Gillian."

For a moment he wanted to argue. Was this the way she planned to tell him that there would be no more children between them because they would no longer sleep as husband and wife? He could understand if she didn't want to get in a family way again. The birth of the twins must have been hard on her. He wasn't there. They'd been sick. She'd said she'd almost died. Only this wasn't fair. They'd had so few nights together when he thought they would have a lifetime.

Gillian stared into his coffee. He'd fought as a soldier for years, but he didn't know how to fight this. "Are you saying that you no longer want to sleep with me as man and wife?"

He held his breath. She'd been his only lover and he'd been hers. It couldn't be fair that they'd had so few nights to hold each other.

"No," she finally whispered as tears rolled down her cheeks. "I'm saying that I can't have any more children. I couldn't write and tell you. I'm so sorry."

His chair toppled backward as he stood and rushed toward her. "Oh, Daisy. My dear sweet Daisy." He pulled her up, holding her to him as if he could take away all the pain of what she'd said.

Understanding and heartache avalanched over him.

# Chapter 31

CLINT NOTICED PATRICK'S RESTLESSNESS AT DINNER. THE kid talked even more than usual and mentioned twice that he'd left something back at one of the houses and planned to ride out after supper to pick it up.

When Annie offered to tag along, Patrick shook his head and argued that he'd just as soon go alone and allow her time to rest. His little bride had been feeling poorly since the funeral.

"I'm sure you'd like a little private time," he said as he kissed her boldly on the lips.

Everyone at the table laughed, knowing that with so many people around, there was no private time.

An hour later, when Truman walked upstairs with Karrisa, he whispered, "I think I'll go with the kid tonight. Something doesn't feel right."

She looked up at him, her blue eyes showing nothing of what she might feel. "Patrick doesn't like you to call him *kid*."

"I know, so I don't to his face, but hell if I can't stop thinking about how young he is. To tell the truth I don't even remember ever being so young even when I was the same age."

"Be careful, old man." She giggled suddenly. "You're starting to make no sense."

He smiled down at her, liking the sound of her happy. "I will, dear. You and little Danny go on to bed. I won't be late." He couldn't help but be pleased that she cared enough to be worried about him.

Once she was settled in their room, Clint checked both his weapons and silently slipped down the stairs. The trading post was dark, but he could hear Harry and Ely playing cards in the corner office. The freight driver and the owner of the trading post were an unlikely pair, but they had age and loneliness in common. Sometimes in this part of the country that was enough to keep a winter's worth of conversation going.

Clint moved out the front door and headed to the barn, thinking he and Patrick were also a mismatched pair to be friends. Even forgetting the ten-year difference in their ages, Clint could not think of one thing they had in common. By the time he'd been Patrick's age he'd fought three years and had grown too hardened to even think of home.

None of that mattered. All Clint knew tonight was that Patrick was worried about something. If there happened to be one chance in a hundred that the kid had a reason for concern, Clint planned to be close enough to keep him out of danger.

Patrick's horse was missing from the corral when he got to the gate. Clint could hear Shelly cleaning and sharpening his tools in the barn. The silent McAllen had skipped supper, as he often did, so he could finish a project or lay everything out for the next day.

Clint didn't worry about Shelly eating; little Jessie always brought him out a plate on the nights his spot at the table was empty. Shelly probably hadn't noticed Patrick had left.

Clint saddled up his horse and headed toward the first building site, his own. For a change, the moon was out and the night calm, but the ground was still wet enough to smother hoofprints as he moved along the wagon ruts everyone now thought of as a road. Just out of sight of the trading post, Clint heard Patrick before he saw him. The tinny jingle of his harness sounded like no other.

"Hey, McAllen, hold up and I'll ride with you." Clint's words were low, but they carried on the still air.

Patrick pulled up on his reins and waited but didn't turn around.

When Clint was even with him, Patrick said in a cold, hard tone. "I'd rather go alone tonight, Truman. I'm not looking for company."

Clint leaned forward in his saddle. "You sure about that? There may be trouble out here that you aren't aware of. Matheson and I thought we noticed smoke from a campfire about an hour before we headed in to supper."

"Trouble probably does wait for me." Patrick still didn't look at Clint. "And I have to face it alone."

"But—"

"No. This is my fight, Truman. You have to promise me you'll stay out of it."

Even in the shadows Clint saw the steel in Patrick's jaw. He wasn't asking that Clint step away, he was demanding. Whatever was out there waiting for him, it waited for him alone and he wanted it that way.

"Fair enough." Clint gave in. "I won't interfere." He turned his horse and rode back toward the trading post.

*Let it go*, he told himself. *Karrisa's right, he's not a kid. He can take care of himself. He didn't ask for or want your help.*

Clint argued with himself for a few hundred yards before he turned around. He'd said he wouldn't interfere, but that didn't mean he wouldn't watch. The kid might not have any idea what he was getting into. He might think his father waited for him, but it could just as likely be Dollar Holt and the one remaining member of his gang. Maybe they were watching the trading post, waiting for the chance to capture one of the men. Then Dollar might try to ransom him for the outlaw tied up in the barn.

As Clint neared the frame of what would soon be his home, he saw Patrick's horse tied to one of the posts that would hold up the porch. Without leaving the shadows of the tree line, Clint slipped from his mount and tied the pinto to a cottonwood by the road, then started walking the last thirty yards.

A mind trained in battle never forgets the skills that kept him alive. His senses turned razor sharp.

Two men stood, their outlines blinking in and out between the studs of the house. One Patrick. One older, stouter. Clint couldn't hear what they were saying, but he could tell they were squaring off like two mismatched fighters in a ring.

Something moved in the trees not far from where he'd left his horse. Clint whirled and pulled his Colt in one liquid movement.

The shadows of three men flashed in the moonlight between the cottonwoods, almost as if they were disappearing and reappearing in the blink of an eye. They walked like farmers pacing off their field, not trained fighters. Their feet were heavy, scarring the earth as they moved, and their breathing rapid and noisy. Clint would bet they'd never known battle.

He stepped into the moonlight just as they trudged from the trees. "Make another move and you're dead, gentlemen." His words were low and deadly serious.

All three men froze. They'd been advancing without their weapons drawn and now were helpless.

"Pull whatever guns you have out slowly and drop your weapons in the mud." Clint stepped closer. He wanted the men to see his face and know that he wasn't the twenty-year-old they came to hurt. He was a hardened soldier who'd kill if he needed to.

The trio looked nervous and did as he said. Two stood tall in defiance, but one began to shiver.

"We're not here to bother you, mister," the tallest of the three had the nerve to say. "We're on the Lord's business, so we'll ask you to step aside."

Clint knew his smile was wicked. "I don't care about the Lord's business—I figure he can take care of that himself—but you're on my land. So that makes whatever you plan to do my concern."

Now two had the shakes, but the courageous one spoke again. "We won't be on your land long. We've just come to beat the devil out of a boy and help his father get him back on the straight and narrow."

Clint moved closer to the one talking and made sure his Colt was pointed directly at the man's middle. "You've come to beat Patrick McAllen. He feared you'd come. Four of you against one. Right? Sounds like a real fair mission to me." He tapped the barrel of his Colt against the spokesman's chest.

Now no one moved. The one who'd been so brave seemed to have lost his voice.

"I could even the odds a bit, but I think we should have a talk first."

Clint wanted them to see the truth, not hide behind a mission they didn't understand. "Patrick McAllen is a married man of twenty, not a boy. He's a fine carpenter and he's my friend. I've a good mind to shoot all three of you in the knees so you'll have to crawl the rest of your lives and won't spend so much time thinking you walk above another soul."

Clint could smell fear. Or maybe it was urine.

"The man you came to hurt is good, unlike you three who sneak up in the dark so you can make sure it won't be a fair fight. He's not like me either. I'd shoot you right where you stand now except for one thing—he wouldn't like it. So how about you all stay here with me and watch? None of us will be in on the fight tonight."

When no one objected, Clint added, "Only one rule. If you move or speak, you're dead. No warning shot. No second chance. Just about like the rules you probably had for Patrick McAllen. I'm guessing you didn't plan on giving him an inch."

The three not-so-wise men stood in the shadows and watched the scene unfolding before them in the skeleton of a house.

PATRICK LIT THE LANTERN AND WAITED. HE KNEW HIS father was close. He wouldn't have to wait long. Solomon was not a patient man.

Footsteps stomped across the boards leading to what would be the front door of Truman's home. Patrick was aware of every movement in the air, every smell in the night. The swish of mud beneath the boards, the huff of his father like a roaring train coming straight toward him. Deep down he knew that he'd been waiting for this confrontation since the night he'd slipped away. His earliest memories were of backing away from his father's rage, only there would be no more backing away tonight.

Tonight, one way or the other, this struggle would be over.

Patrick left the lantern on the ground and stood. He'd face his father as a man, not a cowering boy.

Solomon stepped into the bones of the house and puffed up, like he always did. Chest out. Arms on his hips. Feet wide apart. Like an avenging angel. Once, years ago, he'd been a powerful sight to behold when angry, but his body had widened and softened from lack of work and his black hair had grayed and thinned. He didn't seem so big, so strong, so right anymore. Maybe he never had been, but Patrick was too frightened to notice.

For a minute they simply stared at each other. Patrick wasn't sure Solomon even saw him as his son any longer. Once people fell in Solomon's eyes they were worthless. Simply extra baggage in a world already crowded with sinners. His son was nothing to him now.

The same was true of fathers, Patrick realized. After the beating, he'd always felt he had no father left inside the man. Solomon was not a part of his family.

"You stole Brother Spencer's daughter," Solomon began. "There will be no forgiving for you in that house either."

"I married her."

"You ran out on your family." His voice rose slightly. "Crawled away like a snake."

"I left."

"You dishonored me. You were to walk in my steps. I'd already set your path for you. All you had to do was follow me."

Patrick couldn't help smiling. The man no longer held any power over him. "I'll walk in my own steps now. I don't want to follow in yours. I never did. None of your sons ever did."

Solomon rocked as if about to explode and screamed, "You didn't listen to me. You didn't obey and now you must pay. Even when you beg, I won't forgive what you've done."

Patrick shook his head. "No. Solomon, I won't come back and

I won't beg." He almost smiled. It all seemed so clear now. "To think how I feared this meeting. After you beat me until I was more dead than alive when I was a boy, I used to have nightmares about what you'd do if I ever tried to leave again. Now I see you for what you really are: a bully of an old man who just wants his way. You trapped your daughters by never letting them look at a man, but you couldn't trap your sons. We all slipped from your grip and none of us will ever come home again. Why should we? We never knew love there once our mother died."

Patrick knew he was poking a bear, but he couldn't stop. He had to say all the things he'd felt and never been able to say.

Solomon seemed to swell with rage. "You will return with me! You will or I'll see you dead. I don't care how many days or weeks or years it takes, but I'll make you see what path is right for you or your death will be on your own hands."

Insanity whispered between Solomon's shouts and Patrick knew it had always been there, simmering just beneath the surface. The endless lectures, the beatings, the need to control everyone around him. Solomon's rage had always been so great, everyone had allowed it, knowing he could snap beyond reason any moment.

Patrick shook his head. "I'll never return, and there is nothing you can do about it. Even if you were brave enough to kill me, I still wouldn't be returning. Face the truth for once in your life. You didn't just lose your sons, you drove them away."

Suddenly Solomon raged like a charging bull toward his youngest son.

Stepping to the side just before impact, Patrick watched his father slam against two of the studs, cracking both.

Solomon turned again, grabbing a board and swinging as he charged. "Even when you fight and beg for mercy, I'll crush you as I should have when you were born. I knew you were rotten just like all the others."

Patrick dodged him the second time. "I don't want to fight you," he yelled. "Unlike you, I don't want you dead. I just want you gone. I want to live my life. I have that right. So go away, old man, and peddle your poison somewhere else."

"No! It is my right and duty to kill you. I swear I will." He swung the board, but he was no match for youth. The years and lack of work had slowed Solomon down. Blow after blow swung wild, missing the mark.

In a scream of frustration, Solomon finally stopped trying to hit Patrick, but his eyes flashed with hate. "I've brought others who will do this dirty job for me. They will beat you slowly and painfully to death if I tell them to. I want to watch you suffer and beg for mercy. If I tell them to stand strong against the devil, the fools will offer you no mercy. I'll see you dead before the sun rises. They will have your blood on their hands."

Patrick shook his head, surprised he hadn't seen the insanity in his father's eyes before now. It was there. Maybe it always had been.

Solomon stood in the center of the framed house and lifted his hand as if finishing a sermon. "Even if you survive tonight, you won't be safe anywhere. They'll hunt you down for what you've done to me." He huffed a few breaths and continued, "I wanted them to shoot you today when we found you working. One shot would have done the job, but they thought I should talk to you first, give you a chance to repent. But I say there will be no redemption for you." The hand that had always jabbed at heaven dropped against the stout man's side, and his shoulders rounded.

"I've heard enough." Patrick couldn't stand to see the man inside his father crumbling into pure monster. "I'm leaving, and I promise you one thing. I'll not spend the rest of my life waiting for that bullet."

Turning to walk away, Patrick realized he didn't even hate his father. He almost felt sorry for the old man. If he'd had any followers, they'd have been with him now.

Patrick took a deep cleansing breath as he stepped out of the frame and his past fears. Before the air could leave his lungs, he felt the barrel of a gun poke into his back.

Closing his eyes to the night, Patrick let Solomon's words echo in his ears. "I'll kill you myself and blame it on one of my men. The lazy bastards should have been here by now. They'll pay for their sins as well."

Pure instinct kicked in. With a flash of movement like Truman had shown him, Patrick stepped sideways, swinging his hand down on his father's arm. The gun flew through the air, twirling like a falling star into the pool of muddy water.

Patrick didn't look back. He wanted no more memories of his father. He simply stepped off the planks that served as a walkway to the front door and crushed the gun deep into the mud. Then, with his father still preaching, he walked away.

If others came after him, he'd deal with them, but he'd not give his father one more thought in this lifetime. As he swung onto his horse, his mind filled with Annie and the need to get back to her.

He needed to apologize for lying to her and beg her to forgive him. Then he'd swear he would never lie to her again and hope that she'd believe him. What if she left? She might even go back home to her terrible stepmother.

He had a feeling he could have broken every silly rule they'd made up those first few weeks, but not this one. This one rule she'd made him swear to keep. Telling her he'd lied to protect her might not help. He'd have to make her believe.

For a moment he thought of not mentioning the lie. No one would know. Tomorrow would just be another day. No one saw him leave. No one heard his father's ranting. No one knew they'd talked.

*Except me*, Patrick thought. If he didn't tell Annie somehow, that would be another lie. They were just getting started. Two lies were too many. Even at the risk of losing her, he had to be honest. He loved her too much.

He wanted there to be nothing unsaid between them. He wanted to always look her straight in the eyes. He wanted to tell her how someday he'd be the best father in the world because he knew exactly what not to do.

FROM THE SHADOWS CLINT WATCHED MCALLEN RIDE AWAY. He didn't cross back to the rough ruts of a road where Clint stood with the three men. Patrick rode out across the open land, a free man for the first time in his life, Clint guessed.

Lowering his Colt, he turned to his prisoners. "Don't ever come back—"

The brave one found his voice again. "We won't, and neither will he." He looked over at the frame where Solomon was now walking around the lantern preaching to an absent congregation. "What he told us about his son wasn't true. Solomon isn't the man we thought he was."

"Most men aren't," Clint answered, then turned to see the outline of Patrick almost home. "But now and then one turns out to be more than you thought."

The three nodded at one another, and then the leader said almost in a whisper, "We won't be back this far north again, and neither will Solomon. He would have never found this place without us, and his health isn't good enough for him to make the journey alone. Tell McAllen to live in peace."

Clint grinned. "I think he's already planning to do that."

He holstered his gun and watched as the men disappeared into the night. After a while, Solomon ran out of steam and also walked away, talking to himself.

For a moment, Clint just stood watching the single lantern burn in his home. No one would ever know what had happened here tonight, probably. He'd never tell Patrick that he'd stopped the others, and he doubted Patrick would mention the talk he'd had with Solomon.

A shadow moved from the other side of the stack of lumber.

Clint straightened, ready for any danger that still lingered.

Only, the shadow wasn't coming toward him. He moved, long and lean, into the house. A rifle rested in one hand as he reached for the lantern.

Clint watched in surprise as Shelly blew out the light, turning the night into silent peace. Apparently, Patrick had had two guardian angels tonight and he hadn't even needed them.

# Chapter 32

LONG AFTER MIDNIGHT CLINT PULLED THE SADDLE OFF HIS horse and walked toward the trading post. He needed sleep, but his mind couldn't shake the way Patrick had remained so calm when he knew his father had come to kill him. Maybe he was just tired of worrying about death.

Patrick may have gone to face his father and talk, but Shelly had brought a rifle. He'd been prepared to kill to protect his brother. So had Clint. Maybe he and Shelly were more alike than Clint thought they were.

He wasn't surprised to find Captain Matheson sitting on the porch in the dark.

"Evening," the captain said as if it weren't the middle of the night and they both didn't know where he'd been. "McAllen made it back an hour ago."

"Good."

"Any problem?"

"Nope." Clint walked past him.

Matheson stood. "Then I guess we can sleep easy tonight."

"Yep."

Clint was halfway up the stairs when he heard Matheson mutter, "Nice talking to you, Truman."

Smiling, Clint continued climbing. The captain had been as worried about McAllen as he'd been.

Clint slipped into his room and took in the sight of Karrisa snuggled in bed. She always slept curled up in a ball as if afraid of the night. He realized that he hadn't heard her crying in her sleep lately. Maybe the nightmares were fading.

The urge to slide in beside her tempted him, but he'd wait to be invited. She might like the kissing and touching, but he wasn't sure she'd welcome more.

Pulling off his gun belt and boots, he spread out on the pallet by the window and closed his eyes. He'd missed holding her tonight, but maybe he'd have a night or two before he had to leave. For some reason he wanted to store up memories to hold him over on the long trip to Dallas. A few more nights, a few more touches would never be enough.

He was almost asleep when he heard the bed creak and guessed she must have rolled over. He swore she checked on the baby in her sleep every hour.

One of the floorboards made a slight popping sound, but he didn't move. They were both safe, locked in their little room.

As light as a breeze, she moved in beside him on the pallet and placed her cheek on his shoulder. She hadn't made a sound, but her body molded against his as though she'd rolled beside him a thousand times before.

After a few minutes, he raised his arm and pulled covers over her. She settled against his chest.

He was wide awake and guessed he would be the rest of the night if he didn't figure out why she'd come to him. "Karrisa, dear, what are you doing?"

She wiggled as if irritated he'd woken her. "Sleeping," she whispered.

"Wouldn't you be more comfortable in bed?"

"No." She pushed on his chest as if he were a pillow she could fluff.

"Why?" he tried again, thinking that he'd be in his grave,

lying there under a pine lid, still trying to figure out this woman.

"Because you're not there."

Some people need fancy speeches or romantic words to move them, but all Clint needed was an invitation, and this was probably as much of one as he'd ever get from his quiet wife.

He lifted her away from him, stood, then picked her up and carried her to bed. As he lay down beside her, he whispered, "This night is half over, but I plan to sleep in this bed right next to you until dawn. If you have any objections, dear, you'd better voice them now."

She put her head over his heart and made a sleepy little sound of contentment. Within a few breaths her body had melted against his and he knew she was asleep.

Lying there thinking of all the things he'd like to do now that he'd finally made it to her bed kept him awake until almost dawn, but in the end he did nothing beyond holding her because no matter how grand the fantasies he planned, he was already in heaven and maybe that was enough for tonight.

# Chapter 33

As he sat in the field behind the barn, Patrick watched dawn's glow spread across the land. He smiled, almost thinking he could see the outline of Harmony reflecting in the sparkles of light. He hadn't even bothered to try to sleep after he'd left Solomon talking to himself. He'd checked on Annie asleep in the barn loft, then slipped out the back. All night he'd walked through the days of his childhood and now it was time to put them aside. He had a wife, a new life.

As morning turned golden, he stood. Annie was probably already making breakfast over at the trading post and wondering why he hadn't been beside her when she woke. Usually she woke happy and in a hurry to start the day, but the past few mornings she hadn't felt well and he worried about her. This living in the barn didn't seem to be agreeing with her. Like the others, Annie needed to be in her own home. A woman needs her nest, his mother used to say, but a man only needs his woman. He decided that was true.

Anxious to start the day, he walked over to the trading post and noticed a few extra wagons tied up to the hitching posts. They must have come in very early. Soldiers, he'd guessed, for they often traveled both night and day thanks to extra drivers.

He bumped into Truman as he stepped onto the porch. "Morning." Patrick didn't miss Truman's frown. The man must have had it tattooed on at some point.

"What's good about it?" Truman asked in his typical grumpy mood. "Army wagons are here and Matheson thinks we should hitch up the freight wagons and head out with them. I thought I'd be here to help another couple of days, but it doesn't look like it. The Romas, Harry Woolsey, and I may be on the road in an hour."

"Don't forget your prisoner. He might not talk, but I hear him snoring below us." Patrick tried to look on the bright side. "The sooner you get started, the sooner you'll be back."

Truman looked like he hadn't slept in days. "When I get back, will you have my house finished?"

Patrick smiled and used one of Truman's favorite words. "Hell, we'll probably have the whole town built. You're going to miss it if you don't get back quick."

That finally brought a smile to the hard man. "Good." He pointed with his head toward the kitchen. "Four soldiers mustering out of the army were riding along on the wagons heading toward Dallas. Matheson just talked them into staying around here for a few months, so looks like you got your first real crew."

Patrick jumped with excitement and started moving toward the kitchen. "Are they any good?"

Truman laughed. "Hell if I know. They're bound to be better than me."

Patrick didn't take the time to argue. He rushed to the kitchen to meet his new crew. Daisy and Karrisa were filling plates as fast as they could as a dozen soldiers stood around waiting. The Roma boys had set up barrels and boards to make a long table on the porch for all the extras. Momma Roma, holding Truman's baby, sat between Harry Woolsey and Ely. They already had their plates but she was too busy talking to little Danny in Italian to eat.

"Where's Annie?" Patrick asked no one in particular.

"She's out back," Daisy said as she passed. "Sick again."

Patrick fought his way through the mob and found Annie out back sitting on a tree stump. She looked so small and young. She might be a year older than him, but with her hair in long braids, she could have been sixteen.

He walked up slowly, noticing she was crying. When her brown eyes focused on him he saw fear and uncertainty for the first time in his brave little Annie. She'd been the one from the first who believed in this crazy plan, and now something was very wrong.

The fear that she'd learned of his lie and knew that he'd gone to meet his father last night tightened Patrick's heart. He loved her so much he wasn't sure what he'd do if she walked away from him.

"Annie?" he whispered, knowing he'd have to face her and make everything all right if she knew. And if she didn't know about the meeting, maybe now wasn't the best time to tell her. Something terrible must have happened, for his Annie never cried.

"Annie, you all right?" If she was ill, or dying, the joy would go out of his life. He'd taken her away from all she knew, and now she was sick. This had to be his fault.

"I'm fine," she said, but didn't look at him.

He lowered to one knee beside her and brushed one of her braids over her shoulder. "Talk to me, Annie. You know you can tell me anything."

"I love you," she whispered. "I really do."

"I know, honey. I love you, too." He thought of how easily loving had come to him, and to her, he guessed. "It's just me and you against the world, and as long as I got you, I've got all I need." Her face looked so pale and her eyes were red and swollen from crying. He couldn't stand seeing her like this.

She leaned into him as if too weak to hold her head up. "Could you carry me back to the barn? I don't feel so good."

He lifted her in his arms, wishing he could take whatever she had from her. He was the strongest. He could fight off what was making her sick.

When they made it to the silence of the barn, he helped her up the ladder and spread blankets over her. Fear had burrowed in his heart and seemed to be settling in. Worry over his father was nothing compared to what he felt now.

"What is it, Annie? Tell me where it hurts and I'll make it go away."

She shook her head. "I don't want it to go away, Patrick."

He decided she was delirious. "Of course you do."

"No," she whispered.

"Then give it to me. I'll be the sick one."

She laughed and rolled over to her side. "That would be funny, Patrick. A man having a baby."

It took him a few seconds for her words to swing back across his brain, and then realization hit him between the eyes. "You're going to have a baby?"

"Daisy says I won't know for sure until I miss another time of the month, but it seems I have all the signs."

Patrick fell back on the hay beside her.

"We're going to have a baby. That's impossible. It takes a lot longer than a few months."

"It is possible. Haven't you noticed what we do under the covers? You put a baby in me."

"Me?" Patrick tried to get his brain to stop spinning inside his skull. "I think we both had equal parts."

She laughed. "I'm hoping he has my brains and your looks. Don't worry, we'll have months to get used to the idea, Papa."

Patrick jumped up and ran down the ladder and out the back of the barn. He barely made it to the grass beside the corral before he threw up.

Truman, ten feet away harnessing horses, stopped and watched him. When Patrick finally stood and wiped his mouth, Truman said, "You sick?"

"Nope," Patrick answered. "I'm with child."

# Chapter 34

CLINT ATE HIS BREAKFAST IN SILENCE, HATING THE NOISE and all the people between him and Karrisa. The thought occurred to him to fire off a few shots to clear the room, but all the soldiers were armed and might fire back.

Finally he gave up and headed back out to the corral. Everyone on the place seemed to think it was time for him to leave but him. The Romas were already packed and the ladies had loaded Momma Roma down with enough food to feed an army. Harry must have talked to Ely about hauling just for the trading post because he was hugging the women good-bye and asking what they wanted him to bring back.

Everyone was ready except Clint. He didn't want to leave, not yet. Not without another night with Karrisa. She was in the middle of all the action, helping get everything ready, so he had no hope of getting her alone.

By nine the wagons were lined up, looking very much like a caravan. The army sergeant said he'd take over guarding the outlaw, who'd been complaining about his treatment since being caught. He said the food was good, but not enough, and he planned to come back and kill every last one of them. The sergeant didn't listen. He had men to guard and the knowledge to make sure the man made it to his trial in Dallas. For him, taking over the prisoner was just part of his job.

Clint saddled his horse. He planned on driving his wagon down and back, so he wouldn't have to hire an extra wagon to haul everything he needed for his house. Only Momma Roma's youngest son, Antonio, said he'd like to give driving a try, and everyone agreed he was old enough. They put the boy in the middle of the line so he wasn't likely to get in much trouble.

As the wagons pulled out, one by one, past the trading post, Clint finally saw his wife standing alone between the store and the barn.

He rode close, then jumped off his horse to say good-bye. When he was a foot away, he couldn't think of all he wanted to say to her and, as always, she didn't say anything. She just stared up at him with those haunting blue eyes he'd never get tired of looking at, and he realized how beautiful she was.

He straightened, shocked that he hadn't noticed before. The frail, thin woman he married was still slim, but she was so lovely, like a fine lady, far too good for the likes of him.

"You be sure and eat regular," was all he could think of to say. "And take good care of Danny. I don't want him hanging around those Matheson twins picking up bad habits."

She smiled that tight little smile of hers.

"You don't need to worry; you'll be safe here until I get back." He stared down at her, wishing he were the kind of man who could say fancy words to let her know how important she was to him, but all he could do was stand there as she slipped a piece of paper in his pocket.

"I wrote down a few things I'll need in Dallas. If you have time—"

"I'll have time."

She smiled and patted his pocket. "Come back to me," she whispered.

Circling her waist, he lifted her up. "I will, dear. I promise."

He kissed her then. Not as long or as hard as he wanted to, but long enough to let her know that she'd be on his mind every day he was gone.

"Truman!" Patrick yelled from the corner of the porch. "If you don't hurry up and say good-bye to Karrisa they'll be in Dallas before you catch up with the wagons."

Clint swore, then kissed her again. "When I get back—"

Giggling, she buried her face against his shirt. "I know. I feel the same."

He knew if he didn't pull away, he might not be able to leave this woman. She wasn't just his wife, she'd become a part of him. The best part, he decided.

As he rode off doing his job of scouting, she never left his thoughts. The ache to hold her wouldn't go away. All he could do was get this job over with and get back to her as fast as possible.

Near sunset he thought of the note she'd placed in his pocket. He stopped his horse on a rise where he could watch the wagons and pulled it from his pocket.

Just as he'd expected, the penmanship was perfect. She'd listed exactly what she needed. A special kind of thread he would find only in a dress shop. Ribbon in several colors that Ely didn't carry. The makings for a summer bonnet. A yard of lace that she'd drawn the width of and made tiny circles showing him what it would look like. He could tell she was sewing for the others and wanted to make each dress unique.

Clint laughed when she said she wanted a dress the same shade of green as little Jessie's eyes. He'd barely noticed the girl and had no idea what color her eyes were. She had to have eyes. He would have noticed if she hadn't, but the color?

At the end of the list, she wrote one sentence. *Come back to me, my one and only love. Karrisa.*

Clint stared at the writing. From the beginning he'd known she'd married him because she had no other choice. She and the baby would have starved to death or ended up in a kind of hell on earth. She came with him, cooked his meals, made his clothes, all because it was her only way to survive. Only, somehow in all the work of living, she'd learned to care for him. She loved him even when he told her from the first that he'd never love her.

The sun was too low to offer enough light to see her

words clearly again. He folded the piece of paper and put it in his pocket. He knew he was a hard man, but he'd always tried to be fair. Only, he wasn't a person most folks liked or cared about. He kept to himself and, for the most part, wanted everyone else to do the same.

Only Karrisa had written that she loved him. He didn't want that. If she'd said it, he might have thought she'd just said the words because she was supposed to. But she'd written them down.

He didn't want to hear them or see them written because Clint knew he'd never say them to her. Part of him wasn't free to love. He was too weary of life to fall in love again. He'd never stand the loss again.

All he wanted from Karrisa was for her to be a wife. She'd been doing a good job of that. The bit of passion they'd shared had been more than he'd expected. He liked that, but it wasn't love. He would never let it be. Only how does a man tell his wife to take back the words she wrote?

That night after supper, he sat down next to Momma Roma. When no one else appeared to be listening, he asked, "You know what happened to my wife back a year ago?"

Clint would bet every dime in his money belt that Karrisa hadn't told anyone at the trading post, but he'd seen her talking to Momma Roma in Italian sometimes and knew they were close.

"I know," the tiny woman said.

He took a deep breath. "She could have told me, but all she did was make me promise never to ask. Whatever happened, I would understand."

"You her future, not'a her past. She no want'a you to look at her through that memory."

"If I knew the monster who hurt her, I'd kill him."

Momma Roma patted his arm. "You a hard'a man, Truman, but I think'a you are the one for her and she knows it. She tell'a me you very gentle to her. She say when she in your arms she feels cherished like you think she's great treasure."

He doubted he was gentle enough. The little woman was

right; he should let the past go. It didn't matter that Karrisa had gone to prison. He'd feel the same way about her. It didn't even matter that she hadn't told him about what she'd done to go to prison. He understood that he was her future and what had happened in the past should stay in the past.

It mattered that someone had hurt her. It mattered a great deal to him.

As the days passed Clint looked at the note in his pocket several times. When they rolled into Dallas, he couldn't wait to get headed back home.

Harry Woolsey had the list of tools and supplies Ely and the others had ordered. He agreed to deliver Buford's wagons, make sure the Romas got their pay, and start collecting the supplies. They planned to use Clint's wagon on the journey home. Until they had everything loaded, Harry said he'd sleep in Buford's barn and keep an eye on the wagon.

Clint followed one of the army wagons to the sheriff's office to deliver the prisoner, who had spent enough days tied up and seemed willing to talk. The sergeant had convinced him that if he told all he knew of Dollar Holt's activities, he might not hang. After staying in a barn and riding tied up in the back of a wagon, prison didn't look so bad.

Clint filled out all the paperwork and gave his statement. A heavy fog had settled over Dallas when he left the sheriff's office deep in thought. Two steps out the door, he bumped into a mountain of a man coming up the steps.

"Hell," Clint muttered as the huge stranger almost knocked him down.

"Truman?" the man asked, as if Clint's one word were all the introduction needed.

Sheriff Lightstone was so dirty Clint almost didn't recognize him. His face was covered in mud and his clothes produced their own dust cloud when he moved.

The sheriff's grin spread across his face. "Glad to see you, Truman." He slapped Clint on the shoulder, sending mud flying off his duster. "I was thinking of making a trip up north to check on you. How you and that little gal doing?"

"It's working out." Clint couldn't stop the smile. "I'm

crazy about her and I think she likes me, which probably speaks both to my good sense and her insanity."

"Well, will wonders never cease." The sheriff roped his arm around Clint's shoulder. "I need to talk to you, son. Why don't you get cleaned up and meet me for dinner? I ain't eat but twice today and I'm starving. Soon as I file this report, I'll be over there."

"I don't have much time in town." Clint didn't want to waste a minute, but he owed Lightstone. "But if you can make it quick, I owe you a meal."

"Of course, wait for me next door. I shouldn't be more than an hour. I'm just bringing back some bad guys this sheriff let wander down my way. I didn't want them, so I brought them back up here. They put up a fight every morning as if one day I'd give in and let them run off again."

Clint laughed, knowing that if they fought this mountain of a lawman, they got the worst end of the deal. "I'll be waiting for you," he said, walking toward the little diner next to the sheriff's office.

Before he went in, he noticed that the factory where he'd bought clothes for the trading post was only a block away. On impulse, he headed toward it. Somehow the sad place made him feel closer to Karrisa. This hadn't been where she worked, but it must have been like this place.

The streetlights offered a fuzzy glow in the fog as he moved toward the steps of the side door. It was late—the women would have gone home—but a horse and fancy carriage waited outside the door.

Crossing the street, Clint asked the driver, "You for hire?"

"No." He barely looked at Clint. "I'm waiting on the boss of this factory just like I do every night."

Clint moved into the shadows close to the steps heading up to the factory door. As he leaned against the building, he saw a fancy-dressed gentleman come out pulling a woman behind him. He was cussing, talking at her more than to her.

"Get down the steps, girl," the man in a heavy wool greatcoat ordered. "I haven't got all night. I've important places to be when I'm finished with you."

The woman was crying softly. She was small with scarves tied around her like Momma Roma had worn. When she didn't move fast enough, the man shoved her and she tumbled the rest of the way down the steps. Her hands reached out to grab the railing. Clint saw that they were tied.

She couldn't catch herself and rolled along the last few steps. Her cries grew louder.

The driver stared straight ahead as if he heard or saw nothing as the man in the coat jerked the woman to her feet and shoved her toward the carriage. "Stop your crying, you twit. We'll be finished in a few minutes and you can go on home. This is just part of your job and we both know it."

The owner slapped her hard and the girl's crying turned to sobs. "That's better. Now get in."

The woman scrambled into the carriage, avoiding the man's fist.

Clint could still hear her gulps for air between her sobs. She was frightened to death.

The owner had his foot on the carriage step when Clint reached him, knocking him into the gutter with one powerful blow. Being attacked so fast, the owner had no time to think of defending himself. Blow after blow rained down on him until his shouts for help became cries of pain.

Finally, when Clint pulled a knife from his boot, the man began to beg and offer money.

"I don't want your money." Clint shoved his knife against the man's throat. "But if you ever touch a woman like this again, I swear you'll bleed out in the street."

With one light slash, he cut across the man's nose just deep enough to leave a scar as a reminder. Then he turned and leaned into the carriage.

The girl's eyes were so full of fright, he almost didn't come closer, but he had to cut the rope around her wrists.

"Go home," he said.

When she didn't move, he opened the other side of the carriage and pointed.

She ran like a rabbit.

Clint walked back to the door he'd come from and joined

the man now sitting in the gutter holding his face. Flashing the knife an inch from his now-bloody nose, Clint warned, "I'll be checking on you. If you step out of line again or I see a bruise on any woman walking out of here, I'll lower the blade to your throat next time."

The man nodded but didn't look up as blood dripped through his fingers.

Clint glanced up at the driver. "You see anything?"

"Like I've been told for years, I ain't paid to see anything."

As Clint stood he patted the bleeding man on the shoulder. "I don't know about you, but I feel better. Hope we don't have to have this talk again because if we do, one of us won't be walking away."

The man was too frightened to answer, or maybe too hurt. Clint didn't much care which.

Clint returned to the diner. By the time he'd washed up and drunk his first cup of coffee, Sheriff Lightstone was barreling his way through the door.

"Sorry to keep you waiting, Truman," he bellowed. "Man got knifed not half a block away. Every man at the station is out looking for the troublemaker. Fellow said a crazy man came out of nowhere."

"What did the attacker look like?"

The sheriff shrugged. "The man beat up said he didn't get a good look at him and his driver, sitting up on the carriage, said he didn't even see the fellow, it happened so fast. With the fog we don't know which way he went, but the guy knifed said he was wearing black."

Lightstone looked at his own clothes, then Truman's. "I guess that fits both of us and half of the men walking out tonight. I'd turn myself in, but I'm too hungry."

"Confessing can wait," Clint smiled. "How about we order? I worked up an appetite beating up the guy."

The sheriff laughed as if Clint were joking.

They settled into talking as they ate, but Clint knew the sheriff had something on his mind. He wasn't the type to make small talk.

As the waitress took the plates away, he pulled an

envelope from his pocket. "I've had this for a while. A week after you and your wife left, a man came to Huntsville looking for Karrisa. He said he was her father and he'd come after her."

Clint felt like someone had dumped a hundred pounds of lead on his chest. "Tell me exactly what he said and how he looked."

Lightstone leaned back in his chair. "He looked well off. Stayed at the best hotel, demanded the best room. They said he complained about every meal he was served."

The big lawman leaned closer. "He appeared angry or maybe bothered to have to spend his time looking for her. Like maybe he expected she should have been still standing outside the gate waiting for him. Asked everyone he saw if they'd seen her and, of course, finally got around to me."

"I told him I was there the night she got out of prison and that she was met by the man she married. I didn't want him thinking she was dead."

"Did he ask my name?"

"He did, but there's where my memory failed me. I needed to know he wouldn't cause you two any trouble before I got my memory working, and nothing he did led me to believe he wasn't full-flying trouble looking for a place to nest."

Clint smiled. "I appreciate it, Sheriff."

Lightstone leaned closer. "I need to know she's happy, Clint, before I send her father away. I guess I'll have to ride back with you and ask her, but I hate to because it's bound to cause questions she may not want to answer."

Clint pulled the note Karrisa had given him from his pocket. "Will this help?"

The sheriff glanced at her long list. "Don't see how her list of supplies will help."

"Read the last line."

The big man leaned back in his chair and held the note far enough away so that he could see it. He silently mouthed the words as he read. When he got to the last, he smiled. "I guess that does answer my question, but I want you to take her father's letter to her. That way she'll know that he did come and she wasn't forgotten."

"If I know you, Sheriff, the letter opened itself while it was in your pocket. What did he say?"

Lightstone didn't bother to deny Truman's claim. "Karrisa's father said he wanted to write and tell her that she can come back. He'd take her in and make sure she would have what she needs. He told me she could have a quiet life taking care of his house. He said she never was much for going out and of course with a bastard she wouldn't be welcome in polite society anyway. The old man said that his half brother was right to turn her away when she got herself in bad trouble, but that now she'd done her time, as her father, he'd do his duty and try to straighten her out."

"She doesn't need straightening out, Sheriff." Clint's jaw tightened, but he kept his words calm. "She doesn't have a bastard. The boy is now and forever my son. We named him after my brother who died in the war." Clint stared at Lightstone. "Is her father still waiting in Huntsville?"

The sheriff shook his head. "He had to get back to business, but if she showed up I was to tell her he'd wire her money to come home." Lightstone frowned, then added, "I got the feeling he was just a man doing his duty, not a father who cared what happened."

"What else?" Clint wanted to know it all.

Lightstone shook his head. "Seems to me a father should ask about his daughter, but he only wanted to know where she was. Didn't ask if you were a good man either. I got the feeling if he wasn't taking her home, he just wanted to make sure she was out of his life."

"She is." Clint took the letter. "I'll see she gets this. I think it will make her feel better to know that he tried to find her, but I don't think she'll go back. You're welcome to stop by the trading post any time. Our place is just down the road."

"I might just do that. When you heading back?"

Clint stuffed the letter and Karrisa's note back into his pocket. "As soon as possible. I miss her. She's quiet, hardly says a dozen words a day, but she's not as shy as folks might think." He smiled, remembering how she came to him so easy and asked if he was going to unbutton her dress again.

The sheriff didn't notice his smile as he downed the last of the coffee. "Judge might want you to stay and testify, Clint. I saw the outlaw you brought in tonight. Once he talks, Dollar Holt will be a wanted man."

Lightstone tossed a badge on the table. "They're waiting over at the station. We plan to deputize you before you start back. That new town of yours is going to need some law and I can think of no better man to wear a badge."

"You're joking."

Lightstone smiled. "Nope. I'm serious. You're so mean most outlaws will walk a wide path just to avoid you. Now you've got a wife and kid, you're not likely to wander off or get drunk."

An hour later Clint pinned on the badge and grinned. He'd finally found something he could do and a place to belong. If Harmony needed a sheriff, he'd fill the job.

# Chapter 35

ONE MONTH LATER
THE MATHESON LAND

GILLIAN STARED UP AT HIS TWO-STORY HOUSE ON LAND that would be his in less than two years. After spending all his life where his home was usually a bunk or a tiny room made for single officers, the place seemed huge.

"It's well built, Captain." Patrick twirled his hammer. "It'll stand the storms and wind out here. I made the windows extra wide like you asked so from every direction you can see your land. In a few years there'll be nothing but cattle and kids running around this place."

"It's a grand house." Gillian swelled with pride. He'd helped with the building every morning, then worked in town every afternoon. They had the town square marked off and the foundations started for the first few buildings. "Truman won't believe all the work we've gotten done during the month he's been gone."

"I know. When I didn't have to keep digging out his bent nails, the construction went faster."

Gillian laughed. "You can't wait to mention that to him, can you, Patrick?"

"You're right about that. I love to see him fighting not to cuss almost as much as he loves cussing at me." Patrick shrugged. "Only, Truman is going to be mighty happy when he gets back. His place is ready to move into, but Karrisa says she's not sleeping there until he gets back."

Gillian glanced toward town. He couldn't see the Truman place for the old cottonwoods and elm trees along the road, but he knew it was there. "She may not move in, but she's over there right now marking off a garden. Told Daisy she's got seeds from the apple trees where she grew up. Says Truman and her are going to plant fifty trees on the spot that borders my land."

The rhythm of hammers echoed around them. While Patrick did the final work on the Matheson place, Shelly and the crew of retired soldiers were framing up his place. "This is really going to happen," Patrick whispered. "In a few years we'll have a town and Karrisa will have her orchard. Good luck, by the way, at keeping your boys out of those apple trees."

Gillian slapped Patrick on the shoulder. "Of course it's going to happen. Next month we'll start construction on the town square. Ely keeps changing his mind about what he wants first, but I'm thinking we start with the basics."

"You really think people will come?"

"They already are. A farmer passed by asking if we needed a blacksmith yesterday. His wife died this past winter and he said he hated being out on his land all alone. Ely told him to go pack his things and move in."

Patrick frowned. "Where we going to put people?"

Gillian smiled. "In a few days, the three rooms above the store will be open, at least until Ely's family comes. That and the barn will be a start. The retired army men have already put up a tent down by the creek. They'll be comfortable through summer. While Ely's buying more wood, you build the houses and he rents them. He'll be a rich man and worn out from repainting the population sign every day."

Gillian moved to his wagon and headed home early. The Trumans might not be moving to their land yet, but everyone was probably happy to help the Mathesons load up. Once their four boys left the place, the trading post would settle down. Daisy promised she'd still come over to help out at the store from time to time, and of course, she'd bring the boys. Ely's favorite pastime seemed to be watching them play.

When Gillian and Patrick reached the trading post, Gillian wasn't surprised to find his wife's two wagons with supplies and furniture already ready to go. All the women and children climbed into the wagons and they circled back to what everyone called the Matheson spread.

As the sun set, Gillian and Daisy moved into their house. He'd decided to leave the upstairs one big room and give Jessie the smaller room downstairs. He'd planned the little room as a study, but she needed her privacy at her age. She was so excited she couldn't stop jumping and screaming with delight as furniture was set in her very own space. Karrisa had made her curtains and a warm rug of strips of rags. With little Danny sleeping on a blanket in the corner, Karrisa helped the girl put everything in place.

Daisy had cooked all day so she could serve dinner on her front porch to all who helped, but now she was too busy to stop to eat. Finally, when all were gone and the house glowed from lamps she'd carefully hauled two hundred miles, Daisy walked through the rooms of her house smiling.

"We'll paint the rooms when we have time," Gillian said as he followed her. "I'll hang a rack for your pots and I'll see if Shelly can help me build a few more dressers for the boys. One won't be enough. I'm glad we got their beds up before they fell asleep. Upstairs reminds me of a barracks. Jessie said she'd sleep up there with them tonight just in case one wakes up and doesn't know where he is. In truth, I think she doesn't want to mess up anything in her room just yet."

"It's perfect." Daisy took his hand in hers. "This house is perfect. We're finally all together under one roof."

"It's not perfect. The walls are rough, the floor could stand a stain . . ." He stopped and looked at her. She was as beautiful as the first day he saw her. "You're right. *Perfect* is the word."

Gillian realized that for the first time since he woke up at the trading post, all was quiet. The boys and Jessie were asleep and he heard no snoring from Ely or whispered conversations leaking through the walls.

"We're alone, Daisy."

She smiled. "We are."

He took her hand and moved into the bedroom. "I want to sleep with my wife in this house every night for the rest of my life. And tonight there will be no blankets between me and you."

"Of course, Captain." She stood at attention as if being ordered and then giggled.

"I'm not a captain anymore, but I'm still yours, Daisy, if you'll have me." He took a step toward her, feeling as hesitant as he had on their wedding night. A year was a long time between making love.

She looked just as nervous. "My body's not the same as it was. Carrying the twins left horrible marks and—"

"You're beautiful. You always will be to me." He stood behind her and began unbuttoning her dress. Maybe if they acted as if this were just an ordinary night, they both would relax.

"You don't miss the army?"

"No. That time in my life seems boring compared to living here." He opened the back of her dress and slid the material forward off her shoulders. "Even filling out the paperwork to try to get a post office in Harmony is exciting. We'll have a courthouse if I can get the county seat here and maybe I'll have an office there." As he talked of his dreams for Harmony, his fingers lightly brushed over her bare shoulders.

She held her dress to her chest. "Blow out the lamp first."

He stopped touching her. "Before I build the town or before I finish undressing my bride?"

Giggling, she clarified, "Before you finish undressing me."

Gillian moved in front of her. "No, Daisy. We've never hid our bodies from each other and we'll not start now. We'll make love in the shadows tonight, but I'll see you first." He hesitated and added, "And you'll see me."

He stood staring into her eyes as he removed his shirt. "Look at me, Daisy. I've got a scar on my forehead that will never go away. Last year I was stabbed and it looks like I have an extra belly button. I fell off my horse last winter and he dragged me through a rock bed. The gashes healed red along my back." One by one he showed her his imperfections. "I'm battle scarred and older than I was when we met. Do you still want me?"

She laughed. "Of course I still want you. Though the two belly buttons do bother me a little."

He brushed his hand over hers, lacing his fingers with hers as he pulled her grip away from her dress. The cotton fell to the floor. "And I still want you, Daisy. My beautiful Daisy. Mother of my four sons and love of my life."

She came to him, pressing her imperfect body against his imperfect body as they both moaned at how perfect it felt to be so close.

Without another word, he blew out the light as she climbed into bed. They made slow love as if journeying through their entire relationship from first kiss to wild passion. He knew her body as she knew his and they knew exactly what the other liked. When they made love, it was magically familiar and brand new at the same time.

Deep in the night he got out of bed and put on his trousers. She put on his shirt and they ran like kids to the kitchen, where they attacked all the leftovers in the basket she'd brought.

"You'll always be eighteen to me," he said as they shared the last of the pie.

"And you'll always be my handsome lieutenant."

For a moment they weren't Captain and Mrs. Matheson, founders of the town and parents of four sons. They were simply Gillian and Daisy, two wild kids in love for the first and last time in their lives.

Hand in hand they walked around the house looking at every piece of furniture she'd brought and arguing over where it should go. Finally, they made it back to the bedroom and Daisy insisted he put on a nightshirt.

"This is ridiculous," he mumbled. "I never wear a nightshirt. Why would I put one on now when in a few hours it will be dawn and I'll be dressing anyway?"

"You'll see," she answered, and held the covers back for him to climb in beside her.

For a long while, Gillian just held her, and then he drifted to sleep thinking he was the luckiest man alive.

At dawn, invading forces attacked. They jumped on the bed, screamed and cried and yelled. As fast as he could grab one and set him off the bed, another advanced with full force.

Daisy deserted him, claiming she had to make coffee.

Gillian was left to fight the Matheson gang alone.

# Chapter 36

DALLAS, TEXAS

CLINT LUGGED ALL THE THINGS KARRISA HAD ORDERED plus a brand-new Singer sewing machine for three blocks before he saw the livery. The machine had cost him fifty dollars, a huge price, but he had a feeling she would love it. Sixty to ninety stitches a minute, imagine that. He'd overheard her tell Daisy that she used to sit on her mother's lap and help her sew, and no matter how hard life got for her, sewing always calmed her.

As he stepped into the cool morning darkness of the Buford Livery in Dallas, Clint couldn't stop smiling. His wagon was loaded and ready to go along with Harry's new wagon full of building supplies.

Harry made a trip to the trading post and back in the days Clint had to wait on the trial. It had been hard for Clint to watch him go out with three wagons and a retired lawman they'd hired to guard, but Clint knew Patrick and Shelly were waiting on the supplies and didn't want to have everything held up by the trial.

Harry Woolsey had spent every dime he made last month on the wagon, and now he was working for himself. He planned to make trips back and forth from Harmony to Dallas for half the price Buford charged in exchange for free room and board when he stayed over at the trading post.

"Ready?" Clint asked Harry as he slid the sewing machine into the last open spot on his wagon.

"We are," Harry yelled.

Clint glanced back, wondering who was hitching a ride, and saw an old wagon packed so high it would probably topple over the first time it hit a bump in the road. Momma Roma sat on the bench, grinning from ear to ear. "We go with'a you, Mr. Truman."

Her boys moved from the shadows. All three had horses and Western hats.

"But . . ." Clint had no idea what he planned to say. She knew the journey would be hard and dangerous; she'd made it once before.

"We gonna help build your town. Mr. Ely told me to come back and he'd hire me to cook. There nothing for us here. We go to Harmony."

Clint guessed they'd put together every dime they had to buy the wagon and horses. He didn't want to rain on their dreams. "Then come along. We can use the help."

As they pulled out of Dallas, Clint fought not to push the small group harder. He wanted to be home. He'd unfolded Karrisa's note and read the last line so many times the paper was worn. Just a few words shouldn't matter that much . . . but they did. He was her love, imagine that.

When he got back home he'd try to talk her out of such a fool notion, but it was nice that she thought of him that way, if only for a while.

This trip he didn't feel like he was just going home to a wife; he was going home to Karrisa and she'd be waiting for him. The trail was dry and the weather good. With luck they'd reach Harmony by early afternoon on the sixth day out and he could help Karrisa move their things over to the house. He felt like this was their beginning at a real marriage and he wanted it to be in their home.

Over the past few weeks he'd settled into the idea that if she wanted to make their marriage more than just an agreement, he'd let her. He still wasn't brave enough to love her, but they could have a good life with him being kind to her and her loving him.

Sheriff Lightstone caught up to them before they were an hour out. He climbed off his horse and sat on the bench with Clint.

"You planning to take me up on that visit?" Clint frowned at the sheriff.

"No, I just thought I'd ride along with you for a spell." Lightstone fiddled with a pipe. "I got to thinking after I had supper with you that old Harmon Ely's been up near the panhandle since we came back from the war. Every now and then a friend passes his place and lets me know he's still up there saying his wife and kids are coming someday."

Clint didn't see the point of the sheriff's conversation, but he welcomed the company. "Ely doesn't talk about them much to us. It's hard to form a thought around all the people, much less a sentence. He did build the kids' bedrooms upstairs, so I think he's still hoping they'll make it." Clint fought not to smile as he added, "Karrisa and I are a little cramped in a room built for a child, but we're managing. The bed's too short and really made for one, but we made it work."

He almost added, *for a few hours the last night*, but Clint decided to keep that to himself.

"I don't want to hear about that." Lightstone sounded grumpy, but he smiled.

Clint thought about how close he'd been to Karrisa that night. She'd slept on his shoulder with her slender hand lying over his heart.

The sheriff finally got his pipe going and ambled back into the conversation he'd started earlier, "I remembered Harmon Ely being about ten years older than me, which would make him about fifty by now. When we first met in sixty-one, he showed me a tintype of his kids, two girls and a boy. They were about ten or twelve then. Almost as tall as their mother. The boy might have been a little older, which would make them in their midtwenties to thirty by now."

Clint saw the truth. "They're not children and they are not coming. Right, Sheriff?"

Lightstone shook his head. "I telegraphed the sheriff in Alpine where Ely used to say he was from. He said Mrs. Harmon Ely died several years ago, right after her son was killed during a raid on their cattle. Sheriff said the daughters were both grown and gone by then. Heard they'd married soldiers from Fort Davis and moved up north."

"You think he knows but still holds on to the dream?"

The sheriff nodded. "It's easier than facing the truth. I think he's remembering them just as they were in the tintype."

"Then who is he building the town for?"

"I'm thinking he wants it for the three of you. He took a year looking for the right men. It's going to take strong men to build a town. My guess is you three will have no one to turn to but each other."

Clint shook his head. "It doesn't make sense but I'll tell Matheson and McAllen what you just told me. Now we know no family is coming, we'll watch over him. He's made of old leather and spit, but he's growing on us."

Lightstone propped his feet up and leaned back against the barrels of supplies. "I'm thinking I might just take a little nap before I ride back. You figure you can keep the wagon rolling slow and easy?"

Clint nodded, already deep in thought. How was it possible that he'd become the mother hen of this group? Now he had to worry about Ely. For a man who didn't like people in general, he certainly was getting attached to several.

The sheriff rode off a few hours later with a final warning to Clint about Dollar Holt. Word was he'd been recruiting outlaws and planned a big raid. Clint decided he had his plate full of worry already and would have to move Dollar to a side dish.

A man can only take so many problems at one time when he's not drinking.

Three days later, Clint wished he'd packed a bottle of whiskey with Karrisa's notions.

The problem didn't seem all that complicated at first. They pulled alongside a wagon with a busted wheel. The Roma boys had ridden ahead and were already helping when Clint got there.

Four women, well past marrying age and all taller than most men, waited beside the trail. They were dressed plain with bonnets that hid their plain faces. All four seemed to be talking at the same time. Complaining, worrying, instructing the Roma boys. One was even quoting scripture and yelling at God like this whole mess was his fault.

Clint thought of pulling his gun and firing just to silence them, but Karrisa probably wouldn't think that was a good idea. The ladies might be big, but they were women and probably needed comfort or protection.

He pinned on his badge, hoping that was all he needed to do in the comfort category, and climbed off the wagon.

"Morning, ladies."

They all rushed toward him, and Clint was hard-pressed not to turn and run. When all four started explaining at once, Clint held up his hands and said, "Hold on. One at a time." He pointed to what looked like the oldest. "You, miss, you go first."

"We need help, Sheriff."

"I can see that, miss. The boys will get you fixed up in no time. A broken wagon wheel is just an inconvenience, not a tragedy," Clint said as he tried to settle into being called *Sheriff.*

"We're on our way north to a trading post. Heaven knows how far it is and if we'll make it alive out here in the wilds of Texas."

Worry turned to dread. "It wouldn't be Harmon Ely's place?" Of course it would, he cussed himself. Ely's place was the only one north of here. "And you're right about one thing, this isn't country women should travel in alone."

"Yes that's the place, and we had no choice but to travel alone." The oldest woman smiled, but it didn't improve her looks. "We were in Dallas, staying with our dear departed mother's parents. All four of us take the train from Houston once a year to help with the cleaning and get the garden started. Our father says it's our mission to make ourselves useful."

Clint considered telling her that *yes* would have been enough, then realized she was still going.

"One of the elders from our church wired me to let us all know that our brothers were alive and staying at Ely's Trading Post. He must have known how worried we all were. Elder Price said he was taking our father back to Galveston, but"—she looked back at her sisters—"we all agreed we should travel to live with our brothers. We're sure they need our help in this wild country."

The other three nodded.

Clint didn't dare ask any questions or the oldest one might be talking until dark. Way more details than he needed to know.

"We're heading that way." He managed to at least sound like he cared. "You're welcome to come along with us if you can keep up."

"Thank you, Sheriff." Another one of the women stepped out of the line. She was just as tall and nearly as plain. "Once we get there we only hope we can find our brothers. None of us has ever been alone in an unknown place with strangers."

He thought of telling them that at their height they should be safe enough. "What's your brothers' names? I probably know of them." Down deep he'd already figured it out, but his mind was refusing to accept the obvious.

"McAllen," they all said at once.

Clint almost laughed. He couldn't wait to see Patrick's face when he pulled in with all his big sisters in tow. He almost felt sorry for the kid. A new bride already carrying a baby and four older sisters.

By dawn the next day Clint had everyone up and moving. The McAllen wagon was light and had no trouble keeping up. As far as he could tell they only carried a few carpetbags and one box of food and blankets. If they had a gun of any kind it was kept well out of sight. They'd all four slept in the wagon bed, packed in like green beans. If one had decided to roll over during the night, they'd all have to turn.

The next afternoon, the women didn't say a word when the wagons pulled into the yard in front of the trading post. A few odd wagons were already there and several army mounts were tied to the hitching rail. Apparently word had gotten out that help was needed to build a town.

Daisy and Karrisa came running down the steps. Both women ran straight to the Romas and began hugging them wildly. Then they patted Harry on the back before finally turning to Clint.

He'd climbed down from his wagon and stood in front of the McAllen women. "Ladies." He smiled first at Daisy and then Karrisa. As he'd known he would, once he saw his wife, he couldn't look away. "I found some of the McAllens' sisters along the road."

Daisy played hostess, inviting them in and making all the introductions as people kept filing out of the trading post. She explained that Patrick and Shelly were out at the last homestead finishing off the inside of Patrick's house. Annie had gone out to take them lunch and probably decided to stay and help.

Clint barely paid attention to all the chatter about all that had happened while he'd been gone. Finally, everyone went inside, leaving him and Karrisa alone.

"Did you eat good while I was gone?" he said in his usual rough tone. "Was Danny a good boy? I'll have a talk with him if he gives you any trouble."

His wife smiled that slight smile. "I did, and he was."

He wanted to grab her and kiss her, but a dozen people might be watching. He wasn't a man who showed his affection in public.

She took a step closer to him and reached out to hold his hand. "I've missed you," she said simply.

His rough, callused fingers closed around her delicate hand. "And I've missed you, dear."

She laughed and pulled him toward the wagon he'd just spent five days riding on. "Come on, let's take all the things you bought to our house. I'll open the boxes there."

"But . . ."

"No one will miss us."

He agreed. The four McAllen sisters talked as much as Patrick did. No one in the trading post would probably get in a word for weeks. Hell, for all he knew Shelly could probably talk, just wasn't cvcr givcn thc chancc.

Karrisa winked at him and Clint forgot all about the McAllen sisters or anyone else. All he wanted was to be alone with Karrisa.

She collected the baby off the porch and they headed toward their new house. Neither said a word as they rode out. He could have talked about his trip to Dallas or she might have told him what happened at the trading post, but for this moment, in the bright sunlight, it was enough just to be sitting side by side.

Sometimes a man likes to take his happiness a cup at a time, and Clint decided his was just about as happy as he'd ever been.

After he lifted her down from the bench, his arm rested lightly on her shoulder as they walked up a stone path to the front door. When he'd left, all that had stood in this spot was the framed outline of his house; now the walls and windows and roof stood before him.

"Wait," he said when she stepped on the porch. "I want to carry you in."

She looked shy but didn't protest as he lifted her, baby and all. When he stepped inside, the house cooled in afternoon shadows. The feeling of home surrounded him. "Wait here, dear. I'll bring everything in."

She squealed with excitement at everything he carried. The rocker he'd bought her when they'd first married was already by the fireplace. From floor to ceiling had been scrubbed and within an hour everything was in place. They only had a few dishes, two pots, and one lamp, but it didn't seem to matter. She'd made curtains and a tablecloth for the little table by the window.

Taking off his money belt, Clint placed it on top of an empty bookshelf beside the fireplace. "That's all the money I have, dear. You spend it on what you need. I'll pull what I need for planting a garden and building a fence around your orchard. If this town ever gets a bank, we might consider depositing it. I'd consider myself a rich man if I had money in a bank."

"Won't you need it for cattle or crops?"

He shook his head as he pulled out the badge Lightstone gave him. "We'll raise apples and a garden and even chickens if you like, but I don't want a plow scarring across this land or cattle tromping the natural grass down. I plan on living here the rest of my life and watching the sun rise and set on this land. I'll make a regular wage from being sheriff, so we won't starve. Would that kind of life interest you, Mrs. Truman?"

She nodded. "I think I'd like that kind of life just fine, Mr. Truman."

For the first time in five days the letter from her father didn't weigh heavy in his pocket. He'd show it to her tomorrow. Today, and tonight, he wanted it to just be the two of them.

When he stepped into the bedroom, Clint saw a huge bed, long enough to hold his frame without his feet hanging off the end, and a cradle for Danny rested in the corner. "What's all this?"

"Patrick and Shelly made the bed out of an old cottonwood they had to cut down, and Shelly made Danny a cradle. It's so fine, when he wiggles it rocks him gently back to sleep."

"It's all fine. I'd thought we'd have to make do with a pallet until I had time to hammer something together." He'd thought of buying a table and chairs, a chest, even a cutting board, but he'd forgotten about the bed until he was halfway home.

When he showed her the sewing machine, she whirled with delight, hugged him quickly, and ran back to examine every detail. Clint simply stood watching her. She looked so happy, truly happy. He told himself she would read her father's letter but never go back home. Only, he'd been a last choice, an only choice over two months ago when she'd left prison. Her father was rich. Keeping her father's house in order wouldn't be near as much work as homesteading with him.

He'd tell her about the letter tomorrow, he told himself again. Now wasn't the time.

Much as he wanted to hold her and touch her, he knew now wasn't the time for that either. They climbed back in the wagon and headed to the trading post for supper. A last meal, he thought, before he'd spend his evenings coming home to her.

The evening held the sun's warmth as a huge pot of stew with corn bread and desserts was set out back behind Ely's place on long tables. The group had outgrown the kitchen.

The four retired army men who came a month ago looked like carpenters now, with wood shavings in their beards. Other new people were there too: a blacksmith who'd already set up the forge and a young preacher who was looking for a church. No one seemed to know what religion he claimed, but he had a little organ in his wagon so he must have been real. He'd gladly agreed to help with the building in exchange for his keep. There were others too: a few families living in their covered wagons, more soldiers who must have retired now that they had somewhere to go. And of course the four McAllen sisters.

Clint watched everyone moving around. Old Ely was inching his way past thirty on his population sign. The founder of this soon-to-be town had pulled his chair up near a play fort someone had built about two feet off the ground. Clint walked over to the man.

"You get the prisoner delivered?" Ely asked without turning his head toward Clint.

"Yep."

"Anything interesting happen on the trip?"

"Nope."

"From the looks of it you took on the job of sheriff. When

Lightstone told me you were coming we both figured if you could stay sober, you'd take the badge." Pounding sounds came from inside the play fort, drawing their attention for a moment.

When Clint didn't comment, Ely continued, "From the profits off all these houses and businesses I'm going to sell and rent out, I'll have McAllen build you a sheriff's office."

He pointed to a barrel-chested man in his midthirties. "Blacksmith just wants to rent from me. Already got several orders lined up."

He gestured to a tall, thin man with his collar buttoned to his Adam's apple. "The preacher and I've been talking. He says he'll pay what he can and work for me for room and board if we'll build him a church. I figure we can have a school there on weekdays. Patrick's got another crew coming in at the end of the week. Men coming back from a cattle drive stopped by needing work until the next drive comes along. As soon as they take their money home, they said they'll be back."

"Good. Momma Roma told me she knows men in Dallas who can lay brick when we're ready." Clint didn't really want to get into the town-building part or he'd be talking to Ely forever, but he needed to say something to the man. "We'll need solid buildings for the square. Ones that will last a hundred years or more."

Ely leaned back in his chair. "Of course. We ain't got many kids yet for a school, but it should be brick. I'll have a talk with Momma myself about the bricklayers. If she recommends them, I'll hire them."

Ely watched the boys play awhile and continued, "I was thinking of asking one of the McAllen sisters if they'd like the schoolmarm job. They all look like schoolteachers to me. What do you think?"

"About what they look like or about one teaching?"

Ely scratched his beard. Since the women made him bathe a month ago he couldn't seem to stop scratching. "Daisy tells me Jessie needs schooling, and these four Matheson boys have been raised by wolves up to now. I say we pick the biggest one of the McAllens to be the teacher."

Losing interest in Ely's dilemma, Clint leaned down to look into the fort. "You boys in the army?"

"I'm the captain," Abe the four-year-old said.

"And I'm the supper," Ben added.

Clint smiled. "You mean the sergeant?"

Ben started crying, "No, I'm the supper."

Clint tried distraction before Daisy blamed him for upsetting her three-year-old. "Who are those two?"

The twins were both sitting in the dirt. With broken spoons they appeared to be trying to bury their knees.

"They're the troops," Abe answered for Ben. "New recruits."

Ben joined in. "Don't know where their own asses are yet."

Ely laughed so hard he almost fell out of his chair.

Clint went back to the adults, swearing his son would never act like those twins or cuss like Ben Matheson.

Patrick and his brother were standing next to their sisters as if protecting them from all the single men coming in to eat. In truth the single men didn't look all that interested. Only the preacher talked to the old maids. It occurred to Clint that if the preacher was Mormon he might take them all on.

"I guess you're glad to have more family here?" Clint asked McAllen.

"Sure am. They said they knew my father was heading after me when he sent them to Dallas to stay with our grandparents, and the minute they got away from our stepmother they all agreed they were never going back." Patrick shrugged and pointed to his silent brother. "Shelly's worried about what we're going to do with them. Annie and I are moving into our place and we've only got one bedroom."

"They can stay here at the trading post," Clint offered.

"They could. Ely can use the help, at least until his family comes. All of them are educated."

"Until his family comes," Clint echoed, wishing he'd never learned Harmon Ely's secret.

# Chapter 37

ANNIE WATCHED HER TALL, THIN HUSBAND CIRCLING AROUND his sisters. He might be the youngest, but he was taking care of them. When everyone settled down at the tables for dinner and talk, Patrick moved in beside her.

"How you feeling, Annie?" he whispered as he patted her arm.

She frowned. "If you ask me that every day for the next six months, you'll drive me crazy, Patrick."

"All right. I won't ask, but you got to promise to tell me if you're feeling poorly. This is my first baby and I don't know what to do."

"Me either, but I have a feeling we'll manage."

Annie ate a few bites as she watched Patrick eat two bowls of soup and half a pan of cornbread. They talked about Truman being a sheriff and where the sisters would stay and all the little things that had happened in their day. Every now and then he'd pat her arm, or knee, or shoulder. By dessert she was starting to feel like old Davy.

When dinner was over, the sisters offered to do the dishes and Patrick took her hand. As the spring warmed they liked to take a walk down to where the two streams crossed. Both were silent for a while as they watched a beautiful sunset spread along the western sky.

Something was on Patrick's mind. She could feel it. The silence. The constant touching as if he feared she might disappear at any moment.

Annie finally turned to him, knowing one of them had to say something. "I'm going to be fine."

"I know," he answered, quickly telling her that the baby wasn't what was bothering him.

She tried again, deciding it could be only one other thing. "Your sisters told me that your father came here to kill you. You saw him, didn't you." It wasn't a question. "That night you left after supper and didn't want me to come along. You hadn't left something at the site. You were going out to meet him."

Her husband, for once, had nothing to say. He stood, staring out into the darkening night. Finally, when his voice came, it was low and full of heartbreak. "I didn't lie to you, Annie. I swear I was going to tell you. I just didn't want to upset you, what with the baby and all. I planned to tell you all about it after we'd settled into our own house."

She watched him talk. He looked like his world was shattering before him. They both knew the lie lay in his silence, not in something he'd said.

He told her he was sorry. He never meant to wait this long. He'd never lie to her again. He loved her and if she left him because of this, he might as well have let his father kill him.

Annie listened and watched Patrick. He looked so young. They both were. He was doing all he could to be a man . . . to be her man. When she'd said she wanted to go with him, she'd liked him, known he was a good person, but she'd never dreamed how much she'd grow to love him.

He couldn't sing. He talked too much. He worried about everyone like he was grandfather to each person in Harmony and not a man of twenty. He thought he could read his brother's mind, and he loved her.

"We got to find a way around this, Annie. I know I said

I'd never lie, but you have to give me a chance to make it up to you."

"Patrick." She finally got a word in. "I forgive you. I believe you. I have no doubt that you thought you were protecting me."

He froze, his mouth wide open. "You forgive me?" He grinned when she smiled at him. "I've been worried for days about how to tell you and what you'd do. I even had a plan to drive you nuts begging if you left me. Now, you just forgive me, as simple as that."

Annie nodded. "As simple as that, Patrick. Only now, I'm allowed one free lie to use anytime I want. And when I lie, you have to forgive me just as easy. You'll never know when it will come or what it will be, but someday I'll lie."

Patrick frowned. "You know that will torture me. You know how I worry. Now I'll be double-thinking everything you tell me."

Grinning, she nodded. "I may save my free lie for years, Patrick, and no matter what it is, you'll have to forgive me."

"So, you're going to stay with me and drive me crazy?"

She looped her arm in his. "That was my plan all along."

"There's a wicked spot in you, Annie Truman."

He rubbed her nicely rounded bottom and told her she was beautiful, and Annie believed him, for he'd used his one lie.

# Chapter 38

CLINT TRIED TO TALK TO EVERYONE, BUT HIS GAZE KEPT turning to his bride. He wanted to be alone with Karrisa more than he needed to breathe. The young preacher was funny, the soldiers interesting, and the blacksmith polite, but he wanted the quiet peace of being with only one person.

When Harry and Ely broke out a bottle to pass around, the women moved inside with the children.

Clint took Karrisa's hand. "Let's go home, dear," he said simply.

She lifted Danny from where he slept in Momma Roma's arms and walked out beside him. With all the people talking, no one seemed to notice them leave.

When they reached the wagon, he lifted her up and headed toward the first little house along Lone Oak Road. His place. The Truman farm.

As always, they didn't talk. The moon rose, a giant ball blinking between the cottonwoods. The wagon swayed. His leg bumped against hers and she didn't move it away. Carefully he let his hand rest on her skirt just above her knee. He liked touching her like this, almost as if he'd done it a hundred times and knew his slight advance was welcome.

Her fingers brushed over his hand, lightly pressing until he felt the warmth of her beneath the layers of cotton.

He was half drunk on wanting her when he pulled the wagon close to the house and helped her down.

"I'll unhitch the horses and be in," he said as she walked inside.

The letter in his pocket rested heavy against his chest as he hobbled the horses so they could feed on the tall grass. When there was time, he'd build a barn and put up a windmill.

She had a right to know that her father had gone to Huntsville looking for her. Clint had no intention of telling her what he had told the sheriff, though. Maybe Karrisa's father had been kinder in the letter when he asked her to come home. She was his only child. Surely she meant more to him than just someone to keep his house.

Clint knew he had to tell her before he touched her again. He had to be honest. Whether the father was kind or harsh didn't change the fact that he had to give her the letter. She now had a choice to make.

He couldn't offer her much more than her father did. Passion, he thought. He could offer her that. In time, passion might be almost the same as love.

The cottonwoods down by Lone Oak Road swayed in the night as if calling him near.

Clint walked toward them feeling like his mind and heart were at war with one another. He still loved his Mary and his little girls. They still filled his heart. He could tell himself that the need he felt for Karrisa was just a physical thing, but he knew it was more. He just didn't know what. She deserved better than him, but he couldn't walk away from her.

The trees were tall here but not as old as the ancient cottonwood on his land down by Huntsville. There, the frequent rain and the wet soil made the trees grow wide with roots running along at ground level. Here, with the earth so dry and rain far less frequent, these trees grew tall and the roots dug deep down in the soil.

He seemed to be changing in this land as well. Part of him wanted to grow so deep into this place that he'd be one with the land. One with Harmony.

Shadows began to dance between the cottonwoods. Shadows he'd clung to for three years. He could almost hear his daughters laughing as they blinked in and out from behind the trees.

Clint lowered himself to the ground and watched them. Their sunny curls bouncing, their smiles contagious. They'd been with him all this time. Just beyond his reach, but there.

He loved this haunting memory as much as he hated the one that sometimes came of them crying, begging him to hold them and not go for the doctor. If he'd stayed, he would have been with them when they passed. The doctor had been no help. Heaven had already called their names by the time he'd returned.

As he watched, he saw Mary walking toward the girls, her hands outstretched. He rarely saw her in the cottonwoods, and always before she'd been in the background, only a faded silhouette watching their daughters.

Hand in hand they stepped from the cottonwoods and walked toward him. Clint didn't know if he was dreaming or had gone completely mad. He didn't care. They were coming toward him. Maybe to take him with them. They'd all be together again.

He stood, wanting to run to meet them, but his feet stayed rooted in the earth. Mary stopped a few feet out of his reach and smiled. She seemed to understand. One at a time she released the girls' hands and they ran to their father. Clint hugged them tightly, feeling as if his heart were being pulled from his chest.

"Good-bye, Papa," they both whispered in his ear as they kissed his cheek.

Mary reached out, her hand almost brushing his face as she nodded once. A silent salute. A forever farewell.

He tried to follow, but his feet wouldn't come loose from the earth. He could only watch as the girls danced on either side of Mary as she walked back to the trees.

When they melted into the shadows, Clint knew he'd never

see them again. The vision he'd held in his mind for three years had vanished. He'd had his chance to hug them good-bye.

He hadn't been able to go with them. He'd already planted his roots too deep in this soil.

He walked back to his house feeling light-headed. They'd always been in the back of his thoughts, dancing, smiling, helping him make it one more day. Maybe he couldn't go with them simply because he wasn't finished here yet.

When he walked into the house, Karrisa was just putting Danny in his cradle. She looked up at Clint with those beautiful blue eyes. All the fear was gone. She trusted him. He'd won that battle with her at least; now he had to let her know that she had choices to make about her life.

He wasn't her only chance, her one chance to survive. If she wanted to go live with her father, she could.

Unable to say anything, Clint handed her the letter, then crossed over to hang up his gun belt on a nail by the kitchen door. Everything they had was in order in their little home. They had no pictures or china or frilly things sitting around. This place must look pretty plain compared to where she'd grown up.

Her traveling jacket that she'd walked out of prison wearing lay on the kitchen table. She must have cut the sleeves and cuffs open while she'd waited for him. Tiny apple seeds were lined up in rows of ten as if she'd been planning exactly how she'd plant them.

He picked up one. *Roots*, he almost said aloud. If she planted these, they'd both be planting roots and would never leave this land.

He tried not to stare when she walked into the room that served as their living space, but he figured she knew he was watching her.

For a moment she looked confused, turning the letter over and over in her hands, and then she moved to the one lamp and opened it slowly. Her face was worried as if she somehow thought a letter might hurt her.

He stood in the dark, watching. If she told him she wanted to go back home, could he let her, could he stop her? He knew the answer. He'd promised to be kind. He'd let her walk away even if it shattered what little sanity he had left.

For a while, she didn't move. She just sat at the table and stared out into the night just beyond the window. Clint tried not to think about what was going through her mind. Lighting a fire, he decided to unpack his saddlebags. He placed his rifle on the hooks above the mantel and touched her brush when he put his shaving gear by the washstand.

He was settling in at the same time she was probably thinking about leaving.

When she still hadn't moved, he washed up and shaved simply because he couldn't stand and stare at her. Not that she would notice. Moonlight framed her as she sat as still as stone, the letter tight in her hand.

*Her choice*, he kept thinking. *Her choice, not mine*. He was strong and probably double her weight. They were married by law. She'd promised him she'd be his wife. But he wouldn't stand in her way if she wanted to leave.

In the mirror, he watched her finally rise and walk to the fireplace. She tossed the letter atop the fire and walked into the bedroom. When she came out again, her hair was down and brushing over her shoulders. The hair he'd thought so lifeless that first night moved in midnight waves. When she stopped a few feet in front of him, he had to fight to keep from touching her.

"Will you unbutton my dress, Clint?" she asked, as if unsure of the answer.

She hadn't said she was going. What she asked was a simple request.

He closed the space between them and slowly began opening the front of her dress. "I love doing this," he whispered as he bent and kissed the first button, then let his mouth slide to her throat.

If this was her way of saying good-bye, he'd make it a memory they'd both hold.

She stood straight and still as he continued, her chin high. "The letter was from my father," she finally said.

"I know. Sheriff Lightstone gave it to me." He moved his

hand beneath the cotton of her dress and felt her warm skin. She was shaking slightly, nervous, but she didn't step away as his touch grew bolder.

She took a long breath as Clint kissed his way down her throat, suddenly far more interested in her than any letter.

"He says I can come home," she whispered.

Clint paused and straightened, hating to leave his work with the job of unbuttoning only half done. "What will you tell him?"

His beautiful Karrisa looked up at him and whispered, "I'll tell him I'm already home."

Clint slid his hands beneath her arms and lifted her so high above she almost touched the ceiling. He circled around, laughing. "You'll stay with me, then?" he finally asked.

"Yes, not because you'll let me but because you want me to stay."

"I do." He carried her the few steps to the bedroom, where the candlelight made her glow as he kissed her hard and fast. "I want you to stay forever with me right here."

To his surprise, she wrapped her arms around his neck and kissed him hesitantly on the mouth. He felt her full lips spread into a smile. "And what will we do right here, forever?" Her words whispered between them.

With a laugh, he tumbled atop the bed, taking her with him. "I want you here with me every day and night of our lives. Do you understand what I'm saying?" He rolled atop her, loving the feel of her body beneath him. With each intake of breath he felt her every curve as she shifted, stretching.

"Yes. I'm your wife, Clint. This is where I want to be."

Before she could catch her breath he was kissing her wildly and removing her clothes so rapidly several buttons popped off and *ting*ed on the floor. He needed to hold her close, so close no clothes remained between them.

The sense that this place, this time, this woman was exactly where he was meant to be filled Clint as he held her close, loving the way she melted against him.

Timidly her hand moved over his chest as she unbuttoned his black shirt. "I like this shirt, but I want to touch you."

He stood and removed his clothes and watched her eyes fill with desire. A surprising passion, newborn and strong, flickered as she studied him. They'd spent so much time walking around one another, touching only when necessary. A fire between them had built slowly, encouraged by kindness and thoughtfulness. Now both were lost in the need for the other.

When he returned to her he rolled atop her, letting his weight push her into the soft feather bed. Then he laughed as he rolled over, taking her with him. As she rested on him, he spread his hands out wide and moved along her back and lower until he'd learned her gentle curves. She rested her head next to his, letting him take his time.

"I should tell you, dear, that I was wrong," he whispered against her ear as he made lazy circles along the small of her back. "I said I'd never love you. I think you were already in my heart that first night we met, but my whiskey brain wouldn't let me think it true."

"I know, Truman." She smiled, cupping his face with her hands. "I've always known."

He ran his fingers along her body that was not quite as thin as it had been a month ago. Every dream he'd had about her when he was away couldn't compare to the woman with him now.

He had to say the words. The words he'd sworn he'd never say. "I love you, Karrisa. Whether you sleep with me as my wife tonight or not, that fact won't change."

He could already see the answer in her eyes. He knew he couldn't name the color of another woman's eyes for a hundred miles, but he knew hers. Moonlight blue. His Karrisa had moonlight blue eyes and it was time to show her just how he felt about her.

Her arms wrapped around him and held on tightly. "Make love to me tonight. Love me so completely that all time before this night vanishes."

And he did. He loved her as he'd never loved a woman. She became a part of him. By dawn the house was their home and she was his.

* * *

WHEN HE WOKE HE COULD HEAR HER IN THE KITCHEN AND he couldn't stop smiling. She'd been shy during their loving, and hungry for more. When they'd finished and were curled in each other's arms, she'd cried.

When he'd asked why, she'd whispered that sometimes happiness spills out. He'd held her close all night and, as he dressed, thoughts of the night to come were already on his mind. He might never show his affection in public, but he'd never stop showing his love in private.

As he walked into the kitchen, she was busy making bread. "Morning," she said, without looking up at him.

He moved behind her and moved his arms around her waist until his big hand spread out over her middle.

She straightened and leaned back against his chest.

"I'll never get enough of you." His words brushed her ear.

His shy wife turned slowly in his arms and kissed his cheek. "Luckily we finally have our own house."

Before he could kiss her senseless in the morning light, he heard the bell tolling from the trading post and every relaxed muscle tightened.

"Something's wrong at the trading post." He pulled away and reached for his gun belt. "I need to get there fast."

She ran for Danny. "I'm going with you." It wasn't a request.

"I'll get the team." He could have made it faster riding bareback and she'd probably be safer staying here, but he wouldn't leave her alone. By the time she wrapped the baby and put on her coat, he was waiting.

She climbed in the back and huddled down behind the bench as he covered her with the tarp that had protected their furniture. "Stay down until we get to the trading post, and then run in the back and stay there. If there is gunfire, no matter what, don't come out."

He took the reins and headed toward Harmony.

# Chapter 39

MATHESON WATCHED TRUMAN HEADING TOWARD HIM AS fast as the horses could run. Most of the settlement hid in predawn shadows, but trouble was out there; Gillian could feel it. His Daisy and the boys were tucked into their house and probably hadn't even heard the bell.

He prayed not. Truman was the only one he needed. They'd both faced battles before, and together they'd face the one he feared he saw coming.

Like the soldier he always would be, Gillian took count of his troops. Patrick and Shelly had left before dawn with a full crew, including the Roma boys. Now that his sisters were here, Patrick wanted to finish his house as fast as possible. Their place was farther out than the others, so he'd take longer to get here even if he did hear the alarm.

That left Ely and Harry, still sleeping off a hangover in the store. The four McAllen women and Momma Roma were upstairs. They'd promised to cook breakfast, but no one must have told them it was served at dawn.

Gillian wasn't sure if Momma Roma's youngest boy had left with the men or stayed around to help with his mother's projects. Since there was no movement from the tents down near the creek, he guessed that the soldiers-turned-carpenters were at work with McAllen as well as the blacksmith. There were others scattered around, but he didn't know whether he could depend on them to fight when danger rode in.

Truman pulled his wagon to the side of the building and bounded over the railing on the front porch. He wore his Colt and carried a rifle—exactly how Gillian hoped he'd show up.

"Trouble?" Clint asked.

Gillian tried to keep his voice low. "I rode over early from my place wanting to check on one of Momma Roma's horses. To the north, where no one is camped, I saw a thin line of smoke as if someone put out a fire just before dawn. Too many years tracking outlaws made me suspicious. I spotted six men traveling light, but there could have been more. A wide bull of a man was giving orders in low tones, like he didn't want anyone around to know where they were camped."

"Outlaws." Truman was already ahead of Gillian. "They're watching us. May have been waiting for me to get in or maybe for a chance to catch the men gone."

Gillian nodded. "I didn't want them to see me, so I stayed out of sight and rode here along the creek bed. All the other men are gone and Ely isn't in any shape to return fire, so looks like it's me and you if they try to hit us this morning."

Both men studied the open land to the north as he added, "What I can't figure out is why they seem to be planning a raid here. We've little stock and most of what Ely has in the store wouldn't be worth the time it would take to load up and haul away."

"They're here for me," Truman said in a whisper. "I can almost smell Dollar Holt near. He's coming to even the score after I destroyed his raid on the first wagon caravan I brought in."

"Maybe if you left, or we told them you had, he might go away."

Truman shook his head. "They'd just burn the place down. Dollar Holt has hated me since the war. I knew when I didn't kill him that night on the road that eventually he'd come after me. I not only spoiled his raid, but I captured one of his men—a witness who's already turned against him. If we catch Dollar this time, he knows he'll go to prison for life, so he's got nothing to lose by holding up this place and killing me."

"But why would men follow him just to kill you?" Matheson needed logic even though he knew outlaws didn't always follow any.

"Something's bothered me since I heard it the first time I was in Dallas. Folks think Ely is rich and is building a town to prove it. Maybe they're after his money?"

"Looks like we're about to find out," Gillian said as he watched four men riding slowly toward them. Three were young, green to the bad life, he'd guess. The other looked more hardened.

Truman lowered his rifle but kept it in easy reach. "Holt isn't among them," he said simply.

The door to the post opened and Ely stumbled out, his rifle by his side. Drunk or sober, he'd fight with them.

"How you want to play this, Captain?" Truman asked.

"You're the sheriff. I follow your lead."

"Cover me." Clint stepped off the porch and into the morning light. "Stand ready, but stay in the shadows of the porch until I lift my rifle to take aim; then be ready to fire."

Gillian guessed Truman could probably raise his rifle and take down all four men even from this distance before one bullet could strike him, but the new sheriff waited to see what they wanted first.

When they were thirty feet away, Clint called out, "That's far enough, boys. State your business."

"We're not looking for trouble, Sheriff," one said. "Just came to shop."

The two younger ones laughed.

"Hand over your guns and you're welcome to go in and look around."

Gillian gripped his rifle. The men were far too well armed to be just traveling. They had no bags of food or supplies tied to their saddles, and all wore double gun belts.

The older one pushed his tan hat back and grinned a wide, toothy grin. "I don't believe we're going to do that. See, we heard this place is just like a bank. All we have to do is ride up and make a withdrawal."

Ely limped forward. "You boys need to keep on riding. The store's closed. I've seen your kind before. Ain't nothing free here."

The smiling man tried again. "Now, we don't want any trouble, especially with the womenfolk here. Way I see it, it's four against three and one is an old man." He pointed with his head toward the barn. "I've got two men in the barn loft who'll shoot the first one of you who raises a weapon. So, how about we do this peacefully?"

"I'm all for peace." The preacher walked out of the store eating an apple.

"Stay out of this, Preacher." Clint's voice was low. "This isn't your fight."

One of the outlaws pointed at the tall, thin preacher. "He ain't even got a gun and he's so skinny we could use him as a rope."

The other outlaws laughed, but there was an edge to their laugh as if they were nervous, or afraid and in a hurry to get on with the business of killing.

Matheson couldn't see this ending well. If anyone fired, half the men would be dead in seconds. Truman might get two of the outlaws before he was hit, but casualties would be suffered on both sides. He'd seen it before. Too many guns and not enough reason to go around.

Truman didn't look the least bit worried. He was just as unfriendly as always. "Where's Dollar Holt? He sent you out here to do his dirty work, but he's nowhere around."

"I'm right here," Dollar said as he shoved Karrisa out the door in front of him. "And I'm through listening to all the chatter. This is how it's going to be. The old man gives us his money and we walk away without hurting anyone. Of course, we'll take your wife along with us for insurance."

"No." Clint's one word was a roar of rage. "Take me. Leave her."

Dollar looked like he was considering the possibility. "How about I take you both? A wife has a right to see her husband die, and, Truman, it's about time you died."

Seven men to two, Gillian thought. Not counting the still-drunk Ely and the unarmed preacher. He had to think of something, anything to increase their chances.

About the time he was sure Truman was ready to start firing, a strange rattling sound came from the road.

Everyone turned and watched as a wagon that seemed to be covered with pots and pans and tools came around the bend. One wheel was smaller than the others, so the cart bumped along even on a flat road.

"Morning," a chubby little man yelled, and waved as if delighted to see them awake. "You folks are up early. This a welcoming party or something? If so, I'm mighty glad I came."

Before anyone could stop him, the man rolled his wagon between Clint and the store and bounced down from his seat. The clatter of the pots almost sounded like faraway gunfire.

Gillian watched through the forest of pans and tools as everything seemed to happen at once.

Behind him, Karrisa jerked free and fell onto the ground, disappearing as she rolled off the porch.

Ely swung at Dollar's gun and the outlaw's first bullet fired wild. His second missed them but sent one of the pots hanging from the old wagon spinning.

Gillian raised his rifle to fire, but he was afraid he might hit one of the others on the porch. So, before Dollar could fire another round, Gillian jabbed his rifle into the man's gut. The huge outlaw let go of his weapon as he yelled in pain but before he could shout any orders to his men, he was hit on both sides by Ely's rifle butt to his chest and the preacher's apple to his nose.

Dollar continued to scream as the preacher knocked him down and sat on him while Ely pounded on his face.

Gillian grabbed both his guns and hurried around the tinker's wagon.

Truman stood, his feet wide apart, his rifle raised. The

men on horseback hadn't had time to draw their weapons. "I can drop you all before you'll have time to pull a gun," Truman said, almost calmly. "Maybe you'll get lucky and I'll miss one of you, but the captain won't. So what do you think? Do you fight or leave, swearing you'll never be back to Harmony?"

"We've got men in the barn," the one in the hat said, as if pulling the only ace left.

Gillian heard two thuds hit the dirt by the barn opening. "You mean those two who just fell out of the barn loft?"

All four outlaws looked worried. Between the two shooters out cold on the ground and Dollar screaming, the winds of chance had turned against them.

"We haven't got enough on these four to charge them, Sheriff," Gillian said to Truman in what he hoped sounded like the reasoning of a lawyer. "But if you shoot them I'll swear they drew on you."

Now the outlaws looked frightened. Three of them couldn't have been much out of their teens and the other hadn't lived as long as he had by being a fool.

"Come on, boys," he said to the others. "Let's get out of here."

"Drop your weapons first," Clint ordered. "I don't want you changing your minds and deciding to come calling later."

Reluctantly they did as he said.

Truman finally lowered his gun. "If you come back here, I'll kill you. Do you all understand? I'm a man of my word."

They all nodded as they turned their horses and rode away, picking up speed as if they feared a bullet might yet find them.

Gillian glanced at the barn as the McAllen brothers collected their two fallen angels.

"We weren't as alone as we thought we were, Captain," Truman said as men appeared from several hiding places, all armed, all ready to fight. "Make sure those four don't turn around, would you?"

"I'll watch them. Go check on your wife." Gillian looked at where Truman had stood and realized he was talking to himself.

Two of the ex-soldiers took over Dollar Holt before Ely beat the man to death. The preacher seemed disappointed to lose his seat but found another job in comforting the McAllen sisters, who were all crying.

Gillian walked around the other side of the tinker's wagon and found the man who'd wandered into a gunfight and no doubt changed the outcome. "I don't know who you are, mister, but you may have very well saved a great many lives today."

The chubby little man rocked on his heels. "I wasn't sure what was happening, but I knew if it was trouble and I didn't help I'd never forgive myself." He helped his wife down from the back of the wagon. "We heard you're building a town. Thought there might be work here. I've been hard-pressed to find any these past few years."

Gillian saw the holes in their shoes and the patches on worn-out clothes.

The man straightened. "Names Wright, Timothy Wright, and I'll undertake any honest work."

Gillian shook his hand. "Ely," he yelled at the man behind him. "Looks like we got ourselves an undertaker."

When he looked back to see if Ely was listening, Gillian saw Truman holding his wife close and realized that the hard man knew he'd almost lost his world. Without a word they climbed into their wagon and headed back home. Apparently Truman had done his job and didn't plan on staying around to rehash what had happened.

Ely yelled over all the noise. "Someone wake up Woolsey and tell him we got another outlaw who needs a ride to Dallas." He then looked at the little undertaker. "Come on in, Mr. and Mrs. Wright. When the ladies get breakfast ready, we'll talk. How do you feel about living in town?"

# Chapter 40

THE TRUMAN FARM

BY THE TIME CLINT TRUMAN MADE IT HOME HE WAS SLUMPING on the bench. Karrisa ran the baby inside and then helped him down from the wagon, both her hands already covered in her husband's blood.

"It's not bad, dear. Feels like the wild bullet of Dollar's just slid along my side."

"Hush," she said, with more anger than he thought his Karrisa could be capable of. "You're leaking all over the place. We should have stayed at Ely's."

"No." He bit back pain as they walked up the steps. "I don't want the others to know I'm hurt. The McAllen women were frightened enough, and Dollar would be very happy to know one of his wild shots hit me."

"Well, Clint Truman, I'm going to be very mad at you if you die on me."

He fought down the pain long enough to laugh as she lowered him into one of the kitchen chairs and began stripping off his shirt. "So you like having me around, dear?"

She didn't answer for a while. She just steamed around gathering towels and heating water. The medicine box she'd insisted on putting together after Matheson had been shot was about to come in handy.

When she finally came back to him, her beautiful blue eyes were still filled with anger. As she gently washed the blood away, she whispered, "Clint, I love you. Underneath all the gruff manner and toughness is the kindest man I've ever known, but if you die on me I plan to be furious."

He saw the tears and wanted to hold her, but she was on a mission to bandage him up. When she finally tied off the bandage around his ribs, he pulled her to his knee and held her close.

"When I saw Dollar Holt push you out the door, I thought I'd go mad. If you love me half as much as I love you, I think I understand why you're so angry now. I was so crazy to get to you that I didn't even feel the bullet slice along my side."

Karrisa wiped her tears against his shoulder and pounded on his wide chest. "I love you twice that much. I couldn't believe you were standing out there facing down four outlaws."

He laughed, forgetting the pain. "We going to argue about this, dear? I wasn't alone. Gillian was armed and Ely was there. Even the preacher helped."

She shook her head. "I don't want to argue with you. But first you've got to promise me you won't die on me."

"I promise." Closing his eyes, he wondered what he'd ever done in this lifetime to deserve this shy woman who only showed her temper when she thought he was hurt.

"I'm putting you and Danny both down for a nap while I finish unpacking."

Clint didn't argue. She made him a funny-tasting tea and he slept the morning away. When he woke, he felt much better and managed to down both breakfast and lunch at the same time.

When they climbed into bed that night, Clint held her close and whispered, "I love you."

She kissed his cheek and answered, "I love you more."

He smiled, figuring they'd have this argument for the rest of their lives, and he didn't mind a bit.

# Chapter 41

JUST AS THE SUN SHONE GOLDEN ACROSS THE WESTERN windows, Patrick grabbed one end of the quilt, helping Annie spread it on the floor of their new home. "When I'm a rich rancher someday, I'll build a big house in the center of our land and we'll use this little place as our getaway hideout."

"I like that idea, but will we be getting away from our kids or your sisters?" Annie giggled. "I thought you'd never convince them to stay with Ely last night. They were all sure they'd be killed in their sleep, and what did they wake up to but an outlaw raid on the trading post. They were so upset all day. Every single man who passed by had to take his turn comforting them."

Patrick took the basket packed with supper. "I noticed the more upset they got, the more the preacher circled. I think he might be sweet on Pamela-Anne. He kept patting her hand even after she stopped crying."

"She's twenty-two, Patrick. Plenty old enough to have a beau." Annie set the plates out as if she were setting a fine table and not a picnic.

He shook his head. "I think it should be like it is in the

Old Testament. The oldest daughter has to marry first. Otherwise we'll never get Edna married off. Not only is she scraping six feet tall, she's bossy as all get-out."

"But Pamela-Anne is sweet and the prettiest of your sisters. With all that red hair she's not likely to be lost in a crowd. If the preacher marries her, he'll be able to find her in the congregation."

"Yeah, but she doesn't have the sense of a newborn calf. Everyone back home bossed her around and she let them. My stepmother treated her like she was a personal maid from the time Pamela-Anne was ten. I always felt sorry for her." He took his plate from Annie. "And saying she's the prettiest in my family isn't saying much." He winked. "All the men got the great looks in the McAllen family."

"Well, if the preacher comes asking for her hand, you'd best be thinking of what you plan to say."

Patrick frowned. "I'll tell him he'll have to take a lot more than her hand. I'll threaten him if he ever hits her. I won't want that for my sisters. They've had a hard enough life as it is."

"You'd beat a preacher up?" she asked.

"If he hurts my sister, I'd probably send Shelly over to do the job. Folks don't know it, but he's meaner than me."

They laughed and ate their first meal in their first home.

Except for a bed frame, they had no furnishings. Patrick wanted to build every piece. He hammered up nails to hang their clothes on and built a long counter by the cookstove in the corner. With two rooms they shouldn't have much trouble finding each other, but after living in the tiny bedroom upstairs at Ely's and the hay loft, the house seemed big and quiet.

As she picked up the dishes, he pulled out the box that Mrs. Dixon had given them all those weeks ago when they'd passed by her place and decided to help. They'd both agreed not to open it until they had a home, just like she'd told them.

"What do you think is in it?" Annie whispered.

"It doesn't matter. She was sweet to give us a wedding gift."

"Our one and only." Annie pulled the yard of yarn that kept it closed, and then Patrick slowly lifted the lid.

A tiny scrap of paper rested on top of a huge key. Patrick took the paper. "Fredericksburg, 1836. The bend of Turtle Creek."

Annie looked at the key. "Wonder what this opens?"

Patrick shook his head. "Probably nothing. Maybe the Dixons just found the key." He lifted the scrap of paper. "She probably wrote down the place where she found the old key. If she'd had the chest that went with this, she probably would have sold it. It's a worthless key, I'm afraid."

"No," Annie pulled the key away from him. "It's priceless. It's our only wedding gift."

Patrick set the key and paper back in the box. "All right. It's priceless. We should put it somewhere safe and keep it always."

Like two kids they stepped into the game.

"But where?" she asked.

Patrick pulled a rock from the fireplace. "I built this thinking if we ever got any money, we could hide it in here. Look, the space is just the right size for the box."

Annie slid the wedding gift in place and Patrick put the rock back. "It'll always be there to remind us how lucky we are." He winked at her. "Now for my favorite part of the day."

"What's that?" She giggled as if she didn't know.

"Bedtime," he answered.

# Epilogue

FEBRUARY 1877

THE WINTER WIND MIGHT HOWL OUTSIDE TRUMAN'S BIG new barn, but all were warm inside. A hundred people, dressed in their Sunday best, had come to celebrate. Harmony, Texas, was officially a town with a post office, a church, a ten-room hotel, and Momma Roma's café. Lots had already been marked off for a dozen more homes, and by spring they'd apply to be the county seat.

Gillian Matheson stood with Truman and McAllen watching folks listen as a fiddler tuned up. Over the months the three had become close friends. Brothers in a dream.

"We did it," Gillian announced. "We've become a town." He noticed Ely over near the front already dancing with the children. They were all trying to imitate his funny jig. Truman had told him and Patrick about Ely's family. They voted to keep it to themselves and let the man continue his dream, only slowly they'd each brought him into their own families. The wives fussed over Ely and made sure he ate properly and took a bath monthly. Daisy still balanced his books and

Annie made it over a couple times a week to help Patrick's two oldest sisters cook for all the people Ely was always inviting in for a meal. Even the girl, Jessie, did her part by watering down Ely's whiskey.

Patrick shook his head. "I've still got a lot of work to do," he said more to himself than the other two. "I've got four full crews building and another crew of bricklayers and we still can't keep up with the need. Folks are moving in wanting to start businesses, and tents run a quarter mile along the creek."

Music filled the barn as folks, most with no dancing skill at all, began to twirl around the room. Mr. and Mrs. Timothy Wright led the promenade in their new clothes without patches.

"He'll be the richest man in Harmony one day," Truman commented as they watched Wright linking arms with his wife. "He'll take on any job that's honest."

Truman raised his eyebrow to Gillian. "I heard he even corralled your gang, Matheson, while you took Daisy out for a dinner at Momma Roma's café. It takes a great man to take on your gang."

Gillian nodded. "He charged me double, but it was worth it. Ely had me give management rights to the cemetery to Wright and his family. As long as there is a Wright to manage it, I have a feeling the cemetery will be kept in good shape. Mr. Wright even went down and brought up rocks from the creek for Granny Gigi's grave. Momma Roma cried when she saw how beautiful he'd made the site. Offered him and his family free supper for a month."

Gillian caught his wife's glance and knew she wanted to dance. He looked at Truman and McAllen. "Aren't you two dancing?"

"No." Patrick smiled. "Annie's so big she's about to pop. Our new young doctor claims the baby is overdue, but I don't trust him. How can he be a doctor? I don't think he's even shaving yet."

"You were young once, McAllen," Truman grumbled. "Hell, it seems like only yesterday."

"I'm still young. What about you, Truman, you too old to dance?"

"No. I could dance, only there's just one lady I want to dance with." He nodded toward his wife. "Problem is she told me yesterday that she's in a family way. I told her to be sure and take it easy tonight and not overdo it."

Both Gillian and Patrick slapped Truman on the back and started giving him advice.

When Daisy finally pulled Gillian away to dance, he couldn't turn her down. "You're the prettiest girl at the dance," he whispered as they began.

"Thank you, but Jessie is shining tonight."

Gillian looked over at the girl who'd saved his life a year ago. She'd grown to be taller than Daisy and was turning into a young lady before his eyes. "She's dancing with Shelly?" Gillian said in surprise.

"Shelly can hear the music."

"I know, but she can't even talk to him."

Daisy smiled at her brilliant husband who could plan a town and couldn't see what was right under his nose. "Jessie's set her heart on Shelly McAllen. He'll be twenty-three when she turns sixteen, and I'm guessing it won't be long before she asks him to marry her."

"No. That's not happening."

"Why, because he can't talk?"

"No. I don't care about that. But she's part of our family and I don't want Mathesons mixing with McAllens. There's no telling what would happen. I'd better put a stop to this now. Next thing you'll be telling me is one of my boys is marrying the Truman girl."

"That won't happen for a while, Captain. A Truman girl hasn't even been born yet."

"But she's coming and I plan to start warning my boys now."

"Yes, honey, you can do that later. For a while how about we all just live in Harmony."

And they did.

Read on for a special preview of the next Harmony novel from Jodi Thomas

ONE TRUE HEART

*Available April 2015 from Berkley!*

# Chapter 1

LATE AUGUST
RICK HUSBAND INTERNATIONAL AIRPORT
AMARILLO, TEXAS

MILLANIE MCALLEN USED THE BACKS OF THE AIRLINE SEATS to hop her way from the tiny toilet to the exit as the flight attendant pulled out her crutches from the front storage.

"Sorry, Captain McAllen, I thought everyone was off." The girl apologized with a quick smile at Millanie.

"No problem. I needed a few minutes to change." Millanie's army jacket rested over her arm. Her name bar and ribbons sparkled in the plane's lighting. She traded the attendant her uniform for the crutches as she read the girl's name tag. "Trudi, would you mind folding this into my bag? When I walk off, or rather limp off, this plane and into Texas, I'm no longer in the army."

While the attendant did as she'd requested, Millanie tried to straighten the wrinkled long-sleeve blouse and gathered prairie skirt she'd changed into. They were not exactly her style—far too lacy.

"I could call for a chair." Trudi looked at her with trained sympathy in her eyes. "This time of night they're never busy."

"No, thanks. I can handle this." After four plane changes and an all-night layover at LaGuardia with her leg hurting like they'd left shrapnel in it, simply walking out of the last airport seemed like a piece of cake.

"What time of night is it?" Millanie guessed she sounded a bit crazy, but she'd lost all track of time after flying halfway around the world.

"Almost eleven. The airport will be closing soon. We're the last flight, I think."

Looping her purse over one shoulder so that it was out of the way and wrapping the bag strings around the long strap, the newly decommissioned Captain McAllen hobbled off the plane. She refused to look back and take one more glance of sympathy. She'd had enough to last a lifetime.

THE AIR WAS DIFFERENT IN WEST TEXAS; IT WAS UNLIKE anywhere in the world: thin and pure with the smell of the earth spiced in by the wind. She hadn't been back to Harmony for six years, but she swore she could smell cattle and oil circulating in the air-conditioned breeze even inside the terminal.

Part of the crowd who'd come to stand and wave flags and cheer for hometown warriors returning on her flight were now milling around, picking up streamers they'd thrown and rolling up flags. She'd heard soldiers talking when they'd waited at the USO in Dallas. One had been told about the welcoming group that would be waiting for them when they landed in Amarillo. All the men seemed excited to be going home to a place where they would be welcomed by a crowd of friends, family, and fellow veterans.

Millanie had limped her way down half a mile of crowded gates at DFW to find a clothing store. It sold the gaudiest Western clothes in Texas. Her choices had been jeans with rhinestone crosses on her butt or a gathered skirt that looked like it had been hanging around since the sixties. She chose the one that would go over her cast.

Looking down at her attire, she guessed her great-great-grandmother probably wore the same kind of outfit when she climbed off the covered wagon almost a hundred and fifty years ago to homestead. Patrick and Annie McAllen hadn't been much more than kids when they'd helped found Harmony. Maybe that was why, no matter where she traveled, the little town would always be home.

She took a deep breath and smiled. Two more hours and she'd be able to rest.

By the time she made it downstairs to the baggage claim area, everyone else on her flight was long gone, and she'd sweated so much her black curly hair lay plastered as if it were a swim cap. Her army-issued duffle bag was circling on the carousel like a lonely drunk after last call.

*I can do this,* she set her mind. *Grab the bag. Drag it the thirty feet to the car rental booth.* Somehow she'd manage to get her right leg in the car and drive with her left.

The thought crossed her mind that she was an idiot for not calling Major Katherine Cummings or one of her dozen cousins in Harmony to come get her. But Millanie, as always, had to prove she could handle everything on her own. She'd been that way since she was nineteen and lost both her parents within a year.

Besides, the major had married the local funeral director and had a baby since they'd last seen each other and Millanie had no idea what her married name was. They weren't really friends, just two soldiers who had a town in common. Millanie had listed Harmony as her hometown and Katherine had been going there when she retired.

*And now I'm returning,* Millanie thought. Something she figured she'd do after twenty or thirty years in the army, not after twelve. One stranger in a crowd outside an embassy one night had changed all her plans and ended her career. Nothing personal. She was just in the wrong place when he wanted to kill himself.

Correction, the wound had not only ended her career, but every plan she ever made. Now she had no direction, no life, no future, and no job she loved. She was simply drifting and any direction, even Harmony, Texas, seemed a good place to go.

As she reached down, trying to balance on one leg while she grabbed for the duffle bag, the strap of her purse slid forward, causing her to miss the handle.

"Damn," she mumbled.

A laugh came from just behind her.

She straightened and turned slowly, shifting her weight to regain her balance. No matter the injury, she'd be ready to fight. Twelve years as a soldier didn't wash away overnight.

As she'd been trained to do, she sized up the man standing a few feet away. Tall, lean, in his mid-thirties with hair too long to be stylish and intelligent eyes behind his dark-framed glasses. A teacher or an accountant by the way he dressed, unarmed, and single she'd guess. She relaxed and faked a smile.

"Sorry." He waved his hands in front of him as if erasing his outburst. "I shouldn't have laughed, but for a moment you looked like you were playing some kind of strange game people waste their money on at the county fair. Reaching for the impossible."

"You hang out at a lot of county fairs?" she asked, thinking this guy didn't look like he ever left the library, or study, or lab, or wherever geeks like him hung out. She could almost picture a tiny hoarder's apartment with stacks of books serving as tables. He probably drove one of those little cars that could almost serve as a paperweight when it wasn't puttering along.

"I hang around them all the time. Can't stay away from the great fried food." He was lying, of course. "How about I grab your bag when it comes around again as my apology?"

She nodded her thank-you, guessing he wouldn't be able to lift her bag. But she wasn't a captain in the army anymore; maybe she shouldn't be so critical. She must simply look like a woman, poorly dressed and stranded in an airport. Maybe she'd play the role all the way to the rent-a-car counter. Then she'd say, "Thank you," and he'd leave thinking he'd done his good deed for the day.

The bag circled and, to her surprise, he picked it up.

Without lowering her only luggage to the ground, he said, "Where you headed? I'll carry it for you."

She smiled, thinking this plan was too easy. "I'm headed to a bed-and-breakfast in a little town called Harmony, but that's a little far for you to carry my bag. How about just dropping it at the car counter over there?"

They both started toward the far end of the terminal just as the light above the last car booth blinked twice and went out.

"Great," Millanie muttered. "Now I'll have to find a cab and stay the night here."

The professor type next to her spoke. "You could ride with me. I'm heading that direction and would be happy to give you a lift."

*No* was already on her lips, but when she looked at him she almost laughed. The man couldn't look less like a serial killer. Odds were he'd be a safe driver who never traveled more than five miles over the speed limit. Her mother's warning of not getting in cars with strangers surely didn't apply to this geek.

When she didn't answer, he must have felt the need to testify. "You're in no danger, miss. I have a cabin out near Twisted Creek. It's no trouble to drop you in Harmony on the way." He didn't seem to be trying to talk her into the ride, just stating facts.

"I wouldn't mind paying for half the gas," she offered.

"Oh, no. I'll be happy for the company. A little conversation will keep me awake. I make this flight every month to visit my mother and the road seems endless when I'm driving alone."

Now she knew she was safe. He'd been to visit his mother. How sweet. He'd have to live near Harmony if he knew about Twisted Creek, and everyone out there knew everyone else.

"I'll hike out to the far parking lot and get my car. You wait here by the side door. I'll be right back." He shoved her duffle bag by the side entrance and disappeared.

She blinked. No one was around. She wasn't even sure which way the professor type had gone. Between the pain in her leg and the lack of sleep, she might have drifted off while still on her feet, suspended like a fashion nightmare of a scarecrow between two crutches.

Moving through the side door, she welcomed the cool air of the panhandle plains night. Since she'd been injured, her life had gone completely to hell. The doctors patched her up, but she'd had no one she wanted to call for help. She could handle this part of the recovery on her own. Her one brother lived in New York and would have just complained that she should have listened to him and not joined the army in the first place. Or worse, he'd want her to come to New York.

Millanie needed peace, not people.

She stared up at the full moon, breathing deep relaxing breaths. In a few hours she'd be back to where she'd spent the first ten years of her life. The day before she'd turned eleven, her dad got transferred to Dallas. The family moved to a bigger house, had more money, but she'd never felt at home. Dallas was just where she lived for a while; Harmony would always be home. Harmony was a place where all the world seemed balanced, even if it was mostly just memories in her mind.

Out of the darkness behind the terminal building, Millanie heard movement and tried to focus her tired mind on reality.

The noise came again, muffled laughter, movement. Custodians taking a smoke break? Teenagers painting the outside of the building? Huge rats? She didn't really care. All she wanted to do was get to the room she'd rented at the bed-and-breakfast and sleep for three days.

Then, out of the corner of her eyes, she saw them. Three men advancing in the tall dry grass. For a moment she was back on embassy guard duty. Listening. Standing ready. On alert.

Opening her eyes, and her ears, she took in her surroundings in the circles of light that she stood between. Amarillo, Texas. Not another country. Not a war.

Her vision adjusted. The three men were shadows now, crouched low, moving behind the bushes made from pampas grass. They were keeping off the sidewalk, but she could hear their every move.

She knew the moment they spotted her. Halted footsteps. Lowered voices.

The one in front straightened and slowed his pace. The other two followed. Now, the men who'd been creeping closer appeared to be simply walking toward her. They were young, loose-jointed probably due to drugs or too much alcohol.

"Hey, lady, that door still open?" the leader asked casually as if he couldn't have easily guessed she'd just come out.

She nodded, her tired body feeling adrenaline begin to pump. All three wore old ball caps and dirty, baggy jeans low on their hips. Druggies, early twenties, probably armed but untrained. Her mind filed facts about each out of habit.

Only one came nearer and looked in the terminal. "No one's around," he whispered back to the others.

"Well, let's grab it and go." The second one moved closer, his whisper carrying easily on the wind.

Millanie kept her head down as if she were paying them no attention, but their planning drifted toward her in the midnight air.

"We could grab this woman's purse," one mumbled. "It's probably got more cash in it than we'd get for that laptop Cherie left out."

Millanie fought the urge to glance back and see which one of the car rental counters had a laptop sitting out. She'd bet it was the counter where the last light had blinked twice.

The leader took off his hat and scratched his head as if to stimulate his thinking. Then he nodded and they all three moved toward her.

"You waiting for somebody?" the leader shouted. "We could help you to your car, lady."

She forced her body to relax as she shifted just enough that her purse slipped to the concrete at her feet. The bag followed. "I'm fine." She finally turned her full attention to the pack. "You boys don't want to do this."

"What?" the talky one said, still edging closer. "We're just offering to help a poor lady in distress. How about you let me carry that expensive-looking purse you just dropped? I don't mind taking it off your hands."

"Step away," Millanie said with cold calmness. "I don't want to hurt you."

All three laughed and showed their teeth like wild dogs.

"Step away," she repeated just as the leader jumped forward, bending to grab the bag at her feet.

A defensive reaction, trained into her muscles by practice and combat, fired her movements.

She swung her crutch, hitting the leader in the knee and sending him down hard on the concrete. When the second one advanced from the other side, planning to grip one of her arms, she let the other crutch fall against the building as she swung a chopping blow across his throat, sending him to the ground fighting to draw air.

The third man had crept forward, but hesitated when one of his friends gasped and the other began to cry as he whined that the bitch had broken his knee.

Millanie lifted her crutch as if it were a rifle and shoved it hard into the third man's abdomen before he could react.

When he winced in pain, she said, "Pick up your friends and get out of here. I'm too tired to turn you three in, but if I ever see any of you again, you'll be sorry."

Holding his middle, the coward of the group, and probably the smartest, helped his friends limp away. Within seconds they were no more than whispered swear words in the darkness.

Millanie leaned against the building and closed her eyes as the sound of a car pulling around to the side of the building reached her tired senses. She remained still as the vehicle stopped and the driver jumped out.

"I'm sorry I took so long," said the tall man from Twisted Creek. "Oh, you've dropped your crutch. You poor thing. Let me help you."

His strong arm circled her waist as he helped her to a battered SUV. She made no protest as he settled her into the passenger seat, carefully lifting her broken leg and locking her seat belt. His hands were gentle, a caretaker's hands as he spread a blanket over her and propped her cast up with a huge stuffed toy unicorn.

Of all the questions she could have asked this stranger, the only thing she could think of after he loaded her duffle bag in the back and climbed into the driver's seat was, "You carry a unicorn in your van?"

"It's my little sister's. She still believes in them."

Millanie knew she was safe. No man who carries around his sister's toy could be a threat to her. "How old is your sister?" she asked as he pulled onto the highway.

"Twenty-three. She's a fortune-teller at the bookstore in Harmony. For your own safety I'd advise you to avoid her."

He continued but she was too far gone into sleep to think how strange his words sounded.

# Chapter 2

As he drove through the night Drew Cunningham thought about how much he loved summers in Texas. Almost midnight and still not enough humidity in the air to allow a mosquito to spit.

He glanced over at Sleeping Beauty in the passenger seat. The lady in distress with her broken leg and tired eyes hadn't said a word since she'd settled into his SUV. He could have raped and murdered her a half dozen times by now, or married her off to some guy in a commune so she could be his eighteenth wife. She already had the clothes for that career.

If he wasn't such a nice guy, he could have robbed her, stolen her hundred-pound duffle bag, and rolled her off in a ditch somewhere. She was so sound asleep she probably wouldn't wake up until day after tomorrow if it didn't rain, and it never rained in Texas. Not this year.

*And another thing,* he mentally corrected himself. *I'm not a nice guy.*

Nice guys finish last. Nice guys never get the girl. His sister had been drilling that into his head every time she'd seen him for six months. Only, her lectures were a waste of time. Everyone out by the lake where he lived knew him and they all knew he was a nice guy. So, little hope of changing his image at thirty-four.

He went back to thinking about all the terrible things that could have happened to Sleeping Beauty if he hadn't come along. By the time he saw the first lights of Harmony, Texas, he'd laid out a whole scenario of how the end of the world had hit while she slept and come morning she'd wake up to a town full of zombies and have no idea who to trust.

Drew frowned. Now he'd have to keep her safe and teach her all the facts on how to live among the undead. It wouldn't be easy for her to run in the cast and, with those clothes, she might as well be waving a come-get-me flag at the monsters.

Drew tossed his glasses on the dash and studied her in the blinks of the passing streetlights. She was pretty: the down deep, no makeup kind of way few women are pretty. Smooth skin, dark hair, lips that would probably keep him awake tonight.

He couldn't help but wonder why she'd come to Harmony, a crippled woman with no family to meet her. It wasn't like this little town had healing springs or a world-class health spa. Harmony was barely on the map. If the world came to an end, the people around here would hardly notice.

Drew turned off Main. She'd said she was headed to a bed-and-breakfast and as far as he knew there was only one. The old place was run by the crazy woman who also thought she was in charge of the local writers' club. The group had asked him to speak a few times. Martha Q Patterson made Drew think of stories about serial killers who only preyed on chubby little women who talked all the time. Rumor was she'd had seven husbands. Some said she killed off half by talking them to death.

He smiled. Martha Q had told him that he made her wish for "afternoon delights," which made him even more frightened of her than he usually was of the fairer sex. He had a feeling she wasn't kidding about the delights part, and she had a dozen rooms at her place where they could work out the details. Just driving down her street made him nervous.

He pulled in the Winter's Inn drive just as the image of

old Martha Q, wrapped in a sheet, hanging from her third-story window flashed in his mind. That sight would be a great opening to a thriller. Only, with her weight she'd be like Outlaw Jack Ketchum in the Old West, who'd gotten so fat on jail food while waiting for the hangman to arrive that the rope had snapped Jack's head right off when the floor went out from under him. One of the not-so-romantic Western stories.

Drew shook off his imagination and tried to stay in reality—at least long enough to get Sleeping Beauty delivered.

The porch light at Winter's Inn was burning bright. One-foot-high LED lights, made to look like daisies, lined both sides of the walk. Drew had the depressing impression he was delivering Hansel's sister, Gretel, to the cottage in the woods. Maybe he should run up and ask if there was room at the inn before waking the beauty beside him.

As he stepped out of his van, Martha Q opened the door and waved at him just like the witch in the fairy tale must have done to the siblings.

Having no choice, he circled the car and opened the passenger door. There she was, dreaming away. Her midnight hair, her perfect complexion, her kissable mouth.

Without much thought, he leaned in and brushed her lips with his as he reached to unbuckle her seat belt.

She made a little sound in her sleep and he fought the urge to deepen the kiss.

"That you, Andrew Cunningham?" Martha Q yelled loud enough to awaken the block. "I didn't know you'd be bringing my guest. When she called from London, I was sure she couldn't be from around here even if her name is McAllen." The round little lady had waddled halfway down the walk. "If she was kin to any McAllen, she'd be staying with them, I'd bet. Probably another one of them genealogy types tracing her roots."

Martha Q didn't offer to help but continued to talk.

Drew brushed Sleeping Beauty's cheek. "Wake up, Miss McAllen. We're here." He fought the urge to kiss her again. That first kiss had certainly brought him fully awake.

In the background he heard Martha Q saying that Hank Matheson told her if another person came here claiming kin, he planned to take a power saw to a few branches of the family tree. McAllens and Mathesons reproduced like rabbits around these parts.

"Rise and shine, sleepyhead," Drew whispered near her ear. You're at Winter's Inn."

Green eyes opened and stared at him. "Who are you?" she asked, surprise in her voice but no fear.

"I'm just your driver, miss." He pointed at the backside of Martha Q as she leaned over, straightening one of the daisy night-lights. "And that is the innkeeper at Winter's Inn."

Sleeping Beauty smiled. "Noisy one, isn't she?"

Drew couldn't hold back a grin. "She has to make that noise if there's a chance she might be backing up."

While Martha Q rambled on about how dark it was around her place, Drew helped his passenger out of his van. "Just hold on to me and I'll carry your crutches. I don't think the walk's wide enough to maneuver on crutches in the dark."

She looped her arm over his shoulder and he circled her waist. At six foot one he rarely saw a woman near his height, but she was within three inches. They progressed down the walkway, her cast taking out every other LED light.

"I'm Millanie McAllen," she said as she hopped along.

"Andrew Cunningham. My friends call me Drew."

"Thank you, Drew, for bringing me here. I owe you one."

He knew he was probably being forward, but the lady was plastered against his side. "You staying long, Millanie?"

She looked up with those tired green eyes and he knew she was a woman who never lied.

"I don't know," she finally answered. "Getting here was my first plan of action. I'll think of my second when I've slept the clock around and eaten a few meals."

Millanie McAllen might think she knew exactly where on the planet she was, but Drew saw the truth in those beautiful eyes.

She was lost.

"Andrew!" Martha Q yelled. "Any chance you two are

going to make it in to sign the register before dawn? I can't stand here waiting if she's not interested. I'm missing the *Late Show*."

Sleeping Beauty looked directly at him when she answered Martha Q, "I'm interested."